# THE

# PRICE

OF

# AMBITION

## LUCY BEAUFORT

First published in Great Britain in 2015

A CIP catalogue record for this book is available
from the British Library

ISBN 978 0 9932988 1 3

www.lucybeaufort.co.uk

Front cover design by Emma Haynes – www.designbypie.net

design by Pie

Printed and bound in England by Booksprint

# Chapter 1
## *December 2002*

Izzy sat at the kitchen table, her head resting on her hands. She gazed unseeingly through the window of the holiday cottage that had been home to her family for the past five months, wondering when the phone call would come telling her whether or not she had been successful in her recent job interview. She was feeling sick with nerves and while she knew that she should get up and rescue the kitchen from the bun making mess created by Tatty her youngest child, she was temporarily paralysed by anxiety. Currently Tatty was in the sitting room watching TV with her older brothers Ben and Ed who had just returned from school and she hoped the phone would ring soon, before they grew bored and started fighting and she would be unable to concentrate on having a sensible conversation.

A ray of weak December sunshine penetrated the kitchen, forcing Izzy to focus on the bare garden and the beautiful landscape beyond it. The holiday cottage was set high up with spectacular views looking down the gorge towards Ironbridge. Relocating had not been a straightforward decision, but Shropshire seemed the ideal county with cheaper property and a more relaxed approach to life. Stephen had easily found a new job teaching French and Spanish at a very good grammar school and had nearly completed his first term there. Izzy had known it would take her a little longer to find the right job and she hadn't expected an opportunity to arise so quickly.

Still it was a good thing. She loved living in Coalbrookdale and she had initially enjoyed spending time with the children and adjusting to village life. However, three months of being a stay at home mum had left her feeling like a caged tiger. Looking after the children was all right, but the household chores had quickly become tedious and the simple truth was she really missed working. She'd made the decision to give up full-time work when the children were born but had decided to return when they were all at school; Tatty would be going in September of next year so it was a little earlier than planned but Izzy didn't want to miss a good opportunity when it arose.

Just as Izzy was preparing to move, her mobile phone sprang into action and a shot of adrenaline raced through her body as she whipped it off the kitchen table. She felt her heart rate escalate rapidly and she inhaled deeply before answering.

'Hello?'

'Is that Isabella James?' a deep, confident voice responded.

'Yes, it is.'

'Ahh, right, well, Charles Hambridge here. Thank you for coming to see us. Cut to the chase and all that, good news I'd say. We'd like to offer you the job.'

'Oh, that is wonderful news ...' Izzy paused with a huge grin on her face not wanting to sound over eager, 'and I take great pleasure in accepting.'

'Excellent,' Charles continued, 'I would like you to start as soon as possible. Shall we say the first week in January; get Christmas out of the way? It helps that you don't have to resign from a current position. Let's say Monday the 6th.'

'That sounds perfect, I'll look forward to it,' Izzy affirmed, craning her neck to look at the family planner and wondering why she hadn't written on it which day the boys were due back at school in January.

'Right, well, I'll get my PA to put the paperwork in the post and I'll see you in the New Year. Have a good Christmas. If you fancy popping in to see us before then, please do.'

'Yes, I will. Thank you very much.'

Izzy could barely contain herself. She jumped up and down with excitement as she selected her husband on speed dial and waited impatiently for the dial tone, simultaneously checking her watch to see if Stephen would have finished teaching for the day. Three forty-five, well he should have done by now she thought.

'Hello,' Stephen's voice came on the line, 'do I take it you have news?'

'Yes, as a matter of fact I do,' she paused for effect, unable to hide the excitement in her voice, 'I am, as of January the sixth, a working woman again.'

'That soon, hey? It's good they offered you the job, but it will mean big changes again for the little ones.'

Izzy thought his response was a bit flat and took a deep breath, 'Well, it won't be that bad. With you finishing at three fifteen every day, at least you can pick the boys up from school and ...'

'Actually, I'm a bit busy at the moment Izzy, and I'd rather not discuss this over the phone,' Stephen cut in, his voice taking on a harder edge.'

'You are pleased for me, aren't you? I mean the money will come in handy, won't it?'

'Undoubtedly, although don't take it for granted that childcare will be any cheaper round here. That is, if we can organise any in two weeks. You've not exactly given us much time to sort things out. Anyway I'll see you at home later, goodbye.'

'Stephen...' but the line was already dead. Izzy felt a bit deflated. She wandered into the sitting room where Tatty and Ed were playing snakes and ladders, while Ben had made the most of her absence to watch some hideous wrestling programme on TV. Before she could remonstrate, Tatty was grabbing at her. 'Do you want to play a game with us now?'

'Not right now, Tatty, maybe later. Mummy needs to make a start getting dinner on and I haven't even finished clearing up the mess you made after lunch.' She watched the hopeful expectation on her daughter's face die away and realized she knew just how she felt.

Izzy sighed as she headed back into the kitchen. She was really excited at the prospect of working as a land agent again. Hambridge & Simpson promised to be a progressive and modern commercially orientated firm and being in the centre of Shrewsbury would make a nice contrast to the splendid isolation of the cottage, or the new house for that matter. She knew it would mean long days again and it would be hard on the family but Stephen would do his fair share and be there for the children when she couldn't be. Besides, when they exchanged on their new home, her pay would help them no end.

The property they had found was just what they were looking for, including a bit of land for a pony and some chickens. Properties like this, of course, did not come cheap and were readily snapped up when they appeared on the market, but this one needed a lot of work just to make it habitable and being in a position to buy without the need to sell a property had worked in their favour. She knew Stephen and his father planned to do much of the renovation work, but these things always cost more than one thought. Surely Stephen could appreciate that this would benefit them all. He could be so negative at times.

* * *

'Well, Izzy, I really hope you've thoroughly thought this through and considered all the implications.' Stephen sat abruptly back on the kitchen chair, folded his arms defensively across his chest and glowered at his wife.

'Of course I have and we've discussed this already. You know I've always believed it's good for children to have a working mother. It provides a strong work ethic. I know it's another year until Tatty starts school but the children have always been OK in childcare before and actually, I meant to tell you earlier that I have already sorted that. I've found the most wonderful child minder. She lives on a farm and only takes on a couple of children at a time. It's on your way to school, which is perfect and of course Shrewsbury is only half an hour away if there's any emergency I have to dash back for. I've done the sums by the way and financially it's certainly worthwhile.' Izzy stared down at her hands which were clasped tightly together, thumbs turning over one another. She chewed her lower lip, took a deep breath and continued. 'You yourself said you didn't know how we were going to fund all the work on the house …' she tailed off, glancing up at Stephen to gauge his mood.

'You really have got it all worked out, haven't you? You can dress it up how you like but I'm not happy about this. I think the children will suffer. I don't mind you working part-time but I'm just not sure how you'll cope full-time.'

'Yes, but with you finishing at three fifteen, you can pick them up then…'

'Izzy!' Stephen cut in sharply, fixing her with a cold stare. 'You know full well that I have a lot of homework and marking to do. This is a new job. It's important that I make a good impression. How can you think I'll be available every day at three fifteen? Frankly that's a ridiculous assumption.' He struggled to control his anger: 'I have responsibilities at work and I am fed up with the way you always belittle my job.'

'I do not,' Izzy said indignantly, 'I just thought you could compromise a little and do some work at home in the evenings.' Not for the first time, she wondered why Stephen always made such a fuss about teaching. It was not as if he had the pressure of financial targets like a lot of professionals and, as for the holidays, well how many other jobs gave one that much time off?

Stephen sat up, placing his elbows on the kitchen table, his hands under his chin. He leaned forward. 'Oh right, as long as it fits in with you, is that it? It's not like I might have to concentrate on what I'm marking or have lessons to prepare? But none of that's important to you Izzy, is it? Don't worry; I can do it all standing on my head.'

'Well, all right, maybe I hadn't really thought that through, but never mind because this childminder is supposed to be fantastic.'

'Well, it's a good job because the children are going to be there a hell of a lot.' Stephen stood up, the kitchen chair scraping on the floor, 'I have always supported your decision to work, but part-time only while the children were small – I can't believe you have disregarded my feelings and in effect those of your children.' He stormed out of the room.

Izzy sat in a stunned silence, mulling over the conversation. She thought Stephen was making a big fuss over nothing and she didn't know what had got into him. He was usually so understanding and the children weren't that small now.

Her mobile erupted into life. Great, her mother. Sighing, she pressed the answer button.

'Hola, Isabella!' sang Adriana. '¿Como esta?'

Gracious, thought Izzy, at least someone's in a good mood. 'Hello Madre. Good thanks and you?' Izzy wondered why her mother was phoning as she only did so when she wanted something. There was no such thing as a social call.

'Christmas, I am phoning about Christmas.' Adriana's Spanish accent seemed much stronger over the phone, 'I am organising Christmas,' she stated firmly.

'Ah,' Izzy steeled herself, took a deep breath and carefully said, 'Madre, we sorted Christmas out weeks ago. We've been invited to Stephen's parents and so that's where we are going, as you well know.'

There was a momentary silence. 'But you haven't been to us since we relocated to Italy and that was two years ago,' her mother whined.

'I know, Madre, but we did invite you over to us last year and the year before.

'Yes, yes, but your father and I couldn't spare the time,' Adriana paused before adding, 'I suppose you don't have enough money is that it?'

Izzy wasn't about to admit to that, although flights for five to Milan at this time of year were costly. 'No, Madre, that is not the problem. Anyway, I will be starting a new job in the new year.'

'I knew it! You have no money, that is why you are working again,' Adriana gushed triumphantly. 'I told you, you should have married Alfonzo. You wouldn't have the money worries then and you could have stayed at home and brought up my beautiful grandchildren properly.'

*Just plenty of extra-marital affair worries*, thought Izzy, gritting her teeth. 'Look, Madre, there is no point arguing about this. I *want* to work?'

'So why not get involved in some charity work if you have time on your hands.'

'I enjoy being a land agent. I'm good at it and that's empowering, as is earning a good wage. I like being able to stand on my own two feet, having a career and recognition. It's important to me, for my well being.' Izzy heard the kitchen door squeak. *Shit*, she thought, *how long had Stephen been standing there listening?*

'Madre, are you still there?'

'Yes, I am. I am just shocked. I thought you would have given that all up after you had children.'

'Honestly Madre, most mothers would be proud to have a daughter like me.'

'Well, I just always thought you'd get that out of your system and take on a more traditional role: wife, mother and charity work . . .' Adriana paused and then added, almost to herself, 'I worked so hard to give you the perfect life.'

'Madre, I do have the perfect life. I suppose we will never see eye to eye on certain things. Oh, by the way, we've bought that house I told you about.'

'Oh good. When do you move in?'

'It will be a while. I told you the house needs total refurbishment. Actually, we are going to live in a static caravan while it's being done up.'

'In a what?'

'A static caravan, Madre.' Izzy smiled to herself. This was not going to go down well.

'A caravan? My daughter in a trailer?'

'That's right Madre. That way we can keep up an eye on the work. Lots of people do it.'

'But a trailer, Isabella?' She adopted a dramatic voice, 'I just don't know where I went wrong. Actually I do know. It was when you decided not to go to finishing school but to do that degree. I should have been firmer.'

'Madre, can we stop this? Can't you just be happy for me,' she took a deep breath and added, 'I'm happy, surely that is enough.'

'Well, of course, but what will I tell my friends?' Adriana wailed.

'Don't tell them anything. It's just a temporary arrangement, after all.' Izzy knew the conversation with her mother needed to end now; otherwise they would go round in circles. 'Look Madre, I need to get on so please give Daddy all my news and my love. I'm sure he will be pleased for me.'

'Well, of course, you are the apple of his eye and can do no wrong, but he will be worried too, you know. As for Christmas, we will have to be better organised next year, ciao Isabella.'

'Bye, Madre.' Izzy stared sadly at the handset for a while before gradually becoming aware of a purring. She looked down to see Marmaduke looking up at her. He stood up and began to wind his big ginger body through her legs, but as she bent down to scoop him up he nipped off in the direction of his food bowl and looked at her expectantly.

'Sorry, Marmaduke, you've had enough food for the day.' Marmaduke sat down and scratched an imaginary itch behind his ear and then stalked off in the direction of the sitting room. Izzy thought about her mother's reaction to her news and shook her head. She wasn't going to let her disagreement with Stephen or the conversation with her mother dampen her spirits. She'd done well to get this job. She went to the fridge and took out a bottle of wine. If she had to celebrate alone then so be it she decided, and went to join Marmaduke in the sitting room.

# Chapter 2

Stephen was up and about early the next morning, entertaining the children while seeing to breakfast and making packed lunches. He'd felt bad about getting angry with Izzy and was doing his best to make it up to her. He decided he was going to make the effort to accommodate her wishes for the time being. If, however, as he expected, home life started to deteriorate then he would have to say something about it. Izzy really didn't have to work, after all.

Stephen took his wife her morning cup of coffee. She had always been hopeless in the mornings and Stephen didn't mind her lying in while he sorted the children's breakfast. Not for much longer, he thought ruefully. She was in for a shock in January, it was a while since she'd had to be up and ready for work and even then it had only been two days a week since Ben had been born.

He sat on the bed next to her, looking down at her face which was shrouded in a curtain of dark curls. 'Your morning coffee, Madam, and you will have to get your bottom out of bed as I'm off to work now and the children will create merry havoc if you don't get a move on. In fact, here comes a mini trouble right now.'

'Mum-my, mum-my, get your bot-tom out of b-ed,' sang Tatty, bouncing up and down on the duvet with her long dark curls flying. 'You have to take Ben and Ed to school. I've made their packed lunches and tidied the kitchen,' she added proudly.

'All by yourself little lady?' enquired Stephen

'Nearly all by myself,' Tatty grinned at Izzy and Stephen swinging self consciously form side to side. 'Come on Mum-my, come on Mum-my!'

Izzy stretched and yawned, 'OK, everyone, I'm getting up.'

Stephen got off the bed and bent to kiss her. 'See you later, have a good day. I won't be home too late, all being well.'

Tatty grabbed his hand and they walked out of the room together, leaving Izzy to get herself ready. Stephen hugged Ben and Ed and made a dash for the door, nearly treading on Marmaduke who was already touting for a second bowl of food. Firing up the old Volvo, he was soon making his way to Newport Grammar School. Head of modern languages was a step up the ladder from his previous job. He was teaching predominantly 'A' level students now, which was demanding but rewarding. He really hoped this childminder was as good as Izzy was making her out to be because his workload was certainly more than she had factored in. He swung into the car park; his heart sinking as he saw the only space was next to a certain BMW Z3 which still had its lights on.

'Morning Stephen.'

'Morning Lucy.' The Head Master's PA, slid out of the driver's seat, flicked her long blonde hair out of her face and made a show of pulling down the rather short skirt of her suit.

'Must dash, so much to do,' Stephen mumbled, locking his car and preparing to head off in the direction of the modern languages building.

Lucy put her hand on his arm. 'You will let me know if I can be of any assistance won't you?' she said, through lowered lashes. Perhaps he was the shy type, she thought to herself. She would just have to work a bit harder to progress beyond these social pleasantries. Still she liked a challenge.

Stephen made it safely to his office and began sorting through his immediate priority, lessons for the day. Thankfully, these were already prepared with photocopying arranged into neat piles. He then prepared a brief agenda for the departmental lunch meeting and made a few phone calls concerning work experience in France for some of his 'A' level students. The bureaucracy involved was proving a headache but he was nearly there and he knew the students would be pleased. The bell for registration rang and he whizzed off to his tutor group with lesson one tucked under his arm. As he crossed the courtyard, he was unaware that he was being watched by Lucy from her office window.

'What are you looking at?' asked one of the administrators coming into the office with a pile of paperwork.

'Actually it's a who not what, Gwen.'

Gwen peered out of the window. 'Oh my, the new man is it? Well, he is quite a dish but married, you know?'

'Yes, well, I'm not after marriage as it happens... just a good time!'

'Oh, I see, well you know my feelings on that one.' Gwen dumped the papers unceremoniously on the desk, turned quickly and headed back out of the door, not bothering to wait for an answer.

Lucy watched her quick retreat with amusement. *Ugly bitch*. No wonder her husband ran off with another woman. 'In fact, someone just like me, Gwen,' she said out loud, rather sorry that Gwen couldn't hear her.

Stephen's day passed quickly and just as he was leaving work he received a text from Izzy, asking him to meet her at the new house. He wondered what she was up to. The house was empty and it would be pitch black outside by the time he got there. Izzy was already there by the time he struggled up the dark bumpy track. In spite of the cold, she was leaning on the bonnet of her VW Golf staring at the house, the wind whipping strands of hair out of her pony tail and across her face. As he opened his car door, she bounded up to him and he could see that her face was lit up with enthusiasm.

'Oh Stephen, it's going to be just gorgeous here, we'll have it ready in no time.'

Stephen studied his wife in disbelief. 'Izzy, I'm glad to see you so happy but you know better than I do that it could take years to get this place into shape. It's not going to be easy living. I don't know how we are all going to fit into the caravan for starters.'

'Oh, it'll be fun, all snug and cosy and we'll be on site to keep an eye on the builders.'

'Izzy, have you forgotten that neither of us will be on site now that you've taken this job? Are you sure we're doing the right thing here?'

'God, yes. This is everything I have dreamed of, or it will be when it's finished. You're such a worrier. It's not like it's the first time we've done a place up. I mean, I know this is much more intensive and we have three children now, but we'll be fine.'

'I wasn't worried when I thought you would be here to manage the project. We both know that's a job in itself.' Stephen squinted into the dark night. By day he knew the views were wonderful – a huge vista of rolling Shropshire countryside. The house was beautiful too, and when it was all finished it would be a fantastic place to live.

Stephen had decided to start with the roof on the house, weather-permitting. It needed to have the old thatch stripped off before being replaced with new. This was due to start after Christmas. He hoped it wouldn't snow. He had obtained three quotes and chosen a local firm who, apart from giving the best estimate, had seemed to talk the most sense. 'Izzy, what are we doing out here? It's freezing and surely we need to get the children back and feed them.'

'I just wanted a moment for the two of us. Everything is falling into place, Stephen. You have a good job, Ben and Ed like their new school, we are going to have the most fabulous home and I have a new job, too. See, we're sorted.'

Stephen slid an arm around Izzy's shoulders, drawing her snugly to his body and resting his chin on the top of her head. She's right, thought Stephen, why am I worrying? It will all be just fine. 'Well, we can't stand her all night, we've got little ones to sort out and we need to get on with some packing. I can't believe it's Christmas already!'

# Chapter 3

Christmas day dawned bright and early with Ben and Ed awake at six a.m. Luckily Tatty slept in and the two boys entertained themselves trying to guess what was in their stockings. Stephen decided to go down and make some tea and wasn't surprised to see his mum already in the kitchen.

'Merry Christmas, Mum,' said Stephen, giving her a hug.

'And a Merry Christmas to you, too,' Susan replied.

Stephen sat in the comfy chair next to the Aga, listening absent-mindedly to his mother as she bustled around the rustic kitchen, its oak units lovingly built by his father.

'So, how are things going?' asked Susan as she made a pot of tea.

'Great, Mum, although this year might be really testing with the house and Izzy going back to work full time.'

'Yes, I can see that.' Susan opened the fridge door to retrieve the milk. 'Well, you'll manage, I suppose. Your father and I both worked.'

'I know that, but because you did all the admin and books for dad, you could work from home and be here for us before and after school. I think that's important for children. What about school holidays? What do we do then? I just hate the thought of them in holiday clubs all summer.'

'Well, you get a fair amount of time off over the holidays too and they can come here of course. Now that your father has sold the business, we've got lots more time on our hands. It will be a pleasure to help. I wouldn't be saying that if I didn't mean it and your father will be pleased too.'

'That's great of you to offer Mum. I'm sure the children will be delighted.'

'Right, why don't you take this tea up to Izzy and then we'd better let the little horrors open those stockings before they burst with the suspense.'

The rest of the morning passed quickly with Stephen's parents popping up to the church for the Christmas service, Izzy preparing vegetables and Stephen entertaining the over-excited troops. They had just all congregated in the kitchen and were in the process of opening a bottle of bubbly, when the door bell rang.

'Oh, do answer that would you Izzy, I'm a bit busy,' Susan smiled good-naturedly at her daughter-in-law as she stirred some gravy.

'Oh, of course,' Izzy replied jumping up. She opened the front door.

'Merry Christmas *querida*,' chorused her mother and father. Izzy's face was a picture, surprise turning to joy and she was being hugged by her father before she could say a word. She wiped tears away as her mother swept through the front door and kissed her perfunctorily on both cheeks.

'Don't overdo it, Madre,' Izzy laughed. 'When, why and how did you get here?'

'By plane of course.' Her mother looked her up and down. 'You need to slim down Izzy. You are carrying too much weight.'

The smile fell from Izzy's face but before anything else was said, Susan swept down on them all and ushered them into the kitchen, patting Izzy protectively as they passed by.

'You look gorgeous, my dear, don't listen to your mother. She is much too thin. She can't have any fun at all,' she whispered conspiratorially to Izzy.

Adriana tried her best with her grandchildren but was much happier when the greetings were over and there was no danger of grubby little hands ruining her immaculate and very expensive dress. She sat by the fire in the sitting room, sipping a glass of champagne. 'This is surprisingly good,' she exclaimed to no one in particular.

'So, who organised this?' asked a delighted Izzy, cuddling up to her father on the sofa.

'Well, actually, it was Susan's idea. She invited us over and we accepted. We're staying just up the road in a delightful little hotel. I must say it's awfully quaint round here,' he enthused, 'I thought I might have a ramble up on the common tomorrow.'

'Oh, we'll come, won't we Stephen, it will be good to have some fresh air,' said Izzy.

'Arthur and I will be happy to join you too, John,' said Susan. 'The dogs could do with a good run.'

'We'll go after breakfast then,' said Izzy. 'How long are you staying Dad?'

'Well, we are flying off to Verbier the day after Boxing Day.'

'Oh, that sounds fabulous. We haven't skied for years now. Maybe next year when we are settled?'

'Well, the sooner you start those children the better,' announced Adriana, 'so make sure it is next year.

'I suppose you are all fantastic skiers, having skied all your lives,' said Susan. 'Anyway, I think it's probably time for dinner,' she bustled out to the kitchen. 'Where are my waiters and waitresses?' she called over her shoulder. They all trooped through into the dining room, where the table had been set beautifully, in red, gold and green.

'Oh, how very traditional,' said Adriana. 'I believe the colours this year are purple and silver. So where are we to be seated?' Adriana smiled brightly at Susan, ignoring the uncomfortable silence. Arthur quickly stepped in and seated everyone. Before long the children, closely monitored by Izzy and Stephen, were carefully bringing in dishes from the kitchen and putting them on to the table without dropping or spilling anything. Christmas lunch was a noisy affair with plenty of amicable chattering and marred only by the odd addition from Adriana who seemed unable to join in with the jolly atmosphere.

Stephen studied Izzy and realized that she tried hard to be everything her mother wasn't but at times had that glacial air about her too. She wasn't as affectionate with the children as she could be. He'd hoped things would change if she spent more time with them but that hadn't been the case. Maybe he was being unfair. He couldn't begin to imagine growing up with a mother like Adriana.

'So, Izzy, tell me about your new job,' her father suddenly inquired.

'Well, it's with a firm of land agents in Shrewsbury, Hambridge & Simpson. They're a smallish outfit but I'm quite happy about that. Anyway, they appear to be expanding quickly and I get the impression there is room for progression within the firm. I was told two associates were promoted after only eighteen months. I'm hoping they might be keen to expand their partner base.'

'So, lots of nice country estates to manage, then. Let me know if there's a spot of shooting on offer.' John winked across the table at his daughter.

'Well, a couple of smallish estates, maybe: I'll have to get back to you on the shooting,' grinned Izzy.

'Mummy, who is going to look after us?' asked Tatty, placing her knife and fork down carefully on her plate.

'We're going to the lady on the farm, silly. The one we saw last week, with all the ponies,' Ed said knowledgeably.

'Yes, and we'll be going there after school, too,' Ben said sullenly. 'I don't know if I want to go there every day,' he added for good measure.

Oh, it won't be that bad,' said Izzy airily. 'Mrs Davis is a lovely lady with three of her own children and she said you could ride the ponies any time. Besides, Daddy will be able to pick you up after school some days.' She forced a smile on her face and looked across at Stephen. Stephen felt resentment building in him but kept silent.

'Will you Daddy? Please?' said Ben, staring at his father.

'Ben, I'll do what I can.'

'Oh that'll be nice Stephen,' said Susan placatingly, sensing tension in the air.

'I would have thought boarding school was the obvious answer,' Adriana chipped in. 'Your father and I will pay for them, Izzy. Boarding school produces such well rounded individuals. I'm not at all sure about this childminding business. You don't really know who is looking after your children and it's not good for them to be in day care for long hours.' The irony of what Adriana had just said appeared to be wasted on her.

'Mummy went to boarding school,' announced Tatty. 'She loved it there, didn't you Mummy?'

'Well, yes, I did, but I didn't start boarding until I was thirteen.'

'Actually, I hated boarding school,' said John. 'Up at some ungodly hour, cold showers, dreadful food, packed like sardines into a cold draughty room. Ghastly, the whole thing.'

'Daddy, you aren't going to send us there, are you?' Ben was looking anxiously at Stephen. 'I don't mind going to the childminder's really,' he added, obviously deciding this was the lesser of the two evils.

'Mummy you never said anything about cold showers,' Tatty said accusingly.

'Oh for heaven's sake, no one is going to boarding school at the moment, so stop going on about it,' Izzy stated firmly.

'At the moment?' Ben picked up. 'So we might go then, sometime?'

'Coffee?' Susan quickly stood up and started clearing dishes, anxious to change the subject.

'Yes, excellent idea. We'll move through to the sitting room and sit by the fire,' said Arthur, standing up and making his way out of the dining room. Stephen followed his mother into the kitchen.

'Are you OK Mum?' he asked. 'That was a fabulous meal.'

'Just fine, thank you. Could you get some cups and saucers from the dining room please? They're in the corner cupboard, thanks.' She busied herself warming the cafetiere.

Izzy sat down next to her father, who was chatting to Arthur about shooting, which was a common interest, albeit poles apart with Arthur a member of a small local syndicate which involved aspects of pheasant rearing and beating, while John had access to a number of high-calibre shoots and thought nothing of spending two thousand pounds on a day's shooting. Izzy was glad that John and Arthur got on so well together and that she got on so well with Stephen's parents. She admitted to herself that she didn't like her mother very much. In fact, she couldn't believe that anyone would like her. She was so cold and never said anything positive or constructive and she had very nearly ruined today – but it's not over yet, Izzy thought to herself, we haven't done the presents!

As it happened, the rest of the afternoon passed uneventfully and everyone appeared delighted with their presents, especially the children who were totally spoilt by both sets of grandparents. Adriana had thoughtfully bought a Karen Millen suit for Izzy's new job but unfortunately in a size too small. At least she could change it.

Boxing Day was a great success. Adriana was confined to her hotel with one of her headaches and there was a noticeable change in the atmosphere, for the better. Everyone was visibly relaxed and there was a lot of giggling, especially when Stephen's brother popped over for afternoon tea with his wife and their two daughters.

Izzy was sad to see her father go. He was such fun, particularly without her mother and she really missed him.

'Keep in touch, sweetheart,' he said, 'and don't work too hard, you've nothing to prove you know.'

'I know Daddy. I'll email you. Enjoy Verbier.'

'I'll say goodbye to your mother for you. You don't want to disturb her when she's not quite tickety boo now do you?'

'No, I don't,' Izzy said sadly and watched her father walk briskly up the road and back to his hotel.

# Chapter 4
## *January 2003*

Izzy woke early. It was her first day at work and she'd been too excited to sleep well. That and the fact that they'd finally exchanged on the house. She rolled over in bed, snuggling up to Stephen and pulling the duvet up against the cool winter morning. Stephen stirred, rolling over on to his back and stretching.

'Morning,' he yawned. 'Big day today Izzy, I think we'd better get cracking – do you want first shower? I know how long you take!'

'Thanks,' she said, 'I'm not that slow!' However, she took the opportunity to leap into the hot water, while Stephen woke up the children. She'd laid out her suit the night before and she always kept her make-up minimal so it was only her unruly hair that needed much attention. She hoped she looked smart enough. All her work clothes were a little tight but she hadn't had time to buy any new ones. Oh well, she'd just have to slim down. By the time Izzy got downstairs, all three children were washed, dressed and eating breakfast at the table.

'You look nice Mummy,' said Tatty.

'Thank you, sweetheart.'

Stephen was dropping off the children at the childminder's. Mrs Davis would take Ben and Ed to school and Tatty to playgroup and collect the children after school. Stephen could pick them up from her on his way home. Today was easy as there were no after-school clubs to confuse things. She felt confident she'd organised everything. Now she could concentrate on getting to work and getting through her first day. She'd even just got time for breakfast herself.

Stephen was back downstairs having showered and shaved. He was always immaculately turned out. He'd have to iron his own shirts from now on, though, thought Izzy. She swallowed a last mouthful of coffee and watched Stephen whizz round the kitchen, loading the dish washer and checking the packed lunches. She couldn't decide if Stephen was making a point about how hectic mornings were going to be. Well, she was feeling calm and she was going to stay that way.

'Right, all done,' he announced. 'Quick, in the car, children. Good luck for today, Izzy, I hope it goes well. I'll ring you at lunch time if I get the chance.' He gave Izzy a quick hug and a kiss.

Tatty also wanted a kiss but Izzy noticed a large toothpaste stain on her daughter's sweatshirt and held her firmly away from her suit.

'For goodness sake, Tatty. How hard is it to spit in the sink, rather than on your clean clothes?'

Tatty's face crumpled, at which point a worried Ed piped up, 'Mummy, I got the toothpaste on her top but I washed it off. Please don't be cross.'

'Well I hope you didn't do it on purpose, Ed. I've got a big day today. You're going to have to be more responsible. What if that had got on my suit?'

'OK, that's enough,' Stephen butted in. 'Tatty, Ed, coats and gloves on. Bags. Out! '

'Stephen, she has a clean one upstairs…'

'Sorry, no time for that. Bye.'

Stephen headed out to the car only to find it needed de-icing and Ben drawing faces on the windows. He sprayed his and Izzy's windscreens, while Ed and Ben helpfully began fighting over who was to sit in the front.

'Oh, for goodness sake, nobody is sitting in the front today. Just get in the car and get your seatbelts on.' Stephen scooped Tatty up and strapped her into her booster seat.

'I'm sitting by the window then,' Ed announced.

Ben opened his mouth to reply but, catching sight of Stephen's face, shot into the middle space, jabbing Ed as hard as he could with his elbow as he did so.

'Ow! That really hurt,' Ed yelled and elbowed Ben back.

'BOYS, WILL YOU STOP THAT NOW!' shouted Stephen. 'This is not the way I want to start a day's work.' He silently cursed Izzy for inflicting this on him.

It took Izzy just under thirty minutes to drive to work. The morning traffic had been surprisingly light and she'd enjoyed listening to the radio without the usual din going on in the back of the car. She parked outside the grand Victorian building and, taking a deep breath, walked through the huge front door and up the large flight of oak stairs taking in the aroma of lavender wax polish. The offices of Hambridge & Simpson took up the whole of the first floor. She presented herself to Saffron the receptionist, who was looking particularly chic with her short sharp haircut and slim-fit trouser suit. Izzy felt rather frumpy as she handed Saffron her coat, suddenly very aware of her too-tight waistband.

She was reassured by the sight of Charles Hambridge striding towards her. Attired in dark green cords, a striped shirt and a co-ordinating paisley tie and waist coat, he looked the epitome of the country gentleman. He shook her hand rather firmly.

'Welcome to Hambridge & Simpson. You've met Saffron here obviously, and my PA Jess. Great reference from your old boss by the way. He ushered her into the main office. Hayley, our secretary. Harry, surveyor. Greg, associate. James, student.' Izzy uttered hurried hellos, and shook hands quickly.

'This is your desk Isabella, new computer etc – it's all been set up for you. Right, let's go through to my office and I'll go over a few things with you. Piers, whom you met at your interview is in the one next door, which leaves just Nick for you to meet. They are both out today, though. I've got a couple of jobs for you to go at, an agri-environmental scheme and some advisory work for Shropshire Agri-Development. Harry will assist you. He's currently just completing a grazing agreement; details all in these files here. If you want to know anything, just ask me. Any of the girls will show you how to access the databases etc. I'm off up North later today for a couple of valuations. I thought with this short week it would you give you a few days to settle in. Any problems just ring me on my mobile.'

'That's a fair trek. Do you do many valuations that far afield,' she queried, wondering why she hadn't asked this at her interview.

'Yes all over really; Scotland down to Cornwall and Ireland as well. Plenty of work and very lucrative.'

'That's great,' Izzy enthused, at the same time picturing Stephen's face when she told him she was off to Ireland for a couple of days. On the other hand, how exciting it would be to travel about a bit. She was about to ask some questions about the jobs he wanted her to do, when Jess transferred a call through to him.

'Must take this I'm afraid. Take the files and make a start why don't you?'

Izzy dutifully picked up the files and returned to her desk, hanging her jacket on the back of the chair and sitting down self-consciously at her desk. Not knowing where to start, she fired up her computer.

'Would you like a drink? Tea or coffee? I was just about to make one.'

'Thanks Jess. Coffee would be lovely. Black, no sugar, thanks.' The girl was very pretty. Izzy guessed she was in her late teens or early twenties. Her blonde hair was piled up untidily on her head, with artfully arranged wisps hanging either side of her face. In spite of the season, she was wearing a long flowery summer dress over trousers, as if she were off to a festival rather than the office.

The day passed quickly with Izzy making arrangements to go and visit a couple of farmers for their initial consultation under the Shropshire Agri-Development scheme. She quickly familiarized herself with the set up of the office and noted that the files were kept meticulously up to date. At lunch time she waited to see if anyone would offer to introduce her to a local café, but when no offers were forthcoming, she wandered into the centre of Shrewsbury, bought a sandwich and ate it whilst walking along the banks of the river Severn. Staring into the fast-flowing river, it occurred to her that Stephen hadn't rung and she decided to call him.

'Hello, what are you up to? Can you talk?'

'Just the usual. Are you enjoying the world of work?'

'Yes, it's great. I've already got some farmers to meet. It's always a bit nerve-racking at the start of a new job, though. I've just popped out for a sandwich.'

'I don't suppose you've spoken to the child minder, Sonia? Don't worry, I rang her a few minutes ago. The boys' school run went smoothly and Tatty had a great time at playgroup this morning. She's off pony riding this afternoon.'

'Oh. Well done. I assumed they'd be fine if I hadn't heard otherwise. OK then. I'd better get going.'

'Try not to be too late home. We'd better do some more packing tonight if we're still moving into your dream home on Saturday.'

Izzy forced herself to push the thought of packing boxes and her daughter riding for the first time to the back of her mind as she walked briskly back to the office. She was greeted by Jess as she walked in the door.

'Ah, you're back. Charles wondered if you would be able to do a valuation on Friday morning. It's not far from here. Four-bed property with a bit of a land. It's for remortgaging purposes. Jess chewed the end of her pen thoughtfully and then added 'Griedy Robert & Alright passes on a lot of work to us and Charles likes to keep them sweet.'

'That will be fine, just give me all the details and I'll get on to it.' Jess smiled. 'Already on your desk.'

'Do you want to come along, Harry?' enquired Izzy as she studied the correspondence. 'You might know this area, Lilleshall?'

'Sure.' Harry looked up from his desk, peering over his glasses at her. 'Actually, I live near there.' He smiled, revealing a set of even white teeth. Izzy decided that Harry was probably all right. He was wearing the regulation land agent wear of fawn-coloured moleskin trousers, a striped shirt and brogues. He had a mop of dark blonde hair and big blue eyes and was handsome in a rugged way.

The afternoon passed uneventfully. Izzy left the office promptly at five-thirty and joined the commuters exiting the town and heading home. The bypass was busy but moving and soon she was on her way down the M54 and heading back to Coalbrookdale.

# Chapter 5

Charles drove like a lunatic up his drive, spotlights picking up the monkey-puzzle trees which lined the long gently winding avenue. He was enjoying the smell of 'new car' and fresh leather, having only recently parted with rather a lot of money for this top of the range Porsche Cayenne. Clarissa's black Mercedes was parked outside the house and Charles crunched to a stop on the gravel beside it. He jumped out of the car and a trio of chocolate Labradors shot round the corner of the house in a tangle of legs and bodies, wagging their tails furiously and whining and barking with delight at the sight of their master. Charles bent to ruffle their heads as they vied for his attention and looked them over approvingly; all excellent gun dogs, in tiptop condition.

'Well, ladies,' he said, 'we might have a spot of shooting on Saturday.' The three dogs wagged their tails happily in response and followed Charles noisily up the marble steps, toenails clattering sharply as they entered through the vast and ancient oak front door and into the hall, an immense atrium stretching up to an enormous domed hexagon of clear glass. Charles never failed to marvel at this extraordinary feat of architecture.

'Oh, what are you doing here? Can't you leave those wretched dogs outside?' an ice-cold voice penetrated Charles's consciousness.

'Lovely to see you to see you too, darling,' his voice matched hers. 'Don't worry, I'm not hanging about. Just dropped in to pick up my overnight holdall and then I'm making tracks up to Sheffield. I won't be upsetting any of your arrangements. What are you up to tonight anyway?' Charles eyed his pencil-thin and immaculately attired wife with disdain. *Would you just look at her, the bony bitch. Hard edges inside and out.*

'Never mind about that. How long are you away for this time? Mummy is hosting her "Dinner and a Promise" auction a week on Saturday; I do hope you haven't forgotten.'

'Ohhh yes, how absolutely appalling of me to forget such an important event.' Charles smirked at Clarissa. 'Orphanages in Romania this time, isn't it? Ironic really. All you mothers packing your children off to boarding school so that you have time on your hands for saving other people's. Ours might as well be in Romania for all we see them.'

'Oh Charles, don't be ridiculous. You've never complained about them boarding before – not that your pitiful income covers the fees.'

'Well, of course, sweetheart. That is why I married your money.'

'Well, luckily for me, I didn't let you invest it. Actually, while we are on the subject, I must say Henry has done wonders with my portfolio. I'm now getting returns of between ten and fifteen percent...'

'Ten and fifteen percent?' echoed Charles. 'That is some return. All above board is it?'

'Oh for heaven's sake, of course it is. You can't possibly imagine that my own brother would involve me in anything dubious.'

Charles looked askance at Clarissa and decided not to respond. Privately he thought Henry was a total waste of space but he was very dear to Clarissa for some strange reason. *Who was Henry in with now?* he wondered. At that return, he'd consider investing himself, if only he had some spare funds. Everything was tied up in the business at the moment. Still, there were always ways to get more money.

Resisting further conservation with his wife, he marched up the staircase, whistling to himself as if he hadn't a care in the world. He knew Clarissa would be gritting her teeth. Entering his bedroom, he took a cigar from his secret stash in the back of his wardrobe and sank down on to a leather recliner. It was the one room he'd managed to stop Clarissa letting her interior designer loose on. He had to admit that the new forty-inch plasma screen TV didn't exactly complement the oil paintings, a rather fine collection of shooting scenes he'd inherited, or the other antique furnishings, but it suited his needs. There was a knock at the door.

'Come in!' Charles acknowledged, without removing the cigar from his mouth. It was Sylvie, the family's housekeeper.

'Mr Ambridge, just to say your packing is all done. I left the bag on the bed.' Sylvie had not quite lost her French accent in spite of living in England for the past twenty years.

'Ah, thank you Sylvie, that's fantastic.' Charles took a long drag on his cigar and breathed out smoke rings.

'Mr Ambridge, you will be in trouble with the mistress of the house,' she said, crossing the room to open the windows.

'Sylvie, it's bloody freezing out there. Shut those at once. I don't give a toss what Clarissa thinks. I was just enjoying five minutes of peace.'

'Well, bon voyage Mr Ambridge. I'll air the room when you've gone then.'

'Thank you, Sylvie. How would I manage without you?' He watched Sylvie blush to the roots of her hair. The poor woman had a terrible crush on him, of course, but one needed to keep such people on side. Sylvie went out of her way to ensure that all his needs were met, well nearly all. In fact she would be happy to satisfy literally all of his needs, but unfortunately she just didn't quite cut the mustard. She'd been with the family for ten years now and had never stepped out of line. She was tolerated by Clarissa and adored by the children. Sadly, Clarissa would never have put up with a gorgeous maid. He laughed to himself. They'd all be shocked if they knew what he really got up to. He was booked in for a session tonight and was looking forward to it. Just what he needed to put him in a good mood.

He ticked off everything he needed, before heading back downstairs and across the hallway. The dogs rushed towards him expectantly, but wagged their tails disconsolately as he strode towards the Porsche and not to his Land Rover. He rang Madame Lily from the car to confirm his time of arrival and fired up the engine.

Clarissa was still sitting in the same place, *Country Life* poised in one hand. *'Oh, goodbye, darling,'* she intoned sarcastically. *'Do have a lovely evening, won't you? Oh yes, thank you Charles. Drive safely and see you whenever.'* She snapped the magazine shut and stood up quickly, smoothing her dress down and checked her reflection in the huge mirror above the fireplace. Clarissa had always been obsessed with her physique, which had developed into a neurosis after having her three children. She took great delight in telling people that after the children were born her metabolism changed and she simply couldn't put on weight. The reality was somewhat different, with Clarissa following a rigid diet. On the occasions she had to eat a 'normal' meal, she would ensure that it was regurgitated discreetly at some point. As far as Clarissa was concerned, she could see nothing wrong in this; it was a perfectly acceptable way to manage excess calories. She visited the gym daily, of course and rode twice a day on top of that. Recently, she had embarked on Botox injections to ensure a wrinkle-free complexion and with her regular visits to the local beauty spa; Clarissa felt she was doing everything possible to maintain her youthful looks.

She was just wondering if she should change for the final pre-auction meeting, when her mobile rang. Her mood cheered enormously as she realised she was speaking to a local magazine editor who was hoping for some photos and editorial on the night. With that trump card up her sleeve, she was impatient to get to the meeting and could hardly wait to end the phone call. Picking up her handbag, she headed for the door, all thoughts of Charles forgotten. The three dogs, sitting forlornly in the hallway, didn't even bother to look up as she left – they knew better than to get anywhere near her.

\* \* \*

Sylvie watched from the upper hallway window as Clarissa stalked to her car and slid in. Like a snake, a viper, Sylvie thought and breathed a sigh of relief. She had finished all her chores for the day and thought she'd take the dogs out for a run.

'Walkies!' she shouted as she ran down the stairs and the dogs, hearing her voice, leapt into action, running round in circles and barking excitedly before she'd reached the bottom step. She trotted through the hallway towards the kitchen, with the dogs belting on ahead, and they shot through the kitchen and into the pantry, scattering wellington boots and various outdoorsy paraphernalia in their excitement. Sylvie pulled on a coat and wellies, grabbed a torch, and let the dogs into the yard. Ruffles, Sylvie's West Highland terrier, quickly joined the excited trio and they careered around impatiently. Goodness, they need some exercise, thought Sylvie as she shut the door behind her and walked through the rustic latch gate and into the stable yard.

The yard was partly cobbled which was lethal in winter when it was icy and wasn't much fun in the rain either. The stables were set around the yard, in a classical arrangement with a large gatehouse, complete with clock, separating the stables into two halves. Heather, the head groom, was just riding back in on one of the huge horses; all horses were huge to Sylvie, who was petrified of them.

'Goodness, Ezzer you're riding late tonight!' she exclaimed and flattened herself against the gatehouse wall. Heather drew alongside and jumped off. The horse immediately put a front leg out and dropped his head down to give it a good rub.

'Well, yet again her ladyship didn't ride today. She knows I need to know first thing in the morning so I can plan what to do with all the horses. She told me yesterday she would ride, but wouldn't tell me which horse she was riding or at what time. I still didn't know at lunchtime and well, here I am, six thirty and still messing about, but once this one's in bed I'll be finished. '

'You really can't leave them for one day?' asked Sylvie. She liked Heather but had often wondered if she made too much of the amount of exercise the horses needed.

'No, unfortunately not. This lot are fed a huge amount and need a lot of work. If you don't get them out of the stable daily, you run into all sorts of problems, veterinary and behavioural. Think small children cooped up all day and fed lots of fizzy drinks and sugary sweets and then magnify that into a half tonne animal which by nature should be on the move for sixteen hours a day and not stuck in a stable.'

'Ah, yes, I see,' Sylvie muttered, wishing she hadn't got her started. 'Well Madame shot off to er charity meeting so there's no risk of er visiting the stables tonight.'

Heather raised an eyebrow and stalked off with the horse in tow. Sylvie called to the dogs and headed out past the flood-lit ménage to the dark fields ahead.

# Chapter 6

Izzy and Harry had arranged to meet in a lay-by about half a mile from the house. He arrived in a brand new BMW, just as Izzy was getting out of her rather aged Golf.

'Nice wheels, Harry.'

'Yes but sadly not mine. It's my mum's car. I'm just borrowing it while mine's repaired. It failed its MOT and needs new shock absorbers.'

'Oh dear, that doesn't sound cheap!'

'Well, I have a mate who owns a garage and he gives me a good deal. If you ever need anything doing, I'll give you his number.'

'Thanks, I'll probably be taking you up on that knowing my luck with cars. We'll go in yours shall we?' she said, blowing on her fingers. 'It's more likely to go missing if we leave it here.'

'When did you start work for Hambridge & Simpson then?' Izzy enquired snuggling into the warmth of the car interior as they pulled away.

'Straight after I graduated about three years ago. I qualified with the RICS last year and I've just got my CAAV. I'm still living at home. Actually it's cool. I have the annexe, so I get to do my own thing. I'm putting away quite a bit towards a deposit on my own place but with cooked meals and the washing on offer, it's not such a bad deal.'

'It sounds like you've got it all worked out then.' Izzy thought how easy life must be for Harry – single, no dependents, no financial worries.

'Yes, it does sound like that,' Harry replied. It seemed as if he were about to add something but instead he announced, 'Oops, here we are.' He braked abruptly and Izzy clung on tightly as they skidded onto an unkempt driveway. The car bumped along through frozen puddles before they drew up outside an early Victorian farm house. The house was really beautiful but Izzy knew it required some serious attention. It was Grade II listed, which might worry some buyers but there were always ways around these things.

'Well, down to business,' Izzy said as she opened the car door and climbed out. 'I wonder what the inside of this place is going to be like. I bet those sash windows need replacing for starters and look at that chimney.'

'On the bright side, the rest of the roof looks all right,' added Harry.

'Hello!' They both turned in the direction of the voice and were confronted by a youth, scruffily attired in ripped jeans and a tattered Rolling Stones T-shirt who appeared to be oblivious to the cold morning. Izzy shivered and was glad she'd plumped for cords with a jacket and a thick over coat which she now wrapped more tightly around herself.

'I'm William and you must be from Hambridge & Simpson. Thanks for coming, where do you want to start?'

'Right, well I'm Izzy James and this is Harry Broster,' she offered her hand in greeting. 'We'll look round the house first, if that's okay and then progress outside.'

'Fine, follow me. Excuse the mess. We're having a clear out in preparation for the renovations. Just need to get some money in. The place hasn't been touched for years and is a proper mess.'

'No problem,' said Izzy as she stepped into the Blenheim-design tiled hallway.

'I'll just put the kettle on and then I'll show you round. I've just stoked the Aga up so it will take a moment to boil.' The young man sauntered off down a corridor and disappeared from view. The house smelt of damp and it was nearly as cold inside as out.

It took the best part of an hour to get round the house, which boasted original fireplaces in all of the high-ceilinged rooms, as well as the original dado rails, ornate cornicing and ceiling roses. Izzy tasked Harry with measuring, while she made notes and William filled them in on his plans for the house. He and his brother had inherited the place from their father as joint beneficiaries and were hoping to borrow money against the house to complete the renovations inside and out. William wanted to put in a music studio and rent it out to budding recording artists (which privately Izzy thought was a waste of time), while his brother wanted a herd of milking goats and to go into business making cheese and yoghurt. Trying to get financial backing had proved difficult for the brothers, neither having been in meaningful paid employment, so they had been delighted to find Griedy Roberts & Alright who specialised in providing funds to people in circumstances such as theirs. Izzy was able to advise William that his brother would be eligible for a government grant to set up the goat enterprise, which she knew had gone down well with William and had impressed Harry.

'Well, what do you reckon?' Harry asked her as they got back into his car.

'On the musicians' commune or the price? I can't advise on the former but I'd say the house is currently worth around nine hundred thousand. It's odd because there's a note in the file that Griedy are valuing it at one million even with the repair work, I'm not sure I would go that high. It's a shame I haven't got time to nip into Shrewsbury to check out the estate agents. I need some evidence of similar sales to help with the valuation; although that won't be easy.'

'I can do that, if you want,' said Harry. I'll drop you at your car and I'll see you at the office later.

Izzy returned to the office where Jess pounced on her with a steaming mug of coffee. With no Charles to report to, she went straight to her desk and began to write her report. Re-reading the file, she pondered the Griedy estimate. She'd have to talk to Charles about that when he got back. In the meantime, she hoped that Harry would manage to find some suitable comparables. She made a detailed list of the repair work needed and recommended an immediate inspection of the front left chimney.

Harry came in a while later having managed a find a few properties, although none of them of were a great help. Having got everything in shape, she dictated the report and passed the tape on to Jess for typing.'

Izzy decided to break for lunch. She'd asked Stephen to make her a sandwich today. It would work out cheaper than buying one and save her a trip into town. She'd just taken a bite, when a voice behind her made her jump.

'Ah hello, you must be Isabella.' Izzy spun around to be confronted by a balding giant of a man, scruffily dressed in dark brown chinos and a sweater that looked as if his grandmother had knitted it. 'I'm Nick, how do you do?' He offered his enormous hand and she took it wondering if she'd get it back.

'How do you do?' she said.

'How are you settling in then?' Nick's grey eyes twinkled appreciatively as he eyed Izzy up and down. 'If you need any help, then best not to ask me. I know nothing and that's the way it's staying!'

'Ha, he's finally admitted it then,' Greg piped up from his desk, peering myopically over his glasses at them, 'and mine's a coffee, white no sugar while you're up.' He addressed this to Nick, one eyebrow raised questioningly.

'Right then, do you know where the kitchen is Isabella?' Nick emphasised the 's' of her name.

'No, and I'm not about to find out.' She forced a smile on to her face, privately thinking that if they thought they'd got themselves a new teasmade, they would have another thing coming.

'Well well. A woman with attitude. Jess, darling you're needed. Catch you later Isabella.'

Izzy hoped she hadn't put her foot in it with Nick but he had got her back up. She finished her sandwiches without enthusiasm. She worked on various bits and pieces for the next hour until Jess appeared with the typed-up valuation. 'Blimey, that's was quick,' she exclaimed, catching the faint notes of patchouli oil which emanated from Jess today.

'Well we like to turn those around pretty quickly.'

'Right, I just need to run something by Charles before I sign it off. I'll check it now and then it'll be ready for discussion when I see him. I suppose that will be Monday morning.'

'Probably, but you never know with Charles. Leave the report on his desk with a note, he'll find it when he's next in.'

'Oh, OK I'll do that then.'

'Cool,' said Jess, a serene smile on her face.

* * *

Charles was in his office when Izzy got there at eight-fifteen on Monday morning.

'Morning Charles. I hope you had a good trip.'

'Oh, morning Izzy. Yes, indeed. How's it all going? Any problems?'

'No, everything is fine. I left the valuation that I did on your desk. Jess tells me you like them turned around quite quickly.'

'Ahh, yes, well I've had a brief look. Cut to the chase, you don't need to mention the chimney in your report.'

'Oh, really? I thought the bank might not want to lend any money if the chimney is going to collapse.'

'Well, did you reduce the value accordingly to take that into account?'

'Yes, of course I did.'

'So, you don't need to mention it then,' Charles paused and fixed Izzy with a stare, 'do you?'

'No,' she paused for a moment before carefully adding, 'I suppose

32

if I've reduced the price accordingly then I don't need to draw attention to it.'

'Precisely. Good work. Must get on,' he dismissed her, waving a handful of paperwork at her. Izzy mulled over the conversation as she walked back to her desk.

'Problem?' Harry enquired, dumping his briefcase on his chair and pulling off his scarf.

'Well, just that valuation on the farmhouse. Charles says not to make any reference to the chimney but I think it's important.'

'Well, I'm with you on that one, but Charles is the senior partner and who am I to disagree. I've only been doing this job five minutes.' Harry held his hands up in the air.

Izzy sighed, 'I thought you said you'd been here three years. Anyway, it just doesn't feel right. I like everything tickety boo as they say, and I feel that it should be in the report.'

'Well, if you want my advice, just do what Charles says. He does hundreds of valuations and must know the score.'

'Yes, you're right, no sitting on the fence. Thanks, Harry.' Izzy sat down at her desk purposefully and turned her attention to tweaking the report.

The rest of the day was fairly quiet so Izzy took the opportunity to familiarize herself with the databases and get a general idea of the spread of work. She noted that they did a lot of valuations, particularly for Griedy Roberts & Alright, quite a lot of compensation work for local land owners as one of the utility companies was putting a new drainage system in place, some planning permission and agricultural grant work. She was absorbed in what she was doing and didn't notice Charles approach.

'Right, Izzy, do you have time for a quick drink before you get off home?' he enquired, dragging on his jacket.

'Oh right, yes. Where are you going? I'll finish up and follow on.'

'Five Bells. On your road home. Must know the one. What's your poison?'

'I'll have a diet coke, please, with ice and lemon.'

'Nothing stronger? See you pronto then.'

Izzy switched her computer off and rang Stephen to say she'd be a bit late home. 'So sorry, but I can hardly say I won't go. Anyway I've packed as much as I can till Saturday. I'll try to make it quick so I can get back for Tatty's bedtime. Give her a kiss from me anyway though and tell her I'll make it up to her over the weekend.'

'I will. Just try not to miss the boys' bedtime as well.'

'I won't. I can't think we'll chat for too long, it's just a quick drink and catch up; that's all. See you later.'

'OK, I'll keep some food back for you, unless you're eating out.'

'No, it's definitely just a drink.'


Charles was nursing a glass of whisky soda, and smoking a cigar thoughtfully as Izzy entered the pub. 'Over here, Isabella.' He waved across the room and Izzy walked self-consciously over to join him.

'Found it all right then?'

'Yes, easily.' Izzy sat down opposite Charles and found herself in a cloud of cigar smoke.

'All gone well today? What have you been up to?'

'All coming together nicely. Actually, I've noticed that there could be scope for more grant applications and planning.'

'Hmm, not overly lucrative that type of work is it? Tends to be a lot of leg work for not much reward.'

'Well, yes, but I made some tentative enquiries today and Shropshire Agri-Development are keen and they provide plenty of funding. It's a fantastic service to offer farmers. They only pay a couple of hundred pounds for a full business appraisal and...'

'Yes, yes,' cut in Charles, 'but what's a couple of hundred quid when you can get so much more for valuation work? It's an area of rapid growth, a bullish market with plenty of opportunity. In fact I must introduce you to the directors of Griedy Roberts & Alright. Gary Griedy is a tremendous chap, very into his shooting. Do you shoot?'

'Uhh, yes. My father is a keen gun when he's in the country and I've shot a bit myself in the past.

'Excellent,' Charles spoke cheerfully, 'I am off tomorrow for a bit of sport, you must join us next time; I shoot as often as I can in the season with several syndicates, you must come along.'

'That would be great,' said Izzy, 'who do you shoot with?' she enquired politely.

'Ahh well, obviously on our estate but I'm also in a couple of syndicates managed by a top notch shooting outfit. I also nip down to Exmoor for a couple of days shooting over the season, try and combine it with a day's stag hunting. Do you hunt as well?'

'Well, again, I have done in the past but just not at the moment.'

'Our family is all very keen. You could borrow one of our horses, if you like.'

'I'm afraid I don't know if I'd survive a day in the saddle. I'm not very riding fit at the moment. Besides, I think I'm going to be pretty busy over the next few months with our new place.'

'All going ahead smoothly is it?' enquired Charles

'Well the static caravans have arrived on site. Officially, we complete on Saturday but the house is empty so the owners said it was OK to get it set up. So we move in this weekend. The builders arrive on Monday.'

'Good Lord, that's brave of you.' Charles looked at Izzy with raised eyebrows and an expression of surprise, 'I didn't realize you were taking on a building project of your own. I hope you won't need much time off?'

'Oh my husband will be overseeing the work. It's just a shame it's not the summer holidays so he can be home all day. '

'I can't see my wife living in a caravan,' said Charles. 'She'd be a bloody nightmare, although it would be amusing to see.' With that he downed his drink and stood up. 'Must dash, commitments and all that. Don't forget, valuations the way to go. Good luck with the move and I'll see you Monday.'

Izzy stared at his retreating back in surprise. When he'd said a quick drink, she hadn't anticipated him leaving her with a still half-full glass. Suddenly eager to get home, she grabbed her coat and dashed out to the car park. Her drive home took her longer than usual, adding to her irritation at Charles's dismissal of her ideas. At least the children would be ready for bed. Stephen had done really well so far and the children had been pretty co-operative. By the time she arrived at the cottage, she was feeling exhausted. God, she needed a glass of wine!

As she opened the door, she was greeted by a whiney and very much fully dressed Tatty. The schoolbags were scattered round the hall and there appeared to be a collection of dirty dishes and saucepans on the kitchen surfaces. A bowl of congealed pasta lay on the floor, Marmaduke eyeing it speculatively. 'Marmaduke, leave it!' Grabbing some kitchen towels, she scooped the mess into the bin.

'What the hell's going on?' she said angrily as she walked into the sitting-room to find a red-faced Ben sitting on the sofa and Ed being comforted by Stephen.

'Hello, darling,' said Stephen ignoring the comment, 'Ben and Ed just had a bit of a to-do but it's all sorted now.'

'But it's gone eight o'clock! They've got school tomorrow Tatty should be in bed by seven thirty and what on earth has happened in the kitchen?' Izzy was getting angrier. All she wanted to do was sit down and now she had all this to deal with.

'Do you think Mummy is cross with us Daddy?' she heard Ed ask Stephen as she marched upstairs after Tatty who had disappeared hastily to get ready for bed.

'I think she might be,' whispered Stephen conspiratorially, which annoyed Izzy considerably.

'Mummy, cuddle me.' Tatty wound her arms around Izzy's neck. 'Lie down next to me Mummy, next to Jemima.' She moved her teddy over and patted the bed next to her.

'Mummy hasn't got time tonight, and you should be asleep already so you can't have a cuddle.'

'Oh, please Mummy? Tatty tightened her grip around Izzy's neck which only served to irritate her more and she pulled away abruptly, putting Tatty's hands firmly on the bed. Tatty's eyes filled with tears and she turned away hurriedly to face the wall so that Izzy didn't see them.

'Goodnight Tatty, sleep well.' Izzy kissed Tatty's cheek and relenting gave her a brief cuddle.

'Goodnight boys,' she said as they headed into the bedroom, 'hurry up and get into bed and don't wake Tatty.'

'Am awake,' said Tatty quietly, staring at the wall.
There was much giggling from Ben and Ed as they made their way into bed.

'Quietly!' hissed Izzy. 'Honestly this is too late for you all; you'll be overtired in the morning and grumpy.'

'Is that why you're grumpy in the morning Mummy because you don't get enough sleep?'

There was a stunned silence and then. 'Ben!' Ed whispered in a loud voice, 'Mummy he doesn't mean it, he's just joking.'

'Well, no kiss for you then, Ben.' Izzy bent down to kiss Ed. 'I don't like rude children.'

'Goodnight.' Izzy closed the door, ignoring Ben's plea for a kiss and headed back downstairs to find Stephen on the computer.

'Sorry, stressy day. I thought maybe we'd have a glass of wine with our meal and have a chat.'

'Love to, but too much work to do and I've already eaten. I was hungry so I ate with the children.' He barely looked up from the screen. 'There's food in the oven for you. Pasta,' he added.

'Oh right, like that is it,' Izzy snapped and headed back into the kitchen to find a dried out bowl of pasta in the oven.

'Nice,' she said aloud and opened the fridge to get a bottle of wine out. She poured herself a large glass of wine, then, relenting, poured another and took it through to Stephen.

'Thanks,' he said, eyes still fixed on his laptop.

'Good day?' she asked plonking herself down on the sofa next to him.

'Frantic and, as I said, I've got rather a lot to get through before tomorrow. I need to get on.'

Izzy went back into the kitchen, ate the pasta, and washed and dried up her plate. She knew she ought to wipe down the table and load the dishwasher but if Stephen wanted to be arsey, so could she. She wandered back into the sitting room. She'd have liked to watch TV but feared a lecture about Stephen not being able to concentrate. Retrieving the weekend's paper, she skimmed a few articles, and then headed upstairs to have a relaxing bath. She'd just got into her pyjamas and was hoping for a quiet read in bed, when she heard banging and crashing in the kitchen. *Great idea. Let's wake up the kids, why don't we?* She found it hard to concentrate on her book and kept listening for Stephen to come upstairs. She knew she ought to go and check on the children but it was so warm under the duvet.

Stephen didn't come to bed until well after midnight, and Izzy was sound asleep.

# Chapter 7

Clarissa slipped on her gym kit and raced to her car, slamming the door behind her. Although she had a gym at home, she much preferred to go to her local health club and use the facilities there. She was much better motivated with other people around her; people who stared enviously at her slim physique. She was meeting her personal trainer at eight-thirty.

The Mercedes purred into life. Clarissa loved this car. It took fifteen minutes to drive to the club and she was soon flying through reception, barely acknowledging the receptionist. In the changing room, she shredded her track pants and sweatshirt to reveal a tiny pair of shorts and a crop top, then sauntered through the gym to the treadmill. She enjoyed the admiring glances from the other members, all the fatties huffing and puffing their way round the gym. Tim, her personal trainer, an ex-marine, greeted her and her eyes lit up at the sight of him. He was the only person she tolerated giving her orders and she enjoyed it. She loved pushing her body to the limits.

Tim put her through an intensive forty-five minutes and by the end of the work-out, she felt as if she'd just completed the London Marathon. On her way back to the changing room, she passed the swimming pool and noticed that it was empty. The gentle mass of sparkling blue water looked enticing. Clarissa looked at her watch. She was due to ride Sid at eleven but that could wait.

Having retrieved her costume from her locker, she was soon swimming up and down the pool, enjoying a rare moment of peace. The pool filled up with several young men and Clarissa decided to use the steam room, enjoying the attention as she passed backwards and forwards between the pool and steam room. In the end, it was after eleven before she made her way back out to the car. She rang Heather on the way home and left her a message to say she would ride Sid at twelve and to have him ready. As she drove, she busied herself checking her phone messages.

The house was quiet when she entered the front door. Clarissa dumped her swimming stuff and gym kit on the hall floor and went upstairs to change into her riding clothes. There was a knock at the door and Sylvie called out, 'Coffee, Madame.' Sylvie placed the tray carefully on a gilt, inlaid Victorian side table. 'Can I get you anything else?' she enquired politely.

Clarissa didn't even look up as she ran her eye over her cream and, luckily for Sylvie, spotless breeches. 'You can go.'

Clarissa drank her coffee. As she put the cup back on the tray she spilt a drop on the cream carpet. Careless of her, but Sylvie could get it off. She wondered what the latest in interior design for bedrooms was. It was about time it was done again. She marched downstairs and out through the kitchen to the scullery to put on her boots and half chaps, and was soon standing by the mounting block in the yard.

'Heather, where is my horse? Don't keep me waiting,' Clarissa barked out across the yard. Heather appeared a moment later with Sid immaculately turned out, and Clarissa waited while she tightened the girth and pulled the stirrups down. She held Sid by the mounting block as Clarissa clambered up and settled herself in the saddle. Snatching the reins, Clarissa turned Sid sharply and made her way out to the ménage.

Sylvie appeared in the yard as Clarissa disappeared from view.

'Are we aving a good day?'

'Just bloody great. I lunged Sid for forty-five minutes this morning as Madame did not turn up to ride him. I've bunged him in the horse walker since then, so hopefully he'll behave.'

'I think it would be more fun if e didn't.'

'Yes, you might think that but I wouldn't wish that on anyone. She'll get her comeuppance one of these days.'

'At least she'll be out of your air for the rest of the day. It's the big event tonight which means an afternoon of beautifying.'

'Yes, thank goodness. The added bonus is she won't ride tomorrow either because she'll be hung over.'

Clarissa rode Sid gingerly around the ménage. She kept him on a tight rein and bullied him along, trying to ensure that he cooperated and didn't try any funny business. She was more than a little afraid of him as he was a big horse and she'd seen him performing aerial acrobatics with Heather on more than one occasion. She knew she wouldn't be able to hold him if he tried it with her. Nevertheless, at seventeen one hands high, she enjoyed the prestige of being seen on such an animal and persevered with him. She had a show jumping competition coming up and she enjoyed the kudos of being a 'show jumper'. It impressed her non-horsey friends no end. After twenty minutes of pussy footing around the arena, she decided to call it a day and took him back to Heather.

'Heather, he needs to be jumped. I haven't got time today and we have the competition next weekend.' She jumped off and threw the reins at Heather.

'Yes, I haven't forgotten,' Heather replied politely. 'Do you want me to ride Doucette for you later?'

Clarissa looked at Heather is if she were mad. 'Of course; I thought I just told you I am extremely busy. I do pay you to look after my horses, don't I?' Clarissa turned on her heel, well aware that she hadn't been near her gentle mare in three days, and marched back into the house. Heather grimaced at Sylvie, who'd hidden in one of the empty stables while Clarissa dismounted and was now trying to cross the yard without being seen.

Entering the back kitchen, Clarissa pulled off her boots, leaving the second one still in the boot jack and dumping her hat and whip unceremoniously on the floor. Ruffles, who'd looked up from his warm basket by the Aga, quickly assessed who'd come in and lowered his head back down. She'd kicked him a few times in passing and he now kept his distance. Clarissa headed for her pristine marble bathroom and turned on the shower, stepping in and enjoying the feeling of the powerful jets running over her body and hair. She thought about this evening's event with mounting excitement. Last year it had been a great success with a phenomenal attendance and a huge show of generosity from the guests. The auction itself had raised over sixty-three thousand pounds, which, when added to the total, had exceeded two hundred and fifty thousand. She hoped to do even better this year. She turned off the shower.

'Clarissa darling, are you decent? May I come in? Your hair rescuer is here.'

'Oh Franco, darling, do come in,' Clarissa called out with carefully considered enthusiasm, emerging from the bathroom in a large fluffy robe. There was much air kissing and Franco guided Clarissa over to the dressing table.

'Well, what a week I've had and the gossip from Paris...' his hands twisted in the air above his head and he rolled his eyes to heaven. 'I don't know where to begin, but first your hair, darling, up or down?'

'Definitely up. I'm wearing a strapless dress and I want to show off my neck and shoulders to their full advantage.'

Franco got to work on Clarissa's hair, while updating her with his latest gossip. She listened with great interest. She enjoyed hearing about other peoples' misfortunes: who'd put on weight, whose husband had been caught cheating, whose child had been expelled from school. Franco was a mine of such information and Clarissa was happy to feed him a few juicy tidbits, while being careful to gush about how well Charles's business was doing and how wonderfully the children were getting on at school. She made sure she was always on her best behaviour when Franco was around. It was hard work, especially for an up do that took two hours. The finished result was spectacularly good. Franco cost a small fortune but he was worth every penny. Clarissa knew that several other people had tried to book him but she'd warned him off doing any of her acquaintances' hair. She couldn't risk being upstaged.

She suddenly realized that she was starving, not having eaten a thing since breakfast. She looked at her watch. If she were quick, she'd be able to get something down her before her makeup and nails. She phoned down to the back kitchen 'Soup, tomato and basil, now.' She didn't wait for an answer.

Sylvie sauntered into the main kitchen and was surprised to see Carl, the family's chef, there. 'I thought you were off today as your presence is not required.'

'I am but I left my mobile here so I've just popped in to collect it.'

'Oh right, well her ladyship is after tomato and basil soup. 'Ave you got any?'

'Yup, in the fridge.'

Sylvie rummaged in the fridge and brought out a carton, 'Do you mean this? Waitrose Finest? I thought you made everything from scratch?'

'Yes, I mean that, and no I don't make everything from scratch and believe me she won't know the difference.' He made for the door.

'Oh God, she will, you'll get into trouble.'

'Oh God, she won't,' he mimicked, 'and don't worry, I won't either! Look, I've been feeding her ready bought stuff for ages and she is none the wiser. Just make sure she doesn't find out and everything will be fine. Pour the remainder into another container and bin that carton. I meant to do that earlier, actually, so thank you.' Carl left whistling, leaving an amazed Sylvie standing in the kitchen, the hand holding the soup raised before her. Obviously thinking he was going to get fed, Ruffles suddenly appeared, wagging his tail. His barking galvanised her into action and she hastily poured the soup into a bowl and popped it in the microwave.

'Shhh, Ruffs. Onestly, some people,' she said bending down to stroke him. She prepared a tray and took the soup and a roll up to Clarissa. She knew Clarissa wouldn't touch the roll but it felt good to tempt her with it. The door bell rang as she reached the top step and she popped the tray on a nearby table before racing back down to answer it. Sophie, Clarissa's make-up lady, had arrived and she took her upstairs, picking the tray back up as she went. She knocked on the bedroom door. 'Are you ready for this?' she mouthed to Sophie.

'Enter. About time too, Sylvie. Is that dolt Sophie here yet?'

'Yes, as a matter of fact she is,' announced Sophie, her smile not quite reaching her eyes.

'Ahh, Sophie, good. Nails first, I think.'

'Maybe you'd better eat your soup before I start Mrs Hambridge.' Sophie busied herself with getting her things out.

'What colour dress are you wearing?'

'It's black, strapless, Oscar de la Renta. It's over there.'

'Black, how fitting,' murmured Sophie. 'Shall we do red lipstick and minimal eye makeup?'

'No. I want to emphasise my eyes, so make them smoky and keep the lipstick neutral.'

'Right, if that is what you would like, although red lipstick and lighter eyes would look great.'

'No, I don't think so. I want smoky eyes. Just get on with it.'

Clarissa swallowed her soup, not touching the roll. It always made her feel virtuous to resist. No doubt Sylvie would eat it for her. She indicated to Sylvie to remove the tray. 'Sylvie, do you know what time Charles is getting home?'

'No, Madame, but I should imagine around five o'clock.'

'Imagine? That's no good to me. Are his clothes ready?'

'Of course, Madame.'

'He'd better not be late.' It was imperative that she presented the correct image and that meant having Charles next to her. 'And he'd better not have drunk too much. Did Charles drive his own car today or get picked up?'

'He took the Land Rover so he could take the dogs.' Sylvie failed to add that he'd also taken Dave, his gamekeeper.

Clarissa clapped her hands together, mentally shutting the door on that little worry and turned her attention back to her nails. 'Cream toes and black fingers I think.'

By five o'clock Sophie had finished and was relieved to be on her way out. She wondered how Sylvie put up with Clarissa. If it wasn't for the money or the worry that she'd bad-mouth her, she would tell her where to go.

Sylvie meanwhile was zipping Clarissa into her dress and making suitably admiring noises. Clarissa was being picked up at six. *One more hour and she'd have a bit of peace.* A car pulled up outside. 'That'll be the Land Rover, Madame. I'll just pop down and remind Mr Ambridge to urry.'

Sylvie dashed out to the car, where Dave was letting the dogs out of the boot and shooing them towards the stables. 'Where's Charles?' she asked nervously. Dave indicated the front passenger seat, where Charles was sprawled, seemingly sound asleep. 'Oh Lordy. Madame will go ballistic.'

Between them, they managed to rouse Charles and manoeuvre him out of the vehicle and round to the back kitchen. Sylvie prayed Clarissa wasn't looking out of the window. They removed Charles's boots and gaiters and pushed him up the back stairs. 'Couldn't you get him away any sooner,' hissed Sylvie.

'Well, I did try but he wouldn't budge.' Dave didn't want to mention the fact that he'd been chatting up a new barmaid and had quite lost track of time, and hadn't quite realised how much Charles had managed to consume.

'You'll have to help me get him in the shower,' she whispered. 'We need to sober him up quickly; he's in a terrible state.'

They got him into the bathroom and started to pull off his clothes. 'I can't do this,' said Sylvie.

'Can't do what?' slurred Charles.

'Undress you and get you in the shower to sober you up,' she snapped.

'Oh, you are a naughty thing aren't you? I know all about French maids and what they can do for a man,' he hiccupped.

'Now then,' Dave intervened, 'we'll have none of that. Sylvie you go and make him some strong black coffee and leave him to me. Charles started singing loudly and Sylvie quickly turned on the shower, hoping the noise of the water would act as a disguise. She took great pleasure in turning the dial to cold. She made a quick getaway as Dave wrestled with a now giggling Charles who, having knocked over the laundry basket had crashed into the towel rail.

Having been half frozen in the shower and then warmed up with several cups of vile-tasting coffee, Charles was marginally more coherent. Dave managed to dress him, and propped him on the recliner. 'Thanks Dave,' Sylvie said. 'Well, we've done our best but I don't hold out much hope for him.' Charles let out a large snore as if to agree. At that moment, there were footsteps in the corridor.

'Shit,' whispered Dave.

'In the bathroom,' mouthed Sylvie and Dave flew in and hid behind the door.

'Charles, are you in there?' The door handle rattled but Charles was oblivious. Sylvie stood frozen to the spot, watching the handle and wondering what the hell to do. Thank goodness she'd locked the door. Clarissa hated Dave, who was the only staff member who stood up to her. She was always trying to convince Charles to get rid of him, but so far Charles had resisted, probably just to annoy her, of course. Sylvie knew that Clarissa would milk this one for all it was worth.

'Just coming darling,' Charles slurred. Sylvie let her breath go and turned to look at him. She watched in amazement as he began to sit up, all be it very gingerly.

'Are you drunk? Why is your door locked?' Clarissa barked.

'Won't be long, angel,' Charles sang affably, swaying gently as he got up from the recliner. Sylvie put her finger to her lips and shook her head as he caught sight of her and gave her a questioning glance.

'Oh, for Christ's sake, hurry up. The car's outside and I can't afford to be late. Sylvie! Where are you, you bloody useless woman?'

Clarissa stomped off down the hallway and Sylvie cautiously opened the door. Dave needed no encouragement to leave the bathroom. 'Great shoot. Enjoy your evening,' he got out, without stopping and legged it down the back stairs.

'Will you be OK, Sir? I think her ladyship wants me,' asked Sylvie.

'Yes. Yes. I'll follow on in a minute.'

Sylvie followed Dave down the back stairs and hurried into the hall, trying her best not to seem out of breath. 'Where in God's name have you been?' Clarissa glared at Sylvie. 'Honestly you are on borrowed time. There are plenty of other girls who would love this job and would be in here like a shot. Help me on with my wrap since Charles isn't here.' Sylvie adjusted the fur stole around Clarissa's shoulders, being careful not to touch the hairdo. She'd love to tell Clarissa that her reputation preceded her and that there would be fewer candidates queuing for her job than she thought. She did look amazing, however, which seemed really unfair.

'Have you seen Charles? I thought he sounded drunk. He had the audacity to call me "angel". '

'Yes. I made him some coffee and he was dressed and ready.'

'I expect he's been having one of those bloody cigars then.'

'Ready, ready, let's go,' Charles meandered down the stairs, a foppish mop of hair falling into his eyes. Clarissa eyed him suspiciously before swinging round to face the front door, which Sylvie hastened to open.

Charles trailed behind, winking mischievously at Sylvie as he went past.

Clarissa took some deep breaths in the back of the car. She decided to ignore Charles. She had wanted to get there before the guests but she was confident her planner would take care of everything. 'Look on the bright side, you'll be able to make a grand entrance,' Charles said condescendingly. The Bentley pulled up outside the venue and Clarissa noted with satisfaction that the photographers were ready and waiting.

'Paps and a red carpet! Well, well, we really do have grand ideas!'

'Try not to make a fool of yourself,' Clarissa spat at him as she waited for the chauffeur to open the door. Charles took great delight in giving her bottom a resounding smack as she left the car and he was captured with a big grin on his face, in contrast to his wife's strained expression.

They made a handsome couple as they walked down the red carpet and disappeared into the foyer. Edwina, Clarissa's mother, came bustling over when she saw them.

'Ahh, you're both here, good.'

'Looking gorgeous as ever,' Charles smiled at her.

'You old charmer, you,' Edwina pushed Charles gently and kissed him on both cheeks. 'My, my have you been drinking?' she asked with half a smile. She adored Charles, which annoyed Clarissa intensely.

'Just one or two. Been shooting you know, bagged the most.'

'Ahh, well then,' she said. 'But you'd better behave; you know how upset your wife will get otherwise, so pace yourself.'

'Of course, of course.' Charles was already scanning the room to see who was about. He was good at working a crowd. Clarissa had gone off in search of the planner so he was free to roam.

The evening was a resounding success with the promise auction raising more than the previous year. Clarissa enjoyed the limelight and made sure that the young journalist from the magazine Shropshire Life knew all about her hard work. The photographer had obliging let her guide him, so she knew the magazine would have plenty of shots of her with the right people. Charles also had a successful evening and congratulated himself on pulling not one but two women - one of them married the other a bright young nubile thing. He didn't think he was in any danger of being rumbled and he didn't much care anyway. He looked at Clarissa as the car took them home and wondered if she was involved with anyone. They certainly hadn't had sex for years. Surely, she must be getting it elsewhere. The gym instructor, maybe? Well, it was none of his business, the dry old trout. He was having plenty and enjoying every minute of it.

# Chapter 8

Charles slept in late the next morning, having drunk a pint of water before going to bed to minimize the threatening hangover. He lay dozing and reliving the previous night's activities with a smile on his face. It was just so easy he thought to himself. The first woman he'd seduced was Sarah, an old family friend in an unhappy marriage, who he'd always quite fancied but who'd always thwarted his previous advances. He'd found himself sitting next to her at dinner and had thought how exciting it would be to try it on in front of her husband, an utter bore who probably wouldn't notice if he shagged her there and then on the table in front of him.

'You're looking splendid tonight,' Charles had purred down her cleavage. 'Good enough to eat, I would say,' he'd added. He'd stared intently into her eyes and seen a shift in the way she appraised him.

'Are you flirting with me again?' She'd flicked her hair over to one side and leant into him, to his surprise gently rubbing her foot up and down his leg. She'd obviously had a bit to drink and was feeling less inhibited than usual.

'I'd like to do a whole lot more than that,' he'd whispered in her ear.

She'd stood up suddenly on the pretext of going to the powder room. 'Someone's phone is ringing,' she announced as she left, throwing Charles a meaningful look.

He'd made a great show of listening to his answer phone and Clarissa hadn't been overjoyed when he'd suddenly announced he'd missed an important call. 'Not at the table, for God's sake,' she'd hissed. He'd followed Sarah outside.

'This way,' he'd said to Sarah as he'd made his way up the lift and punched the call button.

'I can't believe I'm doing this,' she'd giggled and then, a little more nervously, 'Where are we going?'

'We'll find an empty room, shouldn't be too difficult,' he'd said confidently and dragged her into the lift before she'd had the chance to change her mind. Finding a room had actually been more difficult than he'd anticipated and he'd had to pay a young chambermaid a handsome sum to open a door. He was a practised lover, having learnt early on to satisfy a woman's desires before his own, which served a number of purposes, not least ensuring that the woman returned to him for sex whenever he so desired. He couldn't get enough and the more women the better. Sarah had been very satisfied and he knew he could add her to his list of repeat conquests.

Leaving Sarah to tidy herself up, he'd returned to the table and feigned surprise that she wasn't back. When someone asked him if he'd seen her, he suggested that maybe Clarissa should go to the ladies' cloakroom to check on her. Clarissa had eyed him suspiciously as she wandered off but she'd found Sarah chatting to an acquaintance.

'Oh, thank goodness for Clarissa,' Sarah announced to the table as she sat down. 'I didn't think I'd ever get away.'

Charles had been impressed.

His next conquest had been a young model named Hannah. He'd had to work considerably harder to seduce her as she pulled that old chestnut about valuing her reputation. 'I value your reputation too darling,' he'd told her, 'and I have a reputation to uphold as well, you know.' He'd run his finger lightly down her neck and along her collar bone and gazed at her as if mesmerized by her beauty. Her lower lip had begun to tremble and he'd known in that moment she would give in. He still had the key to the bedroom which he and Sarah had made such good use of and he led her towards the backstairs before she'd had a chance to change her mind. She had been very exciting as she'd acted coy and slightly unsure of herself throughout which had only increased his ardour. He'd wondered if it had been her first time, in which case she was a lucky girl.

A knock at the door brought Charles back to the present. 'Come in, come in if you bear gifts,' he called. Sylvie appeared at the door and brought in a tray with breakfast on it.

'You did ask to be woken at this time, Sir,' she said.

'Yes, yes I did, and what have you brought me?' The tantalizing aroma of cooked bacon reached his nostrils and he threw back the covers and sat up, stark naked. Sylvie looked away hurriedly and Charles laughed at her discomfort. 'Never seen a man naked before?' Sylvie ignored him.

'Are you riding this morning?' she asked placing the tray carefully down on a nearby table.

'Why? Are you offering?' he asked innocently. 'Yes, tell Heather I'll be down in twenty minutes, will she be coming out?'

'I think so, but I'm not sure. Anyway I'll go and tell her,' Sylvie couldn't wait to get out of the doorway.

* * *

Charles enjoyed his morning ride with Heather. She was good fun and up for a hard gallop. She had rebuffed all his advances until he'd finally realised that she must be a lesbian and given up. It wasn't as if there was a shortage of women after all.  By twelve-thirty he was back and showered and ready for a lunch meeting with Gary at his golf club. Charles was the first one there and was busy chatting up the barmaid when Gary arrived.

'Old habits die hard,' Gary winked at Charles. 'Good night last night was it?' he enquired with a smirk on his face.

'Oh yes,' Charles grinned back. 'Two fine fillies. Well one filly but both fine; very fine.'

'Just the two, Charles? You must be slowing down.'

'Under the circumstances, I did very well.'

'Circumstances?'

'I had rather a lot to drink after the shoot yesterday. Clarissa was furious. It was worth getting squiffy for that alone!'

'You really are something else.' Gary shook his head from side to side, smiling to himself.

'Anyway, cut to the chase, how was the meeting?'

'Bloody fantastic. I think we'll be getting the full sixty million from various investors so, all being well, we should be able to get the banking arm of the business up and running in six months time. Annabelle and Justin having been working really hard on this deal.'

Charles looked impressed. 'That'll give you plenty of flexibility, then.'

'Yes, it will. We should be able to do some mix and match deals and we'll also be able to use the money for bridging finance in order to allow us time to set up a more conventional mortgage. There will be a lot more valuation work for you. How's your new recruit coming along?'

'Well, I think she'll be fine. Compliant sort; needs to get a bit more of a commercial head on her, but we'll work on that.'

Charles was interrupted by the maître d' coming over to find out if they wanted to eat yet. Charles was ravenous and they made their way through to the restaurant area. 'Good God man, I don't know where you put it all,' Gary exclaimed as Charles ordered foie gras, followed by sirloin with stilton sauce.

'I expect it is furring up my arteries nicely,' Charles laughed. 'I may have to have the vanilla crème brûlée and the cheeseboard to finish it off – with a glass of port, of course.'

'Sounds good to me. Anyway, you mentioned something about Henry and a rather good investment. You did mean Clarissa's brother didn't you?'

'Oh, yes, surprisingly. Well I don't know all the details but apparently the returns are currently between ten and fifteen percent per annum.'

'Are you sure about that?' Gary frowned slightly, 'that sounds too good to be true.'

'I agree, but Henry is going to show me some figures and if what he says is true, then I think I'll dip my toe in.'

'What sort of investment is it?'

'Well, it's exclusive for starters. You have to be invited to join and you need to be prepared to invest a minimum of two hundred thousand.'

'OK, well none of that's a problem, but I would like to see some evidence of the investment yields.'

'Absolutely, as would I. As soon as I have details I'll pass them on to you. The invitation is not a problem. I believe the fund is open at the moment for some new investors but they're quite selective.'

'I suppose they don't want any dodgy geezers then.'

'Definitely not. No riff raff! In fact you may have trouble getting in!' Charles laughed out loud.

'Touché,' grinned Gary. 'So, how did halfwit Henry come to be involved anyway?' There was a short silence while both men considered this.

'I think he knows the main guy, wife's uncle or brother or something.'

'Or something?' Gary queried with a raised eyebrow and half a smirk. 'Do you ever listen to anyone when they're telling you something.'

'Yes, well I got bored at that point. You know what Henry's like. He just goes on and on and I lost the will to live.'

'Hmm, well, I've only met him once and that was once too often, but I do think it would be prudent to check it all out. What about Clarissa, how much has she invested?'

'I wish I knew. The old baggage won't tell me but Henry mentioned a couple, and we didn't get to finish the conversation, so I would imagine two hundred thousand, which is the minimum.'

'Or two million,' added Gary after a pause. There was silence as both men digested this. Christ thought Charles, that is a lot of money.

'Hell, that gives her a return of over two hundred thousand a year,' Charles took a deep breath.

'I'm not so sure about this. My business does that as it is and I'm in full control. Gary sat thoughtfully, and then added, 'Actually, if I had any spare, I'd invest it in this business so count me out but I'll ask Annabelle and Justin; they might be interested.'

'Are you sure? It seems like a dead cert to me.'

'Yes, positive, I might regret it, of course. Keep me posted.'

'I will, don't you worry.'

'Looks like dinner is on the way.' Gary sat upright and shuffled the cutlery around on the table, 'and I don't mean the waitress!' He grinned at Charles who quickly looked behind him to check her out, only to be confronted by a waiter bearing the starters. He turned quickly back to Gary who was laughing.

'Sucker,' he said shaking his head, 'you really are incorrigible.'

'Jealous, that's what you are,' said Charles primly.

'I don't think so. You are going to come a cropper one day.'

'No way. I'm very careful. They're always married,' Charles paused, 'well, nearly always married and anyway, it's not as if I force them to do it and I make no promises. I don't wine and dine. It's just sex and some women like that.'

'Look, you don't have to justify yourself to me,' laughed Gary, 'but one day you might land yourself a bunny boiler.'

Charles had developed a niggling headache by the time he left the club. He felt a little irked by Gary. The two of them usually sang from the same hymn sheet but he wasn't sure if that had been the case today. Oh well, he was probably imagining it.

The dogs were waiting for him when he got home. He'd hoped Dave might have walked them but, then again, some fresh air wouldn't do him any harm and there was still an hour or so of daylight left. Whistling to the Labradors, he strode off across the lawn.

# Chapter 9

Izzy and Stephen sat on the sofa, their feet resting on an unopened packing box, both exhausted by the hassle that was involved with moving. The children were cycling about outside, wrapped up against the January chill. Izzy, wearing an old pair of jeans tucked into a bright pink pair of ski socks, a red sweatshirt and no makeup, looked relaxed and happy. Amazing, thought Stephen.

'Well the children seem to be enjoying themselves. How's Marmaduke? In fact where is Marmaduke?' Stephen exclaimed, suddenly noticing the cat basket was open.

'Christ,' exclaimed Izzy, jumping up. She started rummaging about in the remaining boxes but there was no sign.

'Children,' Stephen yelled out of the door, 'have you seen Marmaduke?'

'Ed has, Daddy,' Tatty said breathlessly as she whizzed by on her scooter. Ed came cycling slowly over, looking a bit sheepish. 'Well,' he began, and Stephen prepared himself, 'I was just checking on him, when I accidentally let him out. He went and hid behind a box.'

'Oh, for God's sake!' Stephen exclaimed and stomped back into the caravan.

Izzy, having heard the conversation, went to check again, but her efforts proved fruitless. 'He must have escaped out the door. God knows where he'll be now.' She could hear the children shouting his name.

'Well, he's probably hiding. He won't go far. He never has before. It's been a bit manic around here and he'll turn up when it quietens down.' Stephen was loath to spoil Izzy's good mood.

'Yes, but he's always been kept in for a week at least before he's been allowed out,' said Ben, coming in and sitting next to Izzy.

Izzy cuddled him, 'I'm sure he'll turn up like Daddy says.'

'Ed is such an idiot, why didn't he just leave his cage alone?'

'Yes, well it's easy to say now,' said Stephen. Want to come with me to get some fish and chips? You know Marmaduke. As soon as he smells food, he'll be back. '

\* \* \*

Sunday dawned with clear blue skies. The caravan was a little chilly to say the least.

'It's bloody freezing,' said Izzy, snuggling into Stephen.

'I suppose I ought to go and put the heaters on in case the children are up. I'll put the kettle on, shall I?' It had been decided that for the sake of their sanity they would purchase two caravans. The larger one was a three-bedroomed unit, with a sitting-room with a table to eat at and a kitchen with a washing machine. The smaller caravan they intended to use for extra storage and Stephen's study. The units were interlocked so they could move from one to another without having to touch the ground.

Izzy snuggled tighter into Stephen and managed to delay him leaving the bedroom for a little longer. By the time he finally got up, Tatty and Ed were up and playing 'cars' in a couple of empty removal boxes, while Ben was in bed with his nose buried in a book. Stephen put the kettle on and fired up the heating in the sitting room. He realized the mugs were still next door, and he wandered off to get some. Tatty and Ed were now playing hide and seek and Tatty, opening a cupboard door suddenly screamed.

'Marmaduke! I've found Marmaduke!' Everyone piled into the kitchen area to see Tatty sitting in the cupboard with Marmaduke held firmly in her arms.

'How the devil did he get in there? ' said Stephen. 'OK, are all the doors and windows shut?' Reluctantly Tatty let Marmaduke go and the relieved cat leapt off her lap and stood surveying the scene, before backtracking into the cupboard.

'I think we'd better leave him there for now, he's obviously a bit traumatised,' said Izzy. 'He'll probably come out later.'

'Thank goodness,' a relieved Ed spoke up, 'I knew he wasn't lost.'

'Right,' said Stephen firmly, 'breakfast and I think we'd better unpack the litter tray. Christ it's cold.'

The family had breakfasted, showered and just finished dressing when there was a knock at the door. The children scrambled to answer it, with Ben getting there first.

'Gosh, how lovely, a welcoming committee!' smiled the man on the doorstep, dressed warmly in a thick coat and with a beanie on his head. He was holding a pair of slippers in one hand and a jar of coffee in the other. 'I've come prepared,' he said cheerily.

'Who are you?' asked Tatty, peering around Ben.

'I'm Simon, the builder. I've come to discuss a few things before I start on your new house.'

'Simon! Come in, come in,' said Stephen, hurriedly ushering the children away from the door. Actually, we've found the coffee, but that's really thoughtful.' Izzy rounded up the children. 'OK, how about I put a video on? And remember, no doors to be left open. We're a bit worried about the cat escaping,' she explained to Simon.

'Butter,' said Simon. 'On the cat's feet. Allegedly it stops them running away.'

'Oh, I've not heard that before. Maybe we'll give it a try.'

''Mummy, shall I get the butter now?' Tatty piped up.

'Umm, not right now. Let's go and watch the video with your brothers.'

'Don't want to.' Tatty plonked herself down on the sofa next to Simon. 'The boys are going to watch a boring film. I'll sit quietly and won't speak.'

Stephen brought the coffee over. 'Right, I've got the plans here. I suppose it's the roof first,' Stephen looked up at Simon.

'Best to get it all water tight before you do anything else, but we'll start digging the foundations for the extension at the same time.' Simon sat up and drained his coffee, 'I think we're pretty organised for now, so expect a load of work men for about eight. We can't start much earlier because of the light, but at least the days are lengthening, so that should improve things.'

'Great. I'll be about in the morning but I'm off to work about eightish and Izzy not long after. I'll leave you a set of keys so you can get in and make coffee.'

'Actually Stephen, I've got a meeting up this way tomorrow, so I can probably leave a little later. Or I can take the children if you want fifteen minutes with the builders. '

Stephen looked at Izzy in surprise. She'd kept that one up her sleeve. On the other hand... 'That would be great,' he said quickly.

'Right, I'll be off then, I'll ring if I have a problem?'

# Chapter 10
## *April 2003*

Charles sat nursing a glass of whisky in the hotel lounge. He'd enjoyed himself with Sarah a number of times a week over the last few months. He'd been surprised when she'd contacted him after their first dalliance at the charity ball. He was waiting for her now and had booked a room in preparation for a spot of late afternoon entertainment. Truth to be told, he was starting to tire of her, but she'd been a willing pupil when he'd resorted to a few tactics to spice up their sessions.

*Talking of willing pupils, what was he going to do about Izzy?* The stubborn woman was still prone to finding fault with the properties he sent her to value. He kept reminding her that giving the correct valuation helped clients to continue living in their homes. His thoughts were broken by Sarah approaching and he noted that she was looking radiant; in fact, better than he'd ever seen her looking. *Now there's a grateful woman*, he congratulated himself.

'You're looking pleased with yourself.' Sarah slid into the seat opposite him.

'I'm admiring my handy work. You are blossoming under my ministrations.' He leant forward and reached out to stroke her cheek, but Sarah turned her head away and glanced round the room nervously. She cleared her throat and, sensing a change in her, Charles quickly continued, 'shame it will have to stop.' For good measure he thought to add, 'before we get too attached, you see.'

Charles was relieved to see that Sarah didn't look too upset. So he'd been right, she had been about to finish it and he'd got in first. He'd never been dumped and he wasn't going to let that happen now. 'Yes, I think perhaps you are right. It wouldn't do to get too close and the longer this goes on, the more chance we have of being found out,' Sarah proffered.

'It's been good though. I enjoyed our trysts.' Charles waited expectantly for her affirmation.

'So have I, it's been . . .' Sarah paused as if searching for the right words, 'a fulfilling experience.'

'Yes, well, we can always hook up on the odd occasion if you fancy.'

'That would be lovely.'

Sarah stood up and Charles noted that she hadn't even removed her coat. She bent down and kissed him chastely on the cheek, before making her way to the door without a backward glance. Charles had to admit that he hadn't anticipated that one. Worse, he had an itch that required scratching. He would have to pay Madame Lily a visit on the way home. His mind ran over the possibilities for the weekend. He was hunting on Saturday and, weather permitting, flying on Sunday. A challenge, but one he could rise to no doubt.

He decided to distract himself by putting in a call to Henry.

'Ahh Henry, Charles here. Just wondering how my investment is coming along?'

'Charles, I was just about to ring *you*. Good news, my boy, good news.' Henry guffawed down the phone and Charles had to move his mobile away from his ear. 'You've made seven per cent this quarter, so your initial investment of umm, where is it?...'

'Two hundred thousand,' Charles chipped in, 'has given me fourteen thousand.'

'Yes, that's right. Not bad for three months now is it?'

'Fantastic actually, Henry. Just fantastic. You really have come up trumps with this deal of yours. Well, I don't want any out it's doing much better than it was stuck in that off-shore account. You can reinvest for me, and don't forget I want a statement.'

'Of course, of course, in the post as we speak. You could always put some more money in. I have a feeling the fund might give a return of over twenty-five per cent this year. Tip off a few mates if you like. I'm sure we could arrange a little introductory fee for the right kind of investor.'

Charles digested this information for a while. 'How big a 'little' introductory fee?' he eventually enquired.

'Well, five per cent of whatever they invest. Not to be sniffed at, but remember they will have to satisfy our specific criteria. We won't have just anyone.'

'No, of course not.' Charles was beginning to reappraise Henry. 'Is there a limit to how many we recruit?'

'No, I don't think so, but I imagine two hundred thousand will preclude quite a few.'

'So Clarissa will have done all right as well, I take it?'

56

'Naturally I'm not prepared to discuss other clients but currently the investment is giving excellent returns for all investors.'

'Other clients? Honestly, Henry, Clarissa is my wife…'

'Changing the subject, I might have another little investment up my sleeve. Property, this time, in the Bahamas.'

'Oh right, not time share is it?'

'Good lord, dear boy, of course not.' Henry sounded indignant. 'No this is a lovely development of exclusive homes overlooking the most beautiful bay. I'll email you the website and you can have a look. We are just asking for deposits at the moment but I suggest you pop over and take a look before you buy.'

'Is Clarissa interested?' asked Charles

'I haven't run it by her yet, a little birthday surprise, perhaps?'

'Henry, you really are surpassing yourself.' Charles smiled, a plan forming in his mind. He would take a couple of days off work and pop over for a look. He needed to keep in Clarissa's good books and this would be a neat way of doing it. An extravagant birthday gift would definitely go down well.

'I feel a business trip coming on,' he enthused and began to think about who might be available to accompany him.

'Right, well I'll pass your details on to my agent and she will show you round when you get there and give you some more information.'

'OK. I'll check out the website first and see what this looks like.'

'Oh, you will be impressed. Five-bedroom residences, all en suite, panoramic views of the bay and each with its own swimming pool and servants quarters of course. An acre of garden and well protected with a gated entrance.'

'Yes, yes Henry. I get the picture. How much?'

'About one and a half million dollars each, but you'll get a good rental income and, of course, capital growth.' *Christ!* thought Charles, *I've just closed my off shore account, how am I going to get my hands on more?* As if Henry could read his mind, he added, 'I can sort out finance for you if you need it old boy, being in the family and all that. I wouldn't want you to disappoint Clarissa, now.'

'Thanks, Henry. I'll have a look tonight and let you know.' Charles's phone buzzed, announcing an incoming call from Jess. 'I'll have to go now, my PA is on the other line, but I'll be in touch in the next few days.'

'Excellent dear boy, excellent, cheerio for now then.' Henry disconnected and Charles took the next call.

'Charles, I'm sorry to bother you but a couple of things have come up, unfortunately both concerning Izzy.'

'Fire away,' Charles sat back in his chair.

'Well, the first one concerns the farm at Lilleshall, the one Izzy valued just after she started.'

'Yes, I know the one. I cast my eye over the valuation at the time. So what's the problem?'

'Well, the chimney has just collapsed and apparently it wasn't mentioned in the report so the bank is concerned.'

'Don't worry about that, they'll be covered by insurance. It's not our problem — they should have had a structural report. What's the next issue?'

'GRA has sent a valuation report back because apparently if the value is not two and a quarter million the deal won't go through. They're saying that Izzy has undervalued the property.'

'What value did she put on it?' said Charles

'Oh, sorry...' there was a pause and rustling of papers, 'two million.'

'Right,' said Charles while he considered this. 'Put two and a quarter mill on the report and send it off. I'll talk to Isabella later. It's only twelve per cent.'

'OK, I'll get on with it. They want it yesterday of course!'

'Thanks, that would be great,' Charles paused, 'where is Izzy anyway?'

'She's out with Harry doing a farm appraisal.'

'Oh, right, well I'll speak to her in the morning then. I'll be in first thing.'

'OK, see you tomorrow, have a good evening.'

Charles rang Madame Lily and fixed an appointment before heading out to his car.

* * *

Charles was first in the office the next morning and busy trying to sort through the piles of paper that completely covered his desk. He had a lot of jobs on that needed finishing but he had a tendency to get bored and they were left until the clients made a fuss. Charles really only enjoyed doing valuations and he'd decided to pass on some of his less lucrative jobs to Izzy and Harry. After all, isn't that what junior staff were for? he thought as he paired files with paper work and stacked them ready for passing on.

'Morning Charles,' said Jess brightly, bringing in his coffee and a Danish pastry and placing them carefully on top of a file.

'Yes, morning. Is Isabella in?' he glanced at Jess before turning his attention to the pastry. 'What's this in aid of?' He looked from the pastry to Jess and back to the pastry.

'Nick's birthday, he bought them in for everyone, and yes Izzy is here.'

'Right, send her in then. I'd better have a word about the valuation.' Charles picked up the pastry and took a large bite out of it.

'You wanted to see me?'

'Oh yes, Izzy, come in and take a seat.' Charles took another bite of his pastry. 'Right, well, cut to the chase. The farm at Lilleshall with the dodgy chimney - it fell down,' he said talking with his mouth full.

'What?' said Izzy looking horrified.

'Just the chimney Izzy, not the whole house.' Charles smiled at his own joke, while Izzy continued to look dismayed.

'Of course not. We knew the chimney was a problem.'

'You knew the chimney was a problem, Izzy,' Charles emphasised, 'and you should really have mentioned it in your report, just to be on the safe side.'

Izzy opened her mouth to say something and then shut it again quickly.

'It's not a problem though,' Charles went on, dusting crumbs off his shirt. 'They should have had a structural survey done and they're covered by insurance anyway, so don't lose any sleep over it. Just remember that next time you ought to mention something so significant.'

'Of course,' Izzy said through gritted teeth. Her face was burning and her heart racing as she recalled how Charles had discouraged her from mentioning it. She wished she could be more ballsy about this.

'The other matter is the valuation you did recently for Griedy Roberts & Alright, the farm just on the outskirts of Wolverhampton. You valued it at two million. I looked at the report and I believe it would be worth two and a quarter million and so I have amended your report accordingly. It needed to be finalised, so Jess did it all for you yesterday evening.'

'Oh, really.' Izzy felt stunned.

'I think it might be a good idea if you went back to showing me all your valuations before sending them off to avoid this happening again.' Charles smiled at Izzy and sat back in his chair with his hands clasped behind his head. 'I keep telling you that no valuation is going to be more accurate than ten or fifteen per cent so you can quite legitimately add on ten per cent. It's no big deal. Just gets the job done.'

'Yes, I see that, but... OK, I'll bring you each one for a final check,' Izzy gave in.

'Good, well I'm glad we've sorted that out.'

'Are you busy just now?' a Scottish accent butted in.

'Ahh, Piers, no do come in. Isabella was just leaving.' Charles looked at Izzy who stood up rapidly.

'Right, back to work then,' she said resentfully and left the room, barely glancing at Piers or Charles.

Piers sat down and crossed one leg over the other, revealing black socks and expensive highly-polished black brogues.

'Is everything all right? I heard there was a wee problem with a farm that Izzy inspected recently. Something about the chimney.'

'Yes, we did have a small problem,' Charles sat up straighter in his chair. 'Isabella neglected to mention the chimney in her report, although she did reduce the valuation accordingly. It's all sorted out now and there won't be a problem. In fact Isabella will show me all her valuations in future before they go out, just in case anything like that crops up again.'

'It sounds like she needs careful mentoring, Charles. I hope you are looking after her properly.'

'Of course I am. I've just gone through her latest valuation with her. I don't know what more I can do. She's not a trainee, you know.'

'No, I'm well aware of that, but she hasn't done a huge amount of valuation work and it sounds like she needs guidance.'

'Yes, Piers, and I am guiding her so stop worrying. Now, if you don't mind, I've got a hundred and one things to get through including checking this months' figures, which you will be pleased with.'

'It's been a good month that's for sure. In fact, the first three months of this year have been grand. I just don't want any standards slipping or we might lose work.' Piers gave Charles a penetrating look.

'That's not going to happen. G.R.A are very pleased with the quality of our work and the fact we turn it around so quickly for them,' Charles said indignantly and then added 'as are the rest of our clients.'

'Yes, I did see we were getting a lot of instructions from Griedy Roberts & Alright just now.'

'Gary and I get on well, that's all, and he likes to do business where he knows he is going to get well treated. Really Piers, you don't have to worry. Valuation is my side of the business and it's going well.'

'No doubting that. I just wanted to make sure Isabella was doing all right and settling in as I haven't had much to do with her and you have.' Piers stood up, 'I'd like to meet this Gary Griedy and the other directors sometime as well.

'No problem,' said Charles, enthusiastically, glad to be off the subject of Izzy. 'I'll set a lunch meeting up for you. Jess can synchronize diaries.'

Piers left the room and Charles sat back in his chair and chewed a pencil. He and Piers had set up the business together six years ago, Charles a rural land agent and Piers a commercial surveyor but with considerable experience of the rural market as well. Piers had developed his role as an expert witness in support of litigation cases and did a lot of planning work, while Charles had developed the valuation work.

He decided that it probably would be a good idea for Piers to meet Gary, Annabelle and Justin. He picked up the phone to get the ball rolling.

# Chapter 11

Izzy sat at her desk, fuming.

'Problems?' Harry's voice penetrated her thoughts.

'No, everything's fine,' she said loudly for the benefit of anyone listening and forced a smile on her face.

'Are you sure? You look a bit fed up.'

'No, honestly, I'm fine, just working some things out.'

'Ok then. Here to help if I can, you know?' He smiled and Izzy felt herself weaken. She could use a friend right now. On the other hand, she didn't know Harry that well. He was always easy to work with and seemed sympathetic, but he might be in cohorts with Charles for all she knew.

'Well, it's just... I've been given some work to complete for a Lord Butterton, and it is taking me a while to work out what has been going on,' she fudged, hoping that would appease him for now.

'Bigotted Butterton?'

*Great!* thought Izzy. *What now?* 'I take it you know him then, Harry?'

'Unfortunately our paths have crossed once or twice. He's a miserable old bugger. Oh, and just so you know, he's an outright chauvinist and a dreadful letch. I suggest you take someone with you when you visit him.'

'Wonderful. I wonder why Charles has given him to me then?'

'I shouldn't take it personally. Charles gets bored with jobs and dumps them on whichever of us springs to mind. He's done it to me several times and it's a right pain in the arse; sounds like it's your turn. My advice is make sure you check through everything with a fine-tooth comb.'

'Thanks, Harry. I'll do that. I don't want to make any more mistakes.'

'Anymore?'

*Damn*, thought Izzy. 'Oh, nothing, honestly; I'd better get on Harry.'

She felt a bit guilty as she watched him walk back to his desk. He did seem a nice guy and he'd certainly been the most helpful of her colleagues. She was probably being paranoid. She quickly scribbled

'Lunch?' on a Post-It note. Harry was on the phone when she walked by his desk but he nodded at her as she stuck it in front of him.

Twelve-thirty finally arrived.

'Are you ready?' she asked Harry.

'Yup, come on then, let's get out of here before someone decides to join us. Where do you want to go?'

'Do you mind if we get a sandwich and walk down by the river as it's such a glorious day. Living in a caravan, makes one desperate to stretch one's legs.'

'No, that's fine. I could do with some fresh air, too. You can fill me in on how many woolly jumpers you are going to bed in now?' Izzy punched his arm, playfully. They purchased sandwiches from a nearby bakery and headed down to the river. It was one of those gorgeous spring days which began cold and crisp with clear blue skies, the early frost gradually melting in the warm sunshine. They sat down on a bench and Izzy unwrapped her sandwich. She went to take a bite, but suddenly found that she couldn't eat.

'Spit it out then... and I'm not talking about your sandwich. You've been like a cat on a hot, tin roof all morning,' said Harry.

She sighed. 'Do you remember the valuation we did on that Victorian farmhouse?'

'Yes, of course. You were worried about its chimneys.' Harry took a mouthful out of his sandwich.

'Chimney! Do you by any chance remember the conversation I had with Charles after I'd done the report?'

'Yes, I do. We discussed it. Charles didn't want you to mention the chimney and you weren't happy about it. Why?'

'OK, well I got a bollocking from him today because the chimney collapsed and the bank wants to know why it wasn't in my report. Oddly, Charles wants to know why it's not in my report, too. I'm really pissed off because it *was* in the original report and it should have stayed there, and I just don't believe he'd have forgotten.'

'Oh, he won't have forgotten,' Harry said matter of factly. 'Couldn't really say anything to you before, you being new and so enthusiastic, but I'm afraid Charles likes to pass the buck whenever possible. He's dropped me in it more than a few times.'

'He always seems so bloody charming. You should have warned me. In fact, you told me to do what he said.'

'OK, sorry I spoke, but, really, did you have any option? It's his company at the end of the day.'

'And my reputation!'

'Yeah well, now you know. Get to know Piers better. He may not have Charles's charm, but he does have work ethic.' Harry looked at Izzy's sandwich. 'Are you going to eat that or just stare at it?'

'I'm not hungry.' She handed Harry the sandwich.

'You'll waste away.'

'Not much chance of that,' she responded patting her stomach. 'Mind you, if I lose my appetite on a regular basis, then I might. Every cloud as they say.'

'You're gorgeous as you are. Anything else?'

'Yeah, there is. I did a valuation for Griedy Roberts & Alright which was a bit lower than they were hoping for. Charles went behind my back and upped my value by two hundred and fifty thousand. Actually the value I had in mind after I'd seen the property was about one and three quarter million. I already had to push it to two million and now Charles has it at two and a quarter million. He changed the figures but that valuation still has my name on it, and quite frankly I'm furious. Did you know about this?'

'No. Actually, that is a bit worrying. If the figures don't stack up, people aren't going to be able to remortgage.'

'Well, Charles says the opposite. That we are letting people stay in their homes by erring on the generous side. That's what he keeps banging on about, at any rate.'

'Izzy, believe me, Charles doesn't give a fig for the people. On the other hand, he is head of valuations, he's been doing this type of work for over fifteen years and who are we to argue? At least the market is rising so, with luck, your house will soon be worth the extra.'

'Unless, we are asked to do a revaluation before then,' Izzy stared at Harry ruefully.

'I suppose you could talk to Piers if you are really worried. Otherwise, you are going to have to stay one step ahead of Charles somehow. Make it clear you are not going to be the fall guy.'

'I suppose you're right. Time to get back, I think. Thanks for listening, Harry, I really appreciate it.' They stood up together and Harry looked down at her.

'Anytime,' he said and their eyes locked. Izzy looked away first, smiling a little uncomfortably. 'Oh, by the way, it's drinks down the pub for Nick's birthday? Coming along?' Harry's tone was light and Izzy wondered if she'd imagined things.

'Alright, I'll try.' Back in the office, she sent Stephen a text to say she'd be late home.

* * *

Izzy parked between the static caravan and a huge pile of rubble. She wasn't looking forward to the confines of the caravan tonight. She decided to have a quick look around the house. She switched the hall light on and wandered from room to room, feeling frustration building within her. The cold rooms smelt of damp and there were piles of rubble scattered about. The place looked like a bombsite. Wearily, she shut the front door behind her and made her way across the mud to the caravan.

Stephen was sitting on the sofa with a glass of wine in his hand, reading a book. She balanced in the doorway, reaching down to chuck off her now-filthy work shoes.

'Have they made any bloody progress on the house this week?'

'Hello Izzy. Shut the door, will you? It's cold and the children are in bed. I've saved you some supper.'

'Sorry. I didn't know it was Nick's birthday until today, *really*. I didn't want to seem anti-social if everyone else was going. How was your day?'

'Fine!' Stephen returned to his book. Izzy changed out of her work clothes and heated up her meal in the microwave. She poured herself a glass of wine and sat on the sofa next to Stephen.

'How are the children?'

'Haven't you checked?' Stephen looked at his watch and turned unsmilingly to Izzy. 'You do realize you haven't kissed them goodnight all week.'

'I'm sorry. I just seem to have one thing after another to deal with. Hopefully next week will be better.'

'Well, I hope you haven't forgotten I've got parents' evening on Wednesday and Thursday. You'll have to be back to sort the children out after school.'

'I think Wednesday may be a problem, actually, as I'm away for the day.'

'Well, Izzy, that's tough. You'll just have to sort it out, won't you?' Stephen reached over for his briefcase and put the book inside.'

'Anyway, what is happening with the house?' said Izzy, changing the subject.

'Nothing at present as you saw for yourself. We are still waiting for the matching timber.'

'So why can't the other jobs go ahead?'

'Look, we've been through this before Izzy. If you want things to go faster, come home on time and let me do a couple of hours on it in the evening. I can't do homework and evening meals and bedtime and then start on the house too.'

'And I keep saying let's get the builders back in. At this rate, we'll be living in this godforsaken caravan next year.'

'I'm very sorry if your ladyship is unhappy but that's just the ways it is,' he said coldly. 'Believe it or not, even with your invaluable money, we can't afford a permanent workforce on site.'

'There's no need to be mean, Stephen.'

'Isn't there Izzy? Where would you like me to start? You are never here. You show no interest in the building project, other than to complain. You show no interest in your children — did you even know that Ed's class was doing the assembly today or that Tatty went to play with a friend this afternoon? No, because the slip about the assembly was still in Ed's bag. He told me he didn't give it to me because he knew neither of us would come. How does that make you feel? Or the fact that the nursery mother rang the childminder rather than us to arrange for Tatty to go over and play? Don't give it a thought. You just keep rolling in late night after night. Oh and excuse me for being pissed off, I wonder why?'

'You are being really unfair, Stephen,' Izzy said quietly placing her fork down on the plate. 'I'm actually under quite a lot of pressure at the moment.'

'And I'm not?'

'I do know what it is like. I was doing all the child care before I took this job. I know how demanding they can be. I hope to work my way up in this firm and make big money, so we don't have any more money worries.'

'Izzy, I'm not complaining about the children. I love being around them. My salary was plenty to live on. Why don't you face it, you don't want to be a mum full stop.

'How dare you? And you might think you earn a decent salary but I'm talking about big money - six figures - real money Stephen!'

'And I thought we were on the same wave length. I can't believe how much you've changed in a few months, what is it with you?'

'Ambition, I suppose, there's nothing wrong with that.'

'No, Izzy, but at what price?' Stephen stared at her, sadly.

'Stephen, I feel fulfilled for the first time in a long while, I've hated not working and yes I do think it's dull looking after children. So, maybe I'm not cut out for motherhood. Happy? I want to work and I will.'

'I'm off to bed, Izzy. I don't wish to discuss this anymore but, just think about it, at what price?'

# Chapter 12

Stephen lay on his side in the small double bed. He'd hardly slept – a knot of anger tightening his stomach every time he replayed his conversation with Izzy. As she shifted next to him, her leg brushed against his and he moved away. As she shifted again, he threw back the covers and headed for the shower. God he'd had enough of living in the caravan. It may be mid-April but he couldn't stop shivering. He stared at his reflection in the bathroom mirror. He looked terrible. He rubbed at his stubble, his breath steaming up the glass before he'd had time to reach for his razor. Turning on the shower, he took solace in the fact that at least the underpowered trickle was hot.

The children were awake when he emerged from the bathroom. Leaping into some clothes, he got the heaters on and began making breakfast. Tatty wandered into the kitchen half dressed and busied herself finding spoons for the cereal, rabbitting on as she did so.

'Daddy, you're not listening to me.'

'Sorry, sweetheart, what is it?'

'I've set the table. I want to help do the lunchboxes. I can butter the bread.'

'Fantastic, Tatty.' He closed his eyes. Tatty liked to help him and he usually loved this too brief interaction with her, even if she did make twice the work for him. Today, however, he just wanted to get the lunches done.

'I'll make them with her today, if you like, Dad,' Ben announced, as he threw himself down on the bench seat and grabbed a cereal packet.

'Actually, Ben, I'll take you up on that. Thanks.'

While Ben and Tatty buttered sliced of bread, Stephen swallowed a strong black coffee. Maybe some fresh air would wake him up. 'I'm just nipping outside for five minutes, guys. Be good,' he entreated, tripping over Marmaduke's empty bowl as he took a step towards the door. Just as he shut the door behind him, Ed arrived and set about filling a bowl to the top with Rice Krispies before pouring on a quantity of milk. The cereal flowed over on to the table, heading for Tatty's neatly stacked pile of bread. 'Oops,' Ed giggled as Tatty began to wail. Ben lobbed a spoon at him. 'You are such an idiot,' he sneered, just as the spoon connected with Ed's forehead.

'Oh for goodness sake. Stop that now! Ben look what you've made Ed do? Don't you know better than to throw cutlery? Clear up that mess immediately.' Both boys dived towards the kitchen roll, glaring fiercely at each other as Izzy groped for the kettle.

Stephen returned to find all three children in tears. He was about to say something, but simply scooped what remained of the bread on to the kitchen counter and began furiously shoving ham and cheese between the slices. Izzy was tempted to throw her coffee at him but gritted her teeth and took her mug into the bathroom. She returned feeling calmer and made a point of asking Ed how his assembly had gone.

'Mummy, why can't you stay at home? All the other mummies came to watch,' Ed began.

'Well, darling, if I had known, I could have taken the morning off but you didn't show me the letter. Mummy has to work so we can have a new house and be able to go skiing and have a nice new car.'

Ed brightened up, 'What sort of car, Mummy?'

'Well, I'm not sure yet. I have to work for the company a bit longer before I get a car. It depends on how hard I work I suppose.'

'Oh, so if you work REALLY hard, you could get a REALLY nice car then, what... like a Ferrari?' Ed started jumping up and down with excitement.

'Don't be silly,' said Ben, 'they cost thousands and we wouldn't all fit in it.'

'More like a Mercedes,' said Izzy smiling broadly.

'Wow,' said Ben, his eyes widening in excitement, 'that would be cool.'

'I know, wouldn't it just,' she smirked, tilting her head to look at Stephen.

Stephen shook his head. 'I'm off to work. Kids, Mummy will be taking you to the childminder this morning. Ben, look at those spellings again before school and help Tatty with her reading if you can.'

'But Stephen... I can't, I...' Izzy stuttered in disbelief as Stephen held up his hand, kissed the children and disappeared out the door. She began banging the crockery into the dishwasher, swiping at Marmaduke who chose that moment to leap up on to the kitchen surface.

'Dad forgot to feed him,' said Ben.

'He can have my soggy sandwiches. I won't eat them now,' sulked Tatty.

Izzy grabbed the car keys. 'Come on, let's go. Thanks to Daddy I am going to be late. Ed why aren't you moving? '

Ed sat with his arms crossed over his chest. 'I want you to take me to school, not to Mrs Davis. I don't mind which car we go in.'

'Ed please...' Izzy bowed her head. It was going to be a long day.

\* \* \*

Stephen parked his car and was irritated to see Lucy pulling into the car park. She slid into the spot next to him. He was beginning to wonder if she lay in wait for him somewhere. Well today he most certainly wasn't in the mood for trading pleasantries. As he got out of the car, he waited for her to begin simpering at him, but instead Lucy kept her head down and dashed towards the school. Stephen noticed she looked as if she'd been crying and immediately felt guilty.

'Lucy, is everything all right?' he called after her, hurrying to catch up with her.

'No, not really, but I don't really want to talk about it right now. I might feel up to talking about it later though, if you're offering?'

'Umm; well I'm sorry to hear that. Maybe later if you don't get things sorted out before then.'

'Thanks, Stephen.' Lucy managed a weak smile and walked off to her office. Stephen cursed himself for chasing after her. He had a strong feeling she would want to talk later. Or maybe he was just misjudging her. Turning into his office, he threw himself into his work, deliberately pushing all thoughts of Izzy and Lucy out of his mind. He was just finishing marking an assignment, when there was a knock at the door and Leonora, one of his A-level students, poked her head round.

'Sorry to like interrupt, Sir. May I like have a quick word please?' Stephen sighed inwardly, wondering what Leonora wanted now. The girl was getting to be a pain in the proverbial.

'Yes, come in, Leonora, and tell me what crisis has befallen you this time.' He tried to inject some humour into his voice. Leonora approached in a cloud of cloying perfume and wearing an extremely short skirt with heeled boots and full make up. Stephen couldn't believe that any parent would let their daughter dress like this for school – or that the school let the girls get away with it either, for that matter.

Leonora had an irritating habit of chewing her hair as she spoke to him. 'Well, I kind of like, have mislaid my essay, and I wondered if I could have some extra time to like get it finished?'

'Leonora, this happens too often. And no, there will be no extension because this time there is a deadline with the exam board. You know this. Look you still have a week. Come on, crack on and get it finished.'

'Cool, ok, umm, would I like be able to have some extra sessions with you because I'm finding it like hard to get information?'

'I run extra sessions for all students on Wednesday afternoons and Thursday lunchtimes; you are welcome to attend those.'

'Well, it's like difficult for me at those times. Could you like do a private thing for me?'

Stephen frowned, 'No Leonora, not unless you can get a group of people requiring extra tuition and then maybe I'll consider running another session.'

'Cool, so like if there were others, you would like do another one?' Leonora appeared to cheer up. 'So, like, what day would be good for you?'

Stephen thought for a minute and decided that Tuesday after school would be OK. Izzy would just have to pick up the children for a change, he was already leaving work early to pick up the children three times a week and frankly it was too much. Izzy could do one day and that would only leave two afternoons when they had to go back to the childminder.

'Tuesdays, 4.00 pm. I can do an hour then.'

'Oh that's, like, really cool for me, thank you so much. I know there are other people interested so I'll spread the word. I'm just so grateful.' Leonora rushed out of the door, almost colliding with Marie-Claire who had evidently been waiting to speak to him.

'You want to watch her, Stephen. I think she's developing a bit of a crush on you.'

'You have to be joking. Why would a girl of her age be interested in me? I'm positively ancient.'

'You might think that, but many of the girls think you are hot. I hear them talking and you need to be aware of it.' Marie-Claire laughed. 'I am a woman and if I were their age I might think the same.' She laughed again and Stephen joined her.

'You are obviously mad but thanks, I will be careful. I don't want any more dramas in my life,' he added ruefully.

'Do you have so many dramas then?' Marie-Claire sat on a chair

71

neatly crossing one leg over the other and straightening her scarf around her long, slim neck. She had immaculately bobbed, dark hair. So different from Izzy's wild curls, Stephen found himself thinking. A flash of irritation went through him.

'Oh just at home. I think the house is getting on top of me.'

Marie-Claire nodded. 'Yes, you have a lot on your plate. How much longer do you think it will be?'

'God knows. Quite frankly, sometimes I'd just like to walk away.'

'I'm sorry; it must be hard for you. If I can be of any help then let me know.'

'Thank you, Marie-Claire. It will work itself out.'

'Is your wife's job going well?'

'Oh, yes, fine. She's . . . very pre-occupied with it.'

'Well, it's hard, working and being a mum.'

He wondered how Marie-Claire did it. He knew she was divorced but had never thought to ask what she did with her two children while she was at work. 'I think she's coping fine with the former and not at all with the latter. She's very snappy with the children.'

'That sounds normal to me. It's so difficult trying to manage everything. I speak from experience and my two are that bit older now.'

Stephen smiled gratefully at Marie-Claire wondering what had gone wrong in her life. 'I guess you're right, but I am looking forward to some normality.'

'Whatever that is. Well I'd better get on.'

'By the way, about the Paris trip, have your students all paid up yet?'

'Amazingly, yes Stephen, they have. I've given the money to the bursar to deposit.'

Stephen stood up to get his list of paid-up pupils, just as Lucy popped her head around the door.

'Oh, you're busy. I'll come back later, it can wait,' she said hurriedly and disappeared as quickly as she'd arrived.

'Oooh la la. Another one of your fan club, Stephen?' said Marie-Claire, standing up to leave. Stephen sighed exasperatedly.

He managed to avoid Lucy for nearly all of the day, but just as he thought he'd got away with it, she appeared in his office.

'Gosh, you're here late, Lucy.'

'Yes, I just wondered if I could have a word?' She sat down opposite his desk, her short skirt riding up her thighs.

'Ok, but I don't have long as I've got to pick up my children.'

Lucy frowned and shifted self-consciously in her chair. 'Well, the thing is that I've heard you are doing private language sessions and I wondered if I could have some, to brush up on my French before the trip.'

'But Lucy you aren't going on the trip.'

'Oh but I am. When I told the Headmaster that I was doing French evening classes, he said it would be OK.'

'Right. Well, I'm sorry but I don't do private sessions. I'm sure you must have covered enough in your evening class to get by.'

Lucy's eyes narrowed. 'Are you quite sure about that? I've heard otherwise.'

Stephen stared at her, slightly puzzled. 'Yes, I'm completely sure.' He picked up his jacket. 'Now, you'll really have to excuse me,' he said and opened his office door.

Lucy marched through, head held high. 'So are you ok now by the way?' Stephen proffered as he locked his office door. 'You looked a little upset this morning.'

'I'm fine, thank you.' She walked ahead of him down the corridor, but stopped and held the fire door open.

'Thank you.'

'My pleasure. Any time,' she suddenly breathed into his ear, just as Mr Coombes the bursar came the other way.

'Working late, eh? Say no more, your secret's safe with me,' he smirked. Lucy giggled conspiratorially, while, to his dismay, Stephen felt himself blushing furiously. God, what was it with women?

# Chapter 13
## *May 2003*

Clarissa was fed up. Heather had handed in her notice and, as much as she was loath to admit it, she knew she was losing a good member of staff. Heather had had the cheek to offer to find her a replacement and, worse, had suggested that she should offer the new employee either more money or better working conditions. Well, she knew plenty of horsey people who worked for the love of it. Heather was obviously getting ideas above her station. Clarissa was therefore puzzled when each of the applicants she interviewed declined her job offer. Heather had looked over their CVs, checked references and made them ride the horses even. Maybe she was scaring them off before they'd had a chance. She flicked through the pile of applications which Heather had discounted. Tamara Swinford-Harrington, well she sounded her sort, although she didn't think she knew her. Maybe she'd give the girl a call.

\* \* \*

Tamara was due to arrive for her interview at three o'clock. Clarissa had sent Heather off for the afternoon to buy some new tack which should keep her out of the way and give the girl a fair chance. By three-thirty, however, there was no sign of Tamara, and Clarissa, who had been perfectly poised on the cream sofa in the sitting room, Tamara's CV on the coffee table in front of her, was now furiously pacing the carpet. She grabbed the CV and was just in the act of scrunching it into a tight ball when she heard the sound of blaring music and a car pulling up outside. She hurriedly tossed the CV behind the screen in the hearth and returned to the sofa.

Sylvie was soon ushering in a tall, well-built girl, sun glasses perched on the top of her dyed ash-blonde hair. She was wearing fawn breeches with half chaps and Jodhpur boots and a baby pink Joules T-shirt which was spotless.

'Hello, I'm Tamara Swinford-Harrington for the three-thirty interview,' she announced in perfectly clipped tones.

'Good afternoon Tamara, please be seated.' Clarissa's eyes did a last minute check of the girl's attire as she marched across the cream carpet. 'I trust you found us without difficulty? People don't usually seem to have too much trouble.'

'Oh, yes, perfectly well Mrs Hambridge. I allowed plenty of time in case I got held up,' Tamara smiled winningly at Clarissa and Clarissa actually let herself wonder whether she had said three-thirty after all.

'I understand you went to Benenden and that you have a National Diploma in Equine Studies.'

'Yes, I've ridden all my life. I'm positively horse mad.' Tamara laughed loudly.

'As is my daughter,' said Clarissa, although she didn't add that Amelia's obsession with her horse; annoyed her intensely. Tamara seemed very jolly. She'd certainly be a breath of fresh air, thought Clarissa. Heather's face seemed to be set in a permanent scowl and Clarissa couldn't actually recall if she had laughed once in her four years of employment. 'Tamara, you appear to be just what I need. Would you be interested in the position?'

Tamara was taken aback at the speed at which she'd been offered the job. 'Um, I think so. What sort of package are you offering?'

Good heavens, thought Clarissa, a package? She took a deep breath in. 'Well, obviously free board and lodging, and pocket money of five hundred pounds per month, and three weeks holiday a year to be taken non-consecutively during the summer.' Clarissa smiled encouragingly, having just upped the money from four hundred pounds. Tamara's face fell. The money wouldn't even cover her hair and beauty treatments. However, she needed this job. Horses could be quite good fun and she only needed to prove to her father that she could hold down a job for a year.

'Thank you, that's fine, although three weeks' holiday isn't very much. Could I have four, do you think?'

'Oh, all right then,' Clarissa acquiesced uncharacteristically. 'I suppose you'd better come and look around the yard then.'

The yard looked immaculate and the stabled horses seemed fairly quiet and easy going. Tamara managed to give each of them a good pat and made what she thought passed for appropriate horse talk. She cheered up immensely, when she heard that someone came in each morning to help with the mucking out. She wondered if it were a he and if he were dishy. Of course, she'd have to sort out how to get a boyfriend round here. She hoped Clarissa entertained a lot as the place would be dead as a dodo otherwise.

The arrival of a woman in dirty riding gear brought Tamara back into the present and she smiled brightly when she was introduced to her.

'Ah, Heather, this is Tamara Swinford-Harrington. She will be replacing you. I hope that there'll be some overlap between Tamara starting and you leaving so that you can show her the ropes.'

'Splendid,' said Heather. 'Yep, lots to go through.'

'No need for all that now, though,' Clarissa interrupted, quickly steering Tamara back towards the house. Heather scowled after them. She remembered the girl's application form which had been poor at best. There were holes everywhere in the CV and it was hard to work out exactly what she had been doing since leaving school. Well, it wouldn't be her problem when she left; she just hoped that the girl could ride otherwise things could go downhill fast.

'Shall I show you your accommodation Tamara?' Clarissa moved determinedly towards the annexe off the main house. 'I'll just show you round briefly as Heather hasn't moved out yet. There are two bedrooms with en-suite bathrooms, a kitchen, utility room, living room and study. It's kitted out with all the stuff you'll need.'

'I didn't expect the accommodation to be so spacious,' exclaimed Tamara with forced enthusiasm. Really, the flat was tiny by her standards and she noted that the decor could do with a sprucing up – new curtains and sofa were a must. The kitchen could do with some help too. She looked at Clarissa, 'This could be made really trendy. I noticed you have a real eye for interior design. My mother would love your style.' She watched Clarissa's chest puff out a little. Well if that didn't do it, she thought, Daddy would have to cough up. Even he wouldn't want her living in squalor.

Clarissa decided she was warming to this girl. 'So could you start on June 1$^{st}$ do you think?'

Tamara didn't need her Filofax to know that she'd be in the middle of her month's holiday in Antigua then. 'I'm actually on a family holiday, but I could start on the 14$^{th}$ June.' She gazed earnestly at Clarissa and added, 'I think it'll be the last time I can go and I know Daddy would be terribly disappointed if I didn't.'

'That will be fine.' Clarissa made a mental note to bribe Heather to stay on for longer; her eventing yard would have just to wait. In fact, she wouldn't let her have a reference until she'd finished.

Sylvie let Tamara out so Clarissa didn't get to see the girl's new BMW drive away. She congratulated herself on her find. It was all going to work out splendidly.

Tamara, meanwhile, was laughing with glee. *God that was so easy.* She'd never had a job interview before and she had her employer eating out of her hand. She'd even persuaded the idiot woman that she hadn't been half an hour late. God, she hoped she could stick it in the sticks. She supposed it was something to tell her chums about. They'd think it was a hoot, Tamara Swinford-Harrington bunking up with a bunch of nouveaus. One year and counting and she'd have her inheritance.

Clarissa rang for Sylvie and ordered a large glass of white wine. She felt she deserved it after her successful afternoon. Henry and Constance were coming over for dinner with an up-date on the investments. Not great news, he'd said, but nothing serious to worry about. Her mother and father were also joining them and Charles who'd somehow got wind of Henry's visit. Charles had recently spent a day playing polo and had made up his mind to take it up. Clarissa thought this was a good idea. She was not a fool about her husband's need for stimulating activities, but she preferred to pretend that these took place on the sporting field.

Her mind drifted to the family's summer holiday. They were off with the three children to the south of France for the whole of August. Probably not as glamorous as Antigua, but she'd rented an enormous villa so that the children could all take a friend, which would keep them out of her hair. She was taking Sylvie as well as Carl this year, as you could never get decent local staff. Tamara would have settled in by then so the horses were taken care of. She hoped Charles had told that useless Dave, he'd need to mind the dogs.

'Ahh, Sylvie, my drink, good. Do you know what time Charles is back tonight?'

'I'm not sure. He knows that dinner is at 8.00 p.m.'

'Hmm,' was the only response.

Sylvie paused as she was leaving, 'You must be glad to have sorted out the new groom.'

'Yes, I'm very pleased. She's ideal. In fact I don't know why Heather didn't shortlist her in the first place.'

'I think she'll suit you down to the ground, Madam.' Sylvie hurried out of the room without waiting for a response. *Had she actually just said that?* She hurried to the kitchen to check that Carl was doing something constructive for a change. He was sitting in a chair with his feet on the kitchen table smoking a cigarette and texting on his mobile phone, a bottle of chilled lager next to him.

'You are awful,' Sylvie giggled, 'how do you know that I wasn't Madam? One day you will get caught.' Sylvie reached into the fridge and brought out a bottle of beer. 'I think I'll join you,' she said.

'Drinking on the job?' Carl enquired. '*Quelle horreur.*'

'As you know, it'll be a long night of serving their majesties your courses,' she paused, 'please tell me they aren't all out of packets.'

'Of course not, I've been very busy today as it happens.'

Sylvie raised an eyebrow. He'd certainly been in the kitchen all day, but she was pretty sure he'd spent the morning watching daytime TV. 'Great, I'll look forward to seeing what you've so lovingly prepared.' Sylvie was pleased that Carl and she were going to France together with the family this summer. It made the whole process more bearable having him there and despite her teasing he was great chef although secretly she wondered why he worked for this family as she didn't think it was very fulfilling.

* * *

Henry arrived promptly at 7.30 pm, mouse-like Constance clinging to his arm. Clarissa would never know what had prompted Henry to marry her. Tonight she was wearing a frumpy dress which did nothing for her figure whatsoever; whereas Clarissa was attired in a slick number by Dolce and Gabbana with Christian Laboutin heels.

Poor Constance was scared witless of Charles and Clarissa. Neither of them ever made any attempt to reassure her and she usually spent the whole evening in a state of anxiety, trying desperately not to spill her wine or drop food. Sylvie was well aware of Constance's awkwardness and tried to alleviate this in any way she could. She greeted Constance and Henry with cocktails.

Charles sauntered in a while later. 'Hello all,' he announced and helped himself to a cocktail. 'What in God's name are these?' he enquired, eyeing the pink drink warily.

'You don't have to have one,' Clarissa said hopefully.

'Bottoms up!' Charles downed it in one and swallowed noisily, smacking his lips together for good measure. 'Actually, quite tasty. I'll have another one, anyone else?' he enquired turning to face the group.

'Yes please. They are rather nice, aren't they?' Constance giggled nervously. Charles handed her another drink.

'Interesting dress Connie. Very sort of, baggy. Is it a new fashion?'

78

enquired Charles who was used to seeing his pencil thin wife and most of the women he gravitated towards in figure-hugging clothes.

Constance blushed and looked down awkwardly at her feet, avoiding everyone's eyes. She felt bulky and uncomfortable next to her svelte sister-in-law. Henry stepped closer to Constance and placed an arm protectively around her.

'I chose this dress old boy. I thought it rather appealing and it is by a new and up and coming designer.' Henry smiled at his wife.

'Oh, and whom might that be?' Clarissa peered over her glass at Henry. She looked down at her own slick number, stroking the fabric of the beautiful dress, safe in the knowledge that it was from the latest collection.

Clarissa and Henry's parents made their entrance at that point and thoughts of designers were momentarily forgotten. Edwina glided into the room, the stereotypical matriarch, immaculately coiffured and elegantly dressed. She greeted everyone with a perfunctory kiss on both cheeks. Siegfried was wearing his favourite tweed suit with a waistcoat and tie adorned with pheasants and he was sporting a moustache which looked suspiciously as if had been curled at the ends. He shook hands all round and guffawed loudly. He exuded a persistent odour of tobacco and whisky, despite the fact he'd supposedly given them both up. Charles rather liked his father-in-law. He was an affable sort and there was no doubt he'd run the family affairs efficiently. It was a shame he'd chosen to pass the reins onto Henry but he had to say Henry wasn't doing too badly at the moment.

Dinner passed without anything untoward happening and Carl's food was excellent. While they were savouring a lemon tart, the conversation turned to investments.

'So, Henry how is the Global Investment Fund performing?' Charles opened the batting whilst helping himself to another piece of tart. 'This is delicious, is there cheese coming too?' he turned around in the general direction of Sylvie, who was standing by the sideboard arranging cheese biscuits. 'Ahh, you have answered my question.' He turned his attention back to the table before she could reply and scooped a large piece of tart into his mouth. Clarissa watched him with distaste; his manners were appalling at times.

Henry finished his mouthful and took a glug of wine. He looked around the table at the expectant faces and decided to get a move on. 'Right, well, as you know, last year was a bumper year. We have had several new investors which has allowed the fund manager to buy into a number of new emerging markets which are currently a little slow but should pay dividends over the coming year, literally,' he laughed at his own joke. 'So currently the quarterly payout is not quite as good as it has been. Of course, for most of you who are continuing to reinvest any dividends, this isn't really an issue. If any of you wish to be paid the dividends, that can be arranged, and if anyone wishes to pull out, then, providing they give a month's notice, that is fine too.'

'What to do you mean exactly, by a little slow?' Charles sat back in his chair and studied Henry intently.

'I suppose currently we're looking at seven per cent per for this quarter, which I know is quite a lot lower than anticipated, and I feel slightly aggrieved to be telling you that, particularly after the previous excellent quarter.' He waited for a response.

'Well, that's still ok, I mean we could have made a loss,' said Charles.

'Absolutely,' echoed Clarissa.

Charles was thinking fast, however. If things continued at that rate, he would make more from buying a property and renting it out. 'So what is the outlook?' he asked.

'It's good old boy, in fact it's very good. This was just a temporary blip. But remember, you're not tied in for more than one month with your level of investment.'

'Or three months with mine,' Clarissa smiled smugly at Charles and continued rather haughtily, 'well, I don't think I'll be pulling out yet, it's done well for me so far. I'll continue my investment, thank you Henry.' She grinned across at her brother.

'I think that's the right decision, Clarissa,' Henry returned her smile. 'I am your brother after all and I wouldn't let you get involved in anything that wasn't going to do well, now would I?'

Charles thought for a while and decided to leave his money where it was. 'I won't be pulling out either, but I don't think I'll reinvest any more Henry, until the returns are significantly better.'

'Of course, old boy, of course.'

'It all sounds terribly exciting' said Constance, 'Henry has invested for me too, haven't you darling?'

'Yes,' he patted her hand indulgently.

Sylvie cleared the sweet dishes away and carefully laid out the cheese and biscuits. She fetched the port decanter and placed it next to Charles. She was intrigued to hear about this investment. She had placed her money carefully in tax-efficient TESSAs, and ISAs and she owned two small properties in France, one a gorgeous little house in Provence which had been left to her by her Grandmother and the other a flat on the beach on the Ile de Re. Both were rented out. She hoped she might have time to check on the Provence property when she was in France with the family in August, but she knew only too well that Clarissa had a habit of cancelling days off at short notice. Anyway, the houses gave her a steady income on top of her salary. One of the few advantages of living with this family was the fact that she didn't spend a penny – she never had time.

'So, do you have a breakdown of the portfolio?' Siegfried asked, nursing a glass of port and carefully slicing himself a piece of Stilton.

Henry fidgeted in his seat, 'Oh, the fund manager does all that. He's always buying and selling. I think the portfolio changes quite often.' He coughed and took a drink of port. 'He is exceptionally talented, you know. He's on a par with Nigel Easton, if not better. He's currently investing in emerging markets as I mentioned previously.'

'Who is Nigel Easton and the emerging markets are where?' Clarissa asked.

Charles raised his eyes to heaven, 'Nigel Easton is the top performing fund manager and emerging markets can be anywhere, but currently, I believe, Asia, particularly China and Korea.'

'Gosh, I didn't know China was in Asia,' said Constance, looking at Clarissa for confirmation.

'That doesn't come as a surprise,' Charles responded before Clarissa did, 'but I know of Easton and if this chap of yours is as good, we'll be doing fine.'

Sylvie smiled to herself. She too had heard of Nigel Easton and had invested in one of his funds, which was outperforming many others at the moment.

'Well, I would still be very interested in knowing exactly where my money is going and I could also follow the various stocks in the papers, it makes it more exciting for an old man,' Siegfried stressed his point.

'Yes, of course, father,' said Henry. 'I'll get a breakdown for you, but, like I said, stocks are bought and sold quite rapidly so the picture changes quite a lot.'

'Really Siegfried must you bother Henry so?' intervened Edwina. 'You can see how busy he is and how important all our interests are to him. You're retired, darling. Enjoy it and leave all the financial worries to Henry.'

'I suppose you're right. I can't help needing to be involved. Sorry Henry, you carry on.'

Sylvie left the room, balancing a loaded tray and pondering the conversation. She thought it odd that the investors didn't get a breakdown of where their cash was being sent. She had always known what was happening to her money, and any changes that were made. Maybe it was like an endowment where you had no idea where your money was put? She'd avoided those and she didn't think she'd be enquiring further about this fund. No, it wasn't for her. She returned to find the party had adjourned to the living area to take their coffee. Charles had engaged Henry in a private conversation and she wondered what he was up to now.

# Chapter 14
## *June 2004*

Charles sauntered into work. Gary Griedy had issued yet more instructions for valuations and he was turning them around within five days, priding himself on the service he was providing. He was getting through two to everyone else's one and he wondered what on earth they were all doing. He looked at his desk which was strewn with files, sticky notes and Dictaphone tapes. Jess had refused to touch it after he had pinned the blame on her for a job he'd forgotten about. She'd had no option but to take the flak for the missing documents, but afterwards she'd insisted she would only be responsible for files given to her in person.

Ignoring the mess, he decided to check his emails. There were several that needed addressing and one client had been waiting at least three months for a planning proposal which he'd done nothing with. He forwarded the message to Harry, and then decided to have a quick catch up with Gary before dealing with the rest. Gary was out, however, so he left a message with his secretary, and tried Gary's mobile which went straight to answer phone. He didn't bother leaving a message.

Flicking through his work diary, he noticed that he had a meeting with Lord Butterton coming up. Of course he'd handed that one over to Izzy, but he should probably show up. Lord Butterton liked to know he was dealing with the main man. He couldn't remember if he'd explained to Izzy about the rent review notices on the Butterton estate. He shuffled through the paraphernalia on his desk and was a little alarmed to find the paperwork at the bottom of a pile of papers. Oh well, easily sorted. When Jess came in with his coffee, he handed the paperwork to her. 'Could you file these at the back of the Butterton file, Jess? Izzy might need them for reference. I don't think she's in yet, but I expect the file is on her desk.'

The phone rang and Charles picked up quickly. 'Tania passed on a message that'd you'd phoned. Why didn't you ring my mobile?' Gary enquired.

'I did, it went straight to answer phone.'

'Oh, I was probably out of range then.'

'Where are you?'

'Dublin, on business. Anyway, I've stopped for a minute and I'm just having a coffee. Actually I was going to ring you because we are finalising the deal with those banks so we should be in position to lend more money in a couple of months.'

'That'll be good. Does that mean you'll clear your arrears list for me then?'

'Funny ha ha. It can't be that bad.'

'Well, cut to the chase. According to Christine my book keeper you owe us from quite a while back, maybe two years.'

'Really?' Gary sounded genuinely surprised. 'Right, I'll get accounts on to it.' Gary paused, 'actually I'm glad you phoned, I've got a new policy I'd like to run by you whereby any clients requesting a mortgage will initially take out a bridging loan with me for between say three and nine months. After that, I can organise a remortgage with another bank which will make things smoother for us and ensure we don't have to wait around for a third party bank to make up their minds about whether or not they're going to lend.'

'Interesting,' Charles sat and thought about what Gary had just told him, 'so you are in effect providing short-term finance for them, although it'll cost the client more in the long run.'

'Possibly, but some of these people won't be able to get mortgages anywhere else. They'll have to come to me and actually I'll improve their credit rating because they won't default on any payments.

'Really, how so?' Charles enquired.

'Oh, come on Charles get with it. The client pays up all the fees and interest owed up front. I add it on to the loan so it's all done and dusted and the client can't default.'

'I like that, so when you pass the client on they have a good track record of paying. Yes I see how that could work. Nice one, Gary, I'm impressed.'

'Well, I don't envisage any problems. It will make selling the packages on easier that's for sure.'

'It certainly will. Does that mean more work for us then?'

'Oh yes, so keep that girl of yours up to speed. She's coming up with better valuations but under my new scheme she'll have to keep her values up to enable me to do plenty of deals and make them look appealing to potential mortgage lenders. I'll need safe loan to value ratios, so if the valuation is on the higher end it looks better on paper.'

'No problem. She's really turned around and she's hungry for success. I've dangled the carrot so to speak and she's certainly chasing it at the moment.'

'Well, it pays to motivate your staff. If you want results you have to reward them, that's always been my philosophy and it works.'

'As it happens, I agree with you on that point.' Charles paused… 'there are too many outfits out there who treat their staff like shit and then wonder why they leave.'

'Well, I must get on. No doubt you're off chasing some bit of skirt this afternoon.'

'No, actually. I have taken up polo and will be leaving for a late afternoon's entertainment at the polo ground,' Charles laughed.

'Polo? You have to be kidding? How did you get involved in that?'

'I had a taster day with some of the hunting crew and it was the best laugh I've have had in ages.'

'Expensive hobby from what I can gather.'

'Well, I'm not fully fledged yet. Clarissa is actually keen for me to do it.'

'Does she know about the house in Barbados yet? The one you're borrowing some money off me for?'

'No, not yet, but I'm going out to see it at the end of August so hopefully it'll be a nice birthday surprise for her.'

'Don't worry, your secret is safe with me but I will expect a trip out there at some point.'

'Of course Gary; we'll have a blokes' session over there.' Charles smiled at the thought.

'You old hedonist; I don't know where you get the energy from.'

'It's all about priorities. I work hard but I like to play hard too. You only get one chance at this life. Let's catch up over lunch soon.' Charles hung up. All was well with the world.

Just then, his eye landed on a "notice to quit" request for a tenant of Lord Butterton's. Where had that been hiding? He'd missed the deadline by at least a month. Shit, he thought. Lord Butterton wouldn't take too kindly to being stuck with a non-rent paying tenant for another two years. They'd talked about doing the place up and getting a better rental yield. He was going to look bloody incompetent. He walked out of his office and over to Izzy's desk. It looked like she was still out on a valuation. He pretended to look though her in-tray, while carefully inserting the memo at the bottom. That should do it. Returning to his desk he Googled the rules of Polo until he decided it was safe to leave for an early lunch. He passed Izzy coming into the reception area as he left, 'Looking good, Izzy. Looking good. Enjoy your afternoon. I'm sure I'll enjoy mine.'

'What is it with him at the moment?' asked Izzy. 'He's in far too good a mood.'

'Well, we're supposedly having a good year, haven't you heard?' said Saffron, sarcastically. 'So good in fact that he's off to play Polo. Not that we are supposed to know that,' she said, tapping her nose.

Typical, thought Izzy, wondering what she should do now about the approval for her valuation. Since she couldn't be trusted with them, it would be nice if he stuck around a bit more. She went into the office. 'Anyone else having a good day. I hear Charles is off out again?'

'I was,' said Harry. 'My billing is right up with all these valuation instructions but Charles has dumped an overdue planning proposal on me. I'll deal with it this afternoon.'

Harry came over and perched on Izzy's desk and started twiddling with a pencil.

Izzy looked up at him, 'Shooh, haven't you got any work to do?'

'Of course, but I'm bored.'

'Well, go and be bored somewhere else. I've got another pile of stuff to clear that has accumulated since yesterday by the look of things.'

'And you were only telling me yesterday how on top of things you are.'

'Yes, well. At least I'm up on Lord Butterton's file. I have my frumpiest outfit ready for next week. Go sort your planning proposal.'

Harry grimaced but as he showed no signs of moving, Izzy retrieved the pile from her in-tray, and quickly scanned through it, placing things in order of priority. She was careful to double check everything. She soon found the memo Charles had inserted into the bottom of the pile. As she read it and noted the date, she turned an alarming shade of dark red. How on earth had she missed this? She would swear on her life that this had not been in her in-tray before now.

'What's up?' said Harry. Izzy thrust the piece of paper into his hands.

'Oh shit,' he said as he read through the document.

'I know,' replied Izzy. 'I don't suppose I need tell you that it wasn't there yesterday. or any other day.' She sat silently for a minute, chewing over the problem.

'It might not be too bad, 'Harry ventured. 'It may only be one of the estate cottages, in which case it will only be two months notice so it's not the end of the world if it's late. However...'

'If it's a farm,' Izzy continued for him, 'then I'm in trouble.'

'Well yes. Why don't you look it up? Here I'll do it while you stew nicely.' Harry slid off Izzy's desk and wandered around to see her computer screen. She readjusted slightly so that he could see. The spreadsheet revealed that Mr Averley was a farmer. The notice to quit had been highlighted.

'It's a bloody farm, so that will be two years won't it? Well, I'm not going to take the flak for that. No one said a word to me about it. I'm going to turn up at that meeting with a list of all current and imminent action points and I will mention that I happened to see on our computer files that a "notice to quit" should have been served to Mr Averley but that I could find no evidence of any written instruction. This, she said, waving the memo, is going to find its way back into Charles's office, his wastepaper basket to be precise. '

Harry looked at her with respect. 'Not bad and very devious miss.' He stood up and stretched. 'Be careful, he won't take kindly to having any dirt shovelled his way.'

'Oh, I will.'

'What are you two up to?' Jess wandered over.

'Nothing much. I was just telling Izzy about Lord Butterton.'

'Oh right.' Jess shuddered.

'Jess, do you use this database regularly?' asked Izzy.

'Yes, I do. I update it and I highlight important stuff so Charles can prioritise. I do him a weekly list of all the things that are happening or due to happen too. If anything is really important, I type him up a separate memo so he can action it. He always seems to lose Post-It notes, so now I like to have a copy on my computer. He can't tell me that I forgot to remind him then. Actually there's a notice to quit somewhere on his desk for Lord Butterton's tenant. I did remind him to deal with it. Oh and Charles asked me to file some stuff about rent reviews in the Butterton file this morning. I assume that means he's dealt with them but one can never assume round here. I haven't typed up any letters but he might have sent emails of course.'

*Yeah right*, thought Izzy, reaching for the Butterton file. 'Thanks Jess. That all sounds really efficient – and very helpful.'

'Yeah well. Needs must.' Jess wandered back to her desk.

'Someone's got the measure of him anyway,' said Izzy, pulling out the rent review paperwork.

* * *

The following Monday, Izzy climbed into Charles's Porsche and slipped the seatbelt across her body. It made a satisfying clunk as it locked into place. She sat with her hands in her lap, twiddling her wedding ring and staring through the windscreen. She was both looking forward to and feeling nervous about the impending meeting. She so wanted to see Charles fall on his face; on the other hand, she hoped he wouldn't be too pissed off with her. It might have been a better idea to go in her own car but it would have seemed odd to refuse a lift when they were going to the same place.

She was fed up with men. Stephen was still giving her the cold shoulder and refused to even discuss work on the house. He hadn't cooked her dinner since their argument, or made the beds or done the washing or washing up. So much for sharing their responsibilities. She'd had to pretend more than once that she was going straight to a valuation, when in fact Stephen had given her short notice that he couldn't take the children to Mrs Davis. And she knew he'd taken on the after-school tutoring sessions just to wind her up. The children were also giving her a wide birth. She knew she was being short with them but she couldn't change things by herself.

Charles roared the engine into life and they were soon heading off to Welshpool. He made constant phone calls while driving, which at least saved her from having to make conversation. The Porsche eventually swept off the main road and on to a wide private road lined either side with mature hedges. It wound its way upwards and the hedges stopped abruptly as the vehicle passed over a cattle grid giving way to green open parkland, fenced with post and rail. Mature beech and oak trees were scattered about and there were several thoroughbred horses with foals standing idly about beneath them, tails swishing. They collectively turned their heads and gave the passing vehicle a cursory look. Izzy smiled and George Stubbs the highly acclaimed painter of horses flitted through her mind before the house came into view. *Christ*, she thought, *it's a proper stately home!*

'Gosh, I wasn't expecting this,' she said aloud and felt a little bit intimidated.

'Yes, it is very grand, and Lord Butterton is a very valued customer, Isabella. Be nice to him.' Charles chuckled.

Izzy felt like pushing Charles out of the car. They drove around the back of the house and pulled into the rear yard where an assortment of vehicles were parked. 'We'll be meeting in the estate office which is just off to your left.' Izzy turned to look and at that moment a scruffy old gentleman meandered out, one leg of his trousers tucked into a pair of wellington boots and the other hanging loose. He was wearing an old, navy-blue fisherman's jumper and smoking a pipe. He peered myopically around the yard and focussed on the Porsche as Charles jumped out. Izzy couldn't believe this was Lord Butterton. He looked harmless enough.

'Ahh, there you are, Charles my boy. Thought I heard that car of yours.' He started towards them and Izzy noted that he had a limp.

'I see you've brought along one of your floozies. There'll be no time for that sort of thing on my time. I pay you to work, young man.' Lord Butterton laughed and then began coughing hoarsely. He cleared his throat noisily, which nauseated Izzy, who had managed to ignore the floozy remark.

'Morning Humphrey. This is Isabella, our newest recruit. Well she's been with us since January actually.'

'Has she now? Well you've kept her well hidden haven't you old boy?' Lord Butterton eyed Izzy appraisingly.

'How do you do, Lord Butterton,' she said politely.

'Oh, do call me Humphrey. I must say you have a Mediterranean look about you.'

'I'm half Spanish but I was educated predominantly over here, hence the lack of accent,' Izzy replied, holding Lord Butterton's gaze.

'Spirited young filly I should imagine, hmm,' he said licking his lips lasciviously. 'Right, shall we get down to business?'

Lord Butterton turned and limped back across the cobbles. Izzy and Charles followed him into an office which had at one stage been a barn but was beautifully renovated with a huge window overlooking the yard. Lord Butterton opened an adjoining door and barked orders at someone sitting next door, and then proceeded to plonk himself down at a huge oak desk. Charles sat down in a chair opposite and motioned for Izzy to sit next to him. The chairs were made of heavy oak with worn leather seats and moulded arm rests. Izzy sat back, as if protected by the chair.

Charles and Lord Butterton talked for a while, completely excluding Izzy but she didn't mind as it gave her a chance to listen to what was going on and to make notes. She was determined that she would have her finger on the pulse. The door opened and a thin middle- aged woman with short spiky hair and glasses entered with a tray and not a glimmer of a smile. She dumped the tray unceremoniously on the desk in front of Lord Butterton and walked out without a word. Lord Butterton moved the tray in front of Izzy and continued talking to Charles.

'Izzy, could you pop next door and ask Annette for the file on Troutbeck Farm?' Charles said suddenly. Izzy's heart began to thump but she was ready for this one.

Izzy got up and made her way over to the inter-connecting door. 'Yes?' Annette peered at Izzy over her glasses. 'What does he want?'

'A file for Troutbeck Farm, please.' Izzy smiled at Annette, deciding to see if she could gain an ally. 'I'm Isabella, by the way.' She held out her hand and Annette stood up and took it. She had a firm handshake, 'Annette,' she said still without a smile. She turned and retrieved a file from the cabinet behind her and passed it to Izzy.

'That's it?' She sat down and resumed typing, effectively dismissing Izzy.

'Thank you,' said Izzy, as she turned and headed back to join the men. She flipped the cover over to try to find any information to help her look efficient but as she passed through the door she caught the file edge on the door frame and the file slid out of her hand and hit the floor landing in an untidy heap. Luckily nothing fell out but she felt such a bumbling fool as she retrieved it from the floor, both men having turned to stare at her. Neither one commented as they resumed their conversation and Izzy sat down carefully and placed the file on the desk. She flicked through her notes until she found what she was looking for. Troutbeck Farm, tenancy succession. She would be able to field some questions now, if they arose.

'Charles tells me that you will be handling tenancy agreements for me from now on, do you think you're up to it?' Lord Butterton glared menacingly at her over his spectacles.

'Yes of course,' Izzy replied smoothly.

'Well, maybe you can tell me why Mr Averley has not been served a "notice to quit". Apparently it should have been done by the end of March.' Lord Butterton glared at Izzy as she retrieved a thin file from which she took out a document and followed a table with her finger until she found Mr Averley.

'Yes, I do see that Mr Averley should have been served notice two months ago. I have just compiled a chart to indicate when everything is due and I assumed that would have been taken care of. I have only just taken over your tenancies but will look into it immediately for you. Maybe Charles could enlighten you.'

Charles didn't even blink. 'It is really not the type of mistake I would expect from someone of your standing and supposed experience Isabella,' he said coolly before continuing 'I don't really want to have to keep an eye on you but maybe I will.'

*Boy is he a smooth operator;* Izzy wracked her brains for a response.

'I think that might be best,' Lord Butterton muttered, 'this mess will cost the estate money you know, not that I'd expect you to understand being a woman for starters.'

Izzy sat feeling completely helpless. Charles really was the limit. Should she challenge him? She decided that it would be very unprofessional to say anything in front of Lord Butterton.

'I will prepare another "notice to quit" which will be served in ten months' time which will at least ensure that the tenant realises that he will have to be out in approximately a year from then,' she said with as much as ice in her voice as she could muster.

'Yes, yes well that's all we can do for the time being,' Charles sighed loudly, shaking his head. 'Really Isabella, such an elementary mistake. I do apologise Humphrey and I will personally see to it that it doesn't happen again.'

Izzy sat there quietly seething. She didn't think she had ever despised anyone as much as Charles. She thought about resigning there and then, but decided that wasn't really option for her at the moment.

'Right what's next on the agenda?' enquired Charles looking at Izzy.

Izzy was about to say she didn't know because she didn't have one and didn't even know there was one for today's meeting.

'I believe it is an update on the rent reviews seeing as we are on the subject of things which should have been dealt with,' she replied smoothly and meeting Charles's gaze. His facial expression didn't change. 'I have noted the following.' Izzy proceeded to run through the list and highlighted future events that would need attending to. The meeting rumbled on for another hour and Izzy managed to hold her own, despite Charles trying to trip her up a few more times. Much to Izzy's dismay, Lord Butterton then decided she must have a tour of the estate. Charles opted to stay behind and finish the sandwiches.

'You can sit by me,' he said as they walked over to an old Land Rover. As she climbed in, he pinched her backside. The trip was, unsurprisingly, a nightmare, with Lord Butterton taking every opportunity to fawn over her, in full view of the driver. The driver did his best to keep up an informative account of the estate and its various tenants, although Izzy didn't really want to hear about the people as she would no doubt be the one making unpopular decisions on Charles's behalf.

She was relieved to get back to the office in one piece, no thanks to Charles who drove like a lunatic on the way back. Izzy couldn't believe that they hadn't ended up in a ditch.

'Fun outing?' enquired Harry with a big grin on his face as she walked back into the office.

'What do you think?' she replied pulling a face as she dumped her stuff on the desk.

'That'll be a no then?'

Izzy walked over to his desk and leant against it. 'It was ghastly,' she said finally. 'Lord Butterton is worse than I had imagined, and as for Charles… well I really thought I'd got him this time…' she tailed off. 'Oh it was just horrendous, the whole bloody meeting.'

'Oh dear. We were all hoping Charles was coming back with his tail between his legs. Have you time for a drink after work? You can tell me all about it then?'

Izzy decided she did. She didn't want to get home too early and she wanted to unburden herself and Harry was great for that.

# Chapter 15

Stephen sat at home watching television with Ben and Ed. Tatty was in bed asleep. He hadn't been surprised to get Izzy's text. He looked at his watch. He'd hoped to do another hour or two of plastering tonight. With exams over and the end of term approaching, his marking was much lighter, so in theory he could spare the time. However, he didn't trust the boys alone together. He'd give them five minutes before they started some sort of trouble.

He'd organised for the children to go to his parents for the first two weeks of the holidays, which would help. They were supposed to be sharing a villa in Tuscany with Izzy's parents for a week. Stephen was undecided what to do about this. Half of him hoped that he and Izzy would be able to spend some quality time together and put their differences aside. On the other hand, if he stayed behind he could work on the house and, if he were honest, he wasn't keen on spending a week playing happy families.

'Right boys, time for bed.'

'Oh no, Daddy, do we have to?' Ed looked up at his father imploringly, 'It's only half past seven and everyone at school is allowed to stay up until eight o'clock.' He stopped stroking Marmaduke, who had been sitting quietly purring on his lap. Marmaduke immediately turned to look at Ed, lifted a paw and patted him to remind him to continue.

'Ed, I don't care what happens in other households, you are going to bed now, so just get on with it.'

Ben stood up and yawned stretching. 'Good night Daddy,' he said, 'I'll go to bed and read for a bit.' He looked smugly at Ed and disappeared next door.

'Daddy, Marmaduke doesn't want me to move, he's so happy. Can't I just sit here for another five minutes? I won't be able to get into the bathroom, anyway.'

'Go and get ready for bed. You can put your pyjamas on as that seems to take you forever and by that time Ben will be out and you can brush your teeth.' Stephen picked up an indignant Marmaduke, opened the door and stuck him brusquely outside. He popped on his wellies. 'I'm just going to check something over at the house,' he said. 'Make sure you are in bed when I get back. And Ed, no fighting with Ben or you will be in bed at seven tomorrow.' He shut the door behind him, not letting Ed get the chance to argue and made his way over to the house. The woodwork was looking good, and he was pretty pleased with the plastering so far too. Maybe he could start tiling the kitchen this weekend. His thoughts were interrupted by Izzy's car coming up the drive. He heard the engine cut out, a door slam shut and footsteps approaching.

'Stephen?' Izzy's voice called through the door.

'In here,' he replied. Izzy appeared through the doorway looking tired and slightly worse for wear.

'Is everything all right, Stephen?'

Stephen was leaning against a kitchen carcass and he held out an arm to steady her as she approached. 'Yes, everything's fine, why wouldn't it be? You're just in time to kiss the boys goodnight.'

'Great,' she said and turned towards the door. 'I'm sorry if I've been snappy. I'm going to try to calm down a bit and get home on time. I don't see why I need to work late just to impress Charles... Anyway, I'll try harder from now on, OK?' She petered out.

*Working late or socializing again?* Stephen thought. He looked at Izzy. She did look rather morose. 'OK Izzy. Look it's been a tough year so far for both of us, but I appreciate the apology. We've got to pull together on this. We both know that. The summer holidays are coming up so that should take the pressure off for a bit. Let's spend some time together, without fighting.'

'I think that would be a good idea.' Izzy looked up at him and smiled uncertainly, deciding not to mention that she wouldn't be having any time off other than the week in Tuscany. Charles had told her only last week that he would be away for the entire month of August and that she must be in the office to cover for him. It had been a battle to get the week in Tuscany through.'

'Come on then, let's kiss the boys goodnight and have a drink. I'm starving, aren't you? Shall I rustle something up?'

Izzy poured two glasses of wine. So, busy day for you?' Stephen asked, passing her a plate.

'Well, yes. I had a lot of reports to get done, that's why I'm a bit late,' she muttered, staring down at her plate. 'God it's only Monday and I feel totally done in.'

Stephen noted that she didn't eat much but helped herself to several glasses of wine in quick succession. 'Izzy, you have to get up for work tomorrow.'

'I know, but I just needed that,' she reached across for his hand and held it tightly. 'I'm sorry,' she said again, her eyes filling with tears.

'Look, it's been full on. We knew this was likely to happen. We just need some down time.'

'I know. Charles just keeps swanning off and giving me his work to do.'

'Well, he is your line manager so maybe you should have a word with him,' Stephen said shrugging. 'That's what I'd do.'

'It's not that easy. Charles owns half the place for starters and he wouldn't know what work ethic was if it bit him on the backside. He knows how to make a buck for sure, but he knows even better how to pass one. I thought I'd like him, Stephen, but right now I couldn't care he falls off his bloody polo pony and gets a mallet in his head.' She found herself ranting to Stephen about the meeting with Lord Butterton, the altered valuations and the wretched chimney stack.

Stephen was furious. 'I can't believe you have been pretending everything has been hunky-dory all these months when it sounds as if you have been working for an absolute crook. I think I'd go very carefully. It can't be legal to change someone else's work, especially when they've put their signature to it, can it? And you might get into serious trouble as a consequence. Even if house prices are rocketing, someone along the way is going to find out what's going on, Izzy. What about the other partner? What's his name? Couldn't you approach him?'

'Piers. Calm down Stephen. I don't think it's that bad – well Charles is, but maybe everyone does valuations like this. I don't really have anything to do with Piers and he and Charles may be really good mates…' Izzy tailed off.

'What about Harry? You mention him quite a lot. What does he think?'

'Much the same as me. He can't stand Charles, although he seems to think a lot of Piers. I don't think he's said anything about Charles to him, though. I think it's a case of put up and shut up or leave. You'll get a chance to meet them all because Charles is hosting a summer barbeque in two weeks' time. We're all invited, children as well.'

'Oh, that will be interesting. You actually want to go?'

'I think I should. I'll work it out and I'll be careful. I know I haven't done anything that is not above board. Do you mind if I watch the news? Then I wouldn't mind going to bed.' Izzy grinned at Stephen.

'Sounds good to me.'

* * *

Izzy actually got up smiling the next morning. She wandered into the kitchen with her dressing gown on and sat down with the children.

'Hello Mummy, I like your hair down like that,' said Tatty. 'Can I make you breakfast?' Stephen held his breath but Izzy obliged, not even saying anything when Tatty spilled some of the muesli on the table. He thought she looked better this morning, much more relaxed. He just wished she told him about her work worries before, if that was what had been getting to her. *Maybe it would all be OK after all.*

Izzy decided she would drop the children off which gave Stephen time to get to work a little earlier. His final year A level and GCSE students were finished and he was finalising the details on the work experience placements.

Predictably, Leonora was waiting for him when he got in. He had thought Marie-Claire was over-reacting when she had said he should watch the girl, but he was becoming worried about her behaviour. 'Look Leonora, I can't see you now. I'm busy.' He unlocked his office door and Leonora walked through before he had a chance to stop her. 'Leonora, I'm really sorry but I have just arrived and I have things that I must do before the start of the day. I only saw you yesterday, so I'm sure it's nothing urgent.'

Leonora burst into tears. Stephen looked exasperated and shut the office door, not wanting to attract attention to the situation. 'You'd better sit down Leonora,' he instructed, resignedly pulling a chair out and sitting next to her but before he knew what was happening she had flung her arms around him and was sobbing into his chest. He didn't really know what to do but half-heartedly patted her on the back whilst trying to extricate himself from her grasp. She clung on to him even more tightly.

'I don't know what to do,' she gasped in between sobs.

'About what?' asked Stephen trying to be sympathetic but alarm bells were ringing and he was desperate to get her out of his office. 'Maybe you could come back when you've calmed down. Like I said I'm very busy. And perhaps a female member of staff would be more appropriate for you to talk to.' Leonora wailed even louder at that point and Stephen was busy racking his brain as to what to do when the office door opened slowly. Lucy poked her head round, her eyes rounding in astonishment at the sight that greeted her. Before Stephen had the chance to explain the situation, she was off

'Lucy!' Stephen called after her. Leonora appeared to have suddenly stopped crying and sat up, carefully brushing her hair out of her eyes. She kept her gaze averted from Stephen's and stood up.

'I'll just go and get tidied up,' she said hurriedly and quickly left the office. Stephen was bewildered. He bumped into Lucy later in the corridor.

'Ah Lucy,' he said, 'what was it that you wanted to see me about?'

'Oh, nothing important, it's all sorted out now. Anyway, I could see how occupied you were with Leonora.' She emphasised the word 'occupied' and stared at him menacingly.

'What are you implying Lucy? She's only a school girl and she came to me because someone or something upset her.'

'I suppose if you say it enough you might believe it,' Lucy retorted before stomping off.

'Lover's tiff?' the bursar asked grinning from ear to ear. 'Bit of a ladies' man I hear.'

'Look, you might find this funny, but frankly I don't,' Stephen barked. 'There is nothing going on, despite what anyone seems to think and I would like it to stay that way.'

'All right, keep your hair on. I was only having a laugh.' The bursar walked away and Stephen stomped off to his office, managing to get there without being accosted. He shut the door behind him before sinking into his chair. He leant back with his hands behind his head and wondered what he was going to do. He didn't want malicious rumours being spread around the school. He rang Lucy's extension. She was back at her desk.

'Lucy,' he launched in, 'I don't know what is going on with you but I would prefer it if you didn't insist on making out that I'm engaged in anything inappropriate with either yourself or anyone else, and particularly not a student.'

'Oh for goodness sake get over yourself. What you do in your time is your business. However, we all have a duty of care as far as students are concerned,' she said icily.

'What on earth do you mean?' he asked, outraged at the insinuation.

'I think you know very much what I mean. Extra lessons for Leonora and private sessions in your office. Can you deny it?'

Stephen sat there opened mouthed, but what Lucy said was strictly true. 'She only had private sessions because nobody else turned up. That's hardly my fault.'

'Well, she told everyone that the sessions were for her alone and no one else would be welcome, including me,' she added. 'I'm sure you remember me querying it at the time. You'd better watch your step because most of the students think you and she are having an affair.'

'A what? That is ridiculous. Look, thanks for the warning. At least now I can sort it out once and for all.' He slammed the phone down and sat for a few minutes before he heard footsteps approaching followed by a timid knock at the door.

'Come in,' he called and was actually pleased to see Leonora standing there because he would now be able to sort this mess out. 'I'm glad you stopped by, I need to talk to you about something. Take a seat.' He gestured to the chair in front of his desk and cleared his throat nervously. Leonora flicked her long hair from one side of her face to the other and sat down, exposing as much thigh as possible.

'Right, we need to have a little chat about something,' he paused momentarily as if searching for the right words, 'I have heard that you have been spreading rumours that we are having a relationship and I'm not very happy about it.' Leonora turned bright red.

'I haven't like said anything of the sort,' she retorted and then more softly, 'Well, we do like each other,' she said. 'I can tell by the way you look at me.'

Stephen stared at her aghast. 'But that's ridiculous. Anyway someone is spreading rumours and whoever it is has got to stop. My job could be in jeopardy and I'm a happily married man and wouldn't want that to be put at risk either, so if it's not you then who is it?'

'I have no idea, but it's so not me and I like resent the accusation.' Leonora looked angrily at Stephen. 'Do you like know who my father is?' she continued. 'He's like a lawyer and if I tell him that you're accusing me of something I haven't done he is so like going to go mental.' She sat twisting her hair around her fingers.

'Right, well from now on the one-to-one sessions will cease and you must stop coming to see me all the time. In fact I'd prefer it if you went to see Marie-Claire. You have another year to go and you need to concentrate on your studies,' Stephen said firmly.

'Oh, you so sound like my dad,' Leonora said. 'Actually, I'll do what I want and if you don't like it then that's so not my problem. You're like in denial,' she continued flicking her hair around, 'I mean, who would turn me down?'

Stephen closed his eyes momentarily as he fought for the right words. There was another knock at the door and he looked up wearily.

'Come in,' he called out. At that moment Leonora began to cry, she sat hunched up with her face in her hands. 'Ah, Marie-Claire thank goodness,' Stephen heaved a sigh of relief and gestured helplessly at the suddenly distraught figure.

Marie-Claire looked from one to the other, 'Would you like me to come back in a minute?' she asked hesitantly.

'No!' Stephen spoke hastily, 'No, please stay, there is something that needs sorting out and you might be able to help. Leonora could you just repeat to Marie-Claire... Leonora!'

A now defiant Leonora had stood up and walked coolly out of the office, leaving Marie-Claire and Stephen open-mouthed and gazing at the open doorway.

'Thank God you turned up when you did; you were right about that girl. She is trouble with a capital T. I understand there are rumours going around that we are having an affair?'

'Well none that I've heard. Look it is well-known that Leonora is an attention seeker. Her parents both work and don't have much time for her and she isn't very popular with the other students. My guess is she is chasing you about because it makes her feel important and thinks it will give her some kudos. However, she is playing a dangerous game and it needs to stop immediately. Is that what you were discussing with her when I came in?'

'Yes, she didn't take it too well, as you saw,' Stephen frowned, 'although she only started crying when you came in. Before that she was being a little madam – Daddy's a lawyer and won't like it when I tell him what you've been up to, and such like.'

'Stephen, you are really going to have to watch your step. Don't ever be alone with her, although I appreciate that it's hard when she turns up at your office.'

Stephen nodded in agreement. 'I think I will just reinforce the point that booking an appointment is essential to secure a meeting with me, and when she books I'll insist on another member of staff being present.'

'I think that would be most wise.' Marie-Claire thought a moment, 'You must keep a record of all the times she comes in; you are going to need to protect yourself. Oh, by the way, there are a few rumours going round about you and Lucy. No need to guess who's behind those.'

'Don't worry about Lucy. At least she'd old enough to hear it straight.'

'Maybe. Well, it'll be the summer holidays soon, so at least you'll get a break from your fan club.'

'Oh, ha ha. It's not like I've encouraged them. I've never had this problem before.'

'I think you've been unlucky, but in this day and age it pays to be vigilant.'

'You're right. How could I have been so stupid?'

'Hindsight, it's a wonderful thing. Anyway, don't dwell on it, you have to move on and act positively. Let's hope Leonora and Lucy find themselves nice boyfriends over the summer which will give them something else to think about.'

'Poor blokes,' said Stephen and they both fell about laughing.

# Chapter 16
## *July 2003*

It was the barbeque event at Charles's and Izzy was wondering what to wear. She'd been through her wardrobe, tried on dozens of things and was now sitting on the bed surrounded by clothes. She was wishing that she'd taken the time to go shopping and buy something new. Half her summer clothes were still in storage. She was also mulling over what Stephen had told her when he'd got home the previous night. She half felt sorry for the girl. She remembered that she'd had a crush on a teacher when she was in sixth-form and she could remember how she had created scenarios round everything he said and did. Luckily, she hadn't been deluded enough to think anything could really come of it and had never dreamt of telling anyone. This Leonora, however, seemed to have stepped over the line. *God, the last thing they needed was more hassle right now.*

'Mummy, why aren't you dressed yet?' Tatty came into the bedroom wearing a pretty floral dress and sat down next to her. 'Don't you know what to wear? Don't worry, I'll help you.' Tatty started rummaging around in the wardrobe and brought forth a summer dress. 'This one Mummy, I'll just find you some shoes.' Tatty picked her way through the mess before selecting a pair of sparkly flip-flops. She held them aloft triumphantly, her little face beaming, her dark ringlets bobbing up and down.

Izzy felt a lump in her chest. Tatty looked so pretty in her summer dress, unlike the jeans and wellies she usually wore. She was such a sweet child really. So eager to please everyone. Just like Stephen, she supposed. Beyond caring what she wore, she stood up and put on the summer dress. She'd bought it last year but had never worn it because it was a little tight. The dress slid over her head and glided down her body. She studied herself in the mirror and decided that actually it didn't look bad at all. 'Good choice, Tatty. What do you reckon?' She smiled at her daughter who was now sitting cross-legged on the bed.

'You look really pretty. But, Mummy, you really must tidy your bedroom.'

Izzy laughed. 'You sound just like me!' she said.

Izzy picked a few things up off the floor and hung them on coat hangers before returning them to the cramped wardrobe. She felt irritation rising again. 'I don't know how anyone can be expected to be tidy in here. I so miss having a proper bedroom.'

'Daddy says we will be able to move in for Christmas.'

'Won't that be exciting? Our first Christmas in our new house,' she enthused for Tatty's sake, though she'd believe it if and when it happened. She quickly brushed her hair and found some earrings to wear. Stephen poked his head round the door.

'Come on girlies, we're all waiting. Yes, you look lovely and no your bottoms don't look big!' Tatty dissolved into giggles.

'Your bottom's much bigger than mine, Daddy,'

'That's it Tatty. Don't you let him get away with talk like that,' Izzy said, grinning.

The three children were very excited and talking nineteen to the dozen in the back of the car. Stephen, on the other hand, was very quiet. Izzy hoped he wouldn't say anything to Charles about his shoddy treatment of her. She suddenly felt nervous and began to fiddle with her dress. She hadn't realised that when she sat down it rode up quite high, the wrap-over style resulting in more leg showing than she would have liked.

Forty-five minutes later they turned into Charles's driveway, which was just as well as the children had begun to mess about and were starting to annoy Izzy. 'Wow, this is awesome,' announced Ben, sticking his head out of the car window. 'Blimey, they must be loaded.'

'Shush Ben! That is a really vulgar comment. Please don't say that to anyone here.'

'As if!' said Ben.

'What's vulgar mean?' asked Tatty, as Izzy looked daggers at Ben. *How and when had he started speaking to her like that?*

'It means rude and in bad taste,' said Stephen. 'Ben, we'll speak some more about being rude later. In the meantime, let's have everyone on their best behaviour. We are here to meet people Mummy works with.' Stephen parked the car carefully between an Aston Martin and a Mercedes.

'That's an Aston Martin, Daddy!' Ben shrieked.

'Yes it is, isn't it? Let me open your doors, please.' Stephen got out nervously and let the children out. 'Careful, please!' he entreated.

'Bet that cost at least a hundred grand,' said Ben.

'Which is why we don't want to mark it. Look, but don't touch.' Stephen took Tatty's hand and offered his arm to Izzy. 'Ready to do battle?' he asked. She gave him a wary look but decided now was not the time to start a discussion. They marched across the gravel and up to the front door, which a few moments later was answered by a smiling lady in a maid's uniform.

'Come in. I'm Sylvie. Is there anything I can take for you? This way.'

Stephen and Izzy noted the French accent and they exchanged pleasantries in French which delighted Sylvie. The initial polite exchanges began to develop into a conversation until Sylvie noticed the children were looking bored. 'Who's for a swim?' she said cheerfully. The children perked up instantly. 'Gosh, I didn't realize that there would be swimming,' Izzy said disappointedly. 'What a shame. We don't have any bathing costumes.' The children's faces fell.

'Pas de problème,' Sylvie. 'There are plenty of costumes in the changing room. I'm sure I can find something for everyone.'

'Oh, don't worry about me,' said Izzy hurriedly. She could think of nothing worse than parading around in front of a load of work colleagues in a swimming costume.

'I might take you up on the offer, though,' Stephen enthused, 'but I'd better make some acquaintances first.'

'Bien sûr, this way please.' Sylvie set off through the house and the family followed her down a vast corridor lined with family portraits, until they reached a door which led outside into a walled garden. They could hear voices, laughter and splashing as they followed Sylvie through a gap in the old stone wall and out to a huge terrace with a swimming pool off to one side. Tables and chairs were strategically placed around the garden, the tables covered in white cloths and adorned with stylish arrangements of tea roses.

People were scattered around in small groups, some sitting at tables, others standing around chatting.

Charles came striding over when he saw them, hand extended in preparation to meet and greet. He acted the perfect host, introducing them to his wife and various friends, whilst organising drinks for them. Izzy opted for an apple juice – there was no way she was going to get tipsy and make a fool of herself. She fixed a smile on her face and tried to remember who was who.

She was relieved to spot her colleagues near the pool and she went up to join them while Stephen followed Sylvie and the children to check out the ball pit and bouncy castle. She noted that there were several adults hanging about the pool in designer swim-wear, the women all stick thin and the men fit and toned. Izzy thought she would avoid that area at all costs.

'Going in then?' The familiar voice next to her made her start and she looked up to see Harry.

'Oh, it's you,' she said smiling. 'Not a chance.'

'I'm glad you're so pleased to see me,' he said wryly before adding, 'why ever not? Gorgeous thing like you. I'll bet you look a darn sight better than that lot of walking skeletons.' Harry appraised Izzy appreciatively.

'Have you been drinking, Harry?' Izzy asked him in mock reproach.

'Of course, how else would I get through an afternoon of mind-numbing banality and tedium? Well not totally so, now that you're here, particularly in that dress...' he nodded approvingly.

'Hmm, you really must meet my husband,' Izzy said with a grin on her face

'Must I? Oh well I suppose I can check out whether he is worthy of you or not. So where is he?'

'Coming right this way,' Izzy gestured in front of her. 'Stephen you must meet Harry. I'm sure I've mentioned him.'

Stephen shook Harry's hand and they exchanged how do you do's. Izzy detected a slight undercurrent of animosity between the two and wondered why. They didn't have much to say to each other and before long Harry made his excuses.

'Well, you're obviously having fun,' Stephen said accusingly.

'What's that supposed to mean?'

'You were chatting and laughing together very cosily until I turned up.'

'Oh don't be ridiculous. Harry and I do get on well and he's easy and up front to work with. But there isn't anything more in it. He's ten years younger than me for goodness sake.'

'That doesn't mean anything. I'm a bloke I should know.'

'Stephen, can we not have this conversation. We've been getting on better just lately and I'd like it to stay that way if at all possible.'

'OK,' he said contritely. 'I'm sorry but you are gorgeous and I just want to make you aware of things.'

'Marauding men, you mean?' Izzy asked, laughing now.

'If you like, yes. I'm here to protect you.'

'Thank you, how chivalrous of you.'

'On another note, I thought your Charles very charming, overly so. Are you sure you want to keep working for him?'

'He's a slime ball, but Stephen I've put such a lot into this job so far. I can't give up yet.'

'Talk of the devil, here he comes now.'

'Please help yourselves to food, the steak is very tender.' Charles motioned toward the barbeque and Izzy and Stephen wasted no time in filling their plates. They found an empty table and sat down to enjoy the food.

'Good afternoon chaps. I'm Henry, Clarissa's brother, and this is Constance my wife. May we join you?' It wasn't long before the table filled up. An incredibly good-looking man, with a deep tan, blond hair and bright blue eyes sat down opposite Izzy. 'Archie McGregor,' Henry informed her. 'He's an old friend from the forces, currently residing in Monaco and over here for a visit.'

Unfortunately, Archie was very loud and complained vociferously about the wine, asking Henry if Charles had anything better to drink. From time to time he eyed Izzy up. She had no idea if she was judged to be any better than the wine and he made her feel increasingly uncomfortable. Before long Archie had quite a gathering. 'Well, much as I adore Monaco, it's just not England. If it wasn't for my old enemy the tax man, I would be here all the time,' he said loudly, looking around for sympathetic faces in his audience.

'Henry, you didn't tell me you were bringing Archie.' Clarissa had sidled up and stood with her lips pursed in a little moue. Archie stood up, took Clarissa's arms then held her away from him, looking her over from top to toe. Clarissa looked up at him from beneath fluttering eyelashes, seemingly loving the attention. Izzy wasn't sure what to make of her. She was wearing a pair of very tight boot-cut jeans and an expensive-looking white shirt, which was tied in a knot at her tiny waist to show off a tanned and very flat stomach. She was trendier than Charles, and certainly complimented his good looks. Izzy wondered if Charles treated her better than he did his staff. She should probably feel sorry for her.

Henry coughed. 'Sorry, Clarissa darling. He wasn't supposed to still be here.'

'Is it a problem?' Archie asked Clarissa with a twinkle in his eye.

Clarissa smiled broadly. 'Of course not Archie, you are most welcome any time. Now you must tell me what you're up to because, according to Henry, you have the most exciting life these days.' She looked around for a chair and Constance obligingly got up and went to stand behind Henry. Clarissa sat down and lent in towards Archie, her back deliberately turned to the guest on the other side of her.

Izzy and Stephen exchanged glances and Stephen made an excuse to go and check on the children. Izzy, however, sat back in her chair, thinking that this might be quite entertaining.

Archie poured himself and Clarissa some more wine. 'I've been in Uzbekistan and I'm sure that Henry has been wildly exaggerating about my adventures.'

'Oh Archie, Henry and I really do think it sounds exciting,' interjected Constance and earnt herself a withering glare from Clarissa.

'Indeed! A fabulous opportunity,' Clarissa took hold of the conversation again. 'Tell me, what do you get up to?'

'Skiing, sailing, polo, ice climbing, sky diving, Formula 3000. Just generally having a good time.'

'Actually, I didn't mean that,' said Clarissa punching him on the arm playfully. 'What do you do in Uzbekistan?'

'Oh, I do a bit of procurement and such like for the government, but it's so boring that I really don't want to talk about it. There are much more fun things to discuss.'

'I'm sure,' said Charles, ironically, appearing behind Clarissa. 'Let me remind myself, Archie from the army, isn't it?'

Henry guffawed. 'That's where all my best chums hail from.'

'Ah yes, all those wonderful chaps who left before they actually saw any action, isn't that right?' Charles sat down in Stephen's vacated seat. 'So, what do you think of my little pad then Isabella?'

'It's beautiful,' said Izzy genuinely.

'And it's all mine,' laughed Clarissa.

'Well you had to bring something to the table, darling. Only fair for what you were getting.'

Clarissa ignored Charles's last remark and turned her attention back to Archie. 'So, tell me about your pad in Monaco, Archie. Is it on the sea?'

'My main residence is right on the sea front. It has a huge balcony overlooking the sea, but we mainly use the swimming pool. I also have another two flats which I let out. They net me a small fortune during the grand prix.'

'Oh, do the drivers rent them?' piped up Constance. 'I do like that Ayrton person.'

'Ayrton Senna.' Archie smiled at Constance.

'Yes, that's him!' cried Constance, pleased with herself.

There was a momentary pause before Clarissa responded cattily, 'Senna is dead Constance. Lord where have you been? And most of the drivers live in Monaco, so they don't need to rent.'

'Oh, silly me.' Constance looked crestfallen and Izzy felt really sorry for her.

'I'm not very up on Formula 1 either,' Izzy said encouragingly, at which point Archie started telling everyone about his private race track in France, where he liked to race go-carts and touring cars. Everyone must come to see it - there were more than enough vehicles to go round! Izzy decided she'd heard enough and whispered to Charles she was going to find Stephen.

She found him by the pool. 'Oh my God,' she said under her breath to him. 'That was horrendous. Do you think we can leave yet?'

'Well, the children are having a blast.' Stephen gestured towards the pool where a dozen children were playing about on floats and chucking balls at each other. The water looked inviting and Izzy suddenly thought how much she'd like to dive in.

Sylvie approached. 'Go in, do. Or you are welcome to use the Jacuzzi and sauna if you prefer. There are more costumes in the baskets over there. Changing rooms to the left. Help yourselves to towels.'

'Well, I'm going in,' Stephen announced emphatically, digging around in the basket for a pair of swimming shorts. Izzy was still hesitating but decided she would look at the costumes.

'Will there be any big enough for me?' she asked Sylvie.

'Of course. Obviously very few of our guests are as skinny as Mrs Hambridge so I've stocked up on various sizes.'

Izzy reflected how thoughtful of Sylvie that was. The thought crossed her mind that Clarissa was probably the sort of woman who would enjoy her guests' humiliation as they failed to squeeze into her incy-wincy swimsuits. On the other hand, her friends were probably the sort who never swam. God forbid if their hair or designer costumes got wet. She picked out a bikini which she thought would do and looking in the mirror on her way out of the changing room, she decided she'd pass. It was only Stephen and a bunch of kids in the pool anyhow. She sucked in her stomach and made her way over to a sun lounger.

Just as she was plonking her towel down, she heard her name

being called, and to her horror saw Charles gliding up with a glass in his hand and looking a little unsteady on his feet. She was torn between covering herself up, jumping into the water, or standing there and making the best of it.

'Ahh, Isabella, I have a little business proposition for you, a very good investment deal. Must have a chat with your husband as well.' He eyed her approvingly and Izzy wanted to squirm. She was saved by the reappearance of Sylvie who took the glass out of Charles's hand.

'No glasses by the pool!' she admonished him, 'and leave this poor lady to have a swim.' She took him by the arm and, to Izzy's surprise; he followed her like a lamb. He was weaving all over the place as Sylvie guided him to the house where they disappeared out of sight. Izzy wondered how he could have got that drunk so quickly. Oh well. She got into the pool before anybody else appeared. It was a little colder than she had anticipated but she soon forgot about that as her children paddled over.

The family enjoyed a healthy splash about together before a horde of teenagers appeared and began a game of water polo. They were all impossibly gorgeous: fit, toned, tanned and just into adulthood. They made Izzy feel old and she decided to make a hasty exit, opting to climb out of the pool on to the side nearest her towel. She did a couple of energetic bounces and jumped up on the edge. To her horror, she felt her bikini bottoms come clean off, baring her white bottom. A cheer went up and, mortified, Izzy slid back into the water to retrieve her bottoms. The cheering soon turned to calls of 'encore'.

'Nice one,' said Stephen coming up grinning. 'Why didn't you use the steps?'

'Because I feel self-conscious in this bikini and didn't want to walk round the pool. God, how embarrassing.'

'Well I suggest you exit via the steps and be brave. I would have said that no one was going to be looking but I think they will be now!'

'Mummy, everyone saw your bottom!' Ed swam up giggling.

'Just laugh it off, best thing to do,' advised Stephen, laughing himself and choking on a mouthful of pool water.

Izzy held her head high and managed to make her way out of the pool without further mishap. She retrieved her towel and hurried into the changing-room for a shower. She was towelling herself off when she heard giggling voices, male and female, coming from the room next door to the sauna. She thought one was Charles's, but she wasn't sure. They seemed to be having a good time at any rate. Izzy returned to her sun lounger. She wanted to go but now Stephen had wormed his way into a game of water polo.

'Have you been in? Izzy looked up to see Harry staring down at her.

'Oh yes, and I made a right spectacle of myself getting out.' He sat down next to her and she told him what had happened.

'What a shame I missed that!' he laughed.

'Not a shame at all, it was mortifying, especially in front of that lot.' Izzy gesticulated toward the pool.

'You do have issues, don't you? I don't know why when you're so gorgeous.'

'Flatterer. You're pretty good-looking yourself. How come you didn't persuade some beautiful girl to come with you today?'

'Well, I don't have much time. I look after my Mum she's not very well.'

'Is she alone then?' Izzy asked and wondered why she didn't already know this; some friend she was.

'My father died last year. He used to look after her, but I do most of it now. Well as much as I can with working.'

'Oh gosh, I'm so sorry, I didn't realise. What is wrong with your mother?' she enquired, seeing Harry in a totally new light.

'Cancer. She's undergoing chemotherapy at the moment.' Harry paused, twiddling his thumbs round, 'I think she's giving up though. She says she wants to be with Dad.'

'Harry, I'm so sorry, you should have told me before.' Izzy remembered how she'd envied Harry his responsibility-free life; in fact that couldn't be further from the truth. 'I'm always going on about me and I always thought you had a cushy number living rent free in your parents' flat, no commitments ...' she tailed off.

'It doesn't matter. Everyone has a cross to bear, and you just have to bear it the best you can.' He looked into her eyes and Izzy felt a shift in their relationship.

'You two are looking very serious,' said Stephen, climbing out of the pool and standing there dripping. He looked good in his borrowed trunks, she thought.

'I'll tell you later.' She smiled up at him. 'Do you want to go soon?'

'Yes, I'll go grab the kids out of the water. Can you help Tatty get changed?' He strode off to the shallow end. Izzy noted that he hadn't said goodbye to Harry.

'I'd better go, Harry. I won't say anything about your mum, if you'd rather he didn't know.'

'It's OK, I just don't want everyone at work to know. Any sign of weakness and all that.'

'Sure, I understand.' Izzy stood up and smoothed her dress down.

'I think I'll make a move as well. I suppose I'd better thank the host. Have you seen Charles recently?'

'Well, last time I actually saw him Sylvie the maid was taking him indoors – he looked a bit worse for wear. However, I thought I heard him in the sauna area, when I was getting changed...' she paused, 'with a woman and there was a lot of giggling going on.'

'Oh right. Well he can't be with Clarissa because she's all over that Archie bloke.'

'Yes, I had the pleasure of their company earlier.' She pulled a face. At that moment Charles came strolling out of the sauna, a big smile on his face, followed by a tall brunette wearing a very small bikini and a rather stunning blonde with an hour-glass figure.

'Well, what's going on there then?' Izzy asked Harry.

'You mean you don't know?' Harry looked at Izzy quizzically.

'The question was rhetorical. Of course I know, but both together do you think?'

'God knows. Shall I ask him when I say goodbye?'

Izzy giggled. 'No! Right, I've got to help Stephen with the kids. See you at work, I guess.'

Stephen and Izzy said their goodbyes and headed back to the car. 'Well that wasn't so bad. You didn't introduce me to Piers,' Stephen observed.

'That's because he wasn't there. I wonder why not?'

'You were expecting him, then?'

'Well yes, I suppose so. I assumed everyone would go.' Izzy considered this for a while. 'I'll try to find out. He probably had another social engagement, or maybe he and Charles aren't best pals after all.'

# Chapter 17

Clarissa hadn't felt attracted to anyone for a number of years and the feelings she was now experiencing were very alien to her. They both intrigued and scared her. She didn't like to be out of control and Archie certainly made her go weak at the knees. She'd wandered over to the pool to gather her emotions but she couldn't resist looking over at Archie, people hanging on his every word. Every so often he looked her way too and she experienced a delicious feeling of anticipation – of bodies intertwined. Feeling suddenly very hot, she lay down on a sun lounger, closed her eyes and indulged her imagination.

A scream tore across her erotic reverie and she opened her eyes, irritated to see Tamara running around the far end of the pool, topless. She was trying unsuccessfully to cover her breasts with one hand, while chasing Charles, who was brandishing her bikini top. Clarissa looked on with an impassive expression on her face; only her eyes, as hostile as the North Sea on a winter's day, betrayed her true emotions. After nearly twenty years of marriage, any feelings of love had long since been eroded. The ire she was now experiencing was directed at Tamara who was supposed to be looking after the horses but had somehow managed to wheedle her way into the party, bringing several very loud friends along with her.

Tamara had turned out to be far from the perfect employee. Clarissa couldn't find anything tangible to pick fault with, but the girl left her with a constant sense of unease. Her excuses were always plausible, but there were too many of them for Clarissa's liking. Tamara had Charles wrapped round her little finger. He was always giving her time off and money for this and that. Clarissa had a suspicion that the girl might be earning her money in other ways. She should ask Amelia to spy on her, but if her suspicions about Tamara and Charles were correct, it might not be appropriate.

It dawned on her that she hadn't seen her daughter all day, although this did not worry her unduly as the twelve-year-old spent her every waking moment in the stables. While Clarissa liked riding, she didn't get the pony obsession. Amelia worried her sometimes, unlike Emily and Toby who were much more her sort. Toby had just finished his A levels and was staying in Newquay until they left for France. He looked every inch the surfer dude, and she was proud of him. Fifteen-year-old Emily was staying with a friend in Cannes and had managed just the one text informing her that she was hanging out on some billionaire's yacht. Right now Clarissa envied her.

Constance came bustling over. 'Clarissa dearest, are you all right? Look, that silly girl has lost her bikini top and Charles has kindly found it for her.'

'So it would appear,' Clarissa answered drily.

'Henry and I are just off, thank you so much for the invite, it's been lovely. Archie is going to stay a bit longer if that's all right.'

'Of course. Goodbye Constance,' Clarissa said dismissively. As Constance turned to go, Clarissa suddenly snapped out, 'is Archie staying with you long? I had hoped to talk to him about his investments, but it doesn't seem appropriate at a party.'

'Oh dear. Well you must come over to us then. I'll ask Archie when he is free. I'm not sure how long he is staying, but I expect it's for a few more days.'

Constance scuttled off, no doubt fretting already about what she should cook. Clarissa frowned. She may have engineered another meeting with Archie, but how could she get him alone? Annoyingly Charles hadn't mentioned any overnight trips for the coming week, although he did enjoy springing them on her at short notice.

Clarissa's gaze moved back to Charles who had succeeded in doing up Tamara's bikini top and was now scooping her into his arms and threatening to jump in the pool.

'What's the hostess with the mostest doing here all alone?'

Clarissa swung around to meet Archie's warm gaze. She switched on a megawatt smile. 'Oh, just taking stock, so to speak. I thought you'd be going home with Constance and Henry. I'm glad you're staying.'

'Well, I was rather enjoying myself. I'm sure I can cadge a lift with someone. Or stay the night,' he ended cheekily, plonking himself on the end of the sun lounger. He lifted his hand to move a strand of hair from Clarissa's face and his blue-grey eyes locked with hers. Clarissa took a sharp breath and felt her insides melt.

'That's very presumptuous of you,' she said coyly, willing his hand to touch her again.

'Well, as a rule I'm not presumptuous, but with you...' he tailed off and dropped his hand, running it lightly down Clarissa's arm and leaving a trail of goose bumps. His eyes bored into hers and she couldn't look away. She felt completely helpless in this man's presence and she was momentarily lost for words. She sat up abruptly, swinging her legs round and standing up. Archie stood too and for a moment they were frozen, looking into each other's eyes.

'I wouldn't bother trying anything with her,' yelled Charles across the pool. 'Utterly frigid.' He laughed loudly and Tamara and her entourage laughed with him.

Clarissa didn't even turn to look at them. 'He thinks I'm frigid but that's because he is a lousy lover and I can't bear him touching me.' She laughed slightly hysterically and Archie put a protective arm around her waist.

'Well, maybe you just need a pair of warm hands to thaw you out,' he murmured suggestively in her ear.

Clarissa reluctantly pulled away and headed towards the changing rooms.

'Do you fancy a swim?' she asked as casually as she could, her heart beating wildly. He followed her into the changing rooms and she could feel his breath on her neck as she leant over to retrieve towels.

'It's not a swim I fancy?' he murmured, reaching out to grab her. Clarissa hastily backed up, holding the towels in front of her until she had nowhere to go. Archie continued to advance. 'I do apologise for being so forward. I don't know what has come over me, but there is something between us, isn't there? I'm not imagining it am I? Do you feel it too?'

'Oh yes,' she said seriously, 'but I'm afraid there will be no funny business because I'm a married woman and an honourable person and I have no intention of behaving like my disgraceful husband.' Feeling a little more in control, she went to walk away. Archie grasped her gently and Clarissa felt as if she were in a dream as he pushed his body against hers and bent to kiss her. She didn't move away. The kiss was gentle to start with but grew in ardour and Clarissa felt herself responding in a way that she'd never experienced before. She finally understood the meaning of 'chemistry' and she didn't want the kiss to end.

'Well, well, what have we here?' Charles's sarcastic tones penetrated the room. 'I'll thank you kindly to put my wife down. I think you've outstayed your welcome.'

Clarissa watched as Archie disengaged himself and walked

towards Charles. 'I think that very much depends on your wife,' he stood his ground, eyeballing Charles.

'She'll do as I see fit.' Charles leaned menacingly toward Archie and added, 'so go home before I get a shot gun out of the cupboard.' Archie stood unmoving for a few moments, gathering his thoughts.

'As you wish,' he said unsmilingly and turned his back on Charles. Facing Clarissa, he winked at her. 'I'm sorry if I have caused you any offence. I really shouldn't have taken advantage of you.' He turned back to Charles. 'It was my fault entirely. Please don't admonish your wife, she doesn't deserve it.'

'Oh, don't you worry, she'll get everything she deserves,' Charles said scowling. 'All in good time,' he added for good measure.

Clarissa ignored Charles. 'You don't have to go just because my charming husband says so. This is actually my house and I want you to stay. I have enjoyed your company immensely and I don't wish for it to end yet.' Clarissa stared challengingly at Charles who stared back unflinchingly with narrowed eyes. He said nothing, appraising her much the way a snake might appraise a mouse before pouncing. Clarissa found it slightly unnerving but refused to weaken.

Archie looked from Clarissa to Charles, silently weighing up the situation. 'I'll just go and order a taxi. Maybe it would be prudent for me to leave now.'

'Along the passage there, keep walking and there's a phone on the table in the hall. You can show yourself out. '

'You are such a shit, Charles,' said Clarissa venomously as Archie disappeared into the house. 'Why can't I have a lover anyway? You're always screwing someone.'

'That's irrelevant,' Charles stated coldly. 'You are my wife and you will behave as such. I certainly won't have you showing me up in front of my colleagues.'

Clarissa laughed out loud. 'You have got to be joking. Show you up? I'm sorry Charles but things are going to be changing around here. You are going to have to tow the line, otherwise I'll leave you. Or, more to the point, you'll be leaving and you won't get a penny from me.'

'Oh really.' Charles yawned. 'I'd like to see you try. You won't get far.'

Clarissa stared at him, thinking what an ugly character he was. How had she ever fallen for his charms? A young woman appeared at that moment, dripping with water from the pool. She hesitated in the doorway when she saw Clarissa.

'Charles, you're needed for the water polo final.'

Clarissa eyed her disdainfully. 'Go back to your floozies Charles. I'm going to my room. Tell Sylvie I have a headache and I don't want to be disturbed.' She headed indoors and her thoughts immediately turned back to Archie. She had to see him again. She ran along the corridors, towards the front door and was thrilled to see him standing there speaking into his mobile. He cut the call as soon as he saw her.

'What an arse your husband is,' he said, shaking his head.

'Tell me about it,' Clarissa sighed.

'I have to see you again, can you find a way for us to be together?' he enquired searching her face.

Clarissa thought wildly, her heart hammering. 'Yes, you can stay with me. Charles and I don't sleep together. We haven't for some time now. He won't come to my room. Come on, let's go.'

'What, now?' Archie stared at her as if she were totally mad.

'Yes, now. Charles will think you've gone home. He's too arrogant to think I'm capable of defying him and besides, I've told him I have a headache. He's used to that. I'll lock my door but he won't come in.'

Archie frowned, 'I'm not sure... ' Clarissa took his hand, her heart was racing and she thought she was going to pass out. She'd never done anything like this before but she was determined to have this moment.

'I am,' she stated simply.

Archie nodded. 'Hurry up then, before I change my mind.' He followed her up the stairs to her room, nervously anticipating Charles's footsteps. Clarissa locked her door behind them and they fell into each other's arms.

\* \* \*

The next morning, Clarissa emerged from her bedroom feeling like a new woman. She felt invigorated and strangely liberated. Archie had snuck out early that morning, having persuaded a local taxi driver to pick him up at the bottom of the drive.

Sylvie had left food out in the breakfast room and Clarissa poured herself a cup of coffee and decided to indulge in a piece of toast. She went outside and sat on the terrace in the glorious morning sun. Archie has been an excellent lover and she simply must see him again. Today, tonight, tomorrow! It turned out, Archie was only here for a week before going back to Monaco and then on to Uzbekistan for business. She'd have to make the most of him.

For some reason she found herself thinking back to the early days with Charles. He had been so handsome and charming and he'd pursued her relentlessly, which she'd found flattering, and he'd impressed her parents no end. She supposed she had been swept along on young love's tide. It hadn't taken long after their marriage, however, for the tide to turn. The real Charles was cold, ruthless and unfeeling. He'd taken what he wanted from her and coldly discarded the rest. He'd had no consideration for her feelings, and her younger self had actually believed she'd done something wrong. It was only after the birth of Amelia that Clarissa had decided enough was enough and told him that he could get his satisfaction elsewhere. He'd retorted that he would do so with great pleasure and that he'd been doing that for years anyway to make up for her lack of skill and desire and that she wasn't nearly enough woman for him. It was then she'd retreated into a hard shell where neither he nor any other man could touch her and where she'd remained… until yesterday.

* * *

It was the night before Archie was due to return to Monaco and Clarissa and Charles had been invited round for a meal at Henry and Constance's. Clarissa was like a young teenager in love for the first time, wondering what to wear and whether she'd get any time alone with Archie. When they weren't making love, he had actually been chatting to her about his business activities and she was genuinely keen to be involved. If Charles had been suspicious about her extra gym and beauty sessions, he hadn't said anything and nor about her sudden keenness for tennis. It had all been much easier than she'd expected.

'I do hope you're not going to be fawning all over Archie tonight and embarrassing yourself again, Clarissa,' Charles sneered as they drove away from the house. *Good, so he didn't suspect*, she thought.

'I might or I might not, what's it to you?' she retorted icily glaring out of the window.

'Your parents are going to be there and I don't think they'd be too impressed.'

'No, I don't suppose they would,' she said quietly. 'Don't worry I'll be a model of decorum.'

'Good.'

It wasn't long before they arrived and they were soon seated around the table and tucking into the hors d'oeuvre. 'Oooh

Gravadlax, my favourite,' murmured Clarissa. Constance sat and stared at her open-mouthed.

Henry nodded approval. 'Mine too. Well done Connie for picking my sister's favourite.'

'I'm so pleased,' Constance spluttered, having never received any sort of compliment from Clarissa.

'I too must thank you for your hospitality Constance. You have been most welcoming,' Archie smiled across at her and then at Clarissa, 'and for yours too, Clarissa.' He raised an eyebrow and a glass to them both. Everyone raised their glasses and Clarissa had the decency to blush. She glanced at Charles, who was studying her suspiciously.

'So what have you been doing with yourself this week Archie?' Charles enquired.

'Oh, this and that, keeping myself busy with a bit of work and lots of pleasure,' Archie responded challengingly, returning Charles's stare.

'You've played some rounds of golf, haven't you Archie?' Constance smiled encouragingly at him.

'Oh really? And which golf club would that be?' Charles asked with interest.

'The Wrekin. It's pretty good. Henry booked me in.'

'Right, what handicap do you play off?' Charles continued.

'Oh, Archie's very good – you have a handicap of six don't you?' Constance gabbled enthusiastically.

'Well, I'm okay, I suppose. I have played quite a lot before.'

'Obviously,' said Charles. 'So, Clarissa, have you been golfing this week? Or playing any other sort of ball game?'

'Just tennis, Charles. You know I don't play golf,' she hit back.

'Archie is responsible for getting us all involved in the overseas investment deal,' Henry said changing the conversation.

'Oh, are you now?' Charles sat up straighter in his chair and prepared to grill Archie some more.

'Well yes, as it happens, I am and I hope it continues to perform as well as it has done so far,' Archie replied smoothly.

'So, do I,' said Charles, 'I wouldn't want my money underperforming, particularly in this market.'

'No,' there were murmurs of agreement around the table.

'Well, naturally I'm in the same boat as all of you but of course investments can go down as well as up so make sure you only invest what you can afford to lose and of course you can get money out at anytime. If you are unhappy, then let Henry know.'

'So you're heading back to Monaco tomorrow is that right?' asked Clarissa.

'Yes, but not for long. I'm needed in Uzbek at the end of next week so will be heading off there after I've checked on a few things, changed my clothes, that type of thing.'

'Ah, so just a fleeting visit home then?' Clarissa continued.

'Yes that's right, check that my house keeper has been doing her job,' he laughed. 'No really, I'm trying to set up some short-term trade financing to help the government out with the procurement of some oil pipes.'

'Oil pipes?' enquired Constance. 'I didn't know that Uzbek whatever it is; has oil. I mean you never hear about the country do you?'

'No, I suppose one doesn't,' agreed Clarissa's mother. 'One always tends to think of the Middle East or somewhere like Texas.'

'Oh yes Dallas, I loved that programme,' said Constance.

'Well surprisingly Uzbekistan is a very oil rich country, but the oil is very sulphurous and requires high-quality pipes to transport it. The problem is the pipes are manufactured in America and Japan which unfortunately has suffered poor relations with Uzbekistan. The government is having problems negotiating a contract to purchase the pipes and transport them. I'm currently acting as a go between and propose to purchase the pipe myself, ship it via Dubai, and make a bit of money out of it.'

'How do you propose to do that then?' enquired Charles.

'Well, I can purchase the pipe from Japan for sixteen pounds a metre and the Uzbek government have budgeted for eighty pounds a metre. Allowing for shipping costs and taxes, I can make sixty pounds a metre. The government are looking to purchase two hundred kilometres of pipe per quarter.'

Charles did a swift calculation. 'Twelve million, you make twelve million pounds per quarter?' There was a stunned silence around the table and all heads turned towards Archie.

'Yes that's right, it's good isn't it?' He sat back in his chair smiling. 'But it is not without risk as I have to finance the first procurement myself.' He picked up his wine glass and took a swig.

'Why is that? I thought you said the government would pay,' Henry queried.

'Well, they will pay but only in arrears, so once the first delivery is made I'm laughing.'

'How much money do you have to put up front then?' enquired Clarissa.

'Quite a lot. In the region of three million, well just over.'

'How do you intend to finance it?' Charles enquired with interest.

'I shall finance half myself and look for investors for the rest.' Archie sat back in his chair letting the information sink in and then added, 'the deal is guaranteed for three years.' He let that sink in as well.

'So what is the downside?' Clarissa asked. 'Surely there is one. It sounds too good to be true.'

'The only downside is that any investors will have their money tied up for a year as it will take a short while for the government to pay up.' Archie took another slug of wine. 'It's a pretty failsafe way of making some serious money, so I will consider any offers of investment most carefully.'

'I think I'm in,' said Clarissa.

'I don't mean right now. See me privately if you're really interested and I can run through the details. I can delay my trip back by one day and I'm hoping to pop over in a couple of weeks so you can talk to me then as well.' He sat back smiling and the buzz around the table was tangible. He caught Clarissa's eye and mouthed, 'later, you and me.'

Clarissa smiled back and wriggled in her chair like a naughty child. For the rest of the meal, she couldn't stop thinking about what he would do to her later on; she couldn't believe what had happened to her this week. The dinner dragged by interminably and Clarissa lost her appetite for food. She toyed with it on her plate and contributed half-heartedly to the conversation, which luckily nobody but Constance seemed to notice.

Coffee was served in the sitting-room and the guests had the opportunity to mingle. Unfortunately, most of them made a beeline for Archie. 'That Archie is quite a chap isn't he?' Siegfried came up and stood next to his daughter.

'He is Father. Do you think you'll invest in his latest venture?'

'I'm not sure. Let's leave it to Henry to decide, shall we?'

'Seriously, what's your gut feeling Father? You used to be a good judge of character; unlike his wife he'd always had slight doubts about Charles. Clarissa turned to face him, searching her father's slightly haggard face.

'Oh, I don't know, I'm past all this now, but he's very sure of himself isn't he? Maybe too sure, but then you don't get anywhere in this day and age without being sure of yourself.'

'I suppose not,' Clarissa agreed. 'I'm thinking of investing a bit. I think it would be fun.'

'Well, just remember not to invest...'

'Anything that you can't afford to lose,' Clarissa finished for him.

Siegfried patted Clarissa on the shoulder. 'I'm just popping outside for a breath of fresh air.'

'Not for a puff then Father? Don't worry, I won't tell Mother.'

'Gosh, am I that transparent then?' he enquired.

'Your secret is safe with me, go enjoy!' Clarissa patted him affectionately on the arm and made her away across the room to join the group surrounding Archie who was regaling them with sailing stories.

'I say,' said Edwina sidling up to Clarissa, 'that Archie is quite the fellow isn't he?'

'Gosh Mummy, Father just said the same, but he is, I agree.'

'Where is your father? He was here just now.'

'Oh, he's just popped to the men's room. He'll be back in a moment.' Clarissa patted her mother's arm.

'Hmm, I rather fear he's more likely to have nipped out for a quick smoke.' Edwina shook her head ruefully and glanced towards the patio door.

'Oh, I thought Father had given up,' Clarissa said carefully, assessing her mother's response.

'That's what he'd like everyone to believe. However, I know better and quite frankly I'm not going to admonish him. He's cut down quite significantly which is good but don't let on that I know, otherwise he'll start up again properly and I don't want that.'

'Your secret is safe with me.' Clarissa laughed inwardly as she moved away to sit down. Her mother followed and sat down beside her. They chatted together about various things and Clarissa started to feel agitated as she wanted to speak to Archie. Charles seemed to have monopolized him which she found slightly disturbing, but Archie appeared to be handling him confidently and guiltlessly. Her mother left her alone on the sofa when her father reappeared and she sat quietly mulling things over. She was doubtful now that she and Archie would get a moment alone and she suddenly panicked that he would be gone and the love affair would be over. She had already made up her mind to invest some money which would go some way towards ensuring that she would get to see him again.

# Chapter 18
## *August 2003*

Charles was sunning himself on his sun lounger in the French villa while contemplating his next move. He'd had lots of fun irritating Clarissa over the last few weeks and next week he was off to Barbados to view the house. Clarissa hadn't been at all bothered about him having to leave the holiday a week early and he wondered if she was planning a little something or other.

He eyed Clarissa distastefully as she made her way outside to claim a lounger before the children descended on the pool. Her behaviour was decidedly erratic, ranging from quite affable to downright miserable. He wondered if it was because he'd scuppered her chances of seeing Archie alone on the evening at Henry and Constance's. He'd enjoyed commandeering the twerp, then insisting that he and Clarissa needed to leave. He'd made the decision that when he'd made enough money he was going to divorce her. She'd served her purpose and he could think of no reason why he would need her in the future particularly with the way his business and new investments were doing. For now he would play the dutiful husband to impress the outside world. Buying her the house would impress most people although he was going to put the deeds in his name so he'd keep that as and when.

He had promised to take Tamara with him to Barbados. She had proved to be an excellent sport. He'd replaced her with a temporary groom for the week, so, all being well Clarissa would be none the wiser. He knew she couldn't stand Tamara but she kept out of her way as the girl was too good a match for her. He couldn't understand why Clarissa had hired her in the first place - but it certainly suited him. He would have to keep her hidden from Henry, of course, but as Henry was only there for a day, if it all worked Tamara would arrive as Henry left. He prided himself on his excellent planning.

The children appeared at that moment, Toby leading the way with his mate James, closely followed by a giggling Emily, her friend Scarlett and Amelia's friend Ruby. Amelia trailed behind them. Charles appraised Scarlett who looked and behaved a lot older than her fifteen years. He suspected that she and Toby had been up to no good, but he wasn't about to say anything. They all fell into the pool. Charles was tempted to join them but thought better of it. He decided to go in and get his packing organised for Barbados.

When he reached his bedroom he found Sylvie already folding his shirts. 'Splendid,' he said throwing himself on the bed, 'you pack, I'll watch.' He lay back, head in his hands and shut his eyes.

Charles arrived in Barbados with a spring in his step and greeted Henry as if they were long lost brothers. Henry wasted no time in taking Charles to see the new development. They drove through the gated entrance and up a long road where there was a lot of building work going on and large plots carefully marked out.

'I'll take you up to the top of the development and you can survey the area and take your pick.' Henry spoke enthusiastically, perspiring lightly despite the air conditioned car.

Most of the houses at the top of the hill were completed and it was obvious that they were occupied. 'This is the "footballer" area,' scoffed Henry. 'Best avoided dear boy, lots of plastic women, you know the sort, pneumatic breasts and pumped up lips.'

Charles laughed. 'I know the sort, vacuous gold diggers at best.'

The car stopped and they got out. The sticky heat was intense and enveloped them as they emerged.

'Right, old boy this is the spot.' They were standing in the middle of a large unfinished complex of four houses with their own separate driveways. The views overlooked the bay and the golf course. It was an incredible location.

'I'm buying this one.' Henry walked off towards a gateway and Charles followed him up the extensive driveway which was composed of little more than hard core. The villa comprised six huge bedrooms, all en suite, an open-plan kitchen and dining area, living room, study and games room. It continued outside with a beautiful swimming pool which appeared to flow into infinity, all set in a garden of about two acres. It was sumptuous and Charles was suitably impressed. Henry took Charles to see his potential property.

'This really is most inspiring Henry. When will it all be finished?'

'Well old boy, hopefully by early next year. The building work, as you can see, is well underway, but landscaping and finishing touches can take longer than you think.'

'Do you know who is buying the other two properties?'

'Yes, as it happens I do.' Henry mentioned two friends of his who Charles wasn't acquainted with.

'No riff raff then?' Charles joked.

'Absolutely not, dear boy. Well, discounting the footballers that is! Right, old chum, how about a little drinky?'

Charles followed Henry back to the car, admiring the surrounding area and feeling very excited at the prospect of owning one of these properties. They made their way to the clubhouse and it was a relief to enter the cool, air-conditioned building. They reclined in soft leather club chairs, and drinks and nibbles were brought to them by a smartly attired waiter. Henry retrieved the documentation and carefully went through the figures with Charles. Rental returns were good and Charles was confident that the house would pay for itself and he would still get a fair amount of use out of it himself.

There were a number of young good-looking women hanging around the bar area and Charles thought excitedly about exploring new possibilities.

'Are you still up for investing in Archie's little business?' Henry broke into Charles's musing.

'Well, it all sounded very good, how is it all progressing, I don't suppose much has happened over the summer?'

'Frustratingly slowly old boy, from what I can gather. It's only to be expected, typical eastern European bureaucracy and various goings on within government.'

'Scope for bribery, at least,' laughed Charles.

'Well yes, but of course that's a bottomless money pit and then you might still end up back at square one. However, I believe he's making inroads. Just don't expect much to happen before the year is out. He still needs some more investors as well so if you know of any pass them on. He'll give you something in return.'

Charles raised his eyebrows, 'quick to reward then.'

'He's most generous, always has been.'

'And not just with his money, I'd wager,' Charles winked at Henry over his glass.

'Oh, the ladies. Yes he's never been short of female companionship it must be said, if that is to what you were inferring.'

'Something like that. Cut to the chase and all that but I fear

Clarissa was most taken with him.' Charles tested the water. 'She spent quite a lot of time at your place when he was there.'

'Did she?' Henry sounded surprised. 'Well Constance said they wanted to talk business. That's why she put on the dinner party. Clarissa didn't get up to anything inappropriate that night, she went home with you.'

Charles was about to respond but didn't. He studied Henry and wondered if he lived in a bubble, only seeing what he wanted to see, unaware of the many small dramas playing out around him. Charles switched his attention back to the moment.

'Right, Henry, well I suppose that just about wraps it up for now, what are your plans for the afternoon?'

'I'm afraid I've got a meeting to go to. Will you be all right on your own?'

'Well, I thought I might have a wander around here and get a feel for the place.' Charles avoided looking in the direction of the women. 'If I'm going to invest, I really ought to avail myself of some of the facilities, don't you think?'

'Absolutely old boy; the spa is definitely worth a visit and I can recommend the massage.' Henry paused and added humorously, 'and it's all above board, no funny business,' he winked at Charles, 'so you'll have to behave yourself.'

'Of course, of course,' Charles acquiesced pleasantly. 'Well, don't let me keep you,' he added, fidgeting in his chair, eager to begin the hunt for his next conquest.

'Well, enjoy your stay; are you joining me and Constance for a light supper tonight?'

'That would be lovely, what time shall I pop round?'

'Anytime from eight. We'll nip round to a rather nice little restaurant. I'll book.'

'I thought you said a light supper?' Charles laughed

Henry stood up and shrugged, 'Well, you know me! You don't have to dress up though. Anyway, I'd better motor on, see you later old boy.'

'Cheerio,' said Charles but his mind was already elsewhere as he eyed the three women at the bar speculatively and decided on a game plan. He approached the bar.

'Ah, ladies I do hope you don't mind me interrupting but I'm new to this area and wondered if you could point me in the direction of the health spa.' Three sets of eyes appraised him, taking in his polished appearance and expensive watch.

'I'm Chantelle,' one of the ladies extended a confident, loudly manicured hand across the table and met his eyes, holding the gaze for a little longer than was strictly necessary.

'I'm Charles,' he held her hand firmly, having noted the Essex twang and squeezed it just before he let go, 'and you must be from Essex.' He added with a smile on his face as took in the mountains of gold jewellery and long platinum-blonde, poker-straight hair.

'Oh, how did you ever guess?' she laughed loudly and a bit too harshly for Charles's liking. He turned to one of the other woman.

'Chelsea and I'm from Essex too!' She held out her hand and grasped Charles's firmly. She was a pretty, petite woman with a huge pair of implants and a wide smile revealing a set of perfect Hollywood teeth. She fluttered her eyelashes at him and ran her hands, adorned with rings, through her mane of long blonde hair extensions. Charles turned towards the last lady.

'Lydia-Rose,' she intoned coolly with RP and the merest hint of a smile and I'm not from Essex.' Everyone laughed and Charles took the opportunity to sit down.

'No obviously not, nor am I for that matter.' He found himself immediately drawn to Lydia-Rose who was by far the most attractive of the three women. 'Can I buy some drinks?' he asked, unable to take his eyes off her face. She had huge, dazzling green eyes that gazed at him unsmilingly from her exquisitely carved face, complete with high cheek bones and a perfect nose. Her hair hung in soft auburn waves down to her shoulders.

'Oh how lovely, fank you, we're drinking Chardonnay.' Chantelle's twang brought him back.

'I might have guessed,' he said good-humouredly and signalled a waiter. 'So what are you lovely ladies doing here then?' Charles sat back in his chair and surveyed the three women.

'Well, I own a house here and these two are staying with me. We're having a little holiday.' Chelsea smiled, playing with her hair.

'Very nice too. So have you owned a house here long?' Charles enquired with interest.

'About a year, it's fabulous, and I spend as much time as I can here.'

'Do you rent it out?'

'No, not at the moment. Well, only to friends and family. We like to be able to come over whenever we like and we couldn't do that if it was let out. What about you? Do you own a house here?'

'I'm in the process of buying one. It's being built at the moment.'

'Where is it?' enquired Chantelle.

'At the top of the hill,' Charles said vaguely.

'Past the footballers,' giggled Chantelle, 'vat's where Chelsea lives. She's married to a footballer.'

'Ah, I see.' Charles laughed ruefully.

'And Chantelle's trying to get one too.'

'Well, I'm sorry that I'm not a footballer then.' Charles eyed Chantelle and she giggled behind her glass of wine.

'What about you Lydia-Rose? Are you after a footballer as well?' Charles turned his attention back to her.

'Lord no,' chortled Chantelle. 'She's got a hedge fund husband.'

Lydia-Rose dropped her head bashfully, while Charles appraised her with increased interest.

'That's a shame for you,' Charles said, carefully watching her reaction. Her head shot up and she looked him squarely in the eyes.

'Why do you say that?'

'Long hours at the office and not much time for fun.' He continued to look at her and she dropped his gaze.

'Sounds like my ideal husband,' interjected Chantelle. 'Lots of money, shop until you drop, beauty treatments all you like. I wouldn't complain.'

'I have a very fulfilling life,' Lydia-Rose responded defensively. 'I am a project manager for a local charity and that takes up a lot of my time.'

'Look, you don't have to convince me, but quite a few of my friends are in your husband's line of work, I know the score,' Charles answered softly. 'I know how lonely it can be for the one left at home.' Lydia-Rose raised her eyes to his and held his gaze. Charles smiled. This one was easier than he'd thought it would be.

'Lydia-Rose's not lonely, she's got us,' Chantelle placed a protective arm around her friend.

'How do you three all know each other then?' asked Charles

'Work related fings,' Chantelle answered. 'I'm a receptionist and aspiring glamour model. Chelsea was a beautician and Lydia-Rose met us at a function that she was organising. I was on reception at the hotel where the event was being held and Chelsea was doing a promotion there.'

'We had to work together for quite a bit and we got to know each other. I suppose you fink it's odd that Lyd gets on wiv us two, seeing as she's posh and we're not.'

'As it happens I suppose I did, but I take it all back. Now who's for another drink and then you really ought to be showing me around before it gets dark!'

Charles raised his glass to the women and took a sip. He was interested in Chelsea and Lydia-Rose because they had money. Chantelle would be an easy lay but had nothing else going for her. 'So, Charles, what line of work are you in?' Lydia-Rose's question out of the blue surprised him.

'Well, I'm a land agent but I also dabble in property,' he smiled over his glass at them all, knowing full well that none of them would be any the wiser.

'What firm do you work for?' enquired Lydia-Rose coolly.

'It's my own firm, Hambridge and Simpson. We're based in Shrewsbury and cover most of Shropshire and a little of everywhere else.'

'I haven't heard of you, but then I probably wouldn't have,' Lydia-Rose replied smoothly.

'So what do you actually do then, sell land?' asked Chelsea.

'No, actually I don't, although we hope to start an estate agency at some point. I do mainly valuations and then general surveyor stuff. Not very exciting I'm afraid - not nearly as exciting or as lucrative as Lydia-Rose's husband, I'm sure,' he said demurely.

'Well, whatever,' said Chelsea, 'I still don't know what you do!'

'I wouldn't worry, most people don't!' Charles replied.

'Come on then, let's get going.' Chelsea stood up and the others followed.

'After you,' said Charles as he indicated the door.

The health spa was in fact directly next door and was reached by a covered walkway.

'Gosh I didn't realize it was that close,' laughed Charles. 'You must have thought I was mad asking for directions. How embarrassing.'

'Oh don't worry. You're a man. Nothing would surprise us girls!' laughed Chelsea

The health club was indeed spectacular. 'Well ladies it's been a pleasure to meet you but I must really be off. I've taken up far too much of your time already,' he said solicitously.

'Oh no, really the pleasure has been all ours,' said Lydia-Rose smiling.

'Yes, and you must come over tomorrow night. I'm having a barbeque,' simpered Chelsea.

'Oh, that would be marvellous.' Chelsea fished in her handbag for a piece of paper and scribbled down the time and address.

Charles left feeling mightily pleased with himself. Who knew, he may even have found potential investors? It was a pity Tamara was arriving tomorrow. He would enjoy an afternoon in bed with her, before heading out for the barbeque. She could amuse herself for an evening. Get over her jet lag and all that.

He picked Tamara up from the airport mid-afternoon as planned and whisked her back to the hotel for some entertainment. Of course she wasn't too happy about the fake meeting he had to go to and sat pouting in the nude. She'd turned her nose up at the money he'd offered her as consolation, and he had to shell out an extra two hundred dollars before she cheered up.

The barbeque was in full swing when he got there and he was surprised at the number of guests present, the majority of them designer-clad women. Charles could smell money and he was excited. He wanted to get as many investors for Archie's little deal on board as he could. If he could persuade Chelsea and Lydia-Rose, the rest would follow.

'Ahh, you made it!' Lydia-Rose caught him slightly off guard. The sight of her nearly took his breath away.

'You look absolutely divine,' he said, taking in her elegant figure, clad in a body-skimming silk dress, and kissing her on both cheeks. 'If you were my wife I wouldn't let you out of my sight,' he murmured in her ear, his hand resting tentatively on her bare shoulder.

She smiled demurely, patting her hair which had been put up in a loose chignon. A pair of long dangly earrings swung delicately from her ears, the only jewellery that she was wearing. 'Well you don't look too bad either,' she replied smiling.

'Hello!' a voice shrieked in his ear. 'You must meet some of my friends. They're gonna love you,' Chantelle enthused, trying to drag him away from Lydia-Rose.

'Well, I really ought to say hello to Chelsea first, seeing as she is the hostess.'

'She's vis way, follow me,' giggled Chantelle, teetering precariously on her high heels.

Charles spent most of the evening being entertained by Chantelle and her friends but did manage to work the room and suss out who

128

was worth pursuing. He managed to get Lydia-Rose alone towards the end of the evening. 'Have you enjoyed yourself?' she enquired, slightly slurring her words and leaning toward Charles.

'Very much. You ladies have a lot of friends.'
Lydia-Rose looked up and around the room, her gaze settling on one particular point. 'Well it's Chelsea really, she's such a party animal, and her husband doesn't seem to mind.' Charles turned to look at Chelsea in her tiny animal-print dress, cavorting with a younger man. The bloke was positively drooling over her.

'Would your husband mind?' asked Charles flirtatiously

'Well of course he would… it's just that he's very busy and we don't seem to have quite as much time for each other as we should. Actually, he always seems relieved when I decide to go off for a few days.' She laughed ruefully. 'What about your wife?'

'Ahh, well that's complicated.' Charles shrugged his shoulders and looked suitably doleful. 'The thing is she hasn't been right since the birth of our last child. She had a horrendous time and she hasn't been interested in the physical side of our relationship since then.'

'Oh dear. That must be difficult for you both.'

'Yes, I've been celibate for twelve years now. Lord, I've never admitted that to anyone. You won't say anything will you? Obviously it's quite embarrassing and I do love my wife …'

'No, of course not. It's deeply personal. You don't have to explain anything to me.'

'I know, I just couldn't help myself.' He paused, 'I felt drawn to you from the first moment I saw you. I'm sorry, I shouldn't have burdened you.' He stood up to go but Lydia-Rose grabbed his arm.

'You really haven't. Sometimes we need to voice our problems. Being celibate, isn't that difficult, being a man…' she tailed off.

'It is, but it has become a way of life for me now. I should be a monk!' They both laughed.

'If you must know my sex life isn't great either,' Lydia-Rose confessed. 'My husband doesn't seem interested even when I do see him. He travels a lot for work and when he's at home he can't seem to switch off.'

'Well, we make a good pair then!' Charles smiled. She was going to be ripe for the plucking by the time he was ready. 'I suppose I ought to be going. Maybe we could meet up for lunch before I head back to the UK. I'm quite busy setting up a few business deals but I could find time for you.' He emphasised the last part for effect.

'I think I'd like that,' she said shyly.

'Have you invested wisely?' he asked suddenly. 'To protect yourself for the future, just in case something goes wrong?'

'Oh, well, no my husband does everything for me.'

'I'll give you a hand if you like. I've got some cracking little things going on that are really doing quite well. You know, you should always look after yourself. I of course have made sure that my wife is well provided for with funds and property in her name,' Charles said smugly.

'I don't really think my husband has thought of that,' Lydia-Rose said quietly and then added. 'I think I might take you up on that offer. I get a generous allowance so that would be a good idea.'

'Well perhaps we could meet up tomorrow? I'll come and pick you up and we'll find a nice restaurant unless you know of one already?'

'I'll have a think. What time?'

'What about twelve-thirty?'

'Excellent.' Lydia-Rose smiled.

Charles left the barbeque on a high and was back at his hotel by midnight. Luckily Tamara was fast asleep. He sidled into bed without disturbing her and lay awake planning his next move.

The next morning he was woken early by Tamara, whose body clock hadn't yet adjusted. She'd ordered breakfast and was sitting at a small table overlooking the bay, tucking into a plate of scrambled eggs and mushrooms. He pretended to sleep and he watched her surreptitiously through half-closed eyelids. After eating, Tamara sat drinking a coffee and finally slipped back into bed with a contented sigh. He pretended to wake up and Charles took advantage of her while she was in a good mood, although his mind wasn't really on the job and thoughts of Lydia-Rose kept intruding. It had been a mistake to invite Tamara here. He hadn't realized that the novelty was wearing off. Plus she was becoming too demanding, and sulky to boot. *Hadn't he always said married women were the way to go?*

He toyed with sending her back on the next plane but rejected that idea in case she turned nasty. He would just have to find someone else to entertain her while he got on with pursuing Lydia-Rose.

# Chapter 19
## *September 2003*

Izzy was sitting on a patch of grass in the early September sunshine enjoying the warmth and a cup of Earl Grey tea. The summer had gone well; the house was progressing, she and Stephen had been getting on better and with Charles out of the way for the last month work had been really good. She was managing her workload and she'd gone through all her clients with Jess and ensured that she was on top of everything. There was a three-year plan for Lord Butterton's estate with salient dates highlighted so she wouldn't miss anything. She'd had to get on with a couple of things for Lord Butterton in Charles's absence, and his Lordship had been pleasantly surprised by the way in which she'd handled them.

The house had been plastered and the bathrooms tiled and plumbed in. There was central heating throughout. The kitchen was underway and they were just waiting for cabinets to arrive courtesy of Stephen's father. He'd already done all the woodwork around the house and it looked really good. The children were due back at school next week and Stephen was remarkably calm for the start of a new term. He was currently out with the children buying new shoes and pencil cases and no doubt a new collection of pencils, rubbers and colouring pencils.

She heard footsteps approaching and her face broke into a smile as she recognized her new friend Chrissie. Chrissie and Izzy had hit it off since they'd bumped into each other, literally, in the school playground. They'd both been late for work and after a moment's irritation had both apologised and confessed as much. They'd met up a few times in the summer holiday and were on the way to becoming good friends.

Chrissie was a petite, bubbly brunette who worked as a medical receptionist most mornings and spent the afternoons riding her two horses. Her husband was a partner in a firm of solicitors and they owned a large property with land. They seemed to enjoy the perfect life.

'Hi, Izzy. Just thought I'd pop over for a quick catch up.'

'Lovely to see you,' Izzy responded warmly. 'You've escaped!'

'Well, the outlaws are visiting, so I've left the little darlings in their care for a moment. Hopefully they won't come to any harm. The outlaws, not the children!'

'How are they?'

'Who? The outlaws or the little darlings? They're all fine as it happens. I'm the one who's worn out.'

'Well, four children and working part-time is equivalent to several full-time jobs. Tea?'

'Oh, that would be lovely.' Chrissie plonked herself into a deck chair, arms behind her head and legs out in front of her. 'Maybe I'll just stay here,' she said closing her eyes and raising her lightly-tanned face to the sun. Izzy left her to it as she went to make tea, coming back out with two mugs and a packet of chocolate biscuits under her arm.

'Sorry it's not the best china.'

'How shocking but I'll let you off for the moment! I'm supposed to be buying a vacuum cleaner actually. I loathe them with a vengeance. In fact, I would love to stand at the top of a block of flats and throw every one I've ever owned off the top and watch each one smash into a million little pieces.'

'You're mad. How can you hate a vacuum cleaner?'

'Where do you want me to start? Cumbersome, unwieldy, break down all the time, fall over when you use the hose thingy, wheels fall off, noisy, I could go on and on.'

'I thought you had a cleaner to vacuum for you?'

'I do, but I still hate them! How's work going and when's the ghastly boss back?'

'Sadly, next week. This last month has been great without him interfering. I've finally got to know the other partner and, surprise surprise, he actually advocates that I'm careful to only value a property to the amount I feel it's worth. I knew I was right. Heavens knows how he and Charles became partners.'

'Wasn't he the one who expected you to make the tea?'

'Well, I've been wondering if I was a bit sensitive there. He's actually really professional. I can't believe he knows what Charles gets up to, although he did make some comment about the extraordinary fees he seems to be bringing in.

'Anyway; how about you?' Izzy changed the subject.

'Ooh, let me tell you the gossip. You know Melanie my practice manager — her fourteen-year-old daughter is up the duff!'

Izzy's eyes rounded in shock. 'We're not talking about "the perfect daughter"?'

'The very one, only not so perfect now, of course.'

'Who's the father?' asked Izzy.

'Ahh, well apparently the girl is not telling anyone, and she doesn't have a boyfriend so he can't be blamed. It's a bit of a mystery.'

'Is she going to keep the baby?'

'She'll have to, it's due next month! Scandalous, isn't it?'

'Poor girl. When did she tell her mother?'

'Only just recently. She'd put on a bit of weight apparently but not enough so that anyone guessed. Anyway, it's been great entertainment this week!'

'I can imagine. I wonder who the father is?'

'God only knows, but it turns out she has been out to numerous parties and clubs dressed up to the nines. Not the little goody two shoes we were led to believe she was, after all!'

'Oh dear, her poor mother. I'd be heartbroken if it happened to Tatty.'

'You're right. Who wants to be saddled with a child at that age, when you're still a child yourself? At least Melanie will be a good grandmother so the child will have half a chance in life.'

'That's true, but if I were Melanie I'd have been excited about getting some independence back.'

'Well, I don't think her other daughter has flown the nest yet. She works at the same place as Stephen. She's PA to the headmaster.'

'Oh right. I'll have to ask Stephen about her, he might even know what is going on.'

'Or not as the case may be. He is a man after all. Most things like that pass them by.'

Izzy laughed and nodded in acquiescence. 'Yes, you're probably right.' At that moment Stephen came roaring up the drive and the three children tumbled out of the car laughing and giggling. They scrabbled around the back and opened the boot, retrieving various items. Izzy stood up stretching and Chrissie finished her cup of tea before standing up.

'I'd best get back to Bedlam and rescue the grandparents. I'll catch up with you later.' She hugged Izzy warmly and exchanged brief pleasantries with Stephen before heading back down the drive.

'Did you enjoy some peace and quiet while we were away or did you have that old windbag round the whole time?'

'Yes, thank you, and Chrissie is not an old windbag. The children are all in good humour so you must have had a nice time.'

'Yes, as it happens we did, and we bought some lunch. Shall we eat?' Stephen removed two full carrier bags from the boot and began to walk towards the caravans.

'Can we eat outside Daddy?' asked Tatty.

'Good idea, let's go and get some plates and cutlery,' said Izzy.

Lunch went smoothly for once, and the children were soon finished and went off to play. Izzy's thoughts returned to the conversation with Chrissie and she asked Stephen if he knew the PA in question.

'Oh yes, Lucy. What do you want to know about her?'

'Well, her mother is the practice manager at the surgery where Chrissie works and the younger daughter is pregnant.'

'Right, so lots of women get pregnant,' Stephen said as he munched on a piece of apple.

'Not at fourteen, they don't! The baby is due next month and she's only just told her parents. Anyway what's her sister like?'

'A pain in the proverbial.'

'Why do you say that?' said Izzy, somewhat surprised.

Stephen shrugged. 'Oh, she's just tricky sometimes and needs a lot of attention.'

'Is she pretty?'

'Yes, I suppose so, if you like that sort of thing. High-maintenance girl, always immaculately turned out, not my type at all.'

'Thanks, I do my best,' Izzy said half indignantly. 'You're not painting a very favourable picture of her!'

'No, well that is just how I see it and any sensible male would run a mile in the opposite direction,' Stephen said vehemently.

'Does she have a boyfriend?' asked Izzy.

'I don't know and I don't care. Look, I didn't want to tell you this, on top of the Leonora thing, but I get the feeling she's making a play, so to speak. She makes me feel so uncomfortable that I try to avoid her, but she doesn't seem to get the message that I'm happily married. She's malicious as well and untrustworthy. She always seems to turn up at inopportune moments, like when Leonora was crying hysterically in my office.'

'I didn't realize you were so attractive and popular! You haven't given either of them any reason to think you might be interested, have you?' she asked carefully.

Stephen looked at her incredulously. 'No, of course not and I resent you asking such a thing. You of all people!'

'Actually that came out wrong, sorry. It's just that sometimes you can be unaware of the subtleties of life.'

'Are you calling me naïve? I resent that too. I've been teaching for years. I could imagine this happening when I was younger and nearer their age, but now? God, I'm positively ancient compared to them.'

'Maybe you were more aware of it then and took stronger measures, perhaps you've relaxed too much. Whatever happens, make sure that you don't get yourself in a comprising position with any of them.'

'Thanks for that helpful advice.' Izzy waited for Stephen to fire back at her with some dig about Harry and Charles, but he simply stood up and gestured towards the house.

'I'd better get on with some painting. Are you going to help?'

'Of course, it'll be quicker with two of us,' she responded quickly. 'Just let me clear these plates away.'

# Chapter 20

Stephen sat down and breathed a sigh of relief as the coach driver started the engine. Loading a group of forty excited 'A' level students and their entire luggage had been somewhat stressful. He had checked and double checked all the documentation and just hoped that he hadn't forgotten anything. Marie-Claire sat down next to him.

'Merde,' she exclaimed, 'I'm exhausted already!'

'I know. I always enjoy planning the trip but dread the actual event, it's a nightmare from start to finish,' Stephen said , 'and what bugs me most is the comments about a "jolly little outing" and "off for a skive" that you get from all the staff who've never done this.'

'I agree, but it's good for the students and I love Paris.' Marie-Claire settled herself in her seat and leant back with her eyes closed. She opened them again, frowning as she heard a commotion and watched Lucy falling up the steps of the coach carrying a pile of hand luggage and giggling loudly.

'Gosh, I didn't realize that there would be a limit on luggage in the hold. I'll just have to bring it on the coach with me!'

Marie-Claire looked at her icily. 'We're only going for five days not a fortnight, what on earth have you packed?' She exchanged glances with Stephen who rolled his eyes skyward and shook his head.

'Oh this and that, I want to be prepared for every eventuality,' she paused briefly before adding, 'would you mind if I sat in your place Marie-Claire? You could sit with Helen.' She indicated the seats behind where Helen, one of the classroom assistants was sitting.

'I don't think so. Stephen and I have a lot to discuss on the way.' Lucy frowned but decided not to retaliate.

'Thank you,' Stephen mouthed at Marie-Claire.

'It's no problem,' she said with a smile.

The rest of the trip to Paris was uneventful and it didn't seem long before they were in the foyer of the hotel and Stephen was trying to sort out all the rooms. He had booked single rooms for all the staff and was relieved to get into his own bedroom and lie down on the bed for five minutes. Marie-Claire, Lucy and Stephen had rooms on one floor with the majority of the students, while Helen had the rest on the floor below. Stephen hoped they'd all behave themselves. He sent Izzy a text to say that he'd arrived in one piece and that he had a huge double bed which was sadly wasted under the circumstances. She texted back saying that she was glad they'd arrived safely and what a shame about the double bed, just as long as he didn't fill it with someone else.

The next three days passed quickly. The visits were excellent and the students were well behaved and enjoying themselves. He'd had no problems with either Lucy or Leonora; although he'd made absolutely sure that he was never alone with either of them and tried to stick with Marie-Claire and Helen as much as possible. By the final day Stephen had finally developed an appetite, which replaced the anxious stomach churning that he'd felt since boarding the coach in England.

The staff were enjoying drinks in the hotel bar on the last evening and the students were looking forward to the disco that was set to take place that night. Stephen had had a little too much red wine and was busily trying to sober up with several glasses of water. The students were behaving a little furtively, disappearing into the foyer every now and again, but Stephen didn't pay too much attention until he noticed several girls looking a bit worse for wear.

'Oh dear,' he said nodding in their direction. 'I think there may be alcohol involved somewhere.'

Marie-Claire and Helen turned to look in the direction that he was indicating and then back at Stephen. 'I think you could be right. I'll go and have a quiet word,' said Marie-Claire.

Marie-Claire rejoined them later. 'One of them smuggled a bottle of vodka in and they've been drinking that. They have promised me that they won't touch anything else but I wouldn't be surprised if some of the others are up to no good. We're going to have start patrolling and reading the riot act where necessary.'

The rest of the evening was rather an ordeal and Stephen was glad to retire to his bedroom at just after one o'clock in the morning with everyone safely in their bedrooms. He was just about to get undressed when there was a knock at the door. He opened it and was not best pleased to see Lucy standing outside.

'I'm so sorry Stephen but one of the lads on the floor below is asking for you. He's not feeling well and I thought you'd better sort it out rather than me, I'm not really suitably dressed.' Stephen suddenly noticed that she was only wearing a flimsy, almost see-through negligee.

He hastily thanked her and hurriedly made his way to the lift, anxious to get away from Lucy and not questioning what Lucy had been doing on the floor below. He cursed softly under his breath when he realised that he didn't know which lad or which room. The lift opened at the floor below and Stephen was surprised to see an empty corridor; he had been expecting at least a few people meandering about, in view of what Lucy had said. He made his way down the corridor stopping at each door to listen, but there was total silence. He hung about for several minutes and then carefully knocked on Helen's door. There was no answer and he suspected that she was sound asleep already.

He made his way back up to his room, noting that Lucy's door was now shut. He breathed a sigh of relief as he pushed his door open. The room was in semi-darkness and as he flipped the main light-switch on, he was horrified to see a figure in his bed. The figure did not move as the bright light flooded the room. He stood motionless for what seemed like an eternity before he cautiously approached the bed. Stephen's heart sank as he recognised Leonora. She reeked of alcohol and was either asleep or unconscious. *What the hell was he to do now?* He could try to wake her but she might be difficult and anyway, right now he was in a very uncompromising position. He made his decision and left the room, carefully shutting the door behind him.

There was nobody in the corridor and he walked quietly down the hallway to Marie-Claire's room. He knocked warily and placed his ear to the door while glancing furtively up and down the corridor. He knocked a little louder; worried that Marie-Claire wouldn't have heard him. A moment later a voice called out and the door opened marginally. Marie-Claire blinked sleepily and looked puzzled to see Stephen standing there.

'I'm really sorry to wake you,' he said hurriedly, 'do you mind if I come in? I wouldn't ask normally but I'm really desperate!'

Marie-Claire eyed him and said wryly, 'is that your best chat up line?' She shook her head slightly with an amused expression on her face and backed up, letting Stephen push the door open. 'OK, what is going on?'

Stephen took a big breath, twisting his hands together anxiously. 'I don't know where to begin and this is going to look bad. I was just off to bed when Lucy appeared at my door and said that one of the lads needed my help. She wasn't wearing very much and I was so keen to be out of her way that I rushed to the lift and only realized that I hadn't asked her who he was as the lift doors shut. I thought that it wouldn't matter because it would be obvious when I got down there. However, when I got there, the corridor was deserted and totally quiet. I spent at least five minutes walking up and down listening at doors but there was nothing untoward. I knocked on Helen's door but she must be asleep so I decided to head back to bed thinking that whatever was going on had been sorted out. Our corridor was empty and I was relieved that Lucy was nowhere in sight. Anyway, I went into my bedroom, closed the door and switched the light on and Leonora was in my bed, fast asleep and stinking of alcohol.'

Marie-Claire's eyes widened in disbelief. 'Are you sure?' she asked.

'Well of course I'm sure. She's there now.'

'I mean how did she get in to your room?'

'I have no idea, but I don't know what to do. Can I stay here for the night? I'll sleep on the sofa but I'm not going back to my room. I can't. I mean, I don't think it's a good idea. We should let her sleep it off. Hopefully she'll be okay in the morning. I can't believe this. I thought the trip was going so well. I suppose I shouldn't have breathed a sigh of relief until we got back to England.'

'No,' said Marie-Claire thoughtfully. 'I wonder if that madam Lucy has had something to do with this. Well you can't possibly go back to your room if Leonora's in there but if she's as bad as you say, then I should go and check on her.'

'Oh, yes that would be a good idea and would you mind bringing my holdall so I can at least change? It's at the bottom of the bed.'

Marie-Claire was gone for what seemed like an eternity but returned with the holdall and a toothbrush from the bathroom. She confirmed that Leonora was obviously the worse for wear but appeared to be sleeping quietly enough. Stephen brushed his teeth and tried to arrange himself as comfortably as he could on the sofa.

He hardly slept a wink and he didn't think that Marie-Claire did either. Eventually he saw the dawn creeping up behind the curtains. At six forty-five he got up and crept into the bathroom to take a shower. He finished pulling on his jeans and a pullover, and made his way back into the bedroom to discover that Marie-Claire was up and dressed already.

'I showered last night,' she said disappearing into the bathroom. He waited patiently for Marie-Claire to reappear.

'OK, shall we go together?' Stephen asked wearily, 'I don't think I can face Leonora on my own.' He looked tired and drawn, with dark circles under his eyes.

'I think that would be best,' she said unsmilingly.

The corridor was deserted and Stephen fumbled with the key card trying to get it into the slot. The door opened and they entered silently. The bed was empty. Stephen pushed open the door to the bathroom. That was empty too.

Stephen frowned, puzzled, 'Where has she gone?' he asked.

'Back to her room I suppose,' said Marie-Claire, 'but she was definitely here last night when I checked.'

'What do you think we should do?' asked Stephen sitting down on the bed.

'Nothing, she's not here now.' Marie-Claire sat down next to him looking bleary eyed. 'We'll see what happens when we see her later. She might say something but if she doesn't remember, then maybe it's better if we say nothing. No harm done.'

'I suppose not,' said Stephen. 'How odd.' They sat in silence for a moment before Marie-Claire perked up and said, 'breakfast, I think we deserve some food!'

'Absolutely,' agreed Stephen standing up. 'Maybe we'll get away with this after all.'

'Get away with what?' demanded Marie-Claire.

'Well, you know. The whole teenager in my bed thing. I mean that would take some explaining,' he said worriedly.

'Oh yes, it most certainly would,' said Marie-Claire giving Stephen an odd look.

'You can't think I was up to anything surely?' said Stephen anxiously. 'I mean you of all people know the hassle I've had with that girl and you even warned me about her. Why else do you think I came to your room last night and asked for help?'

'Yes, of course. It's just so odd and does look a tiny bit suspicious, but as you say I do know what she's like.' She shook her head slowly. 'I think we need to prepare for some problems.'

'As if I haven't got enough already,' Stephen said ruefully. They made their way down to breakfast and were the first ones into the dining-room. They helped themselves from the buffet and sat down at an empty table. A waitress approached and took their order for tea and coffee. Stephen picked at his croissant disconsolately and waited for the students to come down. They did so in dribs and drabs, some of them looking distinctly hung over. He was waiting for Leonora and Lucy, neither of whom had appeared yet.

Eventually, he could stand it no longer and he decided to go and brush his teeth and finish packing. As he was on his way out he met the pair coming the other way.

'Good morning,' he said nonchalantly. 'I'd hurry up if I were you. The gannets are clearing the decks.'

'I'm not very hungry,' Leonora said looking very green.

'Nor am I,' said Lucy frostily.

'Well, at least have a drink, Leonora.' He turned to continue on his way before turning quickly back to Lucy. 'Oh, and which lad did you mean last night? I went to find out but the whole floor was quiet.'

'Lad?' enquired Lucy looking puzzled, 'I'm sorry I don't remember.'

'Oh, don't you?' Stephen hissed furiously. 'You came and knocked on my bedroom door and told me a lad was ill.'

Lucy shook her head. 'I'm sorry, but you must be mistaken. You had, after all, had rather a lot to drink.'

Stephen was about to say more but decided against it. What the hell was she playing at? All the way up in the lift he mulled over the conversation. He sat on the bed in his room, wishing he was anywhere but here and longing for Izzy to reassure him. There was a knock at the door.

'Stephen? It's me Marie-Claire, can I come in please?' He got up and went to answer it.

'Everything all right?' she asked.

'Well no. Lucy has accused me of being inebriated last night, and worse than that, she denies all knowledge of being outside my room or telling me about the lad that I had to go and see.'

'I wonder what she's up to? Leonora and Lucy are as thick as thieves at the moment and Leonora in particular looks very unhappy. Mind you, she must have a monumental hangover. Anyway we must get ready to leave.'

Leonora and Lucy sat together on the return coach journey and both completely ignored Stephen. Stephen couldn't wait to get home. His stomach churned constantly and he felt a nagging fear which he knew wouldn't shift easily. He had decided not to tell Izzy anything because he would have to admit to sleeping in Marie-Claire's room and the whole thing sounded unbelievably suspicious.

* * *

The next few weeks were stressful. Leonora kept turning up at his office, and when he refused to let her come in without another member of staff present she would start crying, which seemed to be the cue for Lucy to appear.

Stephen was short with his family and felt like he was on tenterhooks, particularly whenever the phone rang. He looked like a haunted man and several people commented on his haggard appearance. Luckily Izzy just put it down to exhaustion with the start of the new term, and his hard work on the house over the summer.

One Saturday morning he was enjoying a cup of coffee and a piece of toast when there was a knock at the door of the caravan. Tatty ran to answer it. She swung the door open and stood in the doorway staring.

'Hello,' she said and paused before adding, 'are you a policeman?' Stephen froze mid munch and placed the piece of toast back on the plate, fighting the urge to bring his half-eaten breakfast straight back up. He felt sweat starting to break out on his back.

'Yes. We need to speak to Stephen James please.'

'That's my Daddy,' said Tatty importantly. 'Please come in.' She stepped back to let them pass.

'Actually we won't come in,' the voice intoned. 'Could he come to the door do you think?'

Stephen stood up slowly, desperately wondering what to do next. Marmaduke, who'd been sitting on the sofa, jumped down and stretched, before walking slowly to the door, whereupon he sat down and stared at the policemen in a vaguely hostile manner. Tatty watched him before turning back to Stephen. 'Daddy, the policemen want to speak to you.'

'Yes, sweetheart. I'm just coming. Would you go and get your brothers up please and Mummy.' He forced a smile on his face, hoping that Tatty would be out of the way before the policemen said anything to him. He watched her skip off and walked tentatively to the door.

'Hello, can I help you?' Stephen said as confidently as he could to the two policemen squashed up together in the doorway. One didn't look much older than some of his students and the other, older one looked as if he lived on a diet of pie and chips. He looked Stephen up and down through small piggy eyes.

'Are you Stephen James?' he asked.

'Yes, I am. How can I help?' he repeated.

'We are arresting you on the charge of rape.'

Stephen stood there open-mouthed. 'What? You have got to be joking?' he added incredulously.

'May I remind you that anything you say will be taken down in evidence and used against you in a court of law.'

Stephen stood there aghast, his heart racing. 'Look you can't just turn up here and make spurious allegations. I have a family and a responsible job in a school.'

Izzy appeared at that moment, her hair still damp from the shower.

'Oh,' she said when she saw Stephen standing in the doorway, 'What's this about? What's going on?'

Stephen fought to keep control of his emotions, 'Well there is no easy way of saying this but apparently I'm to be arrested on a charge of rape.' He couldn't believe he was actually saying the words.

'What?' said Izzy incredulously, 'rape?' She turned to the policemen. 'That is completely ludicrous. I'm sorry but you must have the wrong man. I've known Stephen for a very long time and I can assure you that he's not capable of such an action,' she instinctively moved closer to Stephen and glared at the policemen.

The pie and chips policeman raised an eyebrow and gave her a withering look. 'Yes, I'm sure, but an accusation has been made and so we will have to take your husband with us to the station for questioning.'

'I don't think so, and I will be taking this matter up with your superiors. It is completely outrageous. How dare you come here and arrest an innocent man like this?' She went to slam the door but Stephen stopped her.

'That's not a good idea, Izzy. They'll end up arresting you for something as well.'

'Surely you're not going along with this?' she demanded, eyes flashing.

'Well, I don't see that I have any choice and anyway, there's obviously been a mix up and the sooner I get it cleared up the better,' he said resignedly.

'But it's their mix up. I don't see why you have to go and sort their mess out, bloody typical!' she exclaimed loudly.

'Daddy,' a little voice piped up in the background, 'are you being rested?' Stephen and Izzy turned to see a sorrowful Tatty standing in the kitchen with a teddy under her arm. She was chewing a lock of hair uncertainly.

'No, sweetheart of course not,' Izzy said sharply and Tatty turned and ran out of the kitchen. She could be heard shouting something to her brothers.

'We really need to be going,' said the pie and chips policeman.

'I'm not at all happy about this,' said Izzy, 'and what exactly is my husband supposed to have done and when?' she demanded angrily, folding her arms across her chest defensively.

'We won't be discussing that here,' the pie and chips policeman said in a bored voice.

Izzy and the policeman glared at each other. 'Right, well I'm coming too. I'll just have to sort out some childcare arrangements.' Izzy unfolded her arms and turned to retrieve the phone which wasn't where it should have been. 'God!' she exclaimed loudly, 'where has that gone now?' She looked around the room swiftly, pushing papers to one side and lifting cushions. Stephen joined in, playing for time and trying to get himself together. *What in God's name was he supposed to have done?* But he knew it was going to come down to the French trip and whatever story Lucy and Leonora has concocted.

'We really must be making a move,' the fat policeman called from the open doorway.

'We'll follow you,' called Izzy. 'You don't have to wait, and I'm not leaving until my children are sorted out.'

'Right, well Mr James you need to come now please, otherwise you'll be on a charge of resisting arrest.'

'That's absurd,' yelled Izzy, getting really worked up and moving towards the open door, hands on hips and her hair flying everywhere, 'and what a nerve, how dare you speak to us like that? We're not criminals. Why don't you go and find some proper ones instead of making preposterous allegations against innocent people? God what is this country turning into?' she ranted.

Stephen found the phone and silently handed it to her. She snatched it from him and dialled quickly. Brief pleasantries were exchanged before Izzy got down to business.

'Chrissie is there any chance you could have the children for me this morning, something has come up and I'm desperate, would you mind awfully?' There was a pause while Chrissie responded and then Izzy again, 'oh thank you so much. I'll be over in ten minutes.'

'Right, let's go,' said the policeman.

At that moment the boys piled into the room, 'Daddy, is there a police car here? Can we see it?' Ben asked excitedly making for the doorway, closely followed by Ed. He stopped short when he saw the policemen and Ed bumped into him from behind. He looked at his father for reassurance.

'It's okay boys, you can go and look at the police car. It's just outside.' Ben and Ed dived past the policemen, who begrudgingly stepped aside.

'I won't have our children seeing their father being dragged off in a police car. It's not fair on them,' Izzy hissed.

'Look, I'm sorry but I'm just doing my job.'

'I know,' said Stephen. 'Please let me leave after the children. They won't be long.'

It took another five minutes of messing around before everyone was ready and Stephen waved Izzy and the children off down the drive, before wearily climbing into the back of the squad car. Stephen sat in silence, listening to the crackling radio in the background and hoping that he wouldn't be spotted by anyone he knew.

On arrival at the station he was asked to turn his pockets out, but apart from his mobile phone there wasn't anything else. He was escorted to an interview room and left alone for what seemed like an eternity, before eventually two people entered the room with a tape recorder and introduced themselves as Chief Inspector Macdonald and Deputy Inspector Smith. They looked grim-faced as they sat themselves down opposite Stephen and switched the recorder on. After preliminaries the interview began.

'Right Stephen, do you know why you are here?' asked the Chief Inspector. He was a tall imposing character with flecks of grey peppering his black hair and Stephen guessed he must be in his mid forties.

'No, I'm hoping that someone will enlighten me.'

'There has been an allegation of rape made.'

Stephen shook his head slowly from side to side: 'Oh, so why am I here?'

'Well according to the victim you are the perpetrator.'

'Well, I'm not. Who is the victim by the way?'

'We were hoping that you'd tell us,' the Chief intoned, his steel-grey eyes boring into Stephen's.

Stephen glared at him resentfully. 'Well I haven't raped anyone so how can I?'

145

'There is a witness,' the Deputy piped up somewhat gleefully. Stephen switched his attention to the other person who was short and wiry with the build of a climber.

'What?' asked Stephen incredulously. 'Who?' He paused, shaking his head. 'So let me get this straight. I have raped someone and someone else watched?' He held his hands up in disbelief. 'This gets more ridiculous by the minute. I must have been set up. When did this alleged incident take place then?' he asked glaring at each of the policemen in turn.

There was a silence and nobody said anything.

'We were hoping you'd tell us,' the Chief Inspector said eventually.

'Well there is nothing to tell because nothing happened. There was no rape, there can be no witness and if there is it is a set up. I am innocent and bloody angry because my reputation is at stake. I am head of languages at the grammar school and this allegation could absolutely ruin everything I have worked for, not to mention the damage that this could do to my family.'

'Well, perhaps you should have thought of that before,' said the Chief coolly. 'Where were you on the night of September the twelfth,' he continued.

Stephen gave a loud sigh, 'I was on a school trip to Paris.'

'And what happened particularly on the twelfth then?'

'We went to the Louvre in the morning and then the theatre in the afternoon.'

'And what about the evening? Can you account for yourself?'

Stephen decided that he might as well be honest and explain what had happened. He didn't want to as he would be dragging Marie-Claire into this, but he realized that he had no choice. How he wished now that he'd told Izzy.

'Well, we finally managed to get the students into bed at one o'clockish and that is when I retired to my bedroom,' he began.

'Alone?' asked the miserable one.

'Yes, alone, but not long after I'd closed my door, there was a knock and another member of staff, Lucy Carlton was standing outside. She told me that one of the lads from the floor below was unwell and asked me to go and sort it out. When I arrived on the floor it was all quiet and I spent a few minutes walking up and down the corridor trying to hear if there was anything amiss. I knocked on the door of the staff member who was in charge of that floor – Helen Roberts – but she didn't answer. She must have been sound asleep, so I decided that Miss Carlton must have been mistaken and returned to my bedroom.'

'Which boy was it?'

'I don't know; I forgot to ask. I was in a hurry to get away from Miss Carlton as she has been hounding me for a while now and she wasn't wearing very much.'

'I see,' the Deputy wrote a few things on a notepad.

'When I got back to my room and turned the light on I found to my horror that a student — Leonora Fielding — had somehow got into my bed. She was sleeping deeply and had obviously been drinking alcohol. I've had problems with her too. I knew that whatever I did it would look bad so I went to the room of another member of staff in our corridor and asked for her assistance. She checked on the girl and I spent the night in her room as obviously I couldn't return to my own. When I went back in the morning, Leonora had gone.'

'So this Marie-Claire would corroborate your story then?'

'Yes, of course. She knows that I've had problems with both Leonora and Lucy.'

'So what time did you first contact Marie-Claire?'

'I suppose at around 1.30 a.m. I can't really remember exactly.'

'And you spent the whole night with Marie-Claire?'

'Yes, and don't forget Lucy saw me before that when she sent me downstairs on a wild-goose chase.'

'Ah yes,' said the Chief staring at him. Miss Carlton doesn't corroborate that bit of your story, I'm afraid. She says that she saw you downstairs earlier in the evening after you drunk several glasses of red wine and that she went to bed not long after that and didn't see you again. She doesn't recall coming to your room or speaking to you.'

'Well she's lying then because she came to my room and asked me to go and check on this lad.'

'Whose name you can't remember?'

'I told you, I forgot to ask. I was in a hurry to get away from Miss Carlton. She has been coming on to me at work and she was dressed very provocatively and I was worried she might try something.'

'According to Lucy you've been harassing her at work and making her life somewhat miserable.'

Stephen sat back in his chair and shook his head. 'Aren't I entitled to a lawyer or something? I can see that I'm being stitched up. I'm going to need legal representation, so I'm saying nothing more.'

The Chief Inspector sat back and turned the tape off after signing off, 'OK as you wish.'

'I want to speak to my wife as well please. She's going to wonder what on earth is going on.'

The policemen left the room and Stephen sat there feeling equally furious and terrified. He seemed to have been left on his own for an age before Izzy appeared at the door, looking grim.

# Chapter 21
## *October 2003*

Izzy stood glaring at Stephen. 'Right, you'd better tell me exactly what's going on. It looks as if we will have to engage the services of a solicitor. That won't be cheap.' She sat down opposite Stephen, who was sitting with his head in his hands and looking as though he'd aged a hundred years. Izzy suddenly felt very sorry for him. She reached out to take one of his hands and he let it fall to the table in hers. They both stared absently at it for a moment.

'Something happened in Paris,' he said quietly and Izzy became aware of an uncomfortable sensation in the pit of her stomach.

'What?' she asked, while dreading what he was going to tell her.

Stephen recounted the whole sorry story, while Izzy listened in silence, her face a mask.

'You did say those women were trouble didn't you?' she said eventually. 'Can we talk freely in here or are we being listened to?'

'I don't know and I don't care. I have haven't got anything to hide,' Stephen said wearily.

'What's happening now?'

'I don't know that either, but I got fed up with the way they were twisting things I said, so I refused to answer any more questions until I had legal representation.'

'I think that's wise, though goodness only knows who we should call. Well, I don't think they can hold you for more than twenty-four hours without evidence. In fact, I bet we could leave now.' Izzy stood up and made her way to the door.

'They are saying there is a witness,' Stephen blurted out.

'What witness? And to what exactly?'

'They won't tell me. They want me to tell them. I suppose it must be Lucy but they won't confirm that and obviously I don't know exactly what I'm supposed to have done. Christ Izzy. How could they do this to me?'

There was a knock at the door and both Izzy and Stephen started as a smartly dressed gentleman in his early thirties came in. He held out his hand to Izzy and then to Stephen. 'I'm Tim Hughes and I will be representing you, Mr James. Gerald Harcombe has sent me,' he added by way of an explanation. A flicker of recognition passed over Izzy's face. Chrissie must have mentioned something to her husband. Tim sat down briskly and took a file out of his briefcase. 'Right, what's been going on? Tell me everything and don't miss out any details.'

Stephen started talking and Tim wrote and stopped to ask questions where appropriate. When Stephen had finished, Tim spent a few minutes appraising what he'd written down.

'Okay, your main problem is the witness, but if you are telling me the truth then she is lying and we should be able to discredit her.'

'I am telling the truth,' said Stephen. 'Don't you believe me?' he asked in a worried voice.

'Whether I believe you or not is largely irrelevant. I'm here to represent you,' he said in a business-like manner. 'Now let's get some more details.'

Tim continued to ask questions and make notes for quite a while before the policemen came back to resume their interrogation. Izzy was asked to leave and was shown to the waiting area. *Please let this be quick!* she thought, selecting a chair in the corner.

She phoned Chrissie. 'Hi, it's me, Izzy, I'm still at the police station,' she said quietly.

'Izzy! I'm so glad you rang. What is going on?'

'Well, I don't really know where to begin. Was it you who arranged for Tim the solicitor?'

'Yes, I had a word with Gerald and he got on to it. I hope that was OK?'

'That's so kind of you,' Izzy said tearfully. 'He seems really good.'

'That's the least I can do. Now can you talk about it?' Chrissie said briskly.

Izzy took a deep breath in, fighting the urge to cry. 'Stephen has been accused of raping a student while on the Paris trip. Of course it never happened but unfortunately it would seem that there is a witness. We don't know what he or she allegedly witnessed and Stephen can't begin to imagine. He had problems with the student at school. She was always trying to see him alone and engineering private meetings. He thought she had a crush on him and he made it clear her behaviour was inappropriate and she became upset and nasty. He told another member of staff about it. A woman.

Apparently the girl's father is some hot shot lawyer though…' Izzy stopped, running out of breath.

'Oh Izzy. That sounds awful. You poor thing. Would you like me to come over? I can leave the children with Claudia, they'll be fine.'

'No, don't worry we should be out soon. Stephen's been in there for ages. Chrissie, he thinks the witness may be your practice manager's daughter; the older one, who works at the school. Stephen didn't tell me but he thought she was making a play for him, too and that she didn't like it when he didn't reciprocate. Small world, hey?' she added with a bitter laugh.

'I think you should come home now,' Chrissie said after a moment of silence. 'The children will need you to be here. Otherwise they're going to worry. You don't know how long they'll be with Stephen and you can't do anything for the moment.'

Izzy did indeed feel helpless. 'OK. Maybe you're right. I'll come home in thirty minutes if he's not out by then.'

'Good,' said Chrissie. 'Stay here for the night. I insist.'

'That's so sweet of you, thank you so much. I'll see you later then and I'll ring if there is any news.' Izzy hung up and sat trying to gain some composure before trying to find someone to tell her how long it might be before Stephen was released. The lady behind the desk was very short with her when she asked how long it might be.

'I have no idea,' she said sharply.

Izzy tried again, starting to feel a bit peeved. 'Well, do you think you could find out for me please? I have a family at home and I need to let them know how long we might be.' She spoke with a tremor in her voice, feeling totally out of her depth.

The lady glared at her disapprovingly, 'Why don't you just go home, then.'

'Well, it's just that if he's going to be out in a short while, I'd like to wait rather than make two trips.'

'It is my understanding that your husband has been accused of rape and that there is a witness, so it is unlikely that he will be going anywhere for the foreseeable future. He constitutes a danger to society and will be kept behind bars.'

She stared at the woman in disbelief, anger mounting until she burst out. 'You have no right to say that; you don't know anything about my husband but I can tell you one thing, he is not a rapist. He's been set up.' Izzy didn't wait for a response but turned sharply on her heel and marched back to her car. She was safely behind the wheel and driving out of the car park before tears started coursing down her cheeks. She could feel panic rising within her and the feeling of an overwhelming loss of control. She started sobbing hysterically and finally pulled over in a lay-by, gripping the steering wheel tightly and letting her head fall forwards on to her hands.

Her mobile rang and she sat up, adrenaline shooting through her. It was only Harry and she ignored it because she couldn't face speaking to anyone right at this moment. It rang again and at that moment she heard a car pull up behind her and a door slam. She looked up to see Harry rapping on her window and wiped her eyes hastily. She opened the window.

'Is everything all right? Why aren't you answering your phone?' He peered more closely at her. 'What's the matter?' he asked more gently.

'It's Saturday, I don't do work calls,' she said without looking at him and feeling irritated. 'I'm fine,' she added for good measure.

'I don't think you are,' said Harry, walking round to the passenger door. 'Let me in,' he mouthed at her. Izzy hastily glanced in the rear-view mirror to check her appearance, which wasn't great. Swollen blood-shot eyes stared back at her. She opened the passenger door and Harry sat himself down next to her. He passed her a handkerchief.

'Trust you to have a hanky,' she smiled at him weakly and wiped the tears from her eyes and cheeks. 'I'll return it when it's laundered, thank you.'

'OK, so what the hell is going on?'

Izzy told him in as few details as possible. 'My God. It all sounds bang out of order. What's going to happen to him now then?'

'I don't know. How did you know I was here? ' Izzy enquired.

'I was driving past and I saw your car parked in the lay-by. I thought maybe you'd broken down and then, when you didn't answer your phone, I thought I'd turn around and check up on you. I wanted to make sure you were all right.'

'Thanks, Harry. When all this gets out, I'll really find out who my friends are, won't I? As for Stephen, well, this is a complete disaster for him. He works in a school for God's sake… At best he'll be suspended while the investigations take place and if he's found guilty then…'

'Don't go imagining worst case scenarios, Izzy. I'm here.' Harry reached out and put his arm around her, pulling her closer to him. She didn't pull away, enjoying the sensation of being protected. They stayed like that for a moment before Harry disentangled himself and opened the door. 'Drive home carefully. I'll be in touch. Promise you'll call me if you need to talk or anything.' Izzy nodded dumbly. She felt bereft as he walked away.

She travelled on to Chrissie's where the children were all playing happily. They were so wrapped up in their activities that not one of them even asked where their Daddy was. The rest of the day was surreal as she fought to keep up a sense of normality. Chrissie kept her propped up with hugs and mugs of tea, and phoned the police station for her a couple of times, but with no more success than she herself had had.

Izzy got a couple of forkfuls of dinner down her but found swallowing almost impossible. In the end, despite Chrissie's protestations, she decided not to stay and managed to round up the children into the car.

'Mummy, what time will Daddy be home?' asked Ed.

'Oh yes, Mummy, is he rested yet?' added Tatty.

'Well I don't quite know but Daddy will be home as soon as he's finished doing what he needs to do,' Izzy got out.

'Might he be away for a while then?' asked Ben. 'You aren't getting divorced are you? That's what happened to my friend. His Daddy started sleeping away and then they got divorced.'

'Don't be ridiculous, Ben; of course not. Mummy and Daddy are fine and Daddy will be home soon.'

'You do argue a lot though, Mummy,' said Ed. 'My friend's Daddy left her Mummy because of that. Are you sure Daddy isn't fed up with you?'

Izzy fought the mounting panic and willed herself to stay calm, 'I know but we've always argued. You lot argue a lot too. It's just part of life when two people can't agree on the same thing.'

Once home the children settled down but were subdued and got quietly into bed. Not one of them asked to watch television or protested that bedtime was later at the weekend. She read Tatty a quick story and told the boys they could read, then kissed them all twice each. 'One from Daddy till he gets home.' She wished she could say 'tonight' but she didn't want to lie to them.

She wandered through to the kitchen area and put the kettle on. She decided to phone the police station again. Luckily the woman on the desk wasn't the same one and Izzy was informed that Stephen was still being interrogated with his solicitor present and that he would probably be detained that night. Izzy put the phone down. *This wasn't happening. What if he didn't come tomorrow either? What would she say to work?* Her eye alighted on Stephen's briefcase. *Did the school know? Should she ring anyone? What could she say? No, this would all go away. It was a stupid mistake and the police would see it. But if they didn't* ... Izzy's mind went blank.

The sound of the phone ringing dragged her back to consciousness. It was Tim. 'Right, well we have confirmation that the witness is Lucy Carlton, the headmaster's PA at Stephen's school. Stephen has a court hearing first thing Monday morning. You ought to be present and can you bring a suit for Stephen, he needs to look smart.'

'Monday! He won't be out until Monday? But surely they can't keep him in; he's innocent for goodness sake. This is awful news.'

'I know. It will be difficult for a while but the truth will come out and then things will get back to normal,' Tim said with forced cheerfulness.

'Really?' Izzy said. 'I don't see how there will there ever be normality again after this? Does it matter if he's innocent? An allegation of rape is not something that can be erased from someone's life easily. It could ruin him,' she said more to herself than to Tim.

'Try to get some sleep and come and see him tomorrow. He's going to need your support one hundred per cent at the moment.'

'I know,' said Izzy. 'Thanks for what you are doing.' Tim rang off and Izzy retreated into a stupor, unable to do anything. She lost track of time and had no idea how long she'd sat there when there was a knock at the door. She jumped, her heart thumping wildly. A traitorous hope popped into her head that it was Harry. She remained where she was, staring at the door.

'Izzy? I know you're in there.'

Izzy was relieved to recognise Chrissie's voice. 'Come in,' she called still sitting huddled up on the sofa. Chrissie bustled into the caravan.

'I wish you'd stayed the night. I've been worried sick about you all since you left, so I thought I may as well drive over and check on you.' She didn't wait for a reply but marched into the kitchen briskly and put the kettle on and then busied herself retrieving mugs and tea bags. Izzy sat in silence, staring into space letting Chrissie take over. She brought the steaming mugs over and sat down next to Izzy.

'I know what's going on. Tim has updated Gerald. It all sounds horrific but Tim thinks Stephen will have a good case. This isn't

154

going to be easy for any of you but you're going to have be strong and I'll help. I'll take the children out tomorrow. We were going to go to the aquarium in Liverpool anyway and Claudia will be helping me. That way you'll be free to spend time with Stephen and the children won't be asking questions. You will need to discuss it with them soon Izzy. This is going to get out and it might filter down to the playground. You should talk to the childminder and their schools as soon as possible.'

'Yes, you're right. Oh Chrissie, this is just horrific. I haven't even dared ring Stephen's parents yet.' Izzy sank her head into her hands with an uncontrolled sob. Chrissie put her arms around her and held her while she cried.

'Why has this happened to us? It's not fair. Stephen is a good man and he hasn't done anything wrong.'

'Well, life isn't fair and this is a big blow but you're strong Izzy and you will get through this. Call Stephen's parents if you can face it. They ought to know and they'll want to help. Then get to bed. I'll be round at eight-thirty sharp as we have an hour's drive. Claudia is doing the packed lunches as we speak.'

'Thank you. You are amazing. How will I ever repay you?'

'Don't be so daft. I'm not expecting payment of any sort. That's what friends do. One day you might be helping me out. You'd better lock up after me.' Chrissie squeezed her arm and went out into the night. Izzy stood there for a while after, staring out into the blackness and filling her lungs with the cool night air. Eventually she forced herself to go in, locked the door behind her and made her way through to the bedroom. She buried her face in Stephen's pillow and cried herself to sleep.

Izzy slept badly with horrible dreams of court rooms and Stephen in prison. She woke, and initially couldn't remember what had happened, enjoying a brief respite from the horror that returned when the recent events came rushing back unchecked. The heavy weariness returned and she lay with her head under the duvet not wanting to get up and face the day. She could hear the children moving about and speaking softly. She didn't want them to come into her room and see her still clothed from the night before. This motivated her to rise, strip and head off to the shower.

As she emerged from the shower, she heard giggling coming from the adjoining caravan. She pulled on some leggings and one of Stephen's jumpers that was lying over a chair and went to see what they were up to. Chrissie was sitting at the table with them, all three stuffing their faces with hot croissants and pain au chocolat. Tatty and Ed had chocolate all round their faces and Izzy smiled in spite of her misery.

'Mummy we're going to the 'quarium!' shrieked Tatty.

'We're going to see sharks,' said Ed. 'If Tatty's naughty we can feed her to them.'

Tatty's eyes rounded in horror. 'You can't really?' she said seeking reassurance.

'Of course not,' said Ben. 'Ed's just teasing you. He's an idiot.'

'No I'm not!' said Ed loudly. 'You're the idiot.'

'That's enough,' Izzy said sharply. 'Or else you'll all stay home with me.' There was an immediate silence. 'Morning Chrissie. Gosh you really didn't have to do all this for them.'

'Actually I'm doing it for me because quite frankly, since Claudia arrived I feel like a spare part in the mornings. She runs everything like a military operation and I just get in her way. So it's nice to come here and do breakfast. Sit down here and eat something.'

'Mummy can you come with us today?' asked Ed

'I would love to sweetheart but I've got a lot of work to do this morning.'

'OK, Mummy but we will miss you,' said Tatty sweetly.

Izzy was relieved when they were all on their way. No one had mentioned Stephen so she hadn't had to lie. She absentmindedly tidied up and then headed off to the police station to see what, if any, developments there had been. She got there at ten o'clock and approached the front desk apprehensively. A middle-aged lady with prematurely greying hair smiled receptively at her as she asked about Stephen. She consulted her computer screen and the smile slowly slipped from her face as she read. 'Mr James is to be detained until his first court hearing which is tomorrow morning,' she said coldly, barely glancing at Izzy. Izzy was starting to feel slightly paranoid about how people were reacting to her when they found out who her husband was.

'May I see my husband please?' she asked forcibly.

The woman responded without looking up, 'I'll find out,' she said and stalked off.

Izzy stood by the window of reception feeling like a criminal and wondering how on earth Stephen was coping. A male voice behind her made her jump and she swung around quickly and was relieved to see Tim.

'Oh, I'm glad you're here. Everyone I have spoken to in this God forsaken place has made me feel like a low-life criminal,' Izzy said ruefully.

'It goes with the territory I'm afraid. Everyone will think you've been harbouring a rapist at home and that you are as much to blame as he is.'

'Well that's ludicrous,' said Izzy. 'What about innocent until proven guilty?'

'Yes well, in theory that is the case but not always in practice and your husband has supposedly taken advantage of a school girl in his care. It's not good.'

'Tell me about it,' said Izzy. 'What are you doing here today?'

'I'm going to prepare Stephen for tomorrow and the possibility he might not make bail.'

Izzy looked aghast. 'You have to be kidding.'

'Well bail is refused for a number of reasons. If the victim decides to issue a Personal Statement which implies that Stephen is a danger to her, then that could be a problem. I don't think that will be the case but we have to be prepared for all eventualities.'

'I didn't think for one minute that he could be kept in jail.'

'Well I'll do the best I can. Come on, let's go and see how he's holding up. A night in the cells can be fairly traumatic to the uninitiated!'

Stephen looked terrible with bloodshot eyes and a hang-dog appearance. 'I'm ruined,' he'd said. 'Everything I have worked for has just gone down the plug hole. I don't deserve this and I don't know why those women decided to do this to me.'

Izzy tried to be encouraging and make him see sense but it wasn't easy and she was totally fed up with the whole thing by the time she left the station. *If only he'd had a bloody bit more common sense, they wouldn't be in this position.* Tim walked her back to her car.

'So what's your gut feeling on this?' she asked looking up at him as she leant back on her car.

'I think your husband will be fine. He's got an alibi for most of the night and in fact there is only a small window when he allegedly got up to anything. Lucy and Leonora are working together and it would be so nice to find out what is going on there. I have a feeling that Lucy is pushing Leonora, but I don't know why. It's a shame nobody saw Stephen and Lucy together to verify his version of events. However, one of my minions is off to retrieve CCTV footage from the hotel. I'm hoping to get my hands on it before the police do.'

157

'Will they have kept it that long?' asked Izzy, 'I thought some of these video things were wiped every twenty-four hours.'

'That's true but luckily this hotel keeps footage for three months, so fingers crossed.'

Izzy brightened slightly. 'So if Stephen is on camera doing the things he says he was then he won't have been allegedly raping someone and that will clear his name.'

'Hopefully!' said Tim. 'Now go home and get some rest and for goodness sake don't forget to dress smartly tomorrow and bring a suit for Stephen.'

'I won't!' Izzy said, looking down at Stephen's jumper ruefully. 'Thanks Tim. I really appreciate what you're doing.'
'That's no problem.' He headed for his car.

On the way home Izzy rang Harry and asked him to cover for her at work. She really didn't want anyone there knowing what was going on. She hoped she'd be able to pop into work in the afternoon and nobody would be any the wiser.

Now she had to call Stephen's parents. She'd spoken to Arthur who had taken the news initially in silence and then mounting anger as she'd relayed the events to him. He'd gone off to speak to Susan and she'd rung back later to offer help.

# Chapter 22
## *November 2003*

Clarissa was sitting in the conservatory enjoying the late afternoon sun. The clocks had changed the previous weekend and soon the daylight would be fading fast. She was feeling distinctly peeved. She hadn't seen Archie again since they'd managed to grab those couple of days in France after Charles had left. They'd spent the time together in a hotel whilst Sylvie looked after the children. Even then, it had all seemed too short and he had spent a ridiculous amount of time on the phone. *All for a bit of pipe, honestly!* She hadn't heard from him in weeks. In fact, she was beginning to have second thoughts about investing. She wasn't sure he deserved her money.

She was also going to have to deal with Tamara. The dratted girl was lording it round the place as if she owned it, even having the cheek to come into the house. Clarissa still couldn't believe that she'd had the flat redecorated for her, with new furniture throughout, only to find that she'd had friends in there partying while they were in France. It looked a mess, with stains everywhere. As for persuading Charles to let her have a temporary groom while they were away! *She had no doubt what Tamara had wanted him for.* She hadn't dared to complain, as Charles would enjoy digging his heels in.

On the other hand, she'd noticed that Charles didn't appear to be chasing Tamara about anymore. She expected he was growing tired of her, which meant he shouldn't object too much when she fired her. He'd probably be grateful. She just had to bide her time until she was certain.

Tomorrow was the opening meet. No doubt Charles was intending to be there, so unfortunately they would have to make a show of companionship. She hoped Sid was fit for riding. Heather had been permanently lunging or jumping him but Clarissa rarely saw Tamara working her horses. She sat up abruptly and decided to go and inspect the horses. The yard was quiet and it appeared that all the horses were in their stables. Those hunting on the morrow were plaited, although Tamara had used rubber bands, which Heather would have never done.

Clarissa walked into the tack room and was surprised to see a girl she didn't recognize cleaning a pile of tack. There were at least five bridles hanging up waiting to be cleaned, along with several saddles on the large saddle horse in the middle of the room. 'And you are?' Clarissa asked. There was no response as the girl carried on rubbing saddle soap into the leather. Clarissa wasn't used to being ignored and she tapped the girl smartly on the shoulder. She looked up startled, and Clarissa noted that she was using an MP3 player. She continued to stare at Clarissa's angry face before shouting, 'Whadoyawan?'

Clarissa ripped the headphones out of the girl's ears and hissed at her. 'Who are you? And where is Tamara?'

The girl glared angrily at her. 'You can't do that!' She picked up her headphones. 'That's abuse,' she said waving them in front of Clarissa.

Clarissa found herself getting angrier. She could easily hit this loathsome child. She tried again. 'I'm Clarissa Hambridge,' she said haughtily and waited.

The girl looked up at her. 'Means nothing to me. I only answer to Tamara, she's the owner.'

'Really?' Clarissa looked up and wondered what on earth had been going on.

'So she employs you?'

'Yeah, to look after her horses,' the girl resumed cleaning.

'*Her* horses?' Clarissa grimaced. 'So where is Tamara at the moment?'

'Gone to a party in London. She'll be back tomorrow to ride. There's a hunt.'

'Well I'm so glad she hasn't forgotten that.' Clarissa stomped off furiously. Enough was enough. After tomorrow, Tamara would have to go.

The sky was a British damp grey when Sylvie pulled back the curtains and Clarissa smiled, knowing it would be a great day for hunting. She lay in bed eyeing her new navy blue hunting jacket, which fitted her perfectly. She knew Sylvie would have polished her boots so that she could see her reflection in them. Her thoughts turned to the two horses she was riding today. Sid first. He looked magnificent and she relished the thought of the admiring glances she always received when bringing him out. At seventeen two he was very impressive. She'd paid a ridiculous amount of money for him but it had been worth every penny in guaranteeing she looked the part.

Sylvie placed a tray on the bedside table next to Clarissa. 'Everything's ready for you Madame,' she said. Without waiting for a response, Sylvie walked downstairs to find Tamara sitting in the kitchen with a cup of tea, reading a celebrity gossip magazine.

'Have you got time to be sitting here?' she asked, surprised. 'Surely you haven't finished everything?'

Tamara stretched. 'Well, I've only got four horses to get ready first thing and then I'll have time to do the other four before change over. I don't know what all the fuss is about. Hadn't you better run along and clean a toilet or something?'

Sylvie eyed Tamara distastefully and didn't reply. Instead she turned to Carl. 'Are the sandwiches and hip flasks ready? Has Amelia eaten breakfast yet? I bet she's been in the yard since day break.'

'Bless,' said Tamara condescendingly.

'Yes, that one actually knows something about animal welfare. Carl, can you make a couple of bacon butties for me? I'll pop one out to her and it will be an incentive to get Toby out of bed. He didn't get back from university until late last night, but he can't lie in if he wants to make the hunt.'

Having showered leisurely, Clarissa donned her buff breeches and immaculately-ironed white hunting shirt. She tied her stock elegantly and popped in the exceedingly old hunting pin which had been given to her by her late grandmother. She patted it affectionately before slipping on her new jacket. She surveyed herself in the huge mirror and liked what she saw: a very slim and elegantly attired lady, hair arranged neatly in a hair net and tied at the back with a discreet navy blue ribbon, face lightly made up, and pearl studs adorning each ear. She looked at the clock. Eleven, time to go down to the drawing room. She picked up her hunting whip and left the room.

Toby and Charles were already waiting when Clarissa joined them and both looked well turned out as she expected. Amelia on the other hand was nowhere in sight. Irritated, she made her way to the boot room and pulled on her boots before going to the stables to look for her daughter. As expected, she found Amelia making finishing touches to one of her ponies.

'For goodness sake Amelia go in and get changed at once! We are waiting to leave and you will not be coming with us, if you're not ready. Toffee is going later anyway so Tamara can finish him off.'

'Tamara is hopeless,' said Amelia, untying her pony and leaving the stable. 'You should have seen the fiasco with loading the horses. It's a good job I was here; otherwise they'd never have got away in time.'

Amelia was changed in five minutes and raced down the stairs and into the drawing-room like a mini whirlwind. 'I'm ready,' she shrieked excitedly. 'Come on let's go!'

'You don't want to be kept waiting then?' asked Toby wryly. Amelia pulled a face at her brother.

'Let's go hunting!' said Charles, putting down his paper and heading for the car.

'Poor old Emily missing the opening meet,' said Amelia as they drove off. 'She was livid when I spoke to her.'

'Well, maybe she should pay more attention to her school work and less to boys and smoking dope,' said Charles.

'Really Charles,' said Clarissa in a horrified voice. 'My daughter wouldn't be mixed up in any of that!'

'Oh, wouldn't she?' said Charles laughing. 'Well she was definitely smoking dope in France and there were plenty of boys texting her. I looked at her phone. Where were you for goodness sake?'

'I don't believe it. Where was she getting the stuff from? I knew that friend of hers was trouble.'

'Actually it was Toby,' said Amelia. 'He had three cannabis plants growing on his balcony that he bought from a local!'

'What! That's outrageous Amelia and I hope it's not true!' She swung round to face Toby who was grinning from ear to ear.

'Sorry Mum,' said Toby shrugging, 'Just a little harmless experiment. Dad enjoyed it though didn't you?'

'Now then Toby that was meant to be our little secret,' he said, smiling at Clarissa and enjoying her horrified reaction, 'and yes, it was good stuff surprisingly enough.'

Clarissa was speechless and couldn't believe this had been going on under her nose and Charles was condoning it. She knew she had been preoccupied with Archie but she must have been going around with her eyes closed. She was totally against drugs of any sort and she thought Charles was too. It seemed however, this wasn't the case any more. He was obviously having a midlife crisis.

By the time they arrived at the meet, Camilla had schooled her face back to one of a proud mother and doting wife. They spotted their horsebox, and went to collect their mounts. Tamara was trying to walk Rubix but he was dancing about like a mad thing and tossing his head up and down so that it took all of her strength to cling on to the leading rein. Clarissa had never seen him like this before. Toby grabbed the horse off her, vaulted on and took him off for a walk to try to calm him down. Sid was nowhere in sight but Clarissa could hear bangs from inside the lorry and she guessed he was still in there. Tamara went to retrieve him, leaving Clarissa standing impatiently, tapping her whip on her boot.

She didn't have long to wait. Sid exploded out of the horse box and leapt sideways off the ramp, landing perilously close to Clarissa who jumped back, startled. Tamara only just managed to keep hold of him as she legged Clarissa up.

Clarissa had just managed to get her feet in the stirrups when Sid set off at a smart trot, snorting and shying as he went. Clarissa was rigid with fear and hung on to the reins for grim death, which only added to Sid's excited state. She made it to the meet in one piece however and managed to negotiate her way through a group of plebs and a variety of common looking horses, pulling Sid up next to some of her own sort. She refused a much-needed glass of mulled wine, fearing for her white stock if she had to steady Sid with just one hand.

Charles was deep in conversation with some young lady, his horse, a hunting veteran, standing quietly. Clarissa wished she was riding him instead. Thankfully, Sid calmed down sufficiently for Clarissa to speak to several people, which she did in a loud voice so that all and sundry were obliged to turn and listen. Several people commented on how magnificent her horse was and she smiled indulgently. She surveyed the scene. There had to be close to one hundred and fifty people mounted on horseback, ranging from a two-year-old sitting on a cute fluffy Shetland pony to an eighty-year-old lady who'd not missed a season in nearly as many years. The huntsmen looked resplendent in their pink coats, standing just to the edge of the crowd and talking amiably with riders and followers on foot, while keeping an eye on the hounds that were milling about excitedly.

With Sid calmer, Clarissa decided she could risk a glass of wine. It would do her nerves good and the riding would work off the calories. They were late starting and she had just downed her third glass when the master sounded the horn calling the hounds to attention. The huntsmen began to move off on their way to the first covert. Excited horses tossed their heads, eager to be off, and riders gathered themselves in preparation.

Sid, realizing that they were finally moving off, was beside himself with excitement and plunged forward, nearly unseating Clarissa. Luckily, he didn't take to bucking and Clarissa managed to hang on as he towed her around from covert to covert, until the hounds finally drew scent and ran. After an hour and a half of having to be kept on a tight rein, Sid exploded like a cork from a champagne bottle and took off at a fast gallop. It took all Clarissa's might not to let him get in front of the master. He was a huge horse with a gigantic stride and he ate up the ground in front of him, pulling like a steam train. Clarissa was beginning to feel absolutely exhausted and couldn't wait to change horses. She most certainly wasn't enjoying herself and she couldn't give two hoots about what she looked like anymore – which was just as well as she was looking somewhat dishevelled.

To add insult to injury, Amelia's pony was going like a dream and even Toby's horse had settled down. Charles and Toby were pushing their horses fast and jumping absolutely everything in their path but Charles's old hunter was beginning to struggle. Clarissa suspected that none of the horses were as fit as they should have been. She casually wondered if Charles wanted to swap, but she swiftly pushed that thought out of her head. She wouldn't give Charles the satisfaction; he'd see through her immediately and any sign of weakness would be used against her at some point.

Clarissa could see hounds disappearing into a wood up ahead and she prayed that the fox would run to ground and she'd have a moment's respite before the next onslaught. Her prayers were answered and the field slowed up and gathered at the edge of the wood, while two of the huntsmen dismounted and disappeared into the wood after the hounds.

Most of the horses settled down to wait but not Sid. He was dripping in sweat and he continued to prance around, yanking at his bit and wrenching Clarissa's arms with monotonous regularity. She moved him away from the rest of the field to try to calm him down and as she turned to face the rest of the field, he reared up suddenly and then plunged forward, sticking his head down between his legs and giving an almighty buck, which sent Clarissa flying through the air and into a huge cow pat. She landed with a squelch and lay stunned for a minute before sitting up, close to tears. The whole field was watching her and she was convinced that quite a few people were smiling surreptitiously. Charles wandered over unhurriedly.

'Making quite a spectacle of yourself, aren't you?' he said mockingly. 'Honestly, the lengths some people will go to just for some attention. Such a shame about the jacket,' he added for good measure.

Clarissa ignored Charles and turned to look for her horse. Sid was careering around the field, still bucking and generally making a nuisance of himself and upsetting other horses. Finally Toby dismounted and gave his horse to his sister to hold whilst he set off to retrieve Sid, who had been partially cornered by three members of the field who were deeply unimpressed by the whole saga.

'I suggest that you don't hunt him until he gets some manners,' one frosty woman said rudely. 'He's dangerous and a liability.'

Clarissa ignored her as Toby legged her back up.

'Aren't we changing horses now?' she asked Toby hopefully.

'Yes, we are. I've just texted Tamara. We're meeting by the old barn in five minutes. We'd best be off while they're digging the fox out,' he said.

'Mummy, are you all right?' asked Amelia, trotting up with a concerned expression on her face.

'Yes, Amelia,' said Clarissa wearily. 'Let's not make more fuss than we need to.'

Tamara was waiting in a lay-by with all four horses. She took one look at Clarissa and laughed. 'Oh dear. Take a tumble did we?' She turned to Charles, smiling as she grabbed his bridle. His horse was blowing hard and dripping from head to foot in sweat.

'Ride hard do we?' she enquired of Charles with a big grin on her face.

'As you well know,' he retorted. 'Now, where's my next horse?' Charles retrieved his fresh mount and was on board before Clarissa had even slid off Sid. 'Get a move on!' he shouted to her. 'I don't want to miss the hunt moving off.'

Charles's horse was dancing round, eager to be off and Clarissa's horse, catching the excitement, wouldn't stand still. It took Tamara several attempts to leg her up on Doucette. Finally she was on, however, and settled down into the saddle of the smaller and more manageable mare, feeling a lot safer. She had bought Doucette for her show jumping ability, but had hunted twice last year like a dream.

They moved off together and headed back the way they'd come.

As they neared the field, the hunting horn startled the usually calm Doucette and she suddenly perked up and began to dance about. Clarissa tensed up and Doucette, sensing the anxiety, began to toss her head, becoming more excited. They arrived just in time – the fox having been dispatched and the hounds re-gathered and the hunt preparing to move off to the next covert. Clarissa noted that both Toby and Charles were having problems with their horses, too. Only Amelia's pony trotted calmly along.

The field assembled near a wood and the hounds disappeared to try and find a fox. Toby, Charles and Clarissa kept their horses to the edge of the field and walked in circles to try to keep them calm. Finally the hounds started baying and set off across the countryside in pursuit, closely followed by the huntsmen. The field set off at a gallop and Doucette took off in hot pursuit. Clarissa tried to slow her down and regain some control, but there was no stopping the mare. To Clarissa's horror, she could see they were heading for a huge hedge and she vainly hoped that maybe Doucette would slow down or stop. However, Doucette was born to jump and the looming five-foot hedge was nothing to her. She'd been cooped up in a stable for weeks and she was enjoying herself immensely. She didn't alter her stride as she approached the huge hedge but kept on, galloping flat out, and launched herself over the hedge in the manner of a steeple-chaser rather than a show jumper. Nevertheless, she cleared it by miles and Clarissa felt like she was flying. The descent seemed to last forever and Doucette, unused to landing on such uneven ground, pecked heavily and somersaulted, rolling on top of Clarissa as she fell. The last thing Clarissa remembered was Doucette stumbling on landing and then nothing.

# Chapter 23

Charles paced up and down the hospital corridor in his dirty jodhpurs, boots clacking on the highly-polished floor. He'd removed his jacket and had rolled up his sleeves and was enjoying the attention he was receiving from various females dotted around the waiting area. Clarissa had not regained consciousness yet and was currently in the CT scanner. After having ascertained that Clarissa was still breathing, Charles had called for an ambulance. He and Toby had decided to carry on with the hunt, leaving Amelia to wait with her mother. 'She did say she didn't like a fuss, didn't she?' Charles had reassured his daughter, patting her on the shoulder.

Luckily a couple of elderly ladies had stopped and offered to hold the horses, while giving Amelia conflicting advice about whether to move her mother into the recovery position or not and what to do about Doucette who had recovered from her fall and was galloping loose.

Charles and Toby had finished the day's hunting and Charles had made his way to the hospital, making all the right noises and looking as if he were concerned. In fact, he was excited. He kept going through all the possible scenarios: Clarissa dying; Clarissa not regaining consciousness and being a vegetable; paralysis; brain damage. He was happily preoccupied with planning his life without her, pleased that he wouldn't have to go through an expensive divorce, when a lady called his name. A particularly good-looking woman wearing scrubs was looking expectantly in his direction. He adopted a suitably worried face and walked in her direction, Amelia following closely behind.

'Come this way, please,' the woman said briskly and they followed her down the corridor and into a side room with several computer monitors scattered about. She indicated for them to sit down. 'I'm afraid it's not good news,' she said softly and then paused, gauging Charles's response. He sat motionless, an unreadable expression on his face. 'She has a subdural haematoma and she will be airlifted immediately to Birmingham to the specialist head injury unit for treatment.'

Amelia gulped and tried to control her emotions as best she could, but she was struggling. Charles sat impassively and waited for the doctor to continue; he wondered what she'd be like in bed.

'What is one of those haema things?' Amelia spoke up. 'Could she die?'

'Basically, it's a bleed on the brain and we have to release the build up of pressure by drilling a hole in your mother's skull. Providing we can stop the pressure, your mother should make a good recovery but there are always risks attached to the procedure.'

Amelia looked a bit happier. 'Oh OK, so it's like a big bruise then?' she said.

'Well, something like that,' the doctor smiled encouragingly at her and then paused, gathering herself to relay the next bit. 'However, that's not all. Your mother has sustained some very severe injuries, not least a fractured neck and we won't know the extent of the damage for a day or two until the inflammation starts to subside.' She looked from Charles to Amelia.

'So what does that mean? Is she paralysed?' Charles asked, trying not to rejoice too soon.

'Possibly. I'm afraid it's quite severe so I would think it likely that some damage will have occurred, possibly long lasting, but I don't want to discuss that now. The most important thing is to stabilize your wife and make sure that she starts to make a recovery. It will have to be one step at a time.'

'I see,' said Charles. 'Well I suppose if that's it for now we'd best be off.' He sat forward on his chair and patted Amelia's knee. 'I have to be somewhere tonight and Amelia you have to get back to school tomorrow so no late night for you.'

The doctor looked surprised and Amelia burst into tears. 'I can't leave Mummy,' she wailed. 'What if she dies?'

'Don't be so ridiculous, Amelia. Your mother's not going to die. She's going to get better and you sitting around here moping is not going to help. So let's get going.' Charles stood up forcibly.

'Can I see her before I go?' she asked the doctor.

'Yes, of course you can,' she stood up smiling kindly at Amelia, 'follow me.'

Charles hesitated and then thought he'd better show willing, so he followed the two women up the corridor and into a side room. Clarissa was covered in wires which seemed to be attached to all sorts of monitors. Amelia gasped as she went over to her mother, the enormity of what had happened finally sinking in. She looked so small and vulnerable lying there and somehow Amelia knew that life would never be the same again. Her mother's eyes were taped shut and her mouth was partly opened with a tube attached. It didn't look like her mother at all. She touched her hand gently, mindful of the drip; it felt cool to the touch. Amelia couldn't remember the last time she'd actually touched or been touched by her mother. Tears welled up and she felt them rolling gently down her cheeks to splash onto the crisp white sheets. A comforting hand alighted on her shoulder and she thought for one minute it was her father but she turned and saw that the doctor was standing just behind her.

'What will happen now?' she asked quietly.

'Your mother is being air lifted to Birmingham. The helicopter is on its way as we speak. You'll be able to see her there.'

'I'm going back to school. I only managed to get this weekend off because of the opening meet,' she said, a note of panic in her voice. 'Mummy will be on her own. Daddy doesn't care about her at all.' Fresh tears spilled on to her cheeks.

'Well, I can't help there, I'm afraid but I'm sure the school will give you some time off. I would have thought this is an exceptional circumstance.'

The doctor turned to look at Charles who was rapidly retreating up the corridor having hastily signed some consent forms. He'd given Clarissa a cursory glance, decided that there wasn't much he could do and turned and left, eager to be off.

'Goodbye,' said Amelia, looking up at the doctor. 'I think I might like to be a doctor.'

'I'm sure you'd be very good,' she said smiling and turned to walk back into Clarissa's room.

Amelia stood momentarily in the corridor before rushing to catch up with Charles. She was silent on the way home and Charles didn't bother to make conversation. He turned the volume up on the radio. 'Beautiful' by Christina Aguilera was playing and Amelia sat listening to the words and thinking sadly of her mother. She turned to study her father and thought how ironic that such a handsome man could be so ugly, because that's what he was inside – a truly ugly person. The realization that she actually didn't like him very much caught like a lump in her chest and she inhaled sharply to try and dislodge the overwhelming feeling growing inside.

Oblivious, Charles was planning his next move and licking his lips in anticipation. He was going to phone Lydia-Rose. He'd been working on her nicely since Barbados and she was close to giving him half a million pounds to invest. He roared up the drive and parked the Porsche in a spray of gravel. The dogs came rushing up as he left the vehicle but he didn't have time for them today. He bounded into the house, leaving Sylvie to deal with Amelia, and hurried up the stairs to shower and change.

He dialled Lydia-Rose's mobile number and waited, lounging on his recliner, feet up on the footstool, whisky and soda in his free hand.

'Hello Charles,' she said softly.

'Hello Lydia-Rose, are you OK to talk?' he asked with a carefully orchestrated tremor in his voice.

'Yes, is everything all right?' she asked cautiously

Charles paused for effect. 'No it isn't,' he said and waited momentarily as if to prepare himself. 'Well, cut to the chase, it's Clarissa. She's had an accident and might not recover.'

'Oh gosh, that's terrible,' said Lydia-Rose compassionately. 'I'm so sorry. Where is she?'

'Birmingham. She's been airlifted there for surgery. She's got a bleed on the brain. She fell off her horse while hunting.' Charles spoke in short sentences, trying to sound as upset as he could. It worked.

'I'm coming to see you. I shall book a hotel and let you know where I am and I won't take no for an answer,' she said firmly.

'Oh, I couldn't possibly ask you to do that for me. You're too kind and you must be so busy.'

'Nonsense,' she said crisply. 'You have been so helpful with my investments. In fact the money should be with you by Tuesday of next week. Anyway, I must get on. I'll see you tomorrow.'

'Thank you Lydia-Rose. What a wonderful person you are.'

'Well, what else are friends for?' she added before ringing off.

Charles punched the air with his fist. 'Result,' he said aloud and relaxed back in his chair and switched the TV on, flipping through the sports channels to find something to absorb him before he made his way off to Madame Lily's. He'd tired of Tamara now and in view of what happened today, he saw no obstacle in getting rid of her. In fact maybe he should do it right now. There was a knock at the door and his mind jolted back to the present.

'Daddy?' Amelia's face peered cautiously around the bedroom door.

'Come in!' Charles called

'I'm going back to school now. Toby will give me a lift to the station.'

'Excellent,' said Charles. 'Such a shame your day's hunting was messed up. You'll be able to go out at Christmas though, won't you?' He took a sip of his whisky, his gaze returning to the TV. Amelia wanted to shout at him that his wife was very ill in hospital and who cared about the hunting. She lowered her head. 'Yes Daddy, of course,' she responded demurely.

'Oh and what are your thoughts on Tamara? I'm thinking of getting rid of her,' he turned back to look at her.

'That would be a good idea. Her care of the horses is terrible and it's probably her fault that Mummy got hurt.'

'Oh that's a bit strong. Your mother could never ride and she would buy horses to compliment her outfit rather than her riding skill. Do you think we could get that Heather back? She was good. Never any problems with her.'

'I don't know Daddy. She was pretty fed up with Mummy and the way she was treated by her.'

'Well, that won't be a problem now will it? I'll give her a ring. What do you say?'

Amelia brightened, 'I think that would be an excellent idea but you'll have to offer her a lot more money. I know she was never given any time off to event her own horse and she will want to do that.'

'I'll bear that in mind,' Charles responded. 'Right, you'd best be off then,' he dismissed her.

Amelia scuttled off to check on Toffee one last time, burying her face in his mane until she heard Sylvie calling her name.

Charles slept in late the next morning. He was exhausted, having not returned home until four in the morning after a long, exhilarating and rather tiring session. Madame Lily had surpassed herself and he'd lost count of the number of women involved. He stretched like a contented cat and contemplated the day ahead. Lydia-Rose; he wriggled in excitement. Today was the day when he would be rewarded and he was looking forward to it. After last night he was fairly spent, but he knew he would be able to go the distance with her and give her a session she wouldn't forget in a hurry.

By the time he'd showered and eaten some toast he'd received a text from Lydia-Rose to say that she had arrived and where she was staying. He knew the hotel; a large impersonal chain where he would have anonymity. He replied saying that he was currently visiting his wife but hoped to see Lydia-Rose this afternoon if that was all right. He then rang the hospital to try to find out if Clarissa was still alive and was disappointed to find out that she was in a critical but stable condition.

He next rang Heather who annoyingly didn't answer. He'd decided that he'd better keep Tamara on until he got Heather back and he left a message. He sat down on his recliner and lit a cigar. He would go for a run shortly but needed some time to chill first.

It was four o'clock before he met up with Lydia-Rose. She was waiting anxiously in the lounge of the hotel. He had not shaved and had dressed appropriately for a harassed and tired husband. He adopted a suitably forlorn expression as he went to greet her.

'Charles,' she said as she hugged him warmly and kissed him on both cheeks. I've ordered tea but would you care for something stronger?'

'No, tea will be fine. I'm driving, after all,' he paused for effect and then added, 'I must apologise for my appearance, I'm in desperate need of a shower. After I spoke to you I headed back to the hospital and I haven't been home yet.'

'Oh poor you,' said Lydia-Rose, 'you must be exhausted. You can shower in my room. I have enough towels for several people.' She smiled at him encouragingly. 'Have you eaten?'

'Well, I ate a mouldy old cheese sandwich in the hospital but I can't remember when that was. Everything is such a blur.'

'Oh poor you,' Lydia-Rose said again, 'and how is Clarissa?'

Charles grimaced as if in pain. He ran his fingers through his hair. 'Well, she's stable but they don't know how much damage has been done yet. They won't know until some of the swelling has subsided.'

'Oh, so you have no idea how long that'll be?'

'Correct. It was touch and go last night.' He dropped his head into his hands for effect.

Lydia-Rose reached out to touch his shoulder and Charles placed his hand over hers. He looked up carefully until his eyes met hers and they gazed at each other momentarily before Lydia-Rose sat back in her chair, retracting her hand.

At that moment a waitress turned up with a pot of tea for two and some assorted cakes. 'I thought you could do with a treat,' said Lydia-Rose as she noticed Charles eyeing them speculatively, 'you've been through so much.'

He grinned back at her and grabbed a large slice of coffee and walnut cake while Lydia-Rose fiddled about with the tea cups. He wolfed the slice down and turned his attention to the rich fruitcake. After two cups of tea, he presented himself as a slightly happier man and he was delighted when Lydia-Rose offered him a shower again.

'I hope this is all above board?' he said to her in the lift on the way to her room.

She giggled nervously and Charles knew he was on to a winner. He had been planning this for so long and Clarissa's accident had sped things along nicely. He nearly didn't make it into the shower, grabbing her gently on entering her bedroom and kissing her softly to gauge her reaction. She responded hesitantly at first, and then with increased ardour. At that point he broke it off and left her standing slightly breathless.

'Lydia-Rose,' he whispered caressing her face. 'We can't do this.' He stared intently at her. 'It's just that it's been so long since I...' he petered out, 'well you know and there's your marriage to think of.' He disappeared into the bathroom and stripped naked before taking a shower. He'd only been in there a couple of minutes when Lydia-Rose opened the bathroom and Charles, glancing out through the glass, could see she was stark naked. She was beautiful and Charles eyed her with appreciation through the stream of water flooding down the glass panel. She knew he was watching her and she undulated slowly over to the shower and opened the door, sliding in next to him. They spent a while just kissing and enjoying the feeling of water sliding over their bodies, getting to know each other more intimately before Charles suddenly switched the shower off and led her out, donning a bath robe to partially dry himself off.

'What!' she exclaimed. 'You can't stop now!' He reached for a towel and began to dry her off sensuously, before she dragged him to the bedroom.

Charles left early the next morning feeling very pleased with himself. Lydia-Rose had been good fun but his tastes were getting more extreme and he knew she wouldn't satisfy him for long. Still, he had to keep her attached for a while to ensure all the financial deals went through. Half a million was on its way to him and he was hoping to get more out of her in the next few months.

He headed into work and arrived by eight thirty. He was the last one in; even Izzy was there, though looking tired. He was going to have to find out how things were going with her; if she wasn't pulling her weight she'd be out of the door. Piers was waiting in Charles's office when he got to work.

'Morning,' he said as he dumped his briefcase on his desk. Piers closed the door behind him and Charles sensed that all was not well.

'I regret to inform you, Charles that I will be resigning from the partnership. I have been offered another job elsewhere that frankly is more appealing.'

'Oh,' Charles looked quite shocked for a moment. 'That was a bit out of the blue. Right, well, I'll get Hugh to sort the financial side out.'

'Is that it?' asked Piers incredulously. 'Don't you want to ask me why I'm going?'

'Not really. There's no point. I think you're mad though, the business is doing exceedingly well.'

'Yes, some might say too well. It's not sustainable. Anyway it doesn't matter as you say.' Piers went to stand up.

'Clarissa's in hospital, she had an accident out hunting on Saturday.'

'Oh no. Is it serious?'

'Fairly. She had a bleed on the brain and she might have spinal damage.'

'Ochh, that's appalling,' said Piers sitting down again. 'I had no idea. I could have given you this news some other time. What are you doing here? For God's sake go and be with your wife.'

'I've been with her since it happened. Need a break from it, frankly, old chap.'

As Piers digested the news about Clarissa, Charles thought quickly about the implications of him leaving. He would have to buy him out and how much would depend on the valuation of the business. They had a fifty-fifty share, so Charles would own one hundred per cent of the business, but he knew that right now he would not have the available money to buy Piers out. He would have to create some new equity partners to buy in and thus create some available cash. He would retain the controlling share of fifty-one percent.

'It might take me a moment to raise the cash,' he said glancing across at Piers. Piers, who'd thought that Charles was probably dwelling on his wife, was surprised by his response.

'Oh right,' he said. 'I'm in no hurry for the money. I'm giving you three months' notice anyway.'

'Yes, of course.' Charles smiled at Piers. 'So what will you be doing?'

'Actually I'm immigrating to New Zealand. We're taking on a skydiving business near Christchurch, South Island.'

'Well I never!' Charles sat back in his chair. 'You've kept that quiet.'

'I know. We wanted to finalize everything before we told people. Katy has a job as a sonographer out there. Her profession is very much in demand, so we'll have a steady income there and then hopefully my business will be good and that'll be us sorted.'

'I'll be out for a visit. I love sky diving. It'll be a good excuse to visit New Zealand!'

'As if you need an excuse. You're always off gallivanting somewhere or other.'

'Well, you only live once and I intend to spend as much time as possible doing fun things. That's why I have to work!'

'Of course, don't we all.' Piers stood up. 'If there's anything I can do let me know.'

'Oh that's fine. I'll get Adam on to it. He'll know how to sort the business out.'

'Actually I meant with Clarissa,' Piers said softly.

'Well there's not very much that can be done at the moment, but thank you for asking.'

Piers looked at him oddly and then retreated back to his office, leaving Charles to mull things over. Piers leaving would give him absolute control of the business and no one to look over his shoulder. He would have a free rein and the possibilities were endless. He would be able to make a serious amount of money. He must ring Garry Griedy as soon as possible.

# Chapter 24

Stephen was moping around the caravan. He had been getting lower and lower over the last month and was frustrated by how slowly everything was progressing. Christmas was looming and he could see no end to the hell that had become his life. He'd been granted bail but only just. The barrister had imposed all sorts of restrictions on him, one of which was the wearing of an electronic tag around his ankle which was utterly humiliating. At least it was the winter and he could keep it covered up with long trousers.

He'd been suspended from school until he'd been cleared of any wrong doing, but he felt that his career was over and that he would forever carry this blight over his head. It waited patiently for him while he slept, greeting him the moment he awoke, and hovered throughout the day, growing in intensity at bedtime and preventing him from getting to sleep. When he did sleep, it was sporadically, and he often awoke at four in the morning to lie motionless, trying not to wake Izzy. He lay there, staring into the darkness, thoughts churning over and over and over. He was exhausted. He knew he was becoming irrational, snappy and intolerant but he no longer had the energy to care.

Izzy had initially been very supportive and had tried to chivvy him along, but her patience had now run out. The work on the house had ground to a halt which probably didn't help matters, and he knew that deep down she suspected that there was more to his relationship with Marie-Claire. He just couldn't find it within him to care. He was currently curled up on the sofa under a duvet with the TV switched on to some inane programme.

'Stephen!' his mother called as she knocked on the door and opened it gingerly. Arthur was hovering on the doorstep, craning his neck to try to get a better view. They both saw Stephen at the same moment as he sat up on the sofa, rubbing his eyes. He looked absolutely dreadful. He hadn't shaved for a week and was very thin and gaunt; he'd aged twenty years. Susan stepped over the threshold and walked meaningfully up to him and Stephen stood up, pushing his unruly hair out of his eyes.

'Mum,' he whispered and the tears started to flow. She put her arms around him and let him sob on to her shoulder. Arthur, who'd followed Susan in, looked around uncomfortably and decided to put the kettle on. After some moments, Stephen stopped crying and wiped his eyes on his sleeve.

'Sorry,' he said and then as an afterthought, 'I'm not coping very well.'

'Tea?' Arthur called out from the kitchen area.

'I'd prefer coffee thanks, Dad,' Stephen sat down again.

'I know you said that you didn't want any visitors but we are your parents and we thought we'd pop over and see you. Izzy phoned yesterday and thought you could do with a visit.'

'Yes,' Stephen replied listlessly. 'I think she's fed up with me.'

'Not you per se Stephen,' Susan said carefully. 'More the situation and how you've let it take control of your life.'

'My life is over,' said Stephen dramatically. 'It has been ruined irreparably.' He had a wild look in his eye that Susan found somewhat disconcerting. She'd never seen her normally composed son looking like this. She exchanged worried glances with Arthur as he walked over with the drinks.

'I think you're being melodramatic.' Arthur sat down opposite Stephen. 'You haven't been convicted and by all accounts you won't be. You are an innocent man and justice will prevail,' he said confidently.

'Your father's right Stephen,' Susan agreed.

'Yes, but even if my name is cleared I can't go back to that school with everyone talking about me and I'll only have to accidently brush up against someone and I could be accused of something untoward. My life is ruined and so is that of my family. They'd be better off without me.' He was shaking now and Susan and Arthur exchanged worried glances again.

'No they wouldn't. They love and need you. Izzy is extremely worried about you and is finding it hard to cope with working, looking after the children and looking after you. She rang to ask for our help because she is exhausted and at her wits' end. This isn't all about you. Your family are suffering too.' Arthur finished speaking and waited for a response.

Stephen frowned, trying to register what his father had just said. 'Oh great, so you're here to look after me then,' he said bitterly and stood up suddenly making for the door. 'And it's my entire fault then that my family are suffering?'

'No, your father didn't say that. You can't help what has happened but you can do something about the way you deal with it. We are not here to look after you. Your father is going to do some work on the house. If you can at least get the kitchen in, and some carpet in the bedrooms, we don't see why you can't move in. I'm going to cook meals and look after the children so Izzy can have some breathing space. You can choose to help your father or sulk in here. It's up to you.'

Stephen had stopped by now and he didn't say anything. He stood silently clenching and unclenching his fists and working his jaw.

Susan stood up. 'Right, well I'll get on with some dinner and have a tidy up,' she said, glancing around the messy caravan.

'I'll go and look around the house and see what needs doing. Will you accompany me Stephen?' Arthur asked hopefully.

'I'm just going to have a shower,' said Stephen angrily.

'He's bad,' said Susan softly, tears collecting in the corner of her eyes.

'I know. He'll need careful handling though. Poor Izzy, she should have told us sooner that things were this bad.'

'I think he might need medication,' Susan added thoughtfully.

'Don't be ridiculous Sue, he's not depressed, he's just let himself go a bit. We'll pull him through. You know my feelings on all these drugs that doctors dispense willy-nilly. Nothing that can't be cured by a few days of hard physical work. I'll get him right.' Arthur stood up, 'I'll make a start.'

Susan watched him go and hoped that Arthur was right. Maybe a bit of physical graft would do Stephen good.

Stephen stood under the hot water. He felt like crap but he was going to have to make an effort if his father had turned up to do some work on the house. He shaved and dressed in clean old clothes and followed his father out to the house. His father was wandering around downstairs.

'You could be in by Christmas easily. There's not so much left to do. We'll get it done in no time if we do it together.'

'I suppose so,' Stephen said unenthusiastically, looking around the kitchen. 'The appliances are in the utility room along with the tiles,' he added disinterestedly. His father poked around, moving kitchen carcasses about.

'I've got the plans and seeing as I made a lot of it, I should be able to remember where it all goes,' Arthur said absently, inspecting a unit door.

Stephen didn't reply. He plonked himself down on an upturned crate and watched his father as he unpacked boxes and shifted units around. He had a pen stuck behind one ear and he kept retrieving it to make notes on a pad that he was carrying. He muttered to himself as he worked and Stephen felt strangely comforted just watching him. He was momentarily taken back to his childhood when he'd spent the odd day with his father during the school holidays and before the business had grown to the extent that his father had employed other people to do the labouring while he quoted and worked on bespoke items.

Marmaduke jumped on to Stephen's lap, where he made himself comfortable and began purring and kneading Stephen's thigh with his front paws. Stephen would have swapped places with Marmaduke for anything at that moment; to lead an uncomplicated and peaceful life without worry. He stroked the cat and scratched him behind his ears. Marmaduke purred louder and gazed adoringly at Stephen through half-closed eyes.

Arthur worked for most of the afternoon and by the end the unit carcasses were all assembled and ready to be put into place. He started on the tiling himself without comment. Suddenly Stephen, who hadn't moved or spoken in all that time, got off the crate, depositing a peeved Marmaduke on to the floor.

'I'll give you a hand,' he said.

'OK,' his father said and carried on with what he was doing.'

By early evening the tiles were in place and ready for grouting. 'They look great Dad. Thank you.'

They made their way back to the caravan, which had been transformed. The place was clean and tidy, and the three children were sitting around the table playing a board game with Susan. A delicious cooking smell permeated the interior.

'Daddy and Gramps!' The three children jumped up squealing and ran to the pair for hugs. Susan watched with a smile on her face.

Izzy arrived home on time for once looking tired and thin. She was delighted to see such order. The meal was noisy and jovial with the children talking nineteen to the dozen and hiding the fact that Stephen was quiet.

'Gramps is going to finish the house, aren't you?' said Ed smiling at his grandfather.

'Yeah, so we can move in for Christmas!' Ben said happily and everyone except Stephen murmured affirmations.

'Daddy you won't be so sad then?' said Ed suddenly.

'Daddy's been sad ever since he was rested,' said Tatty. 'I know why Daddy was rested. It was rape,' she announced importantly. She looked round at the horrified faces. 'Actually, I don't really know what that means,' she whispered, seeking reassurance. There was none forthcoming, just a deathly silence.

Izzy recovered quickly. 'Sweetheart who told you that?'

'They were talking about it at school,' she said quietly, sensing that maybe she shouldn't have said anything.

Stephen got up abruptly from the table and headed for the door. Izzy jumped up and ran after him shutting the door after her. He pushed her off as she tried to take his arm and he kept on striding away from her and down the drive.

'Oh for goodness sake. You can't just run off like this. It's not going to solve anything,' she said angrily after his retreating back. He didn't stop and she didn't pursue him. She just watched him sadly, wondering how they were ever going to get their life back.

Stephen kept walking. He was so angry and he needed to get rid of some pent up frustration. How could his precious little daughter be dragged into this seedy mess and he was sure the boys wouldn't have escaped unharmed either. He had been told to expect this but that was one thing. It was another actually hearing it firsthand. He'd like to kill the little bastard who had said that to Tatty.

He stopped and leant over a gate, wondering for the thousandth time why Leonora and Lucy had done this to him. He tried to remember what life was like before the incident but he couldn't; he tried to remember what happiness was like but he couldn't. It was like his life had just begun and that everything that went before was nothing and everything now was just pain and torment and there was no future.

'Daddy!' Stephen was interrupted from his gloomy musings. He stepped back from the gateway and on to the road to see who was shouting. 'Daddy!' Ben's voice called again and he watched as Ben broke into a run. Stephen stooped to put his arms around him and he hugged his solid body to him with his chin resting on his head, soft brown curls tickling his chin. He could see Arthur following steadily on behind with Tatty and Ed each side holding his hands. Stephen could feel a lump forming in his throat and he wished more than anything to find the strength he would need to carry on.

'Just thought we'd have a walk around the block, didn't we children?' said Arthur positively. 'A bit of fresh air after all that food.'

'That's right Daddy. You must have had the same idea,' Ed smiled cheerily up at Stephen, seeking reassurance. Stephen wasn't sure he could do this right now and Ben, sensing Stephen's reticence, piped up, 'come on Daddy, you're always tell us that walking is good for you!' Stephen sighed inwardly and thought that compliance was probably the best option under the circumstances.

'OK, lead on,' he said to Ben who took his hand and they all proceeded down the lane. Stephen was worried about meeting someone. He was sure the entire village were talking about him and he couldn't bear it. *Stephen James, the local paedo.* Izzy had told him to hold his head up and walk about in a confident manner rather than a victim but it wasn't easy. He was relieved to get home in one piece.

Izzy and Susan were talking in the kitchen area when they got back having tidied up the dinner things. The children headed off to bed and Stephen sank wearily into a chair. The others chatted about various things trying to encourage Stephen to chat but he was struggling to engage his brain. Susan raised the subject of Stephen seeing someone to try to help him come to terms with what was going on.

'Sometimes talking things through with a stranger can be helpful,' she said encouragingly.

'Actually, I'm sick of talking things through. I don't want to discuss my problems and talking about them won't make them go away,' he answered.

'I think it's time you had some help,' Susan said firmly.

'Well, I don't think so,' said Stephen flatly, his eyes flashed a warning at his mother and she backed off.

Izzy didn't see the look pass between Stephen and his mother. 'I happen to agree with your mother,' she said. 'I think it would be most helpful for you and there's no stigma attached to it these days.'

'Izzy, I've just said that I won't do it,' Stephen said vehemently, his eyes boring into hers. 'There's nothing wrong with me. I'm just mightily pissed off about my situation and you are really not helping by making ridiculous suggestions.'

'They're not ridiculous, Stephen,' Izzy swept in angrily. 'You're the one that's being ridiculous. You can't even see what you've become. That's the problem with depression. It creeps up on you and you're not even aware of it. You need help and that's that.'

'Depressed?' said Stephen incredulously. 'You think I'm de-pressed?'

'I probably wouldn't go that far,' Arthur piped up hurriedly. 'Just a bit down perhaps,' he suggested.

'Well, there's quite a lot to be miserable about, isn't there?' Stephen said angrily. 'I mean I'm a criminal, banned from my job and my 5-year-old daughter talks about me being a rapist over dinner,' he said.

'None of this is really helping,' said Susan. 'I think Arthur and I will head off to our B&B.'

Izzy and Stephen were left alone with only silent recriminations for company. Stephen refused to look at her and after a few minutes Izzy got up and went to bed. Stephen lay down on his side with his head on a couple of cushions. Marmaduke jumped up and snuggled against him, purring. Stephen shut his eyes and concentrated on the sound, until his mind went blank.

# Chapter 25

Izzy woke early and discovered Stephen curled up with Marmaduke, fast asleep. He looked contented and Izzy sat down quietly opposite him just watching. He'd lost so much weight over the last two months. He stirred in his sleep and Marmaduke woke up, peered over at Izzy and stood up carefully, stretching before jumping down and heading for the cat-flap.

Izzy made tea and when she went back, she was pleased to see Stephen was awake and sitting up. He looked up and gave her a weak smile as she offered him his tea. 'I'll drink this and then I'll shower so I'm ready for when Dad gets here. We'll crack on and get this house finished.'

Izzy felt surprised. Stephen hadn't expressed an interest in getting the house finished for a while now. 'That's great, Stephen,' she said carefully. 'It'll be nice for Arthur to have you helping him.'

'Well, as everyone keeps telling me, I can't stay around here moping can I?' He stood up, putting his untouched tea on the table and stumbled towards the shower. Izzy sat sipping her tea and feeling distinctly unhappy. At least she wouldn't have to worry about the children today with Susan to help out.

Susan and Arthur arrived just before she left and they exchanged pleasantries before she headed off to work.

\* \* \*

Charles sauntered in at around nine-thirty am, looking suspiciously pleased with himself. Izzy enquired politely after Clarissa. 'No change. Oh I'd like a quick meeting with everyone please in half an hour,' he said over his shoulder, as he disappeared into his office.

'I wonder what about,' Greg said what everyone was thinking.

'Well we will find out soon enough,' replied Harry.

They all filed into the meeting room half an hour later and sat round the large oak table. Piers and Charles came in last and sat down looking serious. Izzy had a feeling that something was up. Piers began. 'There is no easy way to tell you this, but I have decided to resign from the business. An opportunity has come up overseas that I would like to pursue. I'm off to New Zealand, I'm afraid.'

There was a momentary stunned silence. Charles cleared his throat. 'None of you has anything to worry about. Your jobs are secure, but there will be some changes and I would like to speak to you individually afterwards to tell you what I have in mind.'

There was a general chitchat amongst the staff and they quizzed Piers on his new business venture. They felt assured that he was leaving for genuine reasons and not because the business was doing badly. 'On the contrary,' Piers said, 'the business is doing well and I might regret this in years to come, who knows?'

Izzy waited patiently for her interview and wondered what Charles was offering. Greg and Nick had come out smiling and she was in next. Her name was called and she stood up abruptly. Charles was sitting at the end of the table and she sat down nervously, placing her hands on her lap and pressing them down firmly to stop them fidgeting.

'Right Isabella, cut to the chase and all that, what do you think this is about then?'

'The future of your company,' she said coolly, meeting his direct stare.

'Right and how do you think you've been doing?' Charles asked her without smiling.

Izzy squirmed in her chair and then remembered herself. 'Very well,' she said confidently. 'I feel that I'm doing a good job for you.'

Charles considered her answer momentarily before answering. 'Yes, I have to agree with you there. You have been working much better and I have decided to offer you the opportunity to buy into the partnership. I'm offering you twelve per cent, which will cost you one hundred and thirty thousand pounds. It sounds a lot but you should get a good return and you will of course have a company car. I was thinking of an Audi A4 with the company logo emblazoned over it to increase brand awareness. I can get a good deal at the local garage and it would look pretty good if we all had one don't you think?'

Izzy was momentarily stumped and couldn't quite believe her ears. 'Well, yes absolutely. Gosh this is all a bit sudden,' she rushed out.

'Well with Piers going, I thought I'd better rethink the whole business.'

'Of course,' said Izzy. Her heart was thumping wildly in her chest and her thoughts were flying around everywhere. She was finding it hard to concentrate on what Charles was saying: 'I would like to think about it and just work out how to fund it. Can I speak to the accountant about it as well?'

'Yes, that is no problem. I will let everyone think about my proposals and then maybe get you all together for a discussion about how it will all work. You will also get to see some figures then as well.'

'Great, well thank you very much. What a fantastic opportunity,' Izzy gushed, forgetting for the moment what a miserable manipulative git Charles could be. She was focussing on prestige and profit and she was very excited about it.

'Well, I shall expect results of course,' Charles added.

'Of course,' said Izzy. She returned to the office beaming and told Harry it was his turn. Greg and Nick swarmed around her as she sat down and they started discussing the recent turn of events.

'What did he offer you then?' Nick asked, getting straight to the point as he plonked himself on the end of her desk, one leg swinging.

'I'm not sure I want to discuss that with you lot,' Izzy said sitting back in her chair with her arms folded defensively.

Nick sighed. 'Playing it coy are we? Right, well we know Charles' is keeping fifty two percent. He's offered us twelve percent each so that leaves twenty-four percent,' he paused for effect. 'Do you want me to carry on?'

Izzy laughed. 'I have been offered the same which leaves Harry on twelve per cent as well.'

'Based on what each of us will be putting in, that means that the profit for last year exceeded one million,' Greg smiled. 'We'll be doing all right if that continues.'

Izzy felt unbelievably excited. It was the first time in ages that she was actually feeling good about something. Harry reappeared.

'Twelve percent?' asked Nick

'How did you guess?' said Harry with mock surprise, 'and a new Audi A4? Hell things are looking up.'

There was a collective murmur of ascent and the four of them continued talking for some time before a call was put through to Harry and they drifted off back to their desks. Greg let out a sudden yell. 'Appointment at Sadler's. Shit I'm late.' He grabbed his coat and briefcase and rushed out of the office.

'Oops,' Izzy said with a smile on her face. 'I can't concentrate on work, either. Too much to think about.'

'Maybe we should go out for a drink at lunch time and talk things over?' suggested Harry.

'Sounds good.' Izzy smiled at him and she felt her stomach lurch as she met his gaze. He'd been really supportive over the business with Stephen. She didn't know how she'd have got by without him and Chrissie. She kept telling herself that he was just a really good mate but she knew that her feelings for him were more than that.

'So what do you reckon to this turn of events then?' Harry asked settling back in the comfy leather pub chair.

'Really really exciting. We could end up making some serious money. I mean valuations are going through the roof. We can hardly keep up and they are so lucrative. And to be a partner, I can't believe it. I mean maybe in a few years but now? It's a dream come true.'

Harry didn't respond for a moment. 'I agree with all that but I have a niggling doubt,' he said pulling a face. 'I'm just not sure,' he added leaning forward and resting his elbows on his knees.

'What do you mean?' asked Izzy frowning.

'Well, it's Charles. I just wonder about his integrity.'

Izzy leant forward, playing with a tendril of hair that had escaped from her hair clip and thought about this for a moment. 'I know he's a shit to work for but we'll be partners. Surely that'll be better as we'll have a say as well.'

'Maybe, but he will have the controlling share and anyway that's not really what I'm worried about.'

'What then?' asked Izzy

'Well, I know we seem to be in rising market with house prices soaring but it can't go on indefinitely and I am slightly sceptical about this sub-prime lending. It's gone mad in America and we'll follow suit. I think it's already started and then where will it all end?'

'Oh, Harry, you're being pessimistic. It is boom time and we should cash in.'

'Oh God, now you sound like Charles!' Harry laughed hollowly.

'What do you mean by sub-prime? All those low-income families buying their social housing? We don't have anything to do with that.'

'Don't we? What do you think those secondary lender banks are up to?'

186

'I don't know what you mean? What secondary lender banks?'

'Izzy, where have you been? What do you think GRA does?' Harry asked looking mildly exasperated.

'They're mortgage brokers,' Izzy said defensively.

'Yes for banks involved with secondary lenders.'

'So, I still don't see the problem. I haven't done any valuations for properties less than three hundred thousand and most have been considerably higher. Hardly your low income family is it?'

'No, true, but don't you look at the applicants and wonder how they are going to fund their properties?'

'Look Harry, I think you're worrying unnecessarily. I know that mortgage companies have relaxed their rules somewhat when it comes to multiples of income but you still have to jump through all the hoops to secure a mortgage and nobody is going to lend money to someone who doesn't have the wherewithal to pay it back, are they?' Izzy said dismissively.

'I'm not so sure. What about all the self-certified mortgages. You can say what you like and the banks don't care. They're just greedy and want your money.'

'I never had you down as a pessimist, Harry and frankly that's what you're being. The way I see it is, if you are daft enough to take out a mortgage that you can't repay then you deserve everything that you get coming to you.'

Harry shook his head. 'Well, it's just not that simple and I think it's a house of cards waiting to come down. People are borrowing money against their homes in the expectation that the house will increase in value but what if all that stops? Then what? We'll be in negative equity again.'

Izzy shook her head. 'That won't happen again. Interest rates were sky high when that happened before – sixteen percent then. No, I can't see that happening. You're worrying unduly,' she said sharply, feeling irritated with Harry.

'Maybe, but I'm just not sure. At some point the bubble will burst and I don't want to be involved with that.'

Izzy looked surprised. 'Does that mean you're not going to accept Charles's offer?'

'No, Izzy, it doesn't, but it does mean that I will be considering it very carefully and will not be swept off my feet by the offer of a new car. I need to be sure that the business is sound.' Harry shrugged. 'It's a lot of money to invest and I'm not going to take any chances. I'm not surprised Piers has gone.'

'Really?' asked Izzy with raised eyebrows. 'What makes you say that?'

He shrugged again. 'Just something he said not long ago. It was about the business and how it had grown so fast and how much money it seemed to be making. I thought maybe he was worried that he wasn't contributing enough personally and that it was all down to Charles and his contacts, but I'm not so sure that's what he meant now.' Harry mulled over the conversation from a few weeks ago. 'I don't think he was very happy with the way things were going.'

'Well, that's odd when things seem to be going really well. We're all pulling in big fees and we're all exceeding our targets now. How could Piers not be happy with that?'

'Maybe that's the problem. Piers is not at all materialistic. He's more interested in providing a quality service . . . oh I don't know. You're probably right. I am being pessimistic. Maybe I should be making hay while the sun shines, along with everyone else!'

Izzy felt a slight nagging fear and quickly quashed it. 'That's better. I knew you'd come round to my way of thinking! How's your home life?' she asked changing the subject.

'Mum, you mean? She's doing all right. Seems to have stabilized for the moment. What about you? How's Stephen?'

'Don't ask. It's pretty appalling at the moment and no end in sight. I alternate between feeling sorry for him and completely pissed off with him.' Izzy chewed her lower lip.

'Have you got a date for the trial yet?'

'Yes, it's not until 12th February.'

'Good heavens, that's ages away.'

Izzy sighed. 'I know, they have to collate all the evidence and stuff.'

'Well I'm always here to talk to.' Harry gazed at her intently.

'Thank you. I know. You've been a big help. I've really appreciated all your support.'

'Anytime,' he said. 'Perhaps we ought to get back.'

Izzy pulled a face, 'I'd much rather stay here,' with you she thought as she gazed at him. She stood up suddenly, shaking the thought from her mind.

'Are you OK?' asked Harry, standing up and moving to her side, his hand on her upper arm.

'I'm fine. Sorry.' She blushed and turned away from him hurriedly, stooping to retrieve her coat. She straightened up and turned up to find Harry still standing where he was. She was aware of his body close to hers and she felt her heart beat rapidly. She could feel his eyes on her and she willed herself to meet his gaze.

'What?' she breathed

'You tell me,' said Harry, eyes boring into hers. Neither of them moved for what seemed like an eternity to Izzy before she dropped his gaze. 'Come on, we'd better get back.'

The afternoon passed quickly and it wasn't long before she was heading out of the door and driving home. She was excited about the partnership offer and used the current situation with Stephen as justification for accepting the position. After all, she didn't know what the outcome with Stephen was going to be and if it was bad she had to be in a strong situation to support her family. He could end up in prison or unemployed and should they split up in the future she had to be able to stand on her own two feet. Izzy suddenly felt very much in control of her destiny. She was going to be OK. She couldn't wait to tell everyone her good news.

She waited until they were all squashed around the dinner table. Susan had cooked a roast and there was a lot of noise as the food was dished up. Stephen was quiet but Izzy was used to his reticence and general apathy and didn't really pay much attention to him.

'I've some very exciting news,' she said and waited for everyone to stop talking.

'What is it Mummy?' asked Ed his big eyes fixed on her face.

'Well, I've been offered a partnership in the firm and I'll get a new Audi A4,' she said with a big smile on her face.

Stephen didn't say anything but just moved his food around on the plate.

'That's wonderful,' said Susan carefully 'and what exactly does that mean?'

'Well, I've been offered a twelve per cent share in the business which will cost me a bit to buy in but then I'll get a share in the profits at the end of the year. Profits this year were in excess of one million.'

'Well that does sound good,' said Arthur. 'Blimey, what's the turnover?'

'I'm not sure exactly, but we will have a meeting with Charles's accountant and will be able to get all the figures then.' Izzy paused and looked at Stephen for a response. 'What do you think, Stephen?'

'I think you've got what you wanted.'

'The house is coming on well,' said Arthur changing the subject. 'You must come and look after dinner. I've finished the kitchen bar a lick of paint.'

'Oh, wonderful. I'd love to see it.'

'And I've taken the liberty of bringing you some carpet samples from your local carpet shop.'

'Thank you so much Arthur.' Izzy smiled gratefully at him. 'I'm feeling quite excited. I can't believe we are going to move in after all this time. You must come for Christmas. It would be lovely to have you both.'

'We'd love to,' Susan affirmed smiling. 'If you're sure it won't be too much for you.' She directed her gaze at her son who sat apathetic and silent. 'Stephen?' she prompted gently.

'Yes, whatever?' he replied listlessly.

Izzy was beginning to feel really pissed off with Stephen tonight. They were all making an effort, so why couldn't he? So much for getting through this together! God, he should be bending over backwards to apologise for getting them into this mess. She sighed and got up and cleared the table.

Susan and Arthur played cards with the children while she washed up. Her thoughts drifted to Harry. She knew she was becoming increasingly attracted to him and had to admit that she enjoyed his attention. Well, it was hardly her fault she was developing feelings for another man. She and Stephen hadn't had sex for what seemed like months and every time she reached out to him, he blanked her completely. She still wasn't absolutely convinced about the situation with Marie-Claire, either. She'd been very short with her when she'd phoned to speak to Stephen and she didn't think she'd called again. Actually, things would be really good right now if it weren't for Stephen.

# Chapter 26

Clarissa was aware of voices penetrating her thoughts and constant beeping noises. She felt strangely detached, like her body wasn't part of her, and she'd been having some weird and horrible dreams.

'Mummy!' Amelia's voice rang out above the background hum. 'Mummy, can you hear me? Open your eyes.'

Clarissa opened them but everything was white and blurry. She tried to focus but she was having difficulty and she screwed her eyes up against the invasive light. She heard someone shouting excitedly and she decided it was another of those strange dreams. She felt exhausted and yielded to the lure of sleep again, the voices and noises drifted away from her.

Moments later she felt herself being dragged away from the comfort of oblivion. She was aware of voices, snatched conversations, '... she's not fully regained consciousness yet', '... the operation was a success', '... we won't know the full extent of the damage for a while yet'. Clarissa wondered who they were talking about.

'Clarissa can you hear me? Can you open your eyes for me?' a kindly but authoritative voice penetrated Clarissa's fuddled mind. Who is that talking to me she wondered? I don't recognise the voice. She tried to lift her eyelids but they felt so heavy; maybe they were stuck. With some persistence they opened a crack and Clarissa gazed out unseeingly. She felt annoyed that she couldn't move and she frowned in irritation.

'Hello there,' the kindly voice said. 'Welcome back.'

Clarissa wondered if she was talking to her. *Welcome back?* Where had she been for goodness sake?

'You had a riding accident. You hit your head and you're in hospital,' the voice answered her question, as if she'd spoken.

Clarissa could feel anger welling up inside her. She didn't have time for this hospital business. She tried to move but nothing happened.

'You've been in an induced coma while the swelling on your brain went down. Amelia wants to say hello. She has been at your bedside for the last two weeks.'

'Mummy. Mummy you're going to be fine. I'm with you. Don't worry about my school. They know and they've given me this time

191

off because I'm not doing any exams yet. Mummy can you see me?' Amelia's head swam vaguely into view.

Two weeks! I've been here two weeks, thought Clarissa. She tried to speak but her face felt like it was encased in concrete and her lips wouldn't move. She couldn't summon the energy to make a sound and all that came out was a barely audible moan. What the hell was going on?

'She's trying to talk.' Clarissa heard Amelia's excited voice.

'Don't try to speak,' the authoritative voice said. 'You've had tubes inserted down your throat and you'll be very sore. Hopefully you won't need them again and you'll feel better in a day or two.'

'Poor Mummy. Don't worry, you'll be fine. Grandpa and Grandma will be so pleased when I tell them.'

Oh well that explained why she couldn't talk for the moment. Clarissa felt exhausted again and found herself unable to stay awake. She drifted off again.

The next time Clarissa woke up her face felt slightly more mobile but her body still didn't feel like it belonged to her. She wanted to lift her head up but couldn't. She tried to turn from side to side, but her neck was encased in some sort of frame and nothing happened. 'What is going on?' she whispered.

'Hello there, you're awake. That's excellent,' a voice said. 'Now, don't try to move. You've got a nasty fracture in your neck and we've immobilised you for the time being, until the fracture stabilizes.

'Fracture?' she parroted. 'Neck?' And then the awful realization dawned on her.

'I'm paralysed,' she whispered.

'Now, don't go getting upset. It's too early to tell anything and the most important thing is that you rest and give your body time to heal.'

Clarissa could feel mounting panic rising within her and the nurse saw that the heart- rate monitor was climbing rapidly. She came and stood over the bed so that she was in view of Clarissa. 'Don't you worry about a thing. We are using drugs to control your movement to facilitate the healing process. You've also had a severe head injury. You have to give yourself time and stay calm.'

Clarissa wanted to argue, to ask more questions. Where was Charles? She found herself drifting again.

Over the next few days Clarissa began to spend more time awake and tried hard to concentrate on the snippets of information the doctors were giving her. She tried to piece them together but couldn't quite do so. She found it all so exhausting and even when a consultant arrived to inform her of the more important events, she found it hard to concentrate.

Amelia was a quiet and constant presence and her mother came in every day and read to her. Clarissa wished she had the strength to tell her to shut up. On the other hand, her view consisted of the ceiling and there was only so much one could take of white space. There were various indignities to suffer on a daily basis which she was now unable to accomplish on her own. Although she couldn't move any muscles and her limbs didn't feel attached to her body, she sometimes felt sensations as she was being handled and there were also quite uncomfortable spasms and shots of pins-and-needles-like pain which assaulted her limbs with regular monotony.

Clarissa was dimly aware that Christmas was approaching and she asked several people whether she would be fit enough to go home. They all cheerfully avoided the question by telling her what good progress she was making. Clarissa wouldn't have described it as progress but the professionals seemed to be pleased with her. She was being fed through a stomach tube and she wondered how many calories they were feeding her since she could hardly burn any off at the gym.

She longed to be home and wondered if she were being missed. She came to the awful realization that she probably wasn't. Charles had been to see her twice and had done his best to chat up the nurses. Toby and Emily had been in to see her once and had both left as quickly as they could. Henry and Constance had visited twice but Clarissa couldn't bear their overbearing sympathy and she'd asked them not to come back too soon. Only Amelia and her parents had bothered to spend any time with her. None of her so called friends had called in although she'd received several bouquets of flowers and cards wishing her a speedy recovery.

A tear rolled down her cheek and she felt it disappear around the side of her face and into her ear. Her heart-rate monitor obviously detected a change in rhythm because a nurse appeared at her side and peered at her face anxiously. She wiped the tear away with a tissue. 'Now then, we can't have any of that. Not when you're doing so well. Your daughter will be in later. She's a lovely lass that one. A real credit to you.' She patted her shoulder and Clarissa wanted to scream. *Patronising bitch!*

'Well now, how are we doing today?' Clarissa heard a voice that she recognised but couldn't place. She tried to turn her head which she could now move marginally. Her eyes widened in surprise.

'Archie!' she whispered. 'Is it really you?'

Archie smiled and approached the bed, brandishing an enormous bouquet of flowers. 'It's me. Dear oh dear, what have you been up to?' He dropped the flowers on the bed and leaned over to kiss her gently.

'Now, now. No getting Clarissa excited. It's taken us a month of Sundays to stabilize her. I'll go and sort these out for you.' The nurse chuckled and whisked the bouquet away before anyone could say anything.

'Thank you for coming,' she whispered. 'I'm sorry that you have to see me like this.' She searched his face anxiously but she didn't see any repugnance there.

'Well, I would have been here earlier but I got held up in Uzbek. Bloody government officials! It's why I haven't been able to call you in weeks. And then I rush home and hear you're in hospital.'

'How kind of you to come when you're so busy,' Clarissa bit out.

'Clarissa, what are you talking about? If I'd known you'd had an accident, I would have dropped everything, but even Henry couldn't reach me in Uzbek. Where's Charles then?' Archie pulled a chair up close to her bed.

'I don't know and I don't care. I'm going to divorce him. I should have done it years ago,' Clarissa said angrily. 'As soon as I'm up and about that'll be that. I'm not putting up with him any longer.'

There was an uncomfortable silence and Archie leaned in. 'Sweetheart, do you know what's happened to you?'

'Of course. A bit of a head injury and a broken neck but it's an incomplete injury so hopefully I'll be as right as rain in a few weeks, once I get some more feeling back.'

'Right. Well, that's excellent,' said Archie brightly. 'I hear they're going to be sitting you up today.'

'Are they?' asked Clarissa sounding surprised. 'Well there we go then. I'll soon be home.' She smiled at him and he smiled back and stroked her hand. She tried to lift it, but she suddenly felt very tired. 'Oh, I'm always so tired. I think it's the morphine.'

'My poor darling. You've had a really bad time. Don't be surprised if it takes a little while to get well.' Clarissa missed the flicker of anxiety that passed across his face.

A nurse came in. 'You'll have to be off now Mr McGregor. It's time for us to sit Mrs Hambridge up.'

'Oh, can't you stay, Archie. Please? Then I will be able to see you properly,' Clarissa pleaded.

'Not today, Mrs Hambridge. Let's see how you get on shall we?'

'I'm only going to be sitting up for heaven's sake. It's hardly a major event.'

'You've not been well,' the nurse said gently but firmly. 'You don't know how you're going to feel. You may feel a little bit nauseous at first.'

'Be a good girl and do as the nurse says, Clarissa. I'll see you tomorrow. Be gentle with her nurse.' Archie bent down and kissed her goodbye. Clarissa shut her eyes so he wouldn't see her angry tears. Her cheeks burnt red with frustration as she listened to his retreating footsteps.

Before she could give way to self-pity, what seemed like an entire medical team arrived. 'Good God! How many people does it take to sit someone up? Anyone would think I was an invalid,' she exclaimed, as people crowded around her bed getting things ready, including a sick bowl. As soon as the bed started to tilt Clarissa upward from a flat position, she began to understand what the problem was. She immediately began to feel very nauseous and seriously light-headed. She lay there willing herself to feel better and her silence implied that all was well and the bed came higher until she was at forty-five degrees. Anxious faces peered at her and she fought the urge to heave. Just as she was about to ask them to lower the bed, she vomited without much warning and nurses bounced into action, placing the bowl ineffectually under her mouth. She could feel vomit sliding down her neck on the inside of her collar and she shut her eyes as they lowered her back down. Everyone made encouraging noises and cleaned her up as best they could. Clarissa felt utterly defeated and she at last realized that this was going to take a bit longer than she'd first thought.

'Why was I sick and why did I feel so light-headed?' she asked.

'Well you've been lying down for a while now and unfortunately spinal injuries lower your blood pressure, which causes the light-headedness when you sit up. It will take a while to sort out. But don't worry, you're doing very well. We are going to try to sit you up again later on.'

The thought filled Clarissa with horror. She could smell the odour of vomit. She shut her eyes. How on earth had she ended up in this mess? She still had no recollection of the accident and could only remember small things about the whole fateful day. She wondered disconsolately if she'd ever get on a horse again.

# Chapter 27
## *December 2003*

Christmas day dawned grey and gloomy with a blanket of miserable cloud hovering depressingly overhead. Charles, however, was feeling buoyant. He'd recently started moving money about and squirreling it away from Clarissa and into one of his own accounts. Prior to the accident Clarissa had managed all the finances online and Charles had worked out her passwords and username a long time ago. He wouldn't need to divorce her now as he would be able to do what he liked with the money until such time as Clarissa was well enough to check her accounts herself but that would be a long time from now. He'd have no problem leading his own life and doing exactly what he wanted.

He'd spent the previous day with Lydia-Rose playing the concerned and guilty adulterer which she had fallen for hook, line and sinker. His interest in her hadn't waned yet because he didn't see her that often and the trysts were always clandestine, which he enjoyed. She was a little firecracker in bed and her appetites were surprisingly voracious; he hadn't been disappointed yet, especially as there was more of her money coming his way.

Money appeared to be flowing in at the moment and he was pleased with his investments; particularly Henry's schemes which were performing magnificently. He'd received a print-out of the end of year accounts and was encouraged by the results; the forecast was exciting and he was considering upping his stake in the portfolio. He didn't even care if Archie was involved. Now his wife was a cripple he wouldn't be sniffing around her. He was going to use some of the money from people buying into his business to fund part of the Barbados property. Yes, he was incredibly pleased with the way things were going.

Sylvie knocked on the door and entered with a tray. 'Merry Christmas!' she called enthusiastically from the doorway.

'And to you too,' he replied amiably.

'I hear you're going to the hospital after all.' She placed the tray on his bedside table.

'Yes, thought I'd better do the right thing and all that?' Charles laughed loudly. 'I promised a cute little nurse a Christmas kiss and I wouldn't want to let her down.'

'No,' Sylvie's normally indulgent response to Charles' comments was a short because she was finding his attitude toward Clarissa a bit sickening at the moment. She'd never taken to Clarissa finding her a difficult and unlikeable character however, she was beginning to feel a tiny bit sorry for her at the moment. She was also annoyed with the way in which he was treating Amelia who was a total sweetie and didn't deserve it.

Charles reached over and patted her backside as she turned away. She jumped and scolded him as she headed into the dressing-room, picking up discarded clothes.

Charles dressed and went downstairs, admiring the beautiful Christmas tree covered in sparkly lights which dominated the hallway. There was another Christmas tree in the sitting-room with a huge pile of presents under it. His mother had dropped them off the day before determined that the family would not miss out. They would have to open them later. OK, so now he was bored. It may be Christmas but he'd need more than a visit to his wife and a few presents to keep him occupied.

The Boxing Day hunt was certainly something to look forward to but in the meantime... he glanced at the whisky decanter and decided on a drink. The whisky dulled his senses somewhat. He was aware that his need for entertainment and instant gratification was getting a little out of hand. It bothered him somewhat. He poured himself another drink. Toby could drive to the hospital.

Some while later Charles and the three children were climbing into the Porsche on their way to the hospital. Toby and Emily were in high spirits and cared only that they were back in time for Christmas lunch. Amelia sat silently, staring out of the window. Charles was decidedly worse for wear, so Toby drove them, taking the bends far too fast and driving well above the speed limit. Amelia was the first one out of the car and had dashed off before anyone else had got a door open.

'What's with old Misery Melia then?' joked Toby, slamming the door behind him.

'Who cares? It's Christmas,' Charles retorted, rolling out of his door and managing to land on his feet the right way up. Emily giggled and caught his arm.

'Honestly Daddy. Did you have to start drinking before we saw Mummy? You're very naughty.' She laughed good-humouredly. 'She won't be impressed.'

'Well, I needed a little something to get through this next bit. I'm sick of this hospital.'

'Poor Daddy,' said Emily patting his arm. 'Come on; let's get this over and done with.'

Emily and Toby guided Charles into the hospital and down towards the spinal unit. All was quiet when they arrived.

'God it's like a morgue in here,' Charles exclaimed loudly and hiccupped. 'Well it's full of half-dead people who are never going to go anywhere, so I suppose it's only to be expected.'

The nurse behind the station looked icily at him. 'Could you keep the noise down please.'

'Oh, keep your hair on and don't be rude to the customers. I pay your wages remember. You public sector sorts are all the same.' Charles paused with a smirk on his face. 'Anyway where is the cripple? Still in the same place no doubt.'

'Have you been drinking?' the nurse peered suspiciously at him.

'Well of course I bloody well have. It is Christmas Day you sanctimonious old bat.'

'Daddy,' Emily's voice cut in, 'I think we'd better move along. Sorry,' she mouthed at the woman behind the counter who was looking absolutely furious. 'Come on Dad, behave yourself for goodness sake, otherwise we'll be asked to leave.'

Toby dragged his father off down the corridor.

'What a result that would be!' Charles continued loudly.

'Here we are,' said Toby peering through the door into the room.

Charles barged his way into the room and was surprised to see Clarissa partially sitting up, her neck still in a brace. 'Merry Christmas, darling,' he said swaggering up to her and kissing her perfunctorily on the cheek.

'Mummy's nearly sitting upright.' Amelia smiled at her mother before looking at the others for a reaction.

'Oh right, yes, excellent,' said Toby looking around the room distastefully. 'Merry Christmas!' he added and inspected his shoes carefully.

Emily went up and kissed her mother dutifully on the cheek. She'd never seen her mother looking so unkempt, without a scrap of make up on and she found it quite disconcerting.

'Mummy's doing really well,' Amelia patted her mother's arm affectionately.

'I'm not so sure about that Amelia. Merry Christmas everyone and thank you for coming but please don't pretend you want to hang about. It's really not the place to be on Christmas Day is it?' Clarissa wished they'd all disappear, she couldn't stand the humiliation and the total loss of control that she had over the situation.

Charles smiled. 'Well if you insist. I believe your parents are dropping in later. Hell what's that ghastly smell? Has someone just farted?' He screwed up his nose in disgust and turned accusingly to Toby.

'Not me,' said Toby shaking his head. 'God that's rank.'

There was a moment's silence while everyone looked at one another and then Amelia stood up abruptly. 'I'll just go and get a nurse.'

Charles, Emily and Toby stared at Clarissa who sat there mutely, her face bright red. Comprehension dawned on them. Charles couldn't stop himself. 'Oh dear, have you pooed yourself, darling?' He doubled over, laughing. 'Oh good God.' He backed away into the corridor, still laughing.

Toby and Emily looked aghast. 'I'd better go after him,' said Toby. 'He's drunk far too much whisky. Stress of all this and everything.'

'Merry Christmas, Mummy,' said Emily. She bent to kiss her mother and gagged, backing away with her hand over her mouth. Amelia appeared with a nurse and bustled around the bed.

'Just leave. All of you,' said Clarissa bitterly. 'I don't want you here. Go and join your father.'

Tears sprung to Amelia's eyes. The kindly nurse frowned as she caught sight of her distraught face. 'Now, now. Don't you worry. She'll be as right as rain tomorrow, just you see.'

Amelia smiled briefly and turned back to her mother. She kissed her on her cheek, 'I'll see you later on tomorrow.'

'If you must,' said Clarissa avoiding Amelia's eyes.

Amelia ran down the corridor, tears rolling down her cheeks. Why did she have to have the most appalling family? She climbed into the car silently, hating each and every one of them at that moment. She glanced at Emily, who was playing with her mobile phone, her long blonde hair hanging in a curtain so that Amelia couldn't see her face. She wondered who she was texting. She didn't like her sister very much. She was selfish and bitchy and only cared about parties, boys and clothes. Toby she'd always adored, but Toby had changed since going to university. He was very popular and the attention must have gone to his head. Girls seemed to call him all the time and she knew he was going on dates with quite a few of them, which was a shame, as she had liked his long-term girlfriend, Harriet. When he was home, he and her father were now more like playmates than father and son and she didn't like their behaviour at all.

She made a vow to herself that she wasn't going to be like any of them. She was going to do something worthwhile with her life and it would not be based on money and looking perfect.

\* \* \*

The Boxing Day meet was a busy affair with all and sundry attending. Charles was always slightly irritated by the number of children who turned up. However, it was a good day all in all and both his horses went exceedingly well. He'd decided to hunt Sid who was improving with every outing. Charles had finally persuaded Heather to come back by asking her to name her price and conditions. She was starting in the second week of January and Charles was currently paying an agency to cover the horse care for the moment. Tamara had left not long after the hunting incident having decided that looking after all the horses was too much like hard work particularly during the winter and she'd got a job as a hostess on a huge yacht in the Caribbean through one of Daddy's contacts. The horses were all improving with the expert care they were now receiving and as a result were slightly more manageable, although Doucette was proving to be a right pain and appeared to be getting worse not better. Charles thought it would probably be a good idea to get rid of her.

They were off to Henry's later and he was looking forward to hearing all about his investments. The building work in Barbados had temporarily stopped, which he wasn't too happy about, but he'd been assured that he'd be able to move in by Easter. He was looking forward to flying out there and taking Lydia-Rose with him for a few days or maybe a week. At least he didn't have to worry about Clarissa. There was no chance that she'd be going for the foreseeable future.

Charles arrived at Henry's early, hoping to have a chat with him before the others arrived. 'Charles dear boy, do come in,' Henry guffawed as Charles entered. 'Constance!' he shouted the long hallway. 'Constance we have guests.' Henry turned back to Charles. 'Where are the children?'

'Following on. Toby insisted on driving but the girls weren't ready

201

and I just needed to escape.' Henry pulled a knowing face just as Constance came scurrying down the hallway and greeted Charles apologetically.

'So how are things?'

'Oh splendid. Absolutely splendid, except for poor old Clarissa, of course.'

'Yes, so, so terrible, Charles,' said Constance, holding back tears. We have tried to visit but I don't think Clarissa really wants us there.' Charles maintained what he thought was an appropriate amount of chat about his wife's welfare, before turning the conversation to investments. Constance scuttled off to get drinks.

Henry too seemed relieved to change the subject. 'Oh it's all going superbly. Archie really is a whiz at sorting everything out. Uzbek is ready to rock and roll, so after Christmas they're getting under way and we can sit back and let the money roll in. I must say Charles you've done an excellent job getting investors.'

'Thank you Henry. It's been no trouble. Anyone with any business acumen can see a cracking deal when it comes their way.'

'Of course, dear boy, of course. I'm hoping to get out to Barbados soon for a site visit, so I'll let you know how things are shaping up over there. I think the builders should be back on track again. Bloody natives! Honestly it takes them forever to get anything done – if we had good British labour out there it would be a totally different thing.'

'I'm with you on that one Henry. I'm glad you're able to pop out. I've been told Easter and it would be lovely to get away for a week if it were possible. Obviously it will depend on Clarissa, but I am worn out with all the visits to the hospital.'

'Absolutely old boy, absolutely. I'm sure the family can cover for you. Now, where has that drink got to? '

Constance appeared with a tray a moment later. 'Scotch?' she asked Charles. 'I know it's before dinner but it is Christmas after all.'

'Oh why not?' Charles settled into a squishy sofa and made himself comfortable. He helped himself to a handful of nuts that were placed in front of him and begun munching in between mouthfuls of whisky. He felt reassured and relaxed and didn't object when Constance topped up his glass. He was quite the life and soul of the dinner party, rather to the surprise of some of the guests, who, while unable to claim they were fond of his wife, had not forgotten why she was absent.

# Chapter 28
## *January 2004*

The first Christmas in their new house should have been one of happiness but sadly it was far from it. Stephen was glad it was over. Moving in had seemed like a good idea but in reality it had all been a bit much; there were still boxes everywhere. Stephen still found it a huge effort just to get out of bed in the mornings, so how could he be expected to care about where they put the furniture? Stephen knew his parents had been a huge help but he was pleased to see them leave. He just wanted to be left alone. Thank God, Izzy's parents hadn't come over. The last time he'd seen them was in the summer in Corsica where they'd hired a villa with Izzy's brother and family. John was a great host and there was plenty of entertainment on offer whilst Adriana just wanted to lie by the pool and keep herself very much to herself.

Marie-Claire was paying them a visit this afternoon. It was the first time he'd seen her since he'd left the school and he wasn't looking forward to it. Izzy wasn't impressed, thinking that he shouldn't have any contact with anyone at that school and particularly not Marie-Claire.

Marie-Claire arrived on time and if she was shocked by Stephen's appearance, she hid it well. She made complimentary noises about the house which Stephen showed her round unenthusiastically, while Izzy made drinks. They all sat down in the lounge.

'I have some information concerning the allegations that have been made by Lucy and Leonora,' Marie-Clare began without delay.

Izzy sat up. 'Really?' she asked, 'what sort of information?'

'Helpful to your case I think, but I don't know what to do about it. I don't want to pervert the course of justice in any way. Firstly, I think you should know that quite a lot of people are supporting you. Stephen, the students miss you and they want you back at school. I don't know if you've been following the local press, but many of them have been protesting on your behalf. Leonora has been completely ostracized and there's been name calling and notes left. She's lost a lot of weight and has been calling in sick and, I suspect, playing truant.

'My heart bleeds for her,' Stephen interjected.

'Anyway, I overheard a conversation between Lucy and Leonora in the library after school. Lucy was saying that Leonora wouldn't remember what happened to her because she was drunk. Leonora then said she would have been sore the next day if she had been raped, or at least had known something had happened, but Lucy just glossed over it and said that sometimes girls didn't know. Leonora also said that she didn't think it would go this far, and although she was happy about getting her own back on Stephen for rejecting her, she didn't think he deserved this. She started crying of course and Lucy got angry with her and told her that Stephen must be punished and did she realise how much trouble they would be in if she changed her story now.'

'She can't remember a thing? She told the police that I raped her and she can't remember one thing about it!' Stephen started pacing up and down. 'Why haven't you told the police this? Or is it because you're my alibi and, oh God, they're not going to believe you, are they?'

'I'm not sure Stephen. I think you should take advice from your solicitor before we do anything. It's the safest thing to do. Oh, I did tell Leonora that I recorded the conversation on my mobile phone.'

'That's excellent,' said Izzy, I'll ring Tim now. All of this, the support at school for Stephen and this piece of evidence, is the best news we've had in a long time, isn't it Stephen?' She looked at him for his response but he seemed to have retreated into himself once again. Izzy tried again. 'Stephen the news that Marie-Clare has given us; it's really good. We can clear this mess up and move on at last.'

'Really? After what I've been through? Haven't I told you that my life is over; it will always be tainted by this. I won't be able to work in any school without this whole debacle haunting me like an evil presence lurking in the shadows and waiting to pounce on me just when I think it's safe to relax.

'You might feel like that now, but give it time and you will move on. I mean it's not like someone has died or anything.'
'Maybe it would have been better if I had,' Stephen stopped talking eyes blazing.

Stephen! Please don't say that, you have a family who need you, who depend on you.

Marie-Clare threw Izzy a worried glance. Izzy indicated for her to follow her into the kitchen. 'It's just how he is these days, Marie-

Claire. Nothing much lifts his mood. This has destroyed him, you know, and I'm beginning to wonder if I'll ever get my husband back. And the children, their father.'

'Well time is a great healer... '

'Ha! That's easy for you to say. You can't begin to know what this has been like.'

'No maybe not but I know that time will lessen the pain and you will move on. I hope Stephen returns to teaching because he is exceptional and a good colleague. I should go. Let me know what you want me to do about what I heard.'

Izzy put out her hand. 'I'm sorry and thank you Marie-Claire for your help. It's nice to know that someone is looking out for us. '

Marie-Claire said goodbye to Stephen who barely acknowledged her. Izzy saw her out and went back into the kitchen and grabbed the phone. She dialled Tim's number.

'Do you like her?' Stephen asked as Izzy came back into the lounge to collect the coffee cups.

'Who? Marie-Clare? Yes I do. I think she's a very caring person and a good one to have on your side.'

'You didn't like her before though did you?'

'Well, I didn't really know her then, but I get the feeling she's a good person with a decent sense of judgement. I've rung Tim. I had to leave a message so in case he calls back please answer the phone. I need to go and get the children from Chrissie's.'

Stephen liked the children being at Chrissie's. They were so busy and loud and he couldn't bear their constant noise. All he wanted was peace and to sleep.

'Stephen? You look very pale. Maybe you should go for a walk and get some fresh air.'

*He wished Izzy would go away too. Why couldn't they all go away?* He stared out of the window and waited for Izzy to leave. Then he went upstairs to the en suite bathroom and picked up his razor. He turned it over and looked at the blade, then frowned, unable to work out what to do next. After what seemed an eternity, he put it down on the sink and made his way to the bedroom. He lay down on the bed, pulling the duvet over him and shut his eyes.

He was woken by a loud commotion and someone bouncing on the bed, and he lashed out angrily, sending the little body flying backwards off the bed. There was a loud crash, followed by a scream. He looked in surprise as Izzy rushed into the room and gathered something up in her arms before backing away. He heard her talking to someone in an urgent voice but he couldn't make out the words. Great wracking sobs broke from his chest, interspersed with a terrible moaning that went on and on. Then someone was holding him in their arms and a voice he did not recognise was speaking softly to him. He felt a small prick in his arm, followed by wooziness. Then he was being led downstairs and out of the house. He could hear someone crying but he didn't resist as he was directed into the strange car.

He didn't recognize the room they took him too, but he lay down thankfully on the bed and fell into blissful oblivion.

He woke the next morning parched, with a thick tongue and an incredibly sluggish body. He tried to sit up but it was such an effort that he lay back on the pillow and surveyed his surroundings. He was lying in a room with pale blue walls; the curtains were of a non-descript blue pattern and he noted that there were two doors, both closed. It smelt clinical and he realised after a moment or two that he must be in a hospital. At that moment, one of the doors opened and in walked two people — a tall blond gentleman in his late forties and a younger, mousy-haired girl with a clipboard. They were both smiling which Stephen found disconcerting.

'Good morning Stephen. I'm Dr Hill and this is Sarah Fielding, a newly qualified doctor on her first rotation.' The tall gentleman sat down on a chair near the bed. 'How are you feeling?' he asked solicitously.

Stephen looked puzzled and struggled to formulate a sentence. 'Where am I?' he asked finally. 'Is there any water?'

'You're in hospital,' the doctor said carefully. 'You're not well and we are going to help you get better.'

'I just feel so tired,' Stephen lay back on the pillows and shut his eyes. He didn't really want to talk to the doctor about what he was feeling. How could he possibly understand? 'I want to go home to my family?' he said at last. No one responded and he opened his eyes and turned to look at the doctor. 'I want to go home,' he repeated and then added, 'what's wrong with me anyway?'

'You've been under rather a lot of pressure and it has taken its toll on your body and mind. We will give you the opportunity to recover and help you to feel better.'

A nurse came in with a glass of water and a small bowl of medication. Stephen eyed it dubiously but didn't argue when they insisted that he take it. He swallowed the tablets meekly, watched by three pairs of eyes. The doctor and his student then left the room and he was alone with the nurse, who explained that there was a bathroom behind the other door for his use.

Time passed in a haze and Stephen had trouble working out if it was day or night. He could hear other voices shouting at times, but for the most part it was quiet and he relished that. Various people inhabited his periphery: food was brought in by a cheerful lady in her late sixties who chatted away not expecting an answer, his room was cleaned by a ghost of a man who worked unobtrusively and there were the nurses who administered his medication and kept watch on him. He was always amazed how one appeared if he went to the toilet.

After an indeterminate amount of time he began to feel less tired and nearly shocked the food lady by responding to one of her questions. The doctor called on a daily basis and Stephen found himself opening up to the man about his feelings and the sense of hopelessness that pervaded him. The doctor always listened, quietly prompting him with questions when Stephen forgot what he was talking about. The staff began to encourage him to sit in the lounge and to meet other people on the unit. Stephen didn't want to see anyone, however, especially a bunch of patients who all appeared to be in a much worse state than himself.

One afternoon he was told he had visitors. He sat placidly on the bed and looked up cautiously when there was a knock at the door. Izzy walked in hesitantly, her face a mix of anxious anticipation and sorrow. She smiled at him and he held out his arms to her. She rushed to sit on the bed next to him and he enveloped her, crushing her body to him and burying his face in her hair. It smelt so safe and familiar.

'I'm so sorry,' his voice was choked with feeling and he suddenly realised that he was weeping great big tears on to the top of her head. She clung to him and when they finally pulled apart, he could see that her face was wet with tears too. She hastily wiped them away.

'We're a right pair, aren't we?' she laughed.

'I'm so sorry,' he said again searching her face. 'I don't know what has happened to me. I don't feel like myself at all. I feel horrible and when this is over I hope I never feel like this again. It's as if there is a large cloud hovering over me all the time, from the moment I wake up to the moment I go to sleep.'

'It's all right darling,' Izzy said softly, stroking his face. 'There is no reason why you shouldn't have all those positive feelings again. You've been ill and it will take a while to recover.'

'Dr Hill tells me that what I'm feeling is quite normal... it's nice to know that I'm not alone in feeling like this. Where are the children?'

'I thought it would be best if I visited you first. They can come next time.'

'I'd so love to see them,' he said sadly after a moment or two.

Izzy hesitated. 'Actually, they're in the waiting room. Do you think you can manage if I bring them in briefly?'

'Why wouldn't I manage? I've been their main carer all year.'

Izzy sighed. 'Stephen, do you remember the last time you saw the children?' she asked.

'Not really, no. Has it been very long?'

Izzy nodded and looked down at her shoes. 'Why is there something I should know about?' asked Stephen.

'No, it's all fine, don't worry. I'll get them but just for a few minutes.'

The children stood hesitating and silent in the doorway, all clinging to their mother. Stephen's brain struggled to identify what was wrong but when he held out his arms to them they came slowly over and formed a little huddle within in his embrace. The children didn't ask any questions which Stephen thought odd but he didn't pursue it. And then they were gone, leaving Stephen feeling miserable and alone.

Stephen made good progress and it was decided that he should be allowed to return home, on the proviso that he took his medication and attended a weekly outpatient appointment until further notice. He was apprehensive about returning home but Dr Hill assured him that he would be fine and it was perfectly normal to be experiencing feelings of reticence.

He was surprised to find the house quiet and it took him a while to work out that the children were often 'visiting friends'. Izzy had taken some time off work to be with him and she was extraordinarily positive about his recovery. Every morning he forced himself to get up, even when he wanted to remain under the duvet. He'd expected to feel a bit better by now and was worried that he didn't. He hadn't asked Izzy about how his case was progressing and whether the information that Marie-Claire had given them had made a difference. His brain just didn't want to go there.

Izzy organised his day so that he didn't have to think about what to do. There were walks, meals, visits to art galleries and museums and plenty of 'rests'. He obediently went through the motions, though he couldn't have cared about any of it.

'Are you ready darling?' asked Izzy with forced cheerfulness. Her face fell when she came into the sitting room and saw that Stephen was still lying on the sofa.

'No. I'm not coming,' he said without looking at her. 'I'm going to watch TV.'

'But Stephen,' Izzy sighed, 'I thought we were going out for a walk on the Long Mynd and then stopping off on the way back for a nice cup of tea.'

'Well I'm not going. I want to watch TV.'

'Stephen,' Izzy's voice took on a slightly harder edge. 'You are not going back to that. Moping around on the sofa and watching the television is not going to help your recovery.'

Stephen swung around to face her. 'I don't think you're in any position to tell me what will or will not aid my recovery. Quite frankly I'm fed up with having every minute of my waking day organised for me. You tell me when to get up, when to eat, when to rest and I feel like some small child who needs to be kept under complete control for the entire day. I am fed up with it. Watching TV for an afternoon is not going to ruin me. Why don't you sit your backside down and watch a film with me instead?'

'Oh I don't think so. I haven't taken time off work to sit around watching you go backwards. I need some fresh air even if you don't.'

'Whatever,' said Stephen and turned his attention back to the TV screen.

'Please Stephen! Let's go for just a short one.'

'Izzy, I have told you, I do not want to go for a fucking walk. Now please can you leave me alone? You're doing my head in!'

'Well, that's just bloody great. Honestly Stephen, after all I have done for you. Supporting you throughout this whole debacle, with those girls and now this illness. The least you could do is show some gratitude for what I've done. I've tried to be so patient, treading around you as if I'm on eggshells, organising the children so that they are out of your way. I wish I'd stayed at work.' Izzy's eyes welled up with tears of anger and frustration.

'Yes, well, we all know where you'd rather be,' Stephen said sarcastically.

'Fuck you,' Izzy swore at Stephen, before walking out the room.

# Chapter 29
## *February 2004*

Izzy had to admit she was glad to be going back to work. She was still livid with Stephen. She'd done her best and it was up to him now. If he wanted to give up and waste his life watching telly, well that was his problem.

She had decided to proceed with buying into the company and had taken out a business loan. Her parents had offered to lend her the money but she was determined to do this by herself. She'd had to secure the loan against the house, but it wasn't really a big deal. Stephen had barely looked at the document that he'd had to sign. One hundred thousand pounds and he couldn't even be arsed to read the large print, let alone the small. As far as she was concerned it was worth it. She was soon to be a partner in a very up and coming firm and she was proud of her achievements.

She parked her car and walked briskly into the office. She switched on her computer and opened the mail on her desk, which was piled up in a neat stack. She was just organising the post into piles when Harry came in.

'Hello stranger,' he said smiling as he approached her desk.

Izzy's face lit up. He looked good enough to eat. 'Hello,' she said brightly, opening an envelope, 'you're in early.'

'So are you.' Harry perched on the edge of the desk and Izzy caught a whiff of aftershave. God, he smelt good, she thought, as she inhaled deeply and turned back to the letters, pretending to give them her attention.

'I knew I'd have a desk like this,' she indicated the pile.

'You look tired. How are things at home?'

'Not great, but I really don't want to talk about it. I've come here to escape and enjoy some upbeat company.'

'That must be mine then. Well I've got a couple of short appointments this morning but I'll be back for lunch, so we'll pop out for a bite if you fancy?'

Oh yes, thought Izzy, I do very much. 'I'll look forward to it.' She smiled at Harry. 'It's good to see you, you know?'

'Yes and you. It's been kind of quiet here without you.' He stood up stretching and Izzy tried not to stare at his torso as his shirt pulled taught. She shook her head slightly, reorganised her thoughts, and logged on to her computer. One hundred and ten new emails pinged into her inbox and she began wading through them. The morning passed quickly and apart from Jess there was nobody else in the office, which enabled Izzy to rattle through some of the more urgent stuff. She had requests for six new valuations, four of which were up country and she asked Jess to book her accommodation for a night away. She didn't know if Stephen could cope at home but she'd ask his parents to come over or ask Chrissie. Frankly, she relished the idea of staying away from home and any feelings of guilt were quickly replaced by the feeling that she deserved this.

'Are you ready then?' Harry's voice penetrated her thoughts and she swung around to catch him standing right behind her chair.

'Yes, just getting some valuations booked in for the middle of next week. They're near Newcastle and I'm going to stay over on Wednesday night so I only have to make the journey once.'

'Gosh, you're travelling a long way. I've refused to do any valuations that aren't in my area.'

'I've heard that Gary doesn't like using you because you create a fuss about everything,' Izzy smirked at Harry whilst standing up and retrieving her coat.

'I don't give a toss what he thinks. I've plenty of local stuff to keep me going without travelling the length and breadth of the country.'

'Whatever partner,' said Izzy and headed for the door. 'Where are we going anyway?'

'Next door should do. They're doing two for one on their main meals.'

'Sounds good to me, I'm starving.'

They walked in silence and ordered food and drinks at the bar before finding a table to sit down.

'So how are you doing with raising the money for the partnership?' Izzy enquired taking a sip of her shandy.

'I'm not,' said Harry sitting back in his chair.

Izzy frowned, 'What do you mean you're not? I'd have thought you'd have got a bit of a move on. Mine's nearly finalized.'

'No, I mean I'm not buying in.'

Izzy's frown deepened while she digested this bit of news. 'Why not?' she said after a short pause.

'I don't want to be a partner yet. It ties me down and I'm too young.'

'Oh,' Izzy looked visibly shocked. 'I'm disappointed. I thought we'd be partners in crime so to speak.'

'Yes well. I haven't changed my opinion of Charles and I don't have a good feeling about him so I'm not doing it.' He sat back as the waitress appeared with their order and neither spoke as she placed the food, cutlery and condiments in front of them.

Izzy studied her food, having suddenly lost her appetite. 'You are just too cautious,' she blurted out as the waitress disappeared. 'I know Charles is a bit of a pig but the firm is doing well. You saw the balance sheet.'

'I agree it all looks excellent, and you know what they say about that, don't you?' Harry looked at her questioningly.

'That's ridiculous. Charles's accountant wouldn't have approved anything dodgy. He would have gone through all the figures with a fine-tooth comb.'

'Naive, that's what you are. You only see what you want to see.'

Izzy felt angry with Harry. How dare he call her naive. 'You're making a big mistake.

'Time will tell. Let's not argue any more. I want to enjoy lunch with you.'

'Have you told Charles of your decision?'

'No, I'm not looking forward to that.'

'I wonder what he'll do with your share?'

'I expect he'll offer it to you, Nick and Craig – an extra four per cent each. Would you take it?'

'Probably, it's only another four per cent so why not? Or I could be really devious and sneak in early and offer to buy up all of your share. I suppose you think I'm mad? But enough of that. Tell me what you've been up to. Have you found yourself a lady yet?'

'Oh yes,' said Harry staring at Izzy intently. Her pulse rate was starting to climb and she could feel herself breaking out in a mild sweat.

'That's good,' she said breezily. 'Tell me about her?'

'Well,' said Harry, 'she's beautiful, intelligent, funny and perfect in nearly every way.'

'Oh, so what's the not so perfect bit then?' she asked gazing back at him.

'She's married,' he said continuing to stare at her.

'Oh, not so good then.' Izzy pulled a face, her heart was still pounding and her hands felt clammy. 'Is she happily married?' she asked.

'I don't really know. Her life is complicated at the moment.' Harry shrugged and looked down at his plate.

It is me, thought Izzy. 'Oh dear, not so good then.'

'No, not so good.' Harry looked up and stared at Izzy until she couldn't hold his gaze.

'So what will you do about it then?' she asked, pushing her food around on her plate.

'Well, that rather depends, doesn't it?' Harry leant forward and placed his elbows on the table.

'Depends on what?' she whispered.

'You know how I feel about you and I think... I hope, you feel the same...' he stopped and the words hung in the air between them.

Izzy chewed her lower lip and wondered what to say. 'I don't know,' she said after a while and stared down at her plate. 'Maybe,' she added, 'but as you've already said, it's complicated.'

'But you do have feelings for me. I'm sure of it,' Harry persisted.

'That's largely irrelevant. I'm married and I'm not an adulterer. I have a family. You're young free and single. Why choose me?'

'Now that's a million dollar question isn't it? Does anyone actually choose a partner? It just happens. It's chemistry – there's neither rhyme nor reason.'

'Maybe,' she said again.

'Oh for goodness sake. If you say that once more!' Harry groaned and they both laughed, breaking the tension.

Izzy stood up abruptly, her practical side taking over. 'I can't do this right now Harry. I'm sorry I must get back.' She took her purse out and dropped ten pounds on the table. 'My contribution,' she said and fled the pub as fast as she could. She was shaking as she began the short walk back to the office and she was glad of the cold air to clear her head. Part of her was excited at the thought of Harry wanting her, but she couldn't betray Stephen, it wouldn't be right. A little voice nagged at her however, telling her she deserved some fun. Harry knew her situation and if nobody found out it couldn't hurt anyone. Maybe she should offer to take him with her to Newcastle when she went. She discounted that quickly, shaking her head. What was she thinking?

She spent the rest of the afternoon in a highly distracted mood. She was aware of Harry sitting behind her and she could feel his gaze on the back of her neck. They didn't speak much and at four-thirty, Izzy stood up, announcing that she was off to look at a piece of land.

'Where is it again Jess?' she asked loudly from her desk.

213

'It's near Walford,' she called back. 'I've got the address here. From what I can gather you go past the farmhouse and the turning is about a mile from there on the left. It's a farm track of course — hopefully you won't miss it.'

'That's great, thanks,' said Izzy. She picked up the file and her bag and glanced over her shoulder at Harry as she left but he ignored her.

She got into her car and sped off, wondering if Harry would follow. She had announced her intentions so that he would hear where it was she was off to. She didn't quite know why she wanted him to follow. She was feeling strangely elated and very hyperactive.

Izzy arrived and spent twenty minutes looking around a decrepit barn. They'd have to work quite hard to get planning permission to build; the place was a crumbling wreck with no discernible roof left and barely four walls. She tried to concentrate on what she was doing but her mind kept wandering back to Harry. She walked back to the car to retrieve the camera and was rummaging in the boot when she heard a car come up behind her, swirling dust clouds following in its wake. She peered over her shoulder and her heart leapt when she realised it was Harry. She felt her blood sizzling. He pulled up next to her car and turned his face towards her as he climbed out, waving a camera at her.

'Looking for this,' he said staring at Izzy and swinging the camera hypnotically in front of her at face height.

'How did you guess?' she smiled at him and felt the pulse thudding in her neck. She hoped he wouldn't see it. She held her hand out to take the camera and he dropped it into her grasp. 'Thank you,' she said lightly and stared pointedly at the camera not daring to look at him. Neither of them moved for what seemed like an eternity.

'Right,' said Izzy at long last. 'I suppose I'd better get on.' She went to move off past Harry but he put a hand out and caught her arm gently and she looked up startled, heart pounding to meet his intense stare. He pulled her slowly towards him not taking his eyes off her and she felt physically unable to resist him. He slowly reached out with his free hand and ran his fingers lightly down her cheek, stopping momentarily at her chin before sliding his hand around to encircle her neck leaving his thumb resting on her collar bone. She shivered involuntarily and he moved closer. Izzy felt desire pulsing through her arteries as he bent down to kiss her. His lips sought hers tentatively at first and then more urgently as their bodies crushed together and their ardour increased.

Izzy didn't want to stop kissing him. She hadn't been kissed like this in years and she was enjoying every second of it. The moment was broken suddenly by Izzy's mobile phone ringing in her pocket and she jumped back as if she'd been struck. Harry self-consciously dropped his hands to his sides and then folded his arms, turning away to lean on his car as she checked her phone shakily and saw that it was Stephen ringing. She didn't answer it but just stared at it.

'Aren't you going to answer it?' Harry asked watching her intently peering at her from under the crook in his arm.

Izzy looked at him quickly, guilt written all over her face. 'It's Stephen,' she whispered, 'I can't talk to him right now.'

'Fair enough,' sighed Harry and continued to watch her. She wrestled with her conscience and took several deep breaths as if to rid her body of unwanted feelings.

'Harry, that can't happen again,' she said not looking at him.

Harry turned around to face her. 'Why not?' he asked frowning.

'Where do you want me to start? Look we've had this discussion already.' Izzy shrugged helplessly.

'Well, that in itself isn't a problem. I don't want to marry you,' Harry said and tilted his head to one side smiling slightly. 'I just want to devour you.' He raised an eyebrow suggestively.

Izzy looked at him and shook her head. 'Well it's very flattering but really it's a non starter. I've got too many things going on right now and I can't possibly handle any more complications.'

'Thanks. I've never been referred to as a complication before.' Harry laughed ruefully and she watched the smile slide from his face. 'I'll take what you've said on board for now,' he said abruptly. 'I'd best be off home.' He turned and got back into his car without looking at her again. It was all that she could do not to go after him as his car sped back down the track.

\* \* \*

At home that evening, Izzy made a special effort, desperately trying to assuage the guilty feeling that pervaded her every pore. It turned out that Tatty had been feeling unwell. She'd been sick a couple of times and Izzy hoped that the whole family wouldn't pick it up. The next day Tatty stayed home as she was still feeling under the weather and Izzy arranged for Claudia to pop up and check on her. She didn't want to admit that she was a bit worried about Stephen being left with her all day. Izzy managed to get through the day but was aware of the large elephant in the room every time she spoke to Harry and they were almost offhand with each other. She hoped that nobody else noticed. She'd finalised her trip for the middle of the week and she was quite glad to be getting away for a couple of days.

'I hear you're off to Newcastle next Wednesday.' Charles's voice startled Izzy from her reverie.

'Oh yes, I am as it happens,' she said nervously, cursing herself for feeling like that every time Charles asked her something.

'Could you fit in another three valuations?' he asked loitering near her desk. 'Seems a bit of a waste for me to go up, if you're going anyway.'

Izzy thought for a moment and knew that she would be unable to get away with not offering to help Charles out, 'Well, I suppose so. I could stay another night.' The thought of that didn't displease her too much.'

'Don't forget you've got that meeting with the environment agency on Friday morning,' piped up Jess.

Izzy paused before saying distractedly. 'Oh yes, I'd forgotten about that. I can't miss that. I'm putting a tender together…' she tailed off.

'Oh, it's only the bloody environment agency.' Charles blurted out.

'Well, actually, I have identified that there is lucrative compensation work after all,' Izzy said meeting Charles's eyes squarely.

'I could go up with Izzy and take on some of the valuations,' said Harry suddenly. 'I've got to go to Humberside for a meeting so I'd be happy to do those as well.'

'Right,' said Izzy, feeling herself blush and her heart hammering in her chest. She studied something on her desk, willing her colour to diminish; she was convinced that everyone could see her true feelings.

'Well, that's all settled then,' said Charles. 'Jess, sort out accommodation, will you? And hire a car for Harry. He'll need one.'

Izzy couldn't concentrate. Harry coming with her was bad news, but she didn't know what to do about it. She could hardly make a fuss. It was a perfectly reasonable arrangement and she was just going to have to get on with it. She couldn't keep up with her changing emotions – yesterday she'd have been overcome with excitement and latent anticipation.

\* \* \*

The next week passed in a haze for Izzy and she and Harry barely spoke, to the point that Jess asked her if she'd had disagreement with him. She fobbed Jess off by saying that everything was fine and that they were both working flat out which was probably contributing to the atmosphere. Jess laughed and said that if she didn't know them better she'd think they'd had a lovers' tiff. Izzy had laughed at that and giggled conspiratorially with Jess who admitted she'd had a crush on him for ages but he'd never shown any interest in her at all. Izzy said she'd put in a good word for her.

The weekend had been trying although Tatty appeared to be on the mend but was very clingy and got very upset and tearful every time Izzy left to go anywhere. Stephen was moping as usual and the two boys did nothing but bicker and fight.

On Tuesday night, Izzy did not sleep well as Tatty was up in the night complaining of a tummy ache and feeling sick Izzy had decided that Tatty was just attention seeking and was trying to prevent her from going away for a night. She had finally lost her temper with her which had appeared to do the trick as she hadn't disturbed Izzy again that night.

In the morning Izzy was in a rush to get ready and leave. She noted that Tatty did look washed out and pale but that was no surprise considering the night she'd had. At least no one else in the family had gone down with it. Izzy took the three children down to Chrissie's to have breakfast as she had offered to help. The children were all staying the night at Chrissie's too and the two boys were very excited. Tatty was quiet but Izzy passed it off lightly. She heaved a big sigh as she climbed back into the car and sped off to pick Harry up.

The trip up seemed to take forever and the traffic was horrendous. Izzy was late for her first appointment, having dropped Harry off to pick up his hire car, and she raced through the valuation having collected a load of comparables from a local estate agent. She made up a small amount of time but realised that she wouldn't make her last appointment that evening. She rescheduled for the next day, but knew it would mean her leaving much later than she had hoped the following afternoon.

Harry wasn't back when she arrived at the hotel and, feeling relieved, she headed up to her room and ordered room service.

217

She was feeling utterly exhausted and couldn't cope with him right now. She texted him to say where she was and that she was getting an early night. She rang to speak quickly to Stephen and then rang Chrissie to ask about the children. All was well so she then switched her phone off and read in bed before turning the light out to settle down for a good night's sleep.

She woke the next morning feeling very rested and ready to face the day, and Harry. She breakfasted with him and they agreed to meet mid afternoon for the long trip back home. Izzy's appointments all went well and she was right on schedule when she parked outside the car hire centre to wait for Harry. He was late and Izzy sat feeling fed up, looking at her watch every five minutes and wondering where the hell he'd got to. She was keen to get home to her family and she was irritated that Harry seemed to be taking for ever; he didn't have the responsibilities that she did. Maybe absence did make the heart grow fonder.

They set off eventually and the first hour of the journey went without any problems. Unfortunately they then hit a serious jam and spent two hours crawling three miles before they came across an exit. Using the satnav they found somewhere to eat nearby and decided to leave the traffic jam to get some food. It was eight o'clock and Izzy was feeling tired. They still had two hours travelling ahead of them and having heard that the motorway was now shut southbound and there was chaos on the roads, they decided to stay in a travel lodge overnight.

Izzy rang Stephen, while Harry went in to organise rooms.

The home phone rang and rang until finally the answer phone clicked in. She left a message promising to call back later. She met Harry as he was walking back to the car and he didn't look happy.

'They're full,' he raised his eyebrows and pulled a face at her.

'Oh,' said Izzy.

'We're not the only ones who have decided to stop rather than brave the chaos. They have recommended a couple of other places near here but we'll have to be quick otherwise they'll go to.'

'Give me the post code and we'll drive on.'

Izzy and Harry spent the next forty-five minutes driving about until they finally found a B&B which had a vacancy; a double room with an en suite and a full English breakfast.

'Well, we're not a couple, we're work colleagues. Haven't you got anything else?' Izzy asked exasperatedly.

'No, I'm sorry, we only have the one room, but it is large and there is a sofa-bed which one of you can sleep on,' the middle-aged lady smiled encouragingly.

'Right.' Izzy turned to Harry for confirmation. He nodded. They wandered up to the room which was indeed large and contained a sofa which Harry kindly offered to take.

'Fancy a drink?' Harry asked tiredly, as he dumped his holdall on the sofa.

'Too bloody right. I'm in need of something alcoholic. Today has been a nightmare but if you don't mind I'm just going to ring Stephen again. He didn't pick up earlier.'

'OK, well I'll be next door. What do you want to drink?'

'White wine please. A Sauvignon Blanc if they've got one.'

'OK, see you in a minute.'

She dialled Stephen. 'Hello,' his voice came on the line, quiet and cautious.

'Hello, it's me,' said Izzy.

'I know,' replied Stephen.

'How are you doing?'

'Okay. Kids are all in bed. Tatty is a bit off colour again. It could be that she is just missing you.'

'Why are they with you and not at Chrissie's?' asked Izzy cautiously.

'I was missing them, and I didn't see why they needed to stay with Chrissie another night. I am capable of looking after them you know?'

'I know, of course you are. It's just...' she tailed off.

'Just what Izzy? I'm not a lunatic you know and I'm a lot better. In fact, this afternoon I really enjoyed being with them. We went to Pizza Hut for supper. They loved it.' Stephen sounded assertive.

'Oh,' Izzy was surprised. 'Well, that's really good. I'm glad the children had a great time and I'm glad you did too,' she said warmly.

'I wish I were at home with you all and not stuck here tonight,' she said more for her own benefit than Stephen's.

'Well, you'll be home tomorrow. Try not to be too late.'

'No, of course not,' said Izzy grimacing as she thought of the meeting in the morning and hoping that Jess hadn't put anything in her diary for the afternoon. 'I'll see you tomorrow.'

'Good night, sleep tight and don't let the bed bugs bite!' Stephen chuckled down the phone.

'You too,' said Izzy looking around the room and hoping that there weren't any nasty things in the room. 'Love you,' she said, in a small voice.

'Me you,' Stephen responded and the phone went dead.

Izzy made her way over to the pub and found Harry propping up the bar with a pint in one hand and a glass of wine to one side.

'All right?' asked Harry.

'Yes,' Izzy sighed. 'All coping very adequately without me. In fact, Stephen picked the children up from the school and took them to Pizza Hut. He hasn't done anything like that in a long time.' Izzy took a long sip of wine and savoured the taste. 'Very good.'

'I'm glad you like it – it's Chilean.'

'God, now we're making small talk!' Izzy took another sip of wine and looked around the bar. She noted a smallish leather sofa which was just being vacated by a young couple and she indicated to it. 'Fancy sitting over there?' she enquired and didn't wait for an answer but headed off to sit down on it carrying her glass.

Harry picked his glass up and followed. He sat down next to her, snuggling back into the sofa. The sofa was in front of a roaring fire and Izzy felt the traumas of her life melting away until all she was aware of was Harry. He'd managed to sit as far away from her as possible on the sofa but he was still very close and as Izzy relaxed she moved closer to him. The wine was diminishing her inhibitions and her thoughts were turning to those of a carnal nature. Harry went up to the bar to order more drinks and she sat feeling blissfully at ease and happy for the first time in a very long while. She closed her eyes, savouring the moment and would have probably been asleep if Harry hadn't returned with the drinks.

'Gosh, is my company that interesting?' said Harry gently nudging her.

'I was just my resting my eyes,' she giggled, 'and anyway I'm usually tucked up in bed by now with a cup of tea and a book.'

'Very romantic,' said Harry.

'The realities of married life,' Izzy said smiling.

'Well, it doesn't sound that bad. I could cope with that every night especially if you were in my bed with me.'

Izzy sat silently and shook her head. She glanced at him from the corner of her eye appraising his features, and deciding that he really was gorgeous, 'Yes, well…' was all she said.

They sat by the fire for a little while longer and then decided to call it a day. Izzy reached for Harry's hand as they walked back to the B&B, but Harry gently let it go.

'I don't think we want the landlady seeing us walking hand in hand now do we? We are just acquaintances after all.'

'Yes, of course.' Izzy wondered if he'd had second thoughts. He seemed to be avoiding her gaze and was conducting himself in an icy manner.

Izzy felt awkward as they entered the bedroom and she plonked herself down on the bed unsure of what to do. Harry broke the silence. 'Do you want to use the bathroom first? I could do with a shower.'

'Oh right, of course, no you go ahead. I'm just going to have a cup of tea. Do you want one?' she smiled hesitantly at him.

'Yes, that would be good,' he replied, barely looking at her and disappearing into the bathroom hurriedly.

Izzy sat still for a moment, mulling things over. He must have changed his mind she thought and felt quite crestfallen. Sighing, she stood up and wandered over to the kettle only to discover that it was empty. She'd just have to wait until Harry had finished, which as it happened wasn't very long. He appeared freshly washed, wearing a pair of striped pyjama bottoms and a T-shirt. He was towel drying his hair and the sight of him nearly took her breath away. She mumbled something incoherent and rushed into the bathroom to fill the kettle up.

When she came back out Harry was arranging  pillows and a duvet on the sofa. She busied herself making the tea and wondered how she was going to get into bed as she had brought no night clothes, preferring to sleep naked. Harry pulled a book out of his bag and settled himself down with his tea, making it clear that he was not going to be talking. Izzy sipped her tea self-consciously before heading into the bathroom to remove her make up and take a shower. When she walked back into the bedroom wrapped in a large bath towel, the room was in semi-darkness and it was relatively easy for her to slip into bed and discard the towel out of sight of Harry.

Izzy didn't sleep very well. She couldn't believe the change in Harry and she kept wondering what was going on. She had to get up in the night to use the bathroom but couldn't find the towel she'd placed on the bed, so she decided to risk it naked. As she came out, she found Harry standing in front of her. She could only just make out his face in the semi-darkness. She ineffectually covered herself with her hands, all the time staring at Harry. He reached out for her, drawing her to him, a soft moan escaping from his throat and she found herself flattened against him. She could feel her insides melting and legs turning to jelly. He bent down to kiss her and she did nothing to resist him. Her arms found themselves winding around his body pulling him to her with an overwhelming urgency. She felt euphoric as they collapsed on to the bed and she realized that his feelings for her hadn't changed after all.

# Chapter 30

Clarissa was having a particularly awful day and wondering how she could end her life. Things had started badly when she'd fainted on her way to the hand therapy class and managed to be sick into her collar again. She hated hand therapy, where she was surrounded by people in similar states of suffering. Looking at them was a constant reminder of what she'd become. She'd been given a piece of hard blue putty and told to mould it with her fingers but she'd spent most of the time just staring at it. The physios had got the message and had given up on her after she was repeatedly rude to them. *Well how would they like it?*

Clarissa hated her hands, the skin of which had become thickened through lack of use and were now scaly like a reptile. When they went into a spasm, they resembled chickens' feet. Amelia soaked them for her when she visited and brought in a scrub, which she massaged into them. She thought it all a terrible waste of time but it kept Amelia quiet for a good half an hour and saved her having to make conversation with her. Instead, she would study her daughter through half-closed lids and imagine what she would look like when she was older. She really didn't favour her or Charles. Her looks annoyed Clarissa and Amelia didn't make the best of them – all that dull brown hair scraped untidily back into a scrunchy and not a scrap of make-up. She was not as thin as she should be either, in spite of all that mucking out and riding. As for why she always dressed in the same old pair of jeans and a T-shirt with some band emblazoned across the front… Amelia steadfastly ignored her when she tried to offer her advice. If Emily ever bothered to visit she would ask her to take her sister in hand.

Oh it was all such a waste of time. She was useless. Charles was right, she was a cripple and she would be better off dead. She should do the wretched hand exercises, and then maybe she'd be able to pull out all the bloody tubes and it would all be over.

She was still engrossed in plotting how to end it all when Archie popped his head round the door and beamed at her. The sunlight shining in from the opposite window cast a halo of light around his head and Clarissa thought he looked like an angel. Maybe he'd come to claim her and whisk her off to a better place.

'Hello,' he said brightly and came over to sit on her bed. Taking her hand, he stroked it gently.

She didn't respond but just looked down at her hand, sitting uselessly in his.

'What do you want?' she asked brusquely, trying ineffectually to withdraw her scaly hand from his. He appeared not to notice how awful her hands were and she really wished that Amelia had done them for her yesterday.

'Well now, that's not very friendly when I've come half way around the world to see you,' he smiled encouragingly at her.

She glared back. 'No you haven't. Why would you come all this way to see a cripple?' Tears of frustration welled.

Archie winced slightly but kept hold of her hand and continued to caress it softly. 'Please don't use that term, it's not nice.'

'Well tough shit!' Clarissa's voice broke slightly with anger.

'Well, that's better. Sounds more like the feisty Clarissa I know. Now, I hear you've not been making an effort with your physio classes, is that true?' Archie leant over and looked into her eyes.

'Not you too. Why don't you just fuck off if you're here to bully me,' she said nastily. She waited for a reaction from him and when there was nothing, not even a flicker across his face, she felt momentarily unsettled. 'There's no point. I'm not going to get any better and I don't want to waste my time or anyone else's for that matter.' She turned her head away.

'Finished? Right, well if you're referring to the physios, then that's their job and they probably enjoy it, otherwise they'd do something else. Given, it can't be an easy job trying to get you lot back on your feet.'

'That's never going to happen. They're all in dreamland. We're all cripples and that's all there is to it. I can't see the point in trying to do stuff if I can't regain total control of my body. I just want to know the truth. What they are doing creates false hope – pissing about with bits of putty, for God's sake. For what? So I can eventually hold a tin opener? Whoopee bloody do.'

'How do you know you won't regain enough control to lead a good life Clarissa?'

'I just do, it's all pointless. So, anyway what do you want? Money?' she spoke sharply.

'That's a bit rude,' Archie replied.

'Oh, I am sorry,' Clarissa spat at him. 'Well you know where the door is don't you?'

'Yes as it happens I do. I believe I came in that way but thank you for that.'

Clarissa wished he'd go and leave her to wallow in her own self pity. She didn't want him to see her like this; a grotesque caricature of her former self.

'Clarissa, you are a beautiful and normally very driven woman, which is why I'm slightly perturbed to find you not making an effort to get going. Frankly I'm disappointed in you.' Clarissa couldn't believe her ears. *Disappointed? Was he mad?* 'You might not like hearing this but the reality is you've had a serious accident and some nasty injuries but you're not dead and you really need to take the physiotherapy side more seriously. You could get a hell of a lot better, take up riding again, lots of things; but nothing is going to happen if you sit there doing sweet FA. The other thing is, I've heard a rumour that affects you,' he paused and Clarissa turned to look at him for the first time. 'It's about Charles,' Archie continued. 'Did you know he was planning to divorce *you*?'

It took a moment for what Archie had said to sink in 'What?' whispered Clarissa incredulously. 'On what grounds?'

'Adultery,' said Archie quietly.

'Oh you are having a bloody laugh,' Clarissa replied angrily.

'No I'm not laughing at all. However, since your accident he has decided not to proceed and is instead planning on getting his mitts on your money and the house. He is currently making arrangements for you to move into a bungalow that has been carefully adapted to suit your needs. I believe it's quite near to the hospital on one of those new housing estates. He's persuaded Henry and your parents that you'll need to be there so you can continue your treatment at the hospital easily.'

Clarissa was really angry now. 'He can't move me out of my house. That house is mine. A new housing estate? How dare he? How do you know all this?'

'Well I was chatting to your brother. He didn't want to upset you so he'd made a decision not to tell you for the time being. I however, thought you ought to know.'

'I can't believe my own brother's going along with this. He can't stand by and see me turned out of my own house.' Clarissa was furious. How dare they plot behind her back.

'Well, he's trying to keep Charles sweet as there are a lot of investments involved.'

'So, why are you telling me this? What's in it for you?' Clarissa

225

turned her attention to Archie. At that moment the door opened slowly and Amelia appeared with a slightly worried look on her face.

'Hello Mummy, Uncle Archie,' she said hesitantly. 'The nurse told me you were visiting Mummy.'

'Do you know about this Amelia?'

'Know what?' asked Amelia, walking into the room and closing the door behind her.

'That your father is planning to move me out of the house and into a bungalow on some bloody housing estate,' Clarissa spat.

Amelia's eyes widened and it was obvious to both Clarissa and Archie that she didn't know anything.

'Look if you don't mind, Archie and I are having an important discussion. Can't you come back later,' she snapped. Amelia adopted a crestfallen look.

'Yes of course, if that's what you'd like me to do. I've got some prep with me. I'll go and do that first.' She didn't wait for an answer but shut the door behind her and Clarissa turned her attention back to Archie.

'So where were we?' there was a short pause. 'Oh yes. So why have you decided to come here and tell me this?'

'Quite frankly you need someone on your side because your brother won't stand up to Charles and you are in no position to at the moment. I think Charles needs putting in his place, but it's your call. There's nothing wrong with that fine mind of yours, so you can tell me what you want me to do … or not, but I'm damned if I'm going to let Charles stab you in the back, investments or not.' He stopped talking and looked down at his hands.

'Come on Clarissa. Don't let him win. You can fight this – all of it.'

'Yes,' said Clarissa quietly.

'Right then. From now on you will attend all your classes and you will make a huge effort in every single one of them. I'm back next week and I expect to hear that you are making excellent progress. If I hear that you're not trying, or that you're being rude to the staff, I will never visit you again. Understood?'

Clarissa nodded, a startled expression on her face. 'And stop calling yourself a cripple, it's a horrible word.'

'What about Charles?'

'Well, I've done a bit of digging and he can't do anything while you're in hospital.' Archie reached over her collar and cradled Clarissa's face. 'Now you're listening, here's the truth you wanted to hear. The doctor thinks your rehab in hospital will be at least another nine months – don't ask how I came by that bit of info.' He paused and scrutinised her face, observing the shock in her eyes. 'So we're going to call it buying ourselves lots of time to thwart that husband of yours good and proper, starting with getting you a lawyer if you want one. I don't know if you'll ever walk again, but I'll ask them outright if you want. I expect they'll say a lot of the outcome is up to you my love.'

Clarissa looked at Archie's earnest face and for the first time since the accident felt a tiny tingling of hope from somewhere deep within her core. She did have it in her to get better. She may never get her old body back but she could make it the best it could be and with Archie to help her, then anything was possible. She looked at him with brighter eyes.

'Good. That's my girl.' Archie smiled at her and dropped his hands. 'One last thing; I'm worried about Amelia — she's here all the time and her school work is going to suffer. I don't know why she's still off school and what Charles has agreed with them but I think you should restrict her to visiting once a week and obviously not the same day I come over. That way, you'll have two of us fighting for you. '

Clarissa agreed with Archie. Amelia was here just about every day at the moment and she was driving her up the wall with her fussing.

'And be nice to her, she's a good kid. You'll have to tell her to keep quiet about the bungalow and my visits. Otherwise that could jeopardise our plans and we don't want that now, do we?'

'I'll have a word with her when she gets back,' said Clarissa. 'I don't think she's that fond of Charles either, as it happens, so I'm sure it won't be a problem.'

After Archie had left, Clarissa sat and wondered. Did Archie really care for her that much? She wracked her brain for a hidden agenda but couldn't think of one?  It had been so long since she'd met anyone who wanted to be near her, other than for her money. Well, she'd show them all. She was going to get better and then she was not only going to divorce Charles, she was going to ruin him. Ha, he could go and live in the bungalow on the housing estate. It would serve him right. The sound of Clarissa's laughter brought a passing nurse to a standstill and she was still laughing when Amelia slipped back into the room and rushed to her side.

# Chapter 31
## *March 2004*

It was the first of March and Charles was having a good day. He'd finally bought Piers out. His current account was full to bursting with the recent deposits and he was finalising another visit to Barbados. According to reports from Henry, the house was near completion and now that Clarissa was indisposed he had the added satisfaction of keeping it to himself. He didn't think that Clarissa would feel like celebrating her 40th this year in view of what had happened. Lydia-Rose had just given him another five hundred thousand to invest on her behalf and he'd decided to direct it to Archie's Uzbek project. He was continuing to receive good returns on money invested through Henry and on the two occasions when he'd asked to get some money out, he'd received a cheque for the correct amount within a week. All most reassuring! He was confident that the fund was performing well, along with the rest of the stock market of course but he was probably doing rather better out of Archie's schemes than some of the funds investing in blue-chip companies and such like.

He'd only managed to see Lydia-Rose a few times over the past few months but she was proving very fruitful and he'd decided to take her away to Barbados as a treat. He was beginning to wonder if she had access to unlimited funds because there seemed no end to the monies available.

Clarissa was still in hospital, which had surprised Charles but he supposed it was a bonus with the Barbados trip coming up. He hadn't bothered to visit her since Christmas and she hadn't asked to see him. He'd received a call from a nurse to say that Clarissa was worried about Amelia missing school, which he read as her being fed up with Amelia's company. However, Amelia still insisted on bloody visiting every weekend, which was costing a small fortune in taxis and petrol and took up Sylvie and Carl's time in giving her lifts. He knew Sylvie couldn't stand his wife but she had a blasted soft spot for Amelia and felt sorry for her.

Clarissa's parents found the journey too much and Henry and Constance had had enough of being screamed and sworn at he was sure. He'd introduced the idea of the bungalow, close to the hospital and getting Clarissa a live-in nurse. No one had protested. In fact he suspected they were relieved. Naturally he'd asked them all not to tell Clarissa. Emily had already asked if she could move into her mother's room but Amelia had been mad with her and he'd persuaded her to wait. Who knew, he might find someone delectable to move in instead.

On the other hand, he was enjoying openly living as a bachelor. He suspected some acquaintances thought it distasteful, but invitations kept arriving and no one challenged him. In some ways, it was a good job he had the changes in the business to keep his mind occupied; otherwise he could see himself being tempted to never work again.

It was a shame Harry had decided not to buy in, but the others had all been happy to up their share. He'd organised the cars for them and they were being delivered in a couple of months' time. Charles wanted them living, eating and sleeping his business. The market was bullish, there was plenty of opportunity to make money and that is exactly what they were going to do.

The phone rang. It was Gary. 'I was just thinking about you!' Charles laughed and leant back in his chair, swinging it around slightly so that he could put his feet up on the desk.

'Oh, not in a pervy way I hope.'

'No, Gary of course not. You're not my type.' Charles laughed again.

'I've had a little idea.'

'God man, not another one?'

Gary ignored Charles and jumped straight in with his idea. 'I think it might smooth the way if we incentivise all our valuations. I was thinking that I would withhold ten percent of the valuation fee until completion of the loan to which the valuation relates.'

Charles mulled this over briefly before responding. 'I don't think that's much of an incentive for my staff. Surely we need to dangle a bigger carrot than that to get them moving things quicker.'

'Well, I was considering moving my fee up accordingly to say two thousand pounds, which is up from the current fifteen hundred.'

'Ok, sounding better and are you keeping the timescales the same?'

'Actually I'd like the turnaround from instruction to valuation within five working days and the finished report within seven working days.'

Charles thought about this and decided that ten per cent was not enough. 'You'd better make it fifteen percent then. That should get the staff moving.'

'Fifteen percent eh? You drive a hard bargain but I'll do it; it'll be good for business all round. Have you considered anymore about expanding the estate agency business?'

Charles pulled his feet off the desk and abruptly swung his chair back round. 'As a matter of fact I have and it is going ahead. I've just had to sort the restructuring out and I'm taking on some new staff to do the estate agency.'

'Excellent. Maybe we could collaborate on that one as well. I'm sure I can arrange some mortgages for those after their dream home but a little short on funds.'

'Like a deposit you mean,' laughed Charles.

'Yes, I suppose so but some of these high street banks are missing a trick with all their ridiculous requirements. This is the twenty-first century not the dark ages for goodness sake.'

'Well, you are right there. I suppose it's not long before we see mortgages of one hundred percent, particularly with the housing market rising the way it is.'

'Absolutely, but I think that the high street banks will be slow on the up-take. We need to get in there fast and start some advertising campaigns. Snap up all these first time buyers for starters.'

'Sounds good to me. I think the ground floor of my office building is coming up for rent so I might take the lease on it for the estate agency.

'It's a shame the whole lot's not for sale.'

'Yes it is but it's owned by an old dear who probably won't live for much longer.' Charles thought for a moment. 'Actually it might be a good idea to pay her a visit. Yes an excellent idea. Well thought out Gary.'

'Well don't get carried away and finish her off,' said Gary, laughing as he hung up.

Charles rang Jess and asked her to organise a staff meeting the following week. He was going to have to get them on board and up-to-speed with some of the new practices. He also asked Jess to get a couple of adverts in the relevant publications for new staff.

A few minutes later his phone rang again. 'Ah Henry, what can I do you for?' asked Charles.

'Charles my dear boy, how's life?' Charles wondered if he detected a hint of nervousness in his voice.

'Come on Henry cut to the chase and all that, tell me what's bothering you.'

'Well absolutely nothing to worry about dear boy,' Henry paused and cleared his throat. 'Just another little hiccup on the building works in Barbados. Bloody natives downed tools again. If I were you, I would delay going out there just yet.'

Charles scowled. 'Well frankly Henry I'm not impressed and I will be going out to have a look at exactly what is going on out there. In fact you should be out there now creating merry hell.'

'Yes yes dear boy but I've been awfully busy and one of those properties is mine don't forget, so you're not the only one who is fed up. I'm trying to get out there in the next week or two, but I will have to reschedule a few things before I can get away.'

Charles wondered what exactly Henry would have to reschedule: miss one of his boozy lunches at his club more like. Charles was never quite sure what Henry did do for a living. Siegfried and Edwina lived in a huge manor house with over five thousand acres, which Henry would inherit. The lucky bugger probably didn't need to work at all.

'Well, what is the problem this time? We've had Christmas; dodgy foundations; don't tell me it's because of the cricket?!'

'Well, as a matter of fact it probably is. England is playing in the West Indies at present and I believe due in Barbados in April. I forgot you don't follow the cricket.'

'Lord no, it's far too slow for me! Anyway it doesn't alter the fact that we have a problem with the building work. I'm definitely going out to see for myself.

'Good plan, dear boy, good plan and if you change your mind about the cricket I can get you some corporate hospitality on one of the days that England are playing.'

Charles was about to dismiss the idea immediately but his mind raced on to other possibilities. 'I think I might take you up on that one, if you're sure?'

'Absolutely dear boy, absolutely; I'll email you details. How's Clarissa doing?' asked Henry changing the subject. 'Have you got any further along with the bungalow?'

'She's doing fine and I've paid a deposit on the bungalow. Not that you're to mention it to her. It will only be temporary because it's near the hospital so she can continue her treatment but the last thing we want is a setback if she doesn't take to the idea.'

'Of course, dear boy of course. My lips are sealed. Still no idea when they'll let her out?'

'None whatsoever, but I'm sure she's in the best possible place at the moment.'

'I must pop in and say hello this week, if I get time.'

'Excellent idea,' said Charles, knowing full well he would wiggle out of it. 'I'm sure she will be delighted to see you. And Henry, this really had better be the last "blip". I want my house finished and finished soon.'

'As do I dear boy, as do I. Charles, do you think Clarissa will ever be able to see the house, seeing as you bought it for her?'

'Henry, I bought the house as an investment and right now whether Clarissa gets to stay in it or not is not a priority. Just get it bloody built will you!'

Charles slammed the phone down. What the hell was going on in Barbados? Well, whatever it was, he would find out soon. He started to go through the enormous pile of work strewn about on his desk but after half an hour he got bored and picked up the phone.

'Jess could you pop in here please?'

She appeared in next to no time, part of her hair braided with brightly-coloured beads and wearing a loud floral dress. Charles shook his head and wondered if he ought to smarten her up a bit.

'Jess my desk is a mess,' Charles gestured to the untidy pile of files, 'and I can't be bothered to sort it out. Maybe you could be so kind as to do something with it. You know, prioritize it or something.'

Jess stood in front of him with her hands on her hips and looked at him much as a parent might look at a wayward child. 'Charles it was prioritized when I gave it to you,' she replied. You really must attend to some of it and then the pile will get smaller and your desk less messy. She picked up the first file and briefly read out the last piece of correspondence concerning a compensation claim.

'Boring,' announced Charles spinning around in his chair. 'Give it to Izzy or Harry or anyone you feel like. Actually give it to Harry. Next.'

Jess retrieved a letter concerning a rent review. 'I can't be bothered with that. Give it to Harry too. Next.' They continued in that manner until the desk had been sorted out and there were only three files left for him to deal with. Most of the rest he'd passed on to Harry. Teach him not to invest, the little twerp.

'Well now that wasn't too painful was it?' he announced.

Jess looked at him with an eyebrow raised. 'I don't think Harry will be too pleased,' she announced as she left the office, carrying a pile of files.

'Tough shit.' yelled Charles after her. If Harry didn't like it, Harry could go. He obviously wasn't committed to the firm. In fact he was going to make life hell for Piers' little protégé. It would be most entertaining.

The meeting room was full when Charles made his grand entrance. Harry had not been included.

'Right, cut to the chase and all that. I thought I'd fill you in on a few details. Firstly, your new vehicles should be with you in a couple of months.' He then proceeded to tell them about the new changes proposed by Gary.

'Won't there be a conflict of interest if the fees are withheld until the valuation is finished?' enquired Izzy.

'No, of course not Izzy. Your valuation is being handled by GRA not the bank lending the money.'

'Oh…right…,' said Izzy.

'Aren't GRA starting to fund some of these mortgages though?' asked Nick continuing Izzy's train of thought.

'Yes, but they're all separate businesses, there's really no need to worry.' Charles paused, 'I'll tell you what, I'll ask Justin and Annabelle to pop in and get you up to speed. It's really no big deal and they are very progressive that brings me on to the next matter. I have finally decided to go ahead with the estate agency as I think it's an excellent time to be in that market. I'm currently looking to take over downstairs and next year open an office in London.'

'Gosh, rapid expansion then,' said Izzy feeling a little anxious and out of her depth. She would be responsible for any debts incurred.

'Yes, yes, we can't rest on our laurels when there is all this money to be made.'

'Well, I'm all for expansion but estate agency is highly competitive. What sort of market will we be aiming for?' Nick asked.

'High end properties in excess of two hundred and fifty thousand. We will offer a bespoke service with glossy brochures, videos and plenty of marketing; fees of 2%. I am open to suggestions; it's not set in tablets of stone yet.'

'Well, that all sounds pretty positive.' Nick appeared to have no misgivings.

Izzy was worried about how quickly things were moving and she wished she could discuss this with someone more knowledgeable. Charles just seemed to be pushing everything through very fast. The meeting ended and Charles was pleased. It felt good knowing he had complete control over the business. Now he just had to chase up his lawyers and get his darling wife to sign a few forms.

233

# Chapter 32

Stephen read the letter twice. He couldn't quite take in what he was reading. The case against him had been dropped. Lucy and Leonora had confessed to making the whole thing up. Well, Leonora had finally confessed and Lucy had eventually capitulated when she realised there was really no point in continuing. Stephen knew he should have felt elated but he just felt flat and emotionless.

He rang Izzy and left a message on her answer-phone: 'Izzy it's me, Stephen. I just wanted to let you know that the case against me has been dropped. I am in the clear and I can carry on as normal. Speak to you later. Love you.'

He sat on the sofa by an open window, inhaling the cool crisp air that filtered past him. The phone rang and he assumed it was Izzy calling back.

'Stephen, I heard there may be news?' It was Marie-Claire.

'Well I've just received a letter today – all charges have been dropped.' He waited and was rewarded with the expected response.

'Oh Stephen, I'm so pleased for you. I knew it wouldn't be long once they confessed.'

'I wonder what prompted them to eventually see the light.'

Marie-Claire chuckled softly. 'As it happens I got hold of Leonora and told her I knew that she was lying and that she'd better own up before things got even worse. I told her I had a recording of the conversation I'd overheard between her and Lucy and that I would give it to the police. She didn't believe me but when I told her what I'd heard nearly word for word she gave in. I think she put the blame at Lucy's door and unfortunately for Lucy being a member of staff and in a position of authority she is now in a lot of trouble.'

'Good,' said Stephen emphatically. 'What sort of trouble?'

'Well, she has been suspended from her post pending enquiries and she will be hauled over the coals for wasting police time. I don't think we'll be seeing her for a while at any rate.'

'Well, it seems I owe you big time.'

'Oh, not at all. I think it was only a matter of time before Leonora saw the error of her ways. She's still not a nice girl because from what I can gather she is blaming Lucy for everything and I'm not sure she's completely guiltless. Certainly not from what you were telling me and the occasions I found her in your office.'

'No you're right. I still have no idea how I'm going to get my life back on track.'

'Well, it will take time but no one gets through life without some adversity. You've got to get out there and create some positive spin for yourself.'

'Maybe. I'm not sure that's my style.'

'Well hiding away will make people think you've got something to be guilty about. Maybe you can make something good come out of this so that it doesn't happen to any other member of staff. Anyway, I think it would be good for you to come back to work as soon as possible. It will give you a focus and I'm sure the school will want that too. Believe you me; they'll want all this to go away in a hurry.'

'What's happened to Leonora? Obviously I can't be expected to teach her again.'

'Well, I'm not exactly sure. She's been signed off sick. My guess is she won't be back. Silly, silly girl.'

'I suppose I should feel sorry for her; she's just a kid, after all, but it's hard to do so right now.'

'Well she's none of your concern anymore and don't you go letting any other students prey on that big heart of yours. I've recommended that a review of the pupil-support scheme goes ahead. I know it's nice to feel that one has a special relationship with the pupils but times have changed and we have to protect ourselves. Now, have I got your permission to go and spread the good news?'

The thought of returning to school filled Stephen with horror. He didn't even like groups of people at the moment. Well he wouldn't get worked up about it until the head called. Maybe after the summer providing his doctor thought him up to it. He picked up the phone and called his parents.

'Daddy, daddy, we're home!' Chrissie had done the school run today instead of the childminder as Stephen was feeling more able to cope with them.

'Daddy, is there any cake?' asked a hopeful Ben, flying to the cake tin.

'Actually, kids, shall we go out for tea and cake? Or pizza if you prefer?'

'Really Daddy?' questioned Ben with a surprised look on his face.

'Absolutely, why don't you all go and get changed and then we'll go. Daddy's had some really good news today.'

# Chapter 33

Izzy arrived home feeling guilty. She'd supposedly been working late but the reality was she'd been with Harry and enjoying herself rather too much. She shouted a hurried hello and rushed up the stairs to shower before she greeted Stephen face to face. The house was quiet and she realised that yet again she hadn't eaten with her family. Well, she was the main bread winner at the moment so what else could they expect. She was rather enjoying the freedom and with Stephen home all the time, she didn't feel any hurry to get back. Still, spending the early evening in bed with Harry was probably pushing it a step too far she thought ruefully as she stripped her clothes off and stared at her naked reflection in the mirror. So, that's what an adulterer looks like she thought.

'Looking good!' Stephen's voice made her jump and she turned sharply to face him. 'You're looking very trim,' he said admiringly and approached her with an amorous look on his face.

She turned away from him and disappeared into the bathroom. 'I really need a shower,' she added, eager to escape his clutches. Izzy showered quickly and was pleased to see that Stephen had left the bedroom when she came out again. She could hear him talking to the boys. There was lots of laughter and Izzy dressed quickly before going to join them.

'Mummy, Daddy took us out for tea and cake and then pizza and ice-cream, we kept ringing you to see if you wanted to come too,' Ed said as Izzy walked into his room.

'Oh. Did he now?' said Izzy sounding surprised. She was torn between being pleased and wondering where Stephen thought they were getting the money from at the moment.

'Did you get my message?' asked Stephen as Izzy walked into the lounge with a glass of wine.

'Um, no. Was it important?'

'Well, see what you think? He handed her the letter.' She took it off him and began reading and she felt a huge surge of relief as she digested the contents. Finally he was vindicated.

'Darling, that's the best news!' she exclaimed. 'Thank goodness for that. So what happens next? When can you go back to work?'

'I have to wait until the school gives me the go ahead but hopefully from September. If the doctor says I'm up to it of course.'

'Oh, yes of course.' She sat down next to him on the sofa. 'I can't believe it. At long last. Have you told anyone yet?'

'Marie-Claire knows and my parents.'

'I think I would have liked to be the first to know,' she said, feeling fed up.

'Well, I did try to get hold of you but you were typically unavailable and I did leave a message. Marie-Claire phoned soon after that and I couldn't keep her in the dark, she has been so supportive throughout all of this.

'Yes, she has,' Izzy admitted. Feelings of guilt pulsed through her and she felt slightly queasy at the thought of what she'd been up to.

'What's the matter? You look a bit pale,' said Stephen. 'I think we should jet off somewhere this Easter and have a break. How about it?'

Izzy was taken aback. 'Gosh you must be feeling better to contemplate a holiday.'

'I'm trying, Izzy. Most days I wake up feeling lousy and that's the way it is for the rest of the day. However, today I felt different for a while and excited at the prospect of taking the children out. I felt like me again.'

'I'm really glad you've had a better day. I don't know about a holiday. Now I've got the partnership, Charles is really cracking the whip and obviously I've got to pay back the money I borrowed. You could see what's on offer though. Maybe you and the children could go with your parents if I can't get away.'

Izzy spent a sleepless night wrestling with her conscience. She felt cheated not to have been there to celebrate Stephen's good news. When she'd checked her phone, there were missed calls from Tim, Chrissie and even Stephen's parents, all of whom had wanted to share the good news. She arrived at work having come to a decision: the affair with Harry was going to have to stop. She owed it to her family after all they'd been through and her friends. She was also aware that Charles had got it in for Harry and, though she felt bad admitting it, she knew it wouldn't look good if their liaison came to light.

She texted Harry to ask him if he were free for lunch and he said that he was. Izzy struggled to concentrate on her work, which wasn't helpful because there was so much of it and she knew that

Charles would be jumping on her pretty soon. She tried to apply herself and was glad when it was one o'clock and she could escape to the pub.

Harry arrived just as she'd ordered drinks, sat himself down next to her and immediately blurted out, 'I've got some news for you, but I'm not sure you're going to like it very much.'
'Oh, why's that?' Izzy took a swig of her slim-line tonic.
'Well, there's no easy way to say this but I've got another job.' He looked at her with a slightly sheepish expression.
'Oh.' Izzy said again. 'Well, it's the first I've heard of it, so when did this come about?'
'Well, it was confirmed this morning, but I've been organising it for a while now.' He took a drink from his glass.
Izzy felt annoyed that Harry hadn't said anything to her sooner but she didn't want to let on. 'I suppose I'm not really surprised. You didn't buy into the partnership and Charles has been dumping stuff on you left, right and centre. So where is it?'
'Scotland.'
'Scotland!' exclaimed Izzy nearly choking on her drink. 'Scotland,' she repeated, 'but that's miles away.' God he was moving away completely. She felt a jumble of emotions: hurt, sorrow, anger and relief. 'What about your mother?' she said in a small voice desperately trying to hang on to her control. Scotland!
'She's finished chemo and radiotherapy so she will come and convalesce with me until she's fit enough to return to her home.'
'Gosh, you really have got it all worked out. Actually I'm a bit fed up that you didn't run it past me before dropping this bombshell; particularly in view of our relationship.'
'Well, it's not really any of your business what I do with my life.' Harry fixed her with hostile, challenging eyes and Izzy reeled.
'What? After everything...?' she replied, feelings of anger welling up inside her chest. *How dare he treat her like this as if it didn't mean anything at all?* She conveniently forgot that the reason they were sitting here in the first place was because she'd been planning to finish things with him. She felt tears prick her eyes and blinked them away hurriedly.
Harry didn't say anything but continued to stare at her.
'Well, aren't you going to say something?' Izzy asked him.
Harry sighed. 'Look, it's just easier this way. You are a married woman with children and frankly there is no future for us, so I'm

239

walking away. It was fun while it lasted but things would have become very difficult for us. This is for the best, you can't deny it.' Silence followed as they both thought about things.

'Who will you be working for?'

'Well, I'm going to manage a large estate up near Edinburgh.'

'Oh, a resident land agent?' Izzy looked up at him in surprise; that's a big change from the commercial world.

'Yes, that's right.'

'No targets then?' she laughed, 'How big is the estate?'

'It's huge, well over ten thousand acres: several farms, lots of cottages and various country pursuits.

Izzy thought that under the circumstances it sounded idyllic. 'Do you get a house with the job?'

'Oh yes. It's a lovely house, stone built, a couple of hundred years old I should think. You can come and visit if you can get away,' he said with an eyebrow raised and a wry smile playing on his lips.

Izzy stared at him and thought how gorgeous he was and she suddenly felt panicky that she wouldn't see him again. 'I'll miss you,' she said continuing to stare at him.

'And I you,' Harry murmured.

Izzy sighed and tore her gaze from him before she succumbed to the weight of emotion building within her.

'Anyway, what's your news?' asked Harry breaking the uncomfortable silence.

'Umm.' Izzy thought for a moment and decided there was no point in telling Harry that she had been planning to end their relationship. 'Stephen has been cleared of the allegations. Lucy and Leonora confessed to fabricating the whole thing.'

'Well, that's bloody fantastic.' Harry was genuinely pleased. 'Let's drink to new beginnings shall we?'

'New beginnings for all of us,' echoed Izzy, raising the glass to her lips.

Izzy and Harry arrived back at the office to find it in utter turmoil.

'Charles has been arrested,' Jess blurted out tearfully,' they've taken him off in a police car for questioning.'

Izzy had a horrible sense of déjà vu and her mind started racing. 'What has he done?'

'I don't know, two policemen came into the office and asked if they could see him and the next thing he was being taken away. It was awful.'

'So Charles didn't say anything then?' asked Harry.

'No, he was grinning from ear to ear and just said that there had been some mistake and he'd be back later.'

'God, trust Charles to be grinning anyone else would have been terrified,' Izzy said thinking about how Stephen had taken the news of his arrest.

'Well, he's obviously fairly confident that he's done nothing wrong, I wonder what it is all about.' Harry mused.

'Well, knowing Charles it could be anything!' Jess laughed. Izzy and Harry exchanged puzzled looks.

'What exactly do you mean by that?'

'Oh well, you know, he does like to help his clients out and he does get results,' Jess shrugged noting the quizzical look on both Izzy's and Harry's faces. 'Well, I just think he pushes the boundaries a bit but people like that and they pay. Nothing illegal or anything.' She added for good measure.

'Oh well we'll find out soon enough.'

The interrogation room smelt vaguely of floor polish and Charles sat impassively in his chair staring into space. He wondered if he was being watched, he knew that they'd keep him hanging about to try and make him feel uncomfortable but he was quite enjoying himself. The only he thing he knew was that he was to be questioned with regard to underage sex with a minor. He wasn't at all worried because he'd thought through all the possibilities and he didn't think they could possibly have anything on him. Madame Lily would have contacted him if she'd been worried about anything and he changed the pay as you go phone that he used to contact her on a regular basis. So as far as he was concerned he was in the clear. He knew that he had fairly debauched tastes but really what they were insinuating was absolutely out of order.

# Epilogue
## *July 2004*

Sylvie was enjoying some respite having taken herself off to stay in her apartment on the Isle de Re as it was in between tenants and she'd requested a month off which Charles had agreed to. She reflected on her most interesting year to date with the Hambridge family culminating in Charles' arrest over the alleged incident with a minor which had apparently taken place the previous January at the charity ball which Clarissa and her mother had hosted. It transpired that one of the women he'd slept with had only been fourteen at the time. Charles and his legal team were working on this case and hoping to get him off the hook by making it clear that the event had been for over eighteens only and how had Charles known that the consenting and willing lady in question had only been fourteen at the time. There was the slight matter of a baby which Charles was having nothing to do with. He was currently refusing a paternity test because as far as he was concerned it wasn't his problem. He was currently on bail; court case pending.

Sylvie was beginning to find Charles' activities a little distasteful and she'd decided that she would only stay while Amelia needed her. Toby had returned home from university briefly, before heading off to California for the summer and Emily was off to Newquay with some of her friends where apparently the entire cool post GCSE mob hung out. Definitely the place to avoid thought Sylvie dreamily. If Toby and Emily had been Sylvie's children she would have been worried. Emily dressed very provocatively and had recently had long blonde extensions added. She was besotted with boys, clothes and was making plans for breast augmentation and lip plumping. Her whole life was about her. Toby seemed to suffer from major mood swings and was unpredictable swinging between affability and paranoia, she wondered if he was playing with drugs. Amelia had booked herself in for pony club camp and was helping Heather out for the rest of the summer. She'd recently bought a rather large docile looking creature which plodded about and appeared more interested in eating than anything else. A far cry from the rest of the stable yard, thought Sylvie. She had her suspicions that Amelia was planning on getting her mother back on board. That would be most interesting.

Sylvie had seen Clarissa a few times when she'd picked Amelia up from the hospital and noted that Clarissa was being her customary rude and obnoxious self once again having regained some of her inner strength. Sylvie thought this might have something to do with Archie who had re-appeared on the scene. Amelia had inadvertently let that slip and then tried to cover her tracks. She'd made Sylvie promise that she wouldn't tell Charles. Sylvie had decided not to bother for the moment, Charles was far too busy with all his schemes and she didn't really think it could do any harm. Apart from that she wanted to be supportive of Amelia who appeared to adore her mother and was trying her best to get her back on her feet. Sylvie didn't have the heart to tell her that that was never going to happen.

She shut her eyes enjoying the warmth of the early evening sun and drifted off to sleep.